SIX ME...
ONE GLORIOUS LEGAC...
A...

### THE PRINCESS . . . AND ...

TESS GALLATIN . . . A savvy and successful diamond broker, she was also a woman with a mysterious past, full of secrets.

JEOPARD SURPRISE . . . Enigmatic and sexy, he'd slipped aboard Tess's boat to search for the legendary blue Kara diamond. But from the moment he laid eyes on the sophisticated beauty, he was irresistibly drawn to her fire and spirit.

### THE REDHEAD . . . AND THE RENEGADE

ERICA GALLATIN . . . The emerald-eyed, flame-haired builder had come to North Carolina to claim the land that was her birthright—and to convince Cherokee renegade James Tall Wolf that she belonged there.

JAMES TALL WOLF . . . Consumed by desire for Erica, he was determined to drive her away from the reservation he called home—until he was seduced by his elusive prey.

### THE HELLCAT . . . AND THE MAVERICK

KAT GALLATIN . . . The pocket-size Venus knew of the bitter feud between the Gallatin and Chatham clans that stretched back generations—but that didn't stop her from losing her heart to the sensual Nathan Chatham.

NATHAN CHATHAM . . . He'd come to Georgia on a mission of revenge, but how could he resist the honey-skinned hellcat who surrendered to him with such fiery abandon?

### FOLLOW THE SUN

*Other Bantam Books by Deborah Smith*
BELOVED WOMAN

# FOLLOW THE SUN

## DEBORAH SMITH

**BANTAM BOOKS**
NEW YORK · TORONTO · LONDON · SYDNEY · AUCKLAND

FOLLOW THE SUN

A BANTAM FANFARE BOOK/AUGUST 1991

The stories in this edition were originally published under
the titles *Sundance and the Princess,*
*Tempting the Wolf,* and *Kat's Tale.*
They have been edited for this edition.

FANFARE and the portrayal of a boxed "ff" are trademarks of Bantam Books,
a division of Bantam Doubleday Dell Publishing Group, Inc.

ISBN 0-553-29092-4

PUBLISHED SIMULTANEOUSLY IN THE UNITED STATES AND CANADA

Bantam Books are published by Bantam Books, a division of Bantam
Doubleday Dell Publishing Group, Inc. Its trademark, consisting of the
words "Bantam Books" and the portrayal of a rooster, is Registered in
U.S. Patent and Trademark Office and in other countries. Marca Regis-
trada. Bantam Books, 666 Fifth Avenue, New York, New York 10103

PRINTED IN THE UNITED STATES OF AMERICA

RAD          0 9 8 7 6 5 4 3 2 1

# SUNDANCE
## *and the*
# PRINCESS

## CHAPTER 1

T HE REPORT WAS titled simply, "Gallatin, Tess—
Profile of Suspect in Kara Diamond Disappearance." Above that title was stamped the national seal
of Kara. Jeopard Surprise thought that the ornate red-
and-silver seal was very pretentious for such a small
Scandinavian monarchy.

It bolstered his suspicion that Olaf, Duke of Kara,
was a pompous man, who would make a pompous
ruling prince. Jeopard doubted the intelligence of anyone who'd pay twenty thousand dollars to get back a
thirty-thousand-dollar diamond that had been stolen
more than two decades before.

A small yellow note was stuck to the report's plastic
cover. Jeopard eyed it, arched a blond brow at the
message, and laid the report aside for a moment. With
quick, efficient movements he punched numbers into
the cordless telephone resting on his knee and waited
for his brother's hearty hello.

When it came it had an echo, as if Kyle Surprise

were hundreds of miles away, rather than in their office, five miles from Jeopard's apartment.

"Damn cordless phone," Kyle said solemnly.

"Stick your note elsewhere."

"Oh-ho, a direct hit to the Iceman's dignity."

"If I had any dignity, I'd tell people that I was an only child."

Kyle laughed at the barb, as usual. "That's cold, Iceman, cold. I thought you had a plane to catch for California."

"I'm going. Tell me what you meant by 'Don't scare her with your charm?' "

"The babe is used to young, fun-loving guys," Kyle shot back drolly. "Do your best to impersonate one."

And, chortling, he hung up in Jeopard's ear.

"Fun-loving" wasn't even in Jeopard's vocabulary. He raised a glass of brandy to a mouth made too grim by too many years of reading reports such as the one on Tess Gallatin.

He felt nothing but cold, professional curiosity about her. That lack of emotion had earned him harsh nicknames from enemies and respectful ones from friends over the years; it was the trait that made him so good at his work.

It was also the one trait that depressed the hell out of him.

He returned to reading the report. It contained the facts of her life in a concise, unequivocal list. Twenty-six years old. Residence: A sailboat, the *Swedish Lady*, Big Cove Marina, Long Beach, California. Widow of Royce Benedict, age sixty-two, jewel thief, died two years ago, cancer.

Father: Hank Gallatin, Cherokee Indian, Mercenary soldier. Mother: Ingrid Kellgren, Swedish, professional athlete. Both deceased.

*Cherokee Indian?* Jeopard scanned that information twice. She was half Cherokee? Well, at least that was different.

Occupation: Diamond broker. Education: Elementary and secondary—Smithfield Academy, London;

college—UCLA, bachelor's degree in business administration.

Lifestyle/personality profile: Married Benedict when she was twenty; inherited his entire estate over objections of his two daughters; sexually promiscuous both before and after Benedict's death. Business associates rate her tough, manipulative. Approach with caution.

Jeopard almost smiled at that last note. While the brandy seared his throat, his eyes narrowed in a thoughtful squint.

Compared to the assignments he'd been given during his government career, her case was fluff. Even compared to the assignments he took now, as a civilian, her case was fluff. In effect, he was about to take his first vacation in ten years.

He flipped the last page of the report and studied a series of photographs. After he stared at them, mesmerized, for a long moment, he slung them and the report into a nearby trash can and downed his brandy in one painful swallow.


THE CHEAP DOMESTIC rental car wasn't accustomed to Tess Gallatin's Grand Prix driving style. But then Tess Gallatin wasn't accustomed to cheap, domestic cars.

She steered the straining little automobile around a bend bordered by lovely, Victorian-era houses on one side and a tree-shaded college campus on the other. Picturesque little Gold Ridge, Georgia, backed by distant mountains, suddenly appeared before her like an obstacle course waiting to be negotiated.

It was so beautiful that it made her hurt inside with an odd wistfulness, as if she were returning to a home she'd never seen before. There were trees, lots of trees, and a brilliant blue sky untouched by smog.

Tess propped one olive-hued elbow out her open window and zoomed into the town square past a neatly preserved brick courthouse fronted by a dignified sign that read, "Welcome to Gold Ridge, Georgia, home of the first U.S. gold rush, 1829. Courthouse and gold museum open for tours."

In a musical British accent she murmured, "All right, Lawyer Brown, where are you?"

She checked her written directions, then peered at a tourist's mecca of quaint storefronts. Finally she spotted a glass door with "T. Lucas Brown, Attorney At Law" painted on it in gloriously ornate letters. T. Lucas Brown's door was sandwiched between a country café and a dulcimer shop. She swung the rental car into a parking spot so fast that when she braked, it made the tires squeal.

A minute later she was striding up a steep old staircase. At the top of it a ceiling fan hummed and clacked rhythmically over a reception area staffed by a Betty Davis clone wearing a white organdy dress.

Tess politely told her she had an appointment.

"Your cousins are already here," Betty informed her, puffing on a long cigarette. "You're late."

"How kind of you to remind me. I've never visited Georgia before. I left the Atlanta airport, took a right, and immediately got lost."

The receptionist scanned Tess's flowing turquoise dress and white fedora with a curious gaze. "Gawd, you're obviously from California."

Feeling more amused than annoyed. Tess cocked her head to one side and returned the appraisal. "You're obviously not shy around strangers."

Betty grinned, nodded, and punched an intercom line on her telephone. "The third one's here, boss."

A booming voice answered, "Dear Lord! A smorgasbord of beautiful women! Send her on in!"

Tess wondered what kind of lunacy she'd encountered as she went where Betty pointed. A rotund, black-bearded man threw a door open and exuberantly waved her inside. "Ms. Gallatin! Meet Ms. Gallatin and Ms. Gallatin!"

Her heart pounding, Tess stepped inside his office and gazed raptly at the two women seated in scroll-backed chairs by T. Lucas Brown's large desk. They stood, gazing back just as raptly.

The tall one, a lanky Amazon with shoulder-length chestnut hair and fair skin, was very businesslike, in a gray pin-striped outfit. The short one, a curvaceous Kewpie doll with an incredible mane of inky black hair and skin the color of dark honey, was very athletic, in jeans, running shoes, and a baggy T-shirt with a road-race logo.

The tall one smiled, came forward, and shook Tess's hand formally, but with genuine warmth. Her voice droll, she said, "I'm Erica. Born in Boston. My great-grandfather was Ross Gallatin, and that's about all I know concerning the Gallatin Cherokee blood. I own a construction company in Washington, D.C."

The short one grinned, came forward, and pumped Tess's hand merrily. "I'm Kat. Born in a circus trunk. My great-grandfather was Holt Gallatin, and I think he robbed banks for a living. I'm a nomad, although I have a dinky little apartment in Miami." She paused, thinking. "Oh. And I'm a professional wrestler."

After a stunned moment, Tess laughed. She'd known her cousins less than a minute, yet she already felt an affectionate kinship with them. "Tess Gallatin," she announced, and smiled at the double-take they did over her slight English accent. "Born in Sweden, raised in England and California. My great-grandfather was Silas Gallatin, and he owned a shipping business in San Francisco. I'm a diamond broker and I live on a sailboat in Long Beach, which is about an hour's drive south of Los Angeles."

"I'm a plain old country lawyer, and I'm fascinated by all three of y'all," T. Lucas Brown interjected, smiling at them. "Ladies, we have a will to read. Take your seats."

When they were all settled he looked at each of them, shaking his head in awe. "What a smorgasbord," he repeated. "None of you have met before?"

Tess traded apologetic looks with her relatives. They shook their heads almost in unison. T. Lucas chuckled. "Incredible. Do you know that you all share the same birthday?"

Tess turned toward Erica and Kat in amazement. "September twenty-seventh?" They nodded, as intrigued as she was. "But different years, I assume. I'm twenty-six years old."

"Thirty-three," Erica told her.

"Twenty-eight," Kat said.

"This has mystical implications," T. Lucas noted solemnly. "Which brings me to the reading of Dove Gallatin's will. Let's see, you share the same great-great grandparents, Justis and Katherine Gallatin—their sons were your great-grandfathers. That makes you cousins of some sort—third cousins, maybe. Who knows? Dove Gallatin was your great-aunt, Kat, and I'm too confused to figure out what that makes her in relation to Tess and Erica."

"My mother was Swedish. My father told me he was almost full-blooded Cherokee, but I know nothing about his family," Tess admitted. "Including Dove Gallatin."

"Same here," Kat added. "And I'm practically a full-blooded Injun."

"Ditto for me and the Gallatin Cherokee history," Erica said. "I'm only one-sixteenth Injun, umm, Cherokee. The Gallatins in my branch of the family didn't marry back into the tribe, the way Kat's and Tess's ancestors did."

T. Lucas Brown sighed heavily. "I hope Dove's bequest sparks y'all's interest in the family heritage. You can read her will if you want, but it's extremely simple. She left you two hundred acres of land north of Gold Ridge. The three of you are co-owners."

Tess blinked in surprise. "Land?"

"Land that's been in the Gallatin Family for over a hundred and fifty years. It belonged to Justis and Katherine—probably belonged to her parents before that. Anyhow, Katherine's will stated that the land must pass down through the family. It went to her son, Holt Gallatin—Kat's great-grandfather—and then to Dove, his daughter. It can't be sold outside the family. It can, however, be leased.

"And you ladies will be happy to know that the Tri-State Mining Company has come to me with a lease offer for you. They suspect that there's enough low-grade industrial gold on your property to make a mining venture worthwhile. Y'all would get plenty of income to pay the property taxes and a small percentage of the mineral rights."

"Hooray!" Kat said. "Let's do it."

"Sounds terrific," Erica added.

Tess nodded. "I agree."

"Now, hold on, hold on. There's something else to consider." He reached into a desk drawer and retrieved a small cloth bag. Brown opened it and took out three large gold medallions.

Tess found herself gazing at them in open-mouthed wonder. They were nicked and dulled by years of handling, but the craftsmanship was superb. Each was a quarter-inch thick and at least three inches in diameter, and each had a small hole bored in it. The holes were worn as if by long use on a necklace.

Each bore a line of delicately molded symbols stamped in a circular pattern. The messages—if that was what they were—began at the outside perimeter of each medallion and wound to the center.

Brown flipped the medallions over. The strange symbols covered the other sides, as well. Attached to the hole in each medallion was a small white tag. Brown glanced at the tags, then handed the medallions out.

"It's absolutely magnificent," Tess whispered as she smoothed her fingertips over the strange gift. She glanced at her cousins and saw expressions of awe on their faces too.

"Each of you gets one," Brown told them. "Dove specified which of you gets which medallion. That's her handwriting on the tags."

Tess studied the bold, artistic script. "What do you know about Dove Gallatin?"

"Not much. She spent her entire life on the Cherokee reservation up in North Carolina; she was at least ninety when she died. She never married. She considered herself a psychic, I understand. I have no idea how she decided which of you gets which medallion. The symbols are different on each one. I believe they're Cherokee script."

"Hmmm, the tribe had an alphabet, correct?" Erica asked.

"Yes. Actually, it's called a syllabary. A remarkable achievement. Invented by a Cherokee named Sequoyah."

"Like the tree," Kat interjected vaguely, staring at her medallion.

"I believe the tree was named after *him*," Brown said with exasperation. "At any rate, ladies, I think it would behoove you three to track down some family history before you let a mining company tear up the Gallatin land. Supposedly the Cherokees buried their gold around here. These medallions may hold clues to something your ancestors left."

"Who made the medallions?" Tess asked.

"Don't know. Your great-great-grandmother Katherine, perhaps."

"Can you take us to see this land?" Kat asked.

"Sure, if everyone wants to."

Tess looked at Kat and Erica. They nodded eagerly.


TESS KNEW AS soon as she saw the magnificent valley that she wanted to learn more about the people who had loved it. Erica and Kat stood silently beside her, their medallions clasped in their hands. T. Lucas Brown waited beside his Land Rover at the end of the old trail that was the outside world's sole access to this spot.

"I say we go back to our respective homes and do some research into our branches of the family," Erica suggested. "And we meet back here again in, say, a couple of months to decide about the mining lease."

"Good enough, Washington," Kat chimed. She gazed at Tess. "What d'ya say, California?"

Tess smiled. "If nothing else, I want to get to know you two better. Certainly."

She held out her right hand. Erica and Kat placed their right hands on top of it. Tess had the oddest notion that someone, somewhere, was watching with approval.

*WHUMP.*

Tess careened sideways on her lounge chair. The large, ostentatious yacht bullied its way into the berth beside her sailboat, bumped it again, and sent Tess sprawling to the deck on her hands and knees.

This was not how she wanted to spend her first day back from the Georgia trip.

Tess staggered to her feet. Her *Swedish Lady* was forty feet long, big enough to have comfortable living space below deck and room for a patio table with a bright orange umbrella and four chairs above, but the yacht dwarfed it.

Against the sun she could make out only the silhouette of the man seated at the control console on the deck above her head. The yacht's bow plowed into the marina dock and bounced at least five feet backward.

Luckily for the yacht, the thick concrete dock was lined with a wood buffer.

Tess huffed in dismay. He was probably another weekend captain who'd rented a berth at the marina so that he could park his floating mansion and serve cocktails.

The interloper cuts his engine off and stood up. Hmmm, at least this weekender had a nice build. Correction—he was wearing nothing but swim trunks, and he had a *fantastic* build, youthful but filled out.

When he raised his arms to ram both hands through his hair in disgust—the yacht was quickly sliding away from the dock—Tess was treated to an even more marvelous view of his body. He didn't look particularly tall, but he was so perfectly proportioned that she couldn't be certain. He gave "proportioned" a breathless new appeal.

And he was floating back out to sea.

Tess got up, stepped carefully around the *Lady*'s mast, and went to the port rail. She cupped her hands around her mouth and called, "Come to the foredeck and throw me your lines!"

He looked down at her, a dark, intriguing form against the blue sky, his eyes covered by aviator-style sunglasses.

Tess waved toward the bow of his yacht with both hands. The movement opened the unbuttoned white shirt she wore over a black maillot. The newcomer pulled his sunglasses down an inch and studied her rakishly, smiling.

"What's the foredeck?" he asked in a pleasantly deep voice.

The handsome idiot. "The front of the boat!" Tess ran to the bow of the *Lady*, crossed her gangplank to the dock, and went to the neighboring berth. Facing his monstrous boat, she yelled again, "Throw me your lines!"

He was smiling as he came down the staircase from the bridge, and despite herself Tess felt the effect of that smile. What she could see of his face seemed to be older than his youthful body, but that only made it more mesmerizing.

He trotted across his foredeck, and Tess fought to keep herself from gaping as she got a closer look at him. The sun glinted off tousled blond hair that was long and the rich color of wheat on top, short and dark gold around his ears.

The beautiful blond hair and his unforgettable, strong-jawed face reminded her of Robert Redford. Tess glanced up and down the busy Sunday-afternoon marina. Every woman within a radius of a hundred yards was staring at Captain Handsome.

Redford, definitely.

Moving with a fluid grace that stole her concentration, he lifted a heavy rope and carried it to the edge of the deck. A full thirty feet of bilge-green water separated him from the dock.

"Ahoy, me pretty," he yelled cheerfully. "Don't let me line catch you unawares."

*It already has,* she thought numbly. Around the marina she had a reputation as a recluse. One frustrated suitor had called her "the unmerry widow." So why was she staring up at Captain Blond as if she wanted to be his galley slave?

Tess clicked back to reality, stepped to one side, and watched him toss the heavy line with a coordinated strength that came from natural athletic ability. When it plopped on the dock she looped it around a cleat.

"Tow yourself in, captain, before someone clips you."

He clutched a chest covered in curly, dark-blond hair. He staggered around, trying to look pitiful while he tugged at the bow rope and finally secured the yacht close to the dock.

"Thank you for your help, fair lady," he said in a raspy tone. "I just got this boat last week, and this is my first time docking it. You were very gentle with me. I'll never forget my first time with you."

Tess sighed. "You're welcome."

"My name's Jeopard Surprise. I love useful women with English accents and beautiful bodies."

Tess grimaced at the tacky remark. She walked back aboard the *Lady* and picked her book up from the lounge chair. She decided it would be best to go downstairs and avoid Captain Tacky before he disappointed her more.

"You're on your own, Mr. Surprise."

"You saved me from washing out to sea! At least tell me your name, fair damsel!"

Tess pointed to her fawn-colored skin, then to the straight black hair that floated around her face and neck in a simple cut ornamented by softly structured bangs. "I'm hardly a *fair* damsel." The events in Gold Ridge tugged at her in a compelling way, and suddenly she added with pride, ''I'm approximately half Cherokee Indian.''

''Your berth's registered to a Royce Benedict. Are you Mrs. Benedict?''

''Do you always investigate your neighbors?'' she called.

''The information is in the marina's files for anyone who wants to know.''

''Then you know without asking that I'm Tess Benedict and that my husband's deceased.''

''I understand that your husband was a retired diamond broker—''

''Don't play asinine games with me. Good day, cap'n.''

With those cool words, Tess went downstairs and out of sight, where she closed the curtains, stretched out on her queen-size bed, and tried to read her book.

Surprise. Jeopard Surprise. Who was he? What was he—aside from being a Redford imitator? And why did history suddenly seem so dull in comparison to current events?

JEOPARD HELD A cold glass of water against his forehead as if it could ease his pain that way. Gone was the wisecracking facade, and in its place was his true persona—quiet, serious, brooding.

All his smiling at Tess Gallatin Benedict had given him a headache.

He picked up the phone beside his bed, called the shore operator, and had her patch him in to a Florida number.

''Kyle? Yeah, it's yours truly calling from Hell.''

Kyle Surprise laughed until Jeopard cut him off with a terse string of obscenities. ''Is she as beautiful as the pictures in the surveillance report?'' Kyle finally managed to ask.

Jeopard hesitated for a moment, shut his eyes, and remembered long legs, high breasts, and cheekbones a model would envy. He remembered a noble, slightly hooked nose and alluring, deep-set eyes that revealed her Cherokee heritage.

He remembered exotic dark hair that wasn't quite black, and skin the color of a deep, golden tan. He remembered a melodic voice that sounded sweet even when she was annoyed.

He remembered that she was as sleek and expensive-looking as the silver Jaguar she kept in the marina parking lot.

"She'll do."

"Did she seem inclined to fit the report's description? A bed bunny? Ready to hop for every carrot that comes by?"

"She watched me as if she might entertain the notion, but she didn't exactly leap into my hutch. God, she's so young. I felt ancient."

"Chill out, gramps, you're only thirty-eight."

"I'm too old to play a male Mata Hari."

"This is a curse cast by all those poor women who trailed you over the years. For once, you have to be the chaser, not the chasee."

"Remind me to go back to my old career. Busting spies and terrorists was easier than playing private investigator for the rich and famous."

There was dead silence on Kyle's end of the phone. Then finally, softly, "Not for me, bro. Not for me."

Jeopard winced. "Hey, kid, what did the doc say yesterday?"

"A few more operations and I'll only resemble Frankenstein when I'm in *bright* light."

Jeopard felt a familiar ache of regret. Kyle had been badly hurt a year before during a mission in South America. A Russian agent had tossed him into a locked room with a pack of kill-trained dogs.

It had been the end of Kyle's enthusiasm for security work, and Jeopard had seen the end coming for himself as well. Millie, their youngster sister, had begged them both to give it up, but particularly Jeopard.

The years of danger, of losing friends and lovers to an honorable but deadly game, had taken a toll on him.

Never one to mince words, Millie had told him that he was becoming something worse than the enemy he fought. He was becoming a machine.

And so he and Kyle had formed Surprise Import/Export, Inc., based in Fort Lauderdale, Florida. The innocent facade hid a quiet, lucrative trade in high-level investigative work. It could be dangerous at times, but compared to the old career, it was easy.

Or so it had been, until now. This fluffy Tess Benedict job was perfect for Kyle—charming, outgoing, fun-loving Kyle. Only, Kyle didn't think his face qualified him for such work anymore.

Jeopard hinted hopefully. "Even with scars, bro, you'd be better with this Benedict woman than I am."

Kyle's jaunty tone returned. "Oh, no, Jep. You're gonna learn to enjoy being coy and cute. I insist. Consider it a challenge."

"Maybe I can find out if she has the Kara diamond some other way."

"Oh?"

"Yeah. I'll threaten her with my Cary Grant routine. She'll have to tell me about the diamond or die laughing."

Kyle was still guffawing when Jeopard hung up the phone.

THE ANTLER CHARM. Tess was sitting on her cabin floor the next morning, surrounded by more history books, when she remembered it. Chastising herself for being senile at twenty-six, she hurried into the galley, went to a dining booth built into the wall, and knelt under the table.

She slid aside a specially designed panel and reached into the base of the booth, where a small safe was secured. A tiny light fixture, keyed to the opening of the panel, illuminated the safe's well-worn dial.

The safe had belonged to Royce for many years, and in its time had protected jewels worth millions of dollars. He had given it to her as a sentimental wed-

ding present, and along with it the promise that he'd
teach her everything he knew about diamonds.

Tess spun the dial quickly, and the door popped
open. She reached in, pushed aside personal jewelry,
personal papers, and a cloth bag containing a hundred
thousand dollars' worth of uncut Brazilian diamonds—
she had to deliver the diamonds to a wholesaler in Los
Angeles the next week—and grasped a piece of deer
antler the size of her thumb.

Her heart pounding with excitement, she quickly
closed the safe and remained crouched under the table, studying the gift her father had given her not long
before his death.

The amulet had been caressed by respectful fingers
until it was nearly white. It was made from the curving tip of a deer antler, and the blunt end was covered
by a cap of gold topped by a tiny ring, so that the
amulet could be worn on a chain.

Her father had told her that the amulet had come
to him from his father, Benjamin Gallatin, a blacksmith on the Cherokee reservation in Oklahoma. It
might have been made by Benjamin's father, Silas, the
half-Cherokee son of Katherine and Justis.

Enchanted, Tess studied the most important aspect
of the amulet—the Cherokee symbols carved deeply into
its surface. She went back to the cabin and retrieved the
gold medallion she'd left laying among her books.

The symbols on the medallion were undoubtedly
separated into words or phrases, and she squealed
with delight when she saw that one of the phrases
matched the symbols on the antler amulet.

The security buzzer sounded, meaning that someone had stepped on a detection panel hidden in the
bow deck. Tess went aboveboard and met a tall teenage boy carrying an enormous arrangement of cut
flowers in a ceramic base.

"Hiya, Tess," he said, peeking through the flowers.
"Some guy called the shop and ordered these for ya.
Mom said to tell ya she's thrilled to have a partner

who gets guys to order two hundred dollars' worth of flowers.''

"Brandt, good lord, who sent these?"

"Uh, uh . . .'' He nodded toward a card stuck in the jungle of blossoms.

Tess opened it and read, ''I'd like to bump into you again and throw you some more lines. How about coming aboard for that margarita? Jeopard.''

She groaned at his determination. Dammit, why did this gorgeous, mature-looking man have the silly technique of a lounge lizard?

JEOPARD HATED PEEKING out the yacht's window. In the old days his agents had called him the Iceman, because of his emotionless facade and unbending dignity. The Iceman had confronted Third World dictators face to face without breaking into a sweat; he'd impressed the most brutal terrorists with his utterly cold demeanor; he'd traded urbane witticisms with powerful women and watched with objective pleasure while they turned into purring kittens.

And now he was hiding behind a curtain and cursing forcefully because the teenage delivery boy was still in Tess Benedict's cabin twenty minutes after delivering *his* flowers.

Jeopard smiled sardonically.

If Mrs. Benedict was a cradle robber, then he might as well pack his gnarled old body back to Florida.

But there *was* hope—if he could impress her enough. After all, this was the self-serving woman who, at twenty, had married a wealthy man almost three times her own age.

It was definitely no love match, judging by the information Jeopard had received. She'd known from the beginning that Royce Benedict was dying of cancer. He'd taught her what he knew about diamonds and used his contacts to get her started as a respected broker. Which was hilarious, considering that before his illness Benedict had been a jewel thief of international renown.

Jeopard sighed, hating the sordid business of prying into her life and wishing that his old cynicism would overwhelm him so that he wouldn't *care* whether Tess Benedict was a gold digger—or in this case, a diamond digger.

For the first time in years Jeopard felt human and vulnerable. He pinched the skin on his stomach, poked his thigh muscles, flexed his biceps, and went to study himself in a mirror.

"SORRY ABOUT THE shower problem, Brandt."

Brandt rolled his eyes and shrugged. "No problem. At least it's fixed now."

"Poor kid. I owe you one. Want to drive the Jag to school next week?"

He whooped loudly. "All week? We get out for the summer on Friday. Until Friday?"

"Sure. If I need a car, I'll borrow my granddad's station wagon."

"You're great! You're really out there, Tess! You're fantastic!"

After Brandt left she stood beside Jeopard Surprise's yacht for nearly a minute, composing a firm speech. Her gaze drifted to the yacht's name, painted on both sides of the bow in black script edged in gold. She hadn't noticed it before.

*Irresistible.*

She shook her head in amused disgust. Tess climbed a wide gangplank to the bow deck and followed a canopied side deck toward the stern.

The yacht's windows were at knee level along the deck. Tess knelt down, one hand raised to tap on them. She really didn't mean to peer inside, but the curtains were thin.

Jeopard Surprise, wearing nothing but an air of concentration, stood in his luxurious bedroom admiring himself in a full-length mirror.

S HE'D SEEN HIM in nothing but swim trunks the day before, but, oh, what a difference the loss of that simple covering made. His rapt scrutiny of himself confirmed her notion that he was vain. But in his case, vanity was justified.

His bedroom was small; after all, the yacht might be impressive, but it wasn't the *Love Boat*. So he was less than ten feet from her, and the sheer window curtains made him more tantalizing by screening him with gauzy white.

Tess remained by the window, her fist frozen in a tapping gesture, her insides dissolving into worrisome sensations of elemental attraction, her eyes riveted to the most undeniably beautiful male body she'd ever seen.

He wasn't beautiful in the sense of a sleek, boyish Greek statue; for one thing, he had a generous supply of hair on his chest, arms, and legs. He had the torso of a boxer—blocky and compact, not top-heavy with muscle. His upper body tapered only a little into his flanks, but there wasn't a spare ounce of flesh around his waist.

No. Jeopard Surprise's beauty came from a combination of muscle, grace, and virility that epitomized masculine charms. The virile part lay docile right now, but it was awesome, nonetheless. Like a sleeping lion, it looked ready to spring up majestically.

She doubted that hc was more than six feet tall, but his legs were long, like a runner's, and they gave him the illusion of more height. They were wonderful legs, and the parts they adjoined, both front and back, were enough to make Tess sigh with plaintive admiration.

He might be preening in front of the mirror, but at least he was dignified about it, she admitted. He seemed very serious and intense.

Turning from side to side, he rubbed his hands up and down his stomach, stopping just short of the luxurious triangle of blond hair low on his belly. He nodded solemnly at himself, then twisted to look over his shoulder at his rump. He slapped it on one side as if he were testing for tone. Then he braced his legs apart and slipped a hand between them to poke his inner thighs.

Tess groaned in dismay as Jeopard stretched languidly, every muscle taut and inviting. He stared at himself in the mirror, nodded again, then slapped both hands on his chest as if to say, *Good stuff*. He had obviously concluded that his appearance was acceptable.

She more than agreed. And she had to get off the *Irresistible* before she went overboard, she thought raggedly.

Tess leaped to her feet. Just as she did, she saw his head snap up sharply toward the windows. Ice water poured into her veins. Had he seen her?

She tiptoed along the side deck and heard his cabin door bang open.

Stepping onto the dock, Tess halted. A dull, leaden feeling filled her stomach, while her face burned.

He could now be heard running across the bow deck.

She turned around slowly, her chin tucked, and gazed up sheepishly. He came to a stop at the edge of the bow. Her mouth dropped open, and she gasped.

Had this man ever smiled at her? Impossible. This man had nothing lighthearted inside him.

He was carrying a small cannon of a handgun, and the fact that he held it pointed in her direction didn't help her feelings. But he'd put on a robe, thank heavens—at least she wouldn't have to deal with his other weapons.

Tess backed across the dock another couple of feet, clasping her hands protectively over her chest. Jeopard Surprise stared down at her, and a deep frown formed between his brows.

"It was only me," she called in a high, unnatural voice. *Please don't blast little old harmless me, captain. I swear I'll never peek at you again.*

After he scrutinized her for several seconds, the deadly look began to fade from his eyes. He blinked. His stance wavered, then relaxed, and he quickly lowered the gun.

"You? What the hell were you doing?"

She stared at the gun. "Fearing for my life."

He glanced at the frightening piece of artillery in his hand. A weary, self-rebuking expression crossed his face. "I apologize. Don't worry. I rarely shoot anyone I've sent flowers to."

"I'm very glad."

He remained still, studying the gun as if lost in thought. Tess watched with growing fascination as she realized that he was still rebuking himself for his reaction. Though frightened and puzzled, she felt drawn to him in an entirely new way.

Royce had often commented, with approval, that she loved to tease the limits of safety. It was evident in the way she drove a car, he said, and in the fact that she had married a jewel thief.

She hadn't believed Royce until that moment. Now she admitted that she liked a hint of danger, and the complex man above her offered not only that, but mystery.

"Don't get the wrong idea. I, umm, I came over to thank you for the flowers, and I . . . heard my boat's alarm system buzzing, so I had to hurry. . . ." She paused, frowning.

She was no good at such ridiculous lies. Tess lifted her chin and said defiantly, "Oh, hell, captain, I was coming to tell you where to shove your flowers. I accidentally looked into your bedroom window. After I enjoyed the show for a few seconds I decided to leave before you realized that you were being ogled. My only problem was that I decided too late. I do apologize, but you should buy thicker curtains."

With that she turned and marched back to the *Lady*.

Jeopard stared after her while his senses slowly returned to a lower level of alertness. Ogling him, she'd said. Enjoying the show.

He began to smile sincerely, and it was such a foreign thing that he didn't even notice.


TESS LAY ON her stomach in the middle of her queen-size bed, crying without a sound, the antler amulet clasped in one hand, Dove Gallatin's medallion clasped in the other, a book open in front of her.

When the bow alarm buzzed, she brushed at her eyes hurriedly and said a small thanks for the fact that she didn't wear any makeup and therefore wasn't smearing any across her face.

A warm California night had descended, and the dock was a sultry place of shadows and pools of light from regularly spaced lamps along the water's edge. The other side of the dock abutted a thick concrete wall, and past it was a grassy lawn dotted with tall palms, beyond which was the marina parking lot.

Tess climbed the stairs from her cabin and found Jeopard Surprise standing on the bow, framed by a background of palms and suggestively shadowed by the dock lamps.

She halted at the top of the steps, her heart kicking into overdrive. He stood with one leg angled out, his hands shoved casually into the pockets of camel-colored trousers. He wore Docksiders and a white polo shirt.

"Well, Peeping Tess," he said solemnly, "the least you can do is walk over to the Zanzi Bar with me and have a nightcap."

She laughed, then applauded. "Bravo to your diplomacy and sense of humor."

He nodded, his attitude quiet and thoughtful. "I understand this place, the Zanzi Bar, is an up-scale hangout for the boating crowd around here."

"Yes." Tess tilted her head to one side and studied him curiously. "You seem different. Subdued. Did my ridiculous antics unnerve you?"

He chuckled ruefully. "I haven't met many women who'd have admitted what they were up to. It's unfair. My standard approach won't work on a woman as honest as you. I'll just have to be myself and hope for the best."

"Marvelous! I knew there was a likable, no-nonsense person behind that frivolous facade."

"Honesty," he grumbled. "I love it."

"I'm too honest, and it gets me in trouble sometimes. But I do like your new attitude."

"Good. Then let's make friends. Come along, Cherokee princess."

She gestured toward her shorts. "Give me time to change."

"Should I alert the cavalry?"

She arched a brow. "After seeing you in action, I don't think you need help."

"In the bedroom, or chasing trespassers?"

Tess chuckled, felt her stomach drop languidly, and stifled a desire to answer, "Either." She pointed over her shoulder. "You may wait at my patio table, captain. I promise to hurry."

"I promise to wait."

She kept her word, and came back above deck to

meet him less than ten minutes later. He sat at the table, slowly folding and unfolding a gum wrapper she'd left there, his head bowed in an attitude of deep thought.

Ah, yes, this side of Jeopard Surprise was more intriguing by the minute.

"I'm ready, Sundance. Stop thinking so hard."

He looked up, stood gracefully, and swept a slow gaze over her softly draped sundress of earth-tone shades. His assessment was bold enough to make her breasts tingle but debonair enough to avoid offense.

"Sundance?" he repeated.

"Surely people have told you that you could be Robert Redford's younger brother."

"Hmmm. I don't feel like a *younger* anything."

"How old are you?"

"Thirty-eight."

She hadn't yet gotten a close look at his face. During the events of the past two days he'd either been a few yards away from her, or wearing sunglasses, or camouflaged by his bedroom curtains.

Even now the light was dim, making it difficult to study him. On impulse Tess reached for his hand and tugged. "Step forward, pops, and let me have a look at your wizened old face."

He smiled a little and did as she asked.

When she stood less than a foot from him in a soft beam of light from the dock lamps, she could only stare up at him blankly, mesmerized. It was a distressful thing to have her mind go on vacation simply because his somber blue eyes were studying her back intently.

Tess murmured something without knowing what she said.

"Thank you," he answered. "I feel so much better."

She broke the spell by laughing softly and stepping back. But he wasn't through stunning her, and he stepped forward.

"If I put on some Ella Fitzgerald and we do this repeatedly, we'll be dancing," she quipped.

"I like your taste in singers. Okay, where did you get those silver-blue eyes?"

"Daddy married a Swedish girl and took her off to his teepee. Pardon me, his wigwam. Cherokees didn't live in teepees." Tess gazed up at him in silence, trembling inside, her eyes riveted to his. "Yours are a darker shade of blue."

They were beautiful, intelligent eyes, she thought, and yet there was something shadowed about them, a coldness deep beneath the surface. But since the coldness wasn't directed toward her, she wouldn't worry about it yet.

He brushed a fingertip along the soft underside of her left eye, then her right.

Tess didn't know whether the boat was rocking or her equilibrium had just faltered. He'd touched her with incredible gentleness, using the same fingertip that had curled so expertly around the trigger of a deadly gun. The thought somehow reassured her that she had no reason to fear him, though others undoubtedly did.

She took a slow, reviving breath.

"Yes, my mother was Swedish. How's that for intriguing? A Swedish mother and a Cherokee father—I don't know whether to say *Yah?* or *How?*"

His mouth quirked up in delight. He seemed surprised that he found her so entertaining. After another second, he tilted his head back and laughed richly. Tess bit her lip and gazed at him with concern. If he kept this more mature charm going, she was in trouble.

"Damn, I haven't laughed like that—" He caught himself, smiled pensively at her, then frowned. He took her chin between his fingers and turned her face to one side and then the other, letting light fall directly on it. "Have you been crying?"

It was hard to remember what she'd been doing. "I was reading an account of the Trail of Tears. You know—when the U.S. government forced the Cherokees to leave the southeast and go to Oklahoma. It happened in 1838. Thousands of people died." She hesitated, then added softly, "My people."

He removed his hand slowly, his fingers almost caressing her as he did, and she had to concentrate to keep from leaning after them.

"I don't know a great deal about Cherokee history," he admitted.

"You probably know more than I do. I'm ashamed to say I don't know much about my heritage."

"Oh?"

"Come on, Sundance. I'll explain while we walk to the bar." She pointed to the medallion that lay between her breasts on a long gold chain. "I'll tell you about my family history."

"Hold my hand. I'm trembling from suspense."

Tess eyed his outstretched hand drolly. "White man speak with forked tongue."

"If you want to know about my tongue I can—"

"I'll hold your hand."

As she led him from the *Lady* she began explaining about Gold Ridge, Georgia, her remarkable cousins, and Dove Gallatin's mysterious intervention in their lives.

"SO, THAT WAS my first foray into my Cherokee heritage," Tess finished, curving her hands around a tumbler of Scotch as she sat at a small table with Jeopard at the Zanzi Bar. "And I'm afraid that it's hooked me. I've been raising my consciousness lately."

*And raising something of mine that I can't name that politely*, Jeopard thought.

"You think I'm whimsical, Sundance?"

"No. I admire your dedication. I haven't run across much dedication lately. Tell me more about yourself."

"I was born in Sweden. My mother died in a skiing accident when I was two. My father was an entirely wonderful man, and he loved me, but his work didn't permit him to raise a child alone. I grew up with my mother's parents, in Sweden, then went to boarding school in England. But I visited my father often, here in California." She paused, smiling at the memories. "The *Swedish Lady* was his boat. He left it to me." Her smile faded. "He died of a heart attack—oh, let's see— seven years ago. When I was nineteen."

"What kind of work did he do?"

The smile came back. "Have you ever heard of Sam Daggett?"

Jeopard chuckled. "He's second in my heart only to John McDonald's Travis McGee character. The Daggett books are classics."

"I'm glad your think so! My father wrote them!"

He looked at her incredulously. "Your father was J. H. Gant?"

"Uh-uh. Hank Gallatin. J. H. Gant was his pen name. And he lived quite a few of the stories he wrote about, I guarantee it. When he wasn't J. H. Gant, author, he was truly Sam Daggett, wanderer and adventurer. That's why I couldn't stay with him. He was always running off to exotic places to help some crony or other get out of trouble."

Jeopard stared at her with new fascination. Her father didn't sound like the mercenary who'd been described in the report.

Hell, this case became more disturbing by the second. Sam Daggett, along with Travis McGee, had inspired his earliest—and most idealistic—dreams of adventure. Those dreams had culminated in a career in Navy Intelligence and eventually in private security work for driven, dedicated T.S. Audubon. His youthful fantasies were the only thing he still cherished about the world's intrigues.

"You look as if I just handed you a Christmas present," she murmured.

"You did."

She took a sip of her drink. "Captain Sundance, I've been babbling about myself and I have yet to learn anything about you."

Professional wariness closed around him like an invisible cloak. "You know a lot. I'm a terrible sailor, I have a bedroom with, ahem, a full-length mirror, and I pack a large pistol for chasing women."

"We're talking about the Magnum .44, you mean," she teased.

Jeopard smiled wickedly. "That too." He couldn't help enjoying her. The fact that she had recognized the gun impressed him. Of course, J. H. Gant's daughter would know about such things.

She laughed in a way that was girlish without being the least bit shy. Her blue eyes held too much authority for that. "What do you do for a living that allows you to buy large pistols and cumbersome boats?"

He fed her his standard story about Surprise Import/ Export in Fort Lauderdale. Her smile tightened, and she searched his eyes intently. Damn, he thought, she knew he was hiding something. Her intuition surprised him, made him feel oddly proud of her but also vulnerable.

"Jeopard, whatever you really do for a living, I hope it's not dishonorable."

He was glad that his control kept her from knowing how much she'd just shaken him.

"You say that because of the way I charged after you with a gun today?"

"Exactly. If your import/export business has anything to do with drugs, you can keep away from me. The farther, the better."

Inside he breathed a sigh of relief. Jeopard laughed with just the right amount of sincerity. "I'm clean, legal, and legit. I'll give you a business card tomorrow, and you can check me out."

She shook her head, smiled, and relaxed visibly.

He held up his right hand so that she could see the heavy gold insignia ring on it. "Naval Academy— Annapolis. The navy was my career until a few years ago. I was a SEAL. Do you know what that means?"

She nodded. "Special forces. Very elite. Also very tough."

"So you see where I get my gun-toting, Clint Eastwood habits?"

"All right." She nodded, satisfied, but after a moment of thought added wryly, "I guess SEALs don't learn how to handle yachts."

He chuckled. "It's not part of military training, no."

"So, importer/exporter, what are you doing so far from Florida?"

"I exported myself here for a two-week vacation."

"You had an, ahem, more experienced captain export your yacht, I hope."

"It's leased. I boarded it off the coast at Laguna Beach."

"Thank heavens you didn't have far to navigate before you rammed my poor *Lady*. The seafaring world wasn't threatened too badly."

"You're hurting my feelings."

"I suspect that few things hurt your feelings. However, I *do* apologize for maligning you."

He grasped his chest theatrically. "You'll have to do better than an apology. You'll have to have lunch with me tomorrow."

She clasped her hands on the table and looked at him formally, much like a schoolteacher addressing an errant boy, he thought.

"Captain Sundance, tell me the truth. Are you married?"

"Would anyone marry such a rotten docker? No."

"Ever?"

"No." He watched her try delicately to hide her curiosity. "Never fear, Tess, I have no desire to do your hair or redecorate your boat."

She gave him a rebuking look, but chuckled, "I wasn't asking for personal reasons."

"Oh? Are you a reporter for the *Marina Enquirer?*"

Her soft laughter crept into his bones and refused to leave.

"You silly lout. I can assume, then, that you're just another carefree playboy?"

"Playman," he corrected. "I passed 'boy' way back."

She laughed again. Jeopard took a slow swallow from his drink and wished like hell that she'd stop. It was not only the most seductive sound he'd ever heard; it was the sweetest. Instinct, observation, and cold, hard facts began to give way to pure affection.

"I believe I *will* have lunch with you, Jeopard." She gazed at him happily.

Jeopard nodded, forcing himself to look pleased. He was too seasoned, too cynical, and too wise to let a job get to him. She was just a job, after all. If she had the Kara diamond, he'd get it from her. And when she realized his deception, she wouldn't have anything to laugh about for a long time.

## CHAPTER 3

S HE COULDN'T WAIT to tell her grandparents about Jeopard Surprise.

At seven the next morning—bleary-eyed because she and Jeopard had sat at the Zanzi Bar talking until four—she parked the Jaguar in front of Viktoria and Karl Kellgren's Spanish-style duplex. The old, exclusive section of Long Beach where they lived was quiet and pretty: small homes and duplexes marched up the street beside tiny front yards exploding with colorful flowers and shrubs.

Karl and Viktoria met her at their door as usual, their arms wide, as if she didn't come every morning for breakfast.

They had followed her to Long Beach soon after Karl retired from a long and prestigious career in the Swedish parliament. Moving to America had been entirely their idea, but she adored them for doing it, and was glad that they were happy in the ultimate American playland that was California.

She didn't have a phone on the sailboat, so they

kept a phone for her, a separate line with an answering machine. And because her relationship with them was so close, she didn't mind that they knew her business and social doings. She led a simple life.

So she sat with them in their bright little kitchen, eating a very Swedish breakfast of pancakes smeared with jelly, not tasting the food, her concentration devoted to telling them an enthusiastic but G-rated account of the intriguing man who'd become her neighbor at the marina.

After a half-hour of nonstop talking in fluent Swedish, Tess realized that their cheerful expressions had gone dark. "What's wrong?" she asked.

Her grandfather spoke first. "Why did you tell him so much about yourself so soon?"

Tess smiled drolly. "*Farfar*, only because the man asked. It could be that he likes me. I am likable, you know." She squeezed Karl's hand. "He's not the kind of man who feels comfortable talking about himself right away. That's the only reason he encouraged me to talk. It was innocent."

Viktoria nervously twisted the hem of the colorful apron she wore over a housedress. "But he wanted to know so much about your work and your family." She frowned. "You didn't tell him that you keep diamonds on your boat, did you?"

"No, of course not."

"And whatever you do, don't tell him about the blue. Don't wear it around him, either."

"That's right," Karl agreed.

Tess stared at her grandparents in disbelief. "You know I don't wear the blue. It's worth too much. What's going on with you worrywarts?"

"The diamond has been in the family for many years," Karl said sternly. "We wouldn't want it stolen."

"Good heavens!" She propped her chin in one hand and looked from Karl to Viktoria slowly. "Why are you worried now, but never before? Why didn't you worry when you gave the diamond to me? I was only eighteen. You didn't even worry when I married Royce, the ultimate diamond fancier.''

"Royce was a friend of your father and mother's. He was an honorable man. We trusted him,'' Viktoria told her. "Since he's been gone you've ignored all the men who've tried to get close to you. Now, suddenly, this Surprise person takes advantage of your loneliness. . . .''

"*Farmor*, Royce has been gone for two years, and I'm lonely, I admit that. But Jeopard Surprise is very special. Besides, neither he nor anyone else knows that I have the blue.''

"Just you be careful,'' Viktoria admonished, waving a finger.

"I could take it to the bank and put it—''

"No!'' both Karl and Viktoria exclaimed.

"Don't show it to *anyone*,'' Karl said emphatically.

"It was your mother's. It should stay close to you,'' her grandmother added.

After a stunned moment, Tess sadly told herself that senility was making its first marks on her beloved grandparents.

"Good. I want to keep it close to me,'' she told them gently. "A thief would have to tear my boat apart to find the blue. I never leave it outside its special safe. Don't worry.''

"I think we'll go down to the marina this morning and sit on your boat until we see this Surprise person,'' Karl announced.

Smiling benignly at their whimsical fears, Tess got up from the table and gave them each a kiss. "You guys do that. I have some phone calls to make, so I'll stay here.'' She paused, feeling mischievous, and added, "If he cranks his yacht's engine, run for your lives.''

SLEEPY-EYED, A cup of coffee in his hand, Jeopard glanced out his galley window a second time just to make certain that they were staring at the *Irresistible*.

Yep. Santa and Mrs. Claus were watching him from the deck of Tess's sailboat.

They both had graying blond hair. Santa wore a Panama hat and didn't have a beard, and their clothes were modern, but somehow the plump little red-cheeked pair evoked thoughts of elves and reindeer.

They sat at the umbrella-covered patio table, looking quite patient, as if they were just waiting for their binoculars to arrive.

They had to be the *morföräldrar*, the grandparents, Tess had mentioned the night before. Karl and Viktoria. The Iceman was under the surveillance of Swedish gnomes.

Jeopard leaned back in his chair and cursed softly at the new wrinkle in what should have been a simple case. Cute little overprotective grandfolks didn't jibe with the background he'd been given about Tess Benedict. Of course, she could be a worthless piece of scum and still evoke love from her family—he'd seen that situation many times in his work.

Sure. Tess was scum. That was why he'd enjoyed every minute of the seven hours they'd sat talking at Zanzi Bar. That was why he'd resisted the urge to seduce her the night before, and had left her at her boat with no more than a quick kiss on the cheek and a joke about being too tired to aim for her mouth.

Sure. He didn't want her. He didn't want to breathe, either. The night before, he'd felt himself permanently slipping over the line that separated professional interest from personal interest.

Hell, maybe it didn't matter. He'd get the job done, regardless.

Where did she go every morning about seven? Work? No, she was dressed too casually to call on diamond wholesalers. A lover? The kid who'd delivered the flowers? Jeopard would rent a car and follow her the next day. It might be important.

Sure. Finding out if she had lovers was crucial to recovering the Kara diamond.

Suddenly he didn't feel like hanging around the marina to be gaped at by cute old people who made him feel dirty for deceiving their granddaughter.

TESS WAS LITERALLY floating on air as she boarded the *Lady*. The two grinning, muscular college boys swung her between them on a seat made of their latched arms.

"You may put me down now, serfs," she ordered, laughing. They set her carefully atop the deck and bowed.

"Anything for you, my queen."

"Anything for a beer, my queen."

"You haven't changed a bit, serfs. Wait here. My castle is a mess, and much too small for a queen and two brawny rugby players." Smiling, Tess went to her cabin. When she came back she carried two bottles of beer and a thick leather scrapbook.

"Oooo, imported brew," one boy crooned.

"Would you expect the king's wife to drink domestic?" the other boy asked.

Tess handed them the beers and the scrapbook, brushing her fingers over the book in a loving goodbye as she did. They assured her that they'd be careful when they photocopied the prized collection of memorabilia and newspaper clippings from the two years Royce had coached a city-sponsored rugby team.

"No hurry about returning it," she called as they tromped away. "But be careful with it."

They blew her kisses out the window of their van as they left the marina parking lot.

Humming, Tess ran back to the cabin and quickly changed from her shorts outfit into sandals, white slacks, and a colorful tank top. She pulled her sleek, chocolate-colored hair back from her temples with white combs.

She went to a jewelry box where she kept her less-expensive items and got a pair of one-carat diamond studs for her ears. She put them on, then slipped a thousand-dollar Lady Rolex onto her wrist.

Next she fastened the antler amulet onto a slender gold chair and proudly hung it around her neck. When she checked her appearance in the mirror of her tiny bathroom, the amulet was all she noticed.

She couldn't wait to tell Jeopard what she'd learned on the telephone that morning.

When the buzzer sounded, Tess burst out of the cabin, looked up the stairwell to the deck, and waved cheerfully.

"Hey, Sundance, I heard that you encountered my grandparents. They said you took the yacht out and didn't hit my boat or the dock even once."

He nodded and tipped a finger to his dark sunglasses in jaunty salute. "I wouldn't dare, as long as they were here. You might say that I was *gnomed*."

Tess laughed giddily as she locked the cabin door and began punching a numbered panel that activated her sophisticated security system. What a perfect day this was going to be!

She glanced up the stairs and sighed at the soul-stirring sight of him. This man probably didn't own a pair of jeans, she decided. He was wearing belted khaki trousers with a blue polo shirt.

But Tess liked his fashionable yet understated style. He had a sexy kind of elegance to him—like a blond James Bond, she thought.

Behind his sunglasses, Jeopard shut his eyes and wished he could do anything but spend the day with Tess. He'd witnessed her exuberant affection with the two college-boy types, and it only added to his troubled emotions.

Whether friends or lovers, they were obviously close to her heart. He hoped they were lovers—he needed some harsh reality to restore his defenses.

She ran up the steps, looking delicious and cool, her white smile beautiful against the fawn hue of her skin. She grasped his hands and smiled at him until he couldn't help smiling back.

"I'm dragging you up to Los Angeles," she announced. "More specifically, to the library at the UCLA campus in Westwood."

"I'm game. What are we researching?"

She was trembling with excitement. Her voice hoarse, she told him, "I spent the whole morning talking to a woman at the Cherokee Cultural Center in Oklahoma. She told me about a biography written by a business associate of my great-grandfather Gallatin—the one who owned the shipping company in San Francisco."

She laughed with delight, threw her arms around Jeopard's neck, and hugged him hard. "And UCLA has a copy!"

Jeopard grimaced as the soft length of her body pressed against him and her delicate perfume filled his senses. Something tore apart inside him, and he was shaken by an all-encompassing desire simply to tell her the truth about his work and his mission there, then do his best to make her not care.

It didn't matter whether she was hoarding a diamond stolen from one of the royal families to Europe, whether she might have married her husband simply to get that diamond and everything else he had, or whether she had a dozen lovers under the age of twenty-five.

Jeopard knew only that he'd been waiting all his life to feel her arms around him.


TESS GOT TEARS in her eyes when a librarian handed her several envelopes of microfiche that contained Silas Gallatin's biography. She and Jeopard found a display machine on a nearly deserted floor of the UCLA library building and sat down at it side by side.

Tess stared at the envelopes as if they were sacred. "It doesn't look like a very long biography," she murmured in disappointment. "Maybe it's just about his shipping business. With a title like *Portrait of a Leader* it could be very impersonal."

"We won't know until we read it."

She looked up at Jeopard, her eyes wetter than ever. "Forgive me for being so sentimental. It's just that I feel as if several important aspects of my life are converging all at once. As if nothing is ever going to be the same again."

Jeopard was very close to her. She saw another odd, unreadable emotion darken his eyes. The man was difficult to decipher, a fact she enjoyed.

"What aspects?" he asked gently.

Tess shivered inside at the effect of his voice. "Meeting my cousins, learning about my Indian heritage." She paused. "Meeting you."

A stillness dropped over him, making him seem poised on the edge of some monumental decision. His gaze went to her mouth. She felt his breath quicken against her face. If he leaned toward her just a few inches, he could kiss her.

But he didn't move.

Tess couldn't stand it. She tilted her head, parted her lips, and kissed him quickly on the mouth. Sensation sleeted through her as his lips responded with a skill that put a world of promise in the brief contact.

"We could get kicked out of the library for doing that," he joked in a gruff tone.

Tess struggled for enough air to speak. "At UCLA? We'd have to do something a lot more shocking."

She took a deep breath and reminded herself why they were there. Her fingers trembling, she put the first sheet of microfiche into the machine and watched her great-grandfather's life reach out to her from the past.


"TAKE DEEP BREATHS. That's it. You're just hyperventilating. Let's sit down over here on the grass."

His arm around Tess's shoulders, Jeopard led her to a small park not far from where they'd left the car.

She clutched the thick handful of photocopied microfiche pages to her chest and kept clutching them even after he'd grasped her by the arms and helped her sit. He sat down beside her, tugged the manuscript away and laid it on the grass, then rubbed her neck gently.

"S-sorry," she managed to say. "We were in there for hours. Everything just hit me as we walked out into reality again. Great-grandmother owned a saloon. And probably a brothel. I never knew the Cherokees allowed such things. I expected Pocahontas, not the Happy Hooker."

She bent her head into her hands and began to laugh.

Jeopard reminded her solemnly. "The writer only said that she ran a house of entertainment in the Oklahoma Territory not long after the Civil War. Maybe she had the historical equivalent of a video arcade."

Tess grasped his shirtfront and chortled loudly into his shoulder. "Pack-saddle Man."

Jeopard's throat contorted with restraint. She made it so easy to laugh. "Wide-Open-Spaces Invader."

When she squealed and thumped his chest with unrestrained mirth, he gave up. They both laughed wildly. She leaned against him and he put both arms around her. They rocked back and forth, gasping for breath.

Tess finally slumped in his embrace, wiping her eyes and reaching up to wipe his. They shared a droll look.

"I really think it's fascinating that my great-*farmor* was a madam," Tess admitted. "She may have done it out of desperation—she was only twenty-two when Silas took her away from her business. It's obvious that the Civil War devastated the Oklahoma Cherokees, and she probably had lost her family. Silas seemed like the kind of man who wouldn't care if he scandalized society, as long as he married the woman he loved. He sounds rather wonderful."

"See? No need to hyperventilate. And think of the other tidbits you picked up."

"It means a lot to me to know that the three gold

medallions were willed to Silas and his brothers by their parents. It's a starting point.''

"Katherine Blue Song. Now you know your great-great-grandmother's maiden name.''

"Katlanicha Blue Song. Katherine was her white name,'' Tess reminded him. "I can't wait to call my cousin Kat. She's named after her—Katherine. I'm sure she'll want to know that her name has a fascinating background.''

"We should fly up to San Francisco this week and find your great-great-grandparents' graves.''

Tess grasped his hand excitedly. "I can't believe they spent their last years in California. Right in my home state! And I have to call my cousin Erica and tell her that Justis Gallatin was described as having 'burnt-red hair, like a chestnut horse.' That's the color of Erica's hair!''

She shut her eyes. "Oh, I don't mind hyperventilating over this. I feel like Sherlock Holmes after a successful case.''

"Without the pipe and tweed hat, thank God.''

Jeopard stroked her back and laughed with her again.

"Jep, I'm very glad you're sharing this with me.''

He looked down at her laugh-flushed skin and happy blue eyes for several long seconds. *Jep*. She had unknowingly chosen the nickname used by his brother and sister, the only two people who loved him and kept him from losing his humanity. Maybe it was a good sign. "I'm glad too,'' he murmured.

He kissed her, kissed her hard, and felt light-headed when she kissed him back with a skill and passion that matched his own. He kept kissing her until a group of students strolled by and hooted at them cheerfully.

"We can't get kicked out of a park for smooching,'' Tess told him when he scowled after the group.

He looked at her, frowning. "I'd like an older audience, at least. How about dinner?''

She was trembling desperately in his embrace. "If

we do this in a restaurant, we'll get kicked out for certain.''

''Very funny. How about dinner aboard my yacht?''

''Can you cook?''

His heart was pounding in his chest. This was stupid, dangerous, and he was in way over his head. He pulled her more tightly against him. ''Does it matter?''

She shut her eyes for a moment, and when she opened them, they were peaceful. ''No. Not at all.''

JEOPARD KNEW THAT she wanted him badly, and his intuition told him that there was something special in the wanting, something that made him unique. His age, he assumed grimly. She was accustomed to kids. Bedding a full-grown man would seem like a novelty to her.

That thought, that he might be nothing more than a change of pace for her, didn't stop him from needing her more than he'd ever needed a woman in his life. Whatever her ugly truths—and he would learn them all before he was through—she hypnotized him with her trusting eagerness.

For another thing, he couldn't resist her cheerfulness. Lord, how many boys had lost their hearts while she perfected her innocent charm?

Nor could he resist her gentle sophistication. No matter how promiscuous she was, there was nothing coy or cynical about her intention to go to bed with him; just a sweet, silent admission in every touch, every look, and every inflection of her beautiful voice.

As they walked hand in hand down the dock toward his yacht, she smiled at people aboard neighboring boats, called to them by name, and swung his hand as if she and he were long-time lovers, not two people who'd known each other only a couple of days.

But she and he weren't strangers, Jeopard conceded silently. He doubted they'd ever been strangers, not even in the first moments when she stood below his bow as he docked the yacht, gazing up at him with amused disgust because of his tacky come-ons.

It was getting too easy to overlook every insinuation in the royal report from the Duke of Kara. What was the duke's idea of promiscuous, anyway? A few lovers—hell, Jeopard thought, he'd had more than a few lovers himself, starting in the tenth grade with a college girl.

Jeopard didn't buy the idea that women ought to be less active than men; he'd known too many strong, intelligent women with the highest moral standards who also, incidentally, loved sex. Two years ago such a woman had died to save his life during an assignment in East Germany.

Jeopard was distracted from his brooding when a redheaded young man with the shoulders of a body builder and the tan of a George Hamilton hopped off a sailboat and swaggered his way down the dock toward them, grinning at Tess. He wore nothing but a bikini-cut piece of blue material masquerading as a decent swimsuit.

Tess smiled at him. "Good afternoon, Timothy."

"Hiya, gorgeous."

"Timothy, this is Jeopard Surprise. He's got the yacht next to me. Jeopard, this is Timothy Taylor. He works for the marina. I hire him to keep the *Lady*'s rigging shipshape."

Timothy shook Jeopard's hand, then winked at Tess and strolled on past.

"He needs to check his own rigging," Jeopard remarked. "He's a sail or two short. You ought to tell him that the kind of swimsuit he's wearing makes people wonder if he's trolling for boyfriends.''

"Jeopard!'' She looked at him in astonishment. "You don't have to worry about Timothy. He's extremely heterosexual.''

He gazed down at her with a carefully neutral expression while disgust and anger grew inside him. He wasn't going to ask how she knew so much about the kid's sex life.

Hell, he could stand her having a lot of lovers, but he couldn't stand the realization that she might have several at once, and that he was only that evening's entertainment.

Suddenly he was furious at Tess, furious that he'd met his Waterloo in a pair of silver-blue eyes set in a face that belonged in a painter's portrait of a Cherokee princess. She'd reduced him to making petty, mean comments and competing for her attention.

For the first time he understood exactly how much she had fouled up his work, his concentration, and his dignity, because he hadn't turned his emotions off.

Jeopard took a deep breath, focused on a cloud drifting over the sun, and cleared his conscience for what lay ahead.

TESS SAT IN Jeopard's lap, one arm draped around his neck, her free hand steering the yacht, the salty ocean wind streaking her hair back and whipping tears from her eyes.

He curled his arm more tightly around her waist, took another swallow from a glass of iced tea, and whenever she looked at him, demonstrated a heart-stopping combination of blond hair, sexy sunglasses, and a perfect masculine smile.

She was sublimely happy.

Finally she bent her head close to his ear and told him. "We've gone far enough from the marina! We don't want anyone to come tearing along the open sea and smash us!''

He nodded and cut the yacht's engine. The yacht began to slow. Tess took her hand off the wheel and circled Jeopard's neck with both arms. She was amazed that she could give him rational instructions about sailing.

The ocean made slapping sounds against the yacht, creating a provocative background of wet rhythms. Jeopard set his tea on a ledge by the control console and removed his sunglasses, then lifted his hand to her own sunglasses, huge lenses with tortoiseshell frames.

He carefully tugged them off her face, laid them beside his tea glass, then cupped her chin with his fingers.

"Well, here we are," he said pleasantly, as if it were an ordinary thing.

Tess's heart thudded roughly. "If you don't drop your anchor it will be *there we go*," she warned.

"Hmmm. Right." He led her downstairs to the main deck, kissed her lightly on the mouth, then went about anchoring the yacht.

The sun was setting behind him, and the sky framed him in deep shades of gold and magenta. Sunlight made a halo around his hair and outlined his body. He was still wearing his polo shirt and khaki trousers, but the outline couldn't have been more enticing had he been naked.

Tess watched him solemnly, her hands clasped behind her back, her knees weak. Privacy—that was what his suggestion to move the yacht had concerned. Neither of them had voiced such a thought, but it had lain between them, nonetheless. It wouldn't have done to stay at the marina, where curious tourists sometimes climbed aboard the boats.

She felt a languid loosening between her thighs, and looked around with breathless amusement for a place to sit.

"I don't know what kind of show I'm putting on, but I'm glad you like it," he called.

Tess looked at him quickly, and realized that she was smiling.

"You drop anchor very well, Sundance."

"You should see how I cook."

"Is it a dramatic performance?"

"It's been known to draw applause."

Much like your other performances, I'll bet, she thought rakishly. She wondered about his past women. Oddly enough, he didn't act the part of a flirt, except with her. She didn't get the impression that he went around bedding just any woman who looked at him.

Good heavens, if he did that he'd have no time for eating or sleeping. Watching other women gape at Jeopard would have provoked her jealousy except that he never noticed their attention, much less returned it.

Her first impression about his vanity had been entirely wrong. He was the least vain person she'd ever known; she even sensed a certain embarrassment on his part, as if he wished he were more average-looking.

A grand *no way* to that, my boy, she told him mentally.

He came toward her, pulling his blue polo shirt off as he did. He tossed it on the deck and spread his arms wide, eyes gleaming with invitation, the sunset making him look like an earthbound angel walking out of heaven. Her heart in her throat, Tess ran to him, and he put his arms around her snugly.

Tess looked up at him with devotion. His eyes became very serious, and he lifted her against him slightly, so that she stood on tiptoe.

"I think you wouldn't mind falling in love with me, Tess." He touched his lips to the tip of her nose and whispered hoarsely, "Even though we don't know each other very well. Tell me you're falling in love with me."

She gasped softly at his desire for this new and very important intimacy. Tess curled her fingers into his chest hair and bent her forehead to his shoulder while she took deep, shuddering breaths.

Finally she tilted her head back and looked at him.

"I am. I don't care if we've just met. I've never felt anything like this before."

"Good." Again, he gave her a perfect, tender smile. "Not even for your husband?"

Tears rose in her eyes. Jeopard seemed to want to extract a commitment out of her in the most painful way possible. But then, she reasoned, it was only because it meant so much to him.

"I did love Royce," she murmured. "We had a beautiful relationship. But it was a mentor-student relationship in some ways—there was no way we could have a typical romance, not with the difference in our ages."

"And he was sick. Physically, he—"

"Jeopard." She grasped his shoulders firmly and looked up at him with pain shimmering in her eyes. "I know that you can do things for me that my husband was too ill to do very well. But I can't tell you that I didn't love or desire him, or that I wasn't happy with him."

"Sssh." He kissed her slowly, deepened the kiss with the erotic exploration of his tongue, then drew back and looked at her. "Say it again for me, Tess. That you're falling in love with me."

She swayed in his embrace, amazed at what had happened to her in the course of two days. "I'm falling in love with you," she whispered.

"There. That came to you as if you said it all the time, see?" He hugged her, nibbled her ear, and slid his hands down her colorful tank top to her white slacks.

He cupped her hips and rubbed slowly. Tess groaned against his bare shoulder and licked his skin with the tip of her tongue. He was delicious, tasting of ocean wind and masculine musk combined with a fading trace of good cologne.

"Does love mean so much to you?" She smiled into his skin.

"Yes." He curved his hands over her waist and drew them up and down her sides, touching her breasts with his thumbs each time. "I want to know everything about you. About your work, your past, about Royce. I want you to trust me and tell me everything."

"Oh, yes, yes," she answered, and put her arms tightly around his neck. "I feel that way about you too. Do you think you're falling in love with me, then?" She laughed sheepishly. "I'm just hinting for you to say so."

His hands tightened on her sides, his grip almost painful. "Oh, yes," he whispered. "I've been falling for you."

Tess looked up at him and lost what remained of her defenses. "I've wanted someone to share with for so long. I've been so lonely."

"Lonely?" He looked a little troubled. "Tess, I don't believe in sexual martyrdom. Please tell me you haven't been celibate since Royce died."

"Oh, of course not," she blurted out. Tess burned with embarrassment. She didn't want to appear foolish in Jeopard's worldly eyes. She managed a sly, teasing look and added, "Now, really, Mr. Surprise. Do I look that prim?"

He laughed, and for a moment she thought she heard a distressing undertone of sarcasm in it. But then he turned one of his mind-boggling smiles on her and she forgot everything except that she was gloriously happy.

"Are you hungry?" she whispered.

His blue eyes glittered with intensity. "The standard reply to that has to be, 'Not for food.' "

"I see." Her knees would turn to Swedish jelly any second now. She'd best take them below, where they could rest on Jeopard's bed. "Then we'll eat dinner later."

They went to his cabin, holding each other so close that their feet kept colliding and they nearly stumbled. "I'm glad we're just going to make love," he teased in a gruff voice. "If we were about to dance, I'd be worried."

So he thought of it as making love. Tess was certain that he could hear her purring.

He opened his cabin door, and she stepped into the small, sumptuously furnished room. He closed the door behind them with a soft click. Tess stood in the shadowy room, her heart racing, listening to him move toward a tiny brass wall lamp.

There was another click, and gentle light turned the cabin into a cosy haven. "Ah, I remember it well," she said, pointing toward the gold-framed mirror on a door at one end of the cabin.

Jeopard stepped up close behind her and grasped her shoulders, pressing himself to her from shoulder to hips. His breath was hot against her neck. "Turnabout is fair play. I'd like to be the audience this time."

She barely recognized her own voice. "That can be arranged."

Tess walked away from him, stopped in front of the mirror, and smiled back over her shoulder. He stood very still, and she knew his gaze was riveted to her. Tess rebuked herself for the twinge of boarding-school-induced modesty that held her back for a second.

Royce had seen her naked, of course, but she'd never stripped for him.

"You're beautiful," Jeopard said softly, as if encouraging her.

She relaxed then. Stripping was no more than shedding a few bothersome clothes. Tess removed her watch and laid it on a small table by the door. She caught her tank top with both hands and raised it over her head, then dropped it with a motion of one jaunty, gracefully curved arm.

He chuckled happily. "You've done this before."

Oh, every day, she thought wryly.

Tess ran her palms over the front of her delicate white bra. The chain bearing the antler amulet hung between her breasts; she cupped the amulet lovingly in her hand.

Her great-great-grandparents, Katlanicha Blue Song and Justis Gallatin, had found each other across two different worlds. Her great-grandfather, Silas Gallatin, had loved Genevieve Walking Light, the madam, despite her troubled past.

Tess didn't know anything about the relationship between their son and his wife—her grandparents— but she did know that her father had loved her mother. It was obvious by the reverent and frequent way he had mentioned her over the years.

She came from a series of great loves, she thought with awe. And now she hoped she had found her own.

She took off the necklace and carefully placed it beside her watch. Then she latched her fingers into the front clasp of her bra and snapped it open. Tess raised her eyes and looked into the mirror, seeing her own flushed skin and gleaming eyes first, then Jeopard's face.

The coldness in it startled her so much that her hands rose to her mouth in alarm. He looked just as he had the other day when he was chasing an unknown intruder on his boat. He looked incapable of emotion.

"What is it?" she murmured. "What's wrong? Do I remind you of someone?"

He blinked in shock. Suddenly his expression was alive again. "My Lord, Tess, did I scare you?"

"Yes."

She cupped her hands over her exposed breasts and turned to face him. He came quickly to her and took her in his arms, cursing himself viciously under his breath.

"I'm sorry," he told her. He shook his head. "I don't blame you for being afraid of that face, Tess. But I swear it doesn't mean anything. It's an old habit from my military training. A bad habit. Don't let it unnerve you."

She chuckled ruefully, but felt herself relaxing because of his sincerity. "If all our troops could be trained to look at the enemy that way, we wouldn't need any other weapons."

He stroked her dark hair gently. "You're not my enemy, Tess."

"For a second, there, I wasn't sure."

His voice was practically an aphrodisiac. "Honey, that's the last way I'd ever feel about you."

*Honey.* With a low moan, Tess leaned against his chest. She laughed. "You might be descended from some Wild West Indian fighter. Those Indian-fighting genes could be hard to ignore."

"No, I'm descended from a Frenchman, remember? In fact, a French pirate who retired to Florida about 1835. He may have fought a few Seminole Indians, though, I admit."

"I forgive him," she said solemnly. "I'm sure the Cherokees fought a few Frenchmen along the way."

Jeopard's laugh was cut short when she raised her mouth to his and kissed him intimately. He shuddered, picked her up, and carried her to his bed.

Tess was overwhelmed by the quickness with which he undressed her and himself.

"Tess," he whispered, drawing the backs of his fingers over her full, firm breasts. "You're fantastic."

Whimpering softly at his words, she raised a hand to stroke his chest. He intercepted it, kissed the palm, then pressed it down beside her on the bed.

"My treat," he murmured hoarsely. "Lie still and let me touch you."

She ached to run her hands over his body, but she was lost in such a daze of emotion and desire that she did as he told her.

He made it worth her while.

His expert touch mesmerized her. He squeezed her breasts rhythmically, raising the nipples so that his incredible mouth could do things to them that made her back arch. He smoothed his hand up and down her stomach, teasing her by almost but not quite reaching the apex of her thighs.

When she was panting and a fine mist of dusky pink colored her skin, he finally slid his fingers into the dark hair between her legs.

"You fit my hand perfectly," he murmured into her ear, then bent his head to nibble her neck.

The sound she made was almost a wail of pleasure. Tess grasped his forearm and stroked the corded muscles quickly, lightly, her touch conveying gratitude for the unforgettable sensations he gave her.

"Sssh, lie still now," he reminded her. He put her hand back on the bed.

"But I want to touch you so much," she murmured plaintively. Tess raised her head and tried to catch his mouth in a kiss.

He drew back, smiling tightly. She read the control in every line of his face. Oh, he was so dear, to give her pleasure this way when she felt the throbbing, hard evidence of his own need against her thigh.

"Now, honey, give me a chance," he said in a low, teasing tone. "I'm not an overanxious kid. I know the value of holding back."

Tess smiled quizzically at his odd words, then shut her eyes and sighed, the sound ragged. "Do with me what you want," she said in an airy, dramatic voice. "I'm yours."

He put his mouth against her quivering stomach and sucked for a moment. As she rose under him, crying out with delight, he murmured, "Good." He moved his magnificently tormenting mouth to another spot. "Mine."

As he placed slow, sucking kisses up her torso he reached for a shelf above the bed and retrieved something.

Tess made a small sound of protest when he stopped kissing her and edged away from her. He held up a small package that she recognized immediately.

He winked at her. "You won't have to worry about anything when you're with me. I believe in responsibility."

She reached out. Her voice was hoarse with desire. "Please. Let me. Just let me do that much for you."

He hesitated, and she watched with dismay as his

jaw tightened. "Jeopard? Do you not want me to touch you?"

Quickly his expression softened. "Honey, of course I do." He laughed low in his throat, but it was a strained sound.

Tess propped herself on one elbow. "What is it?" she said wistfully. "What's wrong?"

He shook his head in mild rebuke. "This couldn't be the first time you've driven a man too close to the edge too soon."

"I . . . oh, I see."

Jeopard kissed her forehead. "Not to worry. I won't let you down."

"Jep, I'm not worried about *that*. You just seem so intense. . . ."

He pressed her down on the bed and kissed her until she couldn't even think about talking anymore. By then he'd finished his preparations, and he slipped his hand between her legs again, stroking first one thigh, then the other.

"Spread your legs for me, Tess," he whispered.

She burrowed her head into the warm hollow of his shoulder and moaned. "Your wish is my command."

"That's it, Tess. You feel so hot and smooth."

He slid his fingers inside her, and Tess's world exploded in response. Everything she felt, everything she was, centered around the sweet destruction he brought to her restraint. She arched her hips and opened her mouth against his throat, calling his name.

Jeopard stroked her harder, adding ecstasy to ecstasy, and she squirmed desperately. Tess began to lick his throat with fervent movements of her tongue, like a wild, loving animal.

He shuddered from head to foot and immediately rolled on top of her. Tess slid her arms around his neck and cried out at the feel of his strong, hard body pressing her down into the mattress and angling between her thighs.

He cupped the back of her head to his shoulder and

slid one muscular arm under her. Holding her almost fiercely, he nuzzled his face against her neck and thrust into her wetness with one smooth stroke.

Tess felt as if he had consumed her totally. She was so deeply wrapped in his embrace that she rocked with every quick, forceful movement he made.

His breath shattered against her neck, harsh and fast. She tried to turn her face to kiss him, but his grip kept her from it.

His embrace was overwhelming. It controlled her; it put her at his mercy. Something about his fierceness touched a small chord of distress inside her, and she kissed his shoulder tenderly, wishing that she understood what provoked him.

Her kiss drew a long shudder through him. He raised his head and gazed down at her with hooded, passion-filled eyes. Tess forgot everything except the raw sensation his gaze ignited in her body.

It amazed her—one look from those searing blue eyes and she rose under him like a magnet drawn to steel. She called his name again and dug her fingers into his lower back. *Jep. Oh, Jep.*

She shut her eyes. The blood rushing in her ears so harshly that she felt deaf, Tess dimly heard him groan and knew that he was watching the uninhibited expressions of pleasure on her face.

He was waiting for her pleasure to crest. She could only imagine what the wild contractions inside her must be doing to him. A second later she knew.

As she clung to him, trembling, he put his head on her shoulder and arched into her so deeply that he seemed to be entering her womb. Again and again he drove into her, then shuddered to a stop, holding her to him as if he'd never let go.

His release was so powerful and erotic that tears of awe came to her eyes. He dragged his head up slowly, like a man just roused from a deep trance and still groggy.

When Jeopard saw her glittering eyes he leaned his forehead against hers and laid his hand against her cheek. His thumb brushed over the moisture on her lower lashes.

"Did I hurt you?" he asked.

"No. Oh, no." Tess stroked his head, raking her fingers through the thick blond hair. "You were wonderful." She hesitated, smiling while a big tear ran under his thumb. "You make me feel so incredibly *lucky*."

After a second he put his arms around her and rested his cheek on her head. She laughed gently.

"Jep, I'm not an oyster. You can't pop me out of my shell."

"Too tight?" His arms relaxed little.

"There. That's perfect, Sundance."

Tess relaxed inside his warm, possessive embrace. It might be more difficult to understand Jeopard Surprise than she'd originally thought, but she didn't doubt that he'd be worth the effort.

Tess stopped reading out loud for a moment and looked at Jeopard with amused disgust. Resting in a white lounge chair on the yacht's upper deck, he reminded her of a lazy cougar. His eyes were shut, and even in relaxation his face was very private. She suspected that he was asleep.

He lay on his back with his hands behind his head, his feet crossed at the ankles. He wore nothing but a pair of low-slung white swim trunks. The sky behind him was as blue as his eyes.

If he'd had his eyes open.

"Sundance, are you listening?" she asked.

"Yes."

"Then why do you have your eyes shut?"

"That black temptation you call a swimsuit distracts me. And I enjoy meditating on the sound of your voice—makes me think of English gardens and tea with crumpets. It's hard to concentrate on Cherokee history."

"Oh." Smiling, she pulled her sunglasses down and

eyed him rakishly. "I don't feel the least bit guilty for distracting a man who cheats at cards the way you did this morning."

"I got you flustered and you made a mistake. That's a legitimate tactic."

"Rubbing your bare toes over my thighs is not a legitimate tactic."

He laughed, the sound low and rich. Tess shifted on her lounge chair, rearranged her history book on her knees, and bit her lip to keep from smiling at him.

As usual he made her feel languid and warm inside, like a flower just waiting for the sun to open it again. More important than that, he had won her trust and friendship completely.

He took pleasure in everything she did, even trivia such as the prim-and-proper way she brushed her teeth—a boarding-school regimen, she informed him. He wanted to know her favorite foods, her favorite books, her favorite *everything*. He was as fascinated with her as she was with him.

As a result, during the past few days the world had shrunk until only she and he were left in a cocoon filled with shared sensation and experience. Lord, she wasn't certain what she and Jeopard indulged in more—long conversations or making love. He was wonderful in both areas.

But Tess noted sadly that his view of the world was as dark as her view was light. That realization had become clear to her the previous night, when they'd discussed Paris. They'd both visited the city several times. Jeopard recalled only terrorist bombings and leftist politics; she recalled the restaurants, the architecture, and the art.

Tess sighed and shook her head. She was working on his cynical attitude and already making progress. Today he seemed almost jovial, and the guarded contentment in his face enchanted her. She smiled to herself. If she hadn't known him for an entire week—and thus gotten a bit accustomed to being enthralled—she would have thrown her history book down and pounced on him.

How could she help it? The man provoked her with tender kisses, affectionate smiles, and a husky way of saying her name.

"I was listening to you read," he assured her again. "Don't stop."

"Ahem. If you've been listening to me, sir, then summarize what I've just read."

He retaliated with a parrotlike recitation. "In 1838 the Cherokees who didn't want to be driven from the Sun Land, as they called their ancestral territory in the southeast, ran to the mountains of North Carolina and hid in caves there." He paused. "Where they developed a subculture of bat people."

"Be serious!"

Hearing the wistfulness in her voice, he stopped teasing. "Where they stayed until the federal government gave up trying to find them. A lot of them died from starvation. Those who survived helped form the eastern Cherokee band, and today they have a reservation in the same mountains where they took refuge a hundred and fifty years ago."

"Very good!"

"We should catch a quick flight up to San Francisco tomorrow and find your great-great-grandparents' graves."

"Would you mind?" she asked. "You must be bored by this personal-history quest of mine."

He rose, stretched, then came to her and tilted her chin up with a caressing hand. "No, I want to learn everything about you and your past."

Tess turned her face and kissed his palm. It didn't matter that he was learning a great deal more about her personal life than she was learning about his. He just needed time to open up.

"I'll make the arrangements," she murmured against the warm hollow of his hand.

"I've already made them."

Tess looked up at him quickly, a pleased smile on

her face. He touched his fingers to her lips and winked at her.

PEOPLE WHO HAVE a good sense of humor usually have a good sense of humanity and of life, an aborigine shaman had once told Jeopard.

The man was a friend of Millie's husband, Brig McKay. In terms of outlook and personality Brig resembled a real-life Crocodile Dundee, and his Aussie friends were as eccentric as anything ever shown on a movie screen.

The shaman, enjoying an extended visit to Millie and Brig's home in Nashville, wore bib overalls and played the harmonica. He owned a grocery store in Brig's Australian hometown, Washaway Loo.

Not exactly a child of nature, Jeopard had thought. But the shaman could predict rainstorms and tell how long the summer would last, and two weeks before Millie noticed any change in her body he'd informed her that she was going to have a baby.

When Jeopard met the shaman, the man had looked into his eyes for a long time and said, "You will be your own destruction."

That prediction had upset Jeopard more than he'd ever admitted. It came back to him even today, in the midst of a breezy, sun-soaked California afternoon while the ocean shushed peacefully outside the open windows of his cabin and sea gulls floated in the sky like small angels.

Jeopard knew the cause of his depression. He was going to make a phone call to Kyle while Tess took care of some minor chores aboard her boat. He felt sneaky, confused, and reluctant to tell Kyle anything ugly about Tess. All bad signs.

He was doing his job, doing it exactly as planned, and with any luck he'd get his hands on the Kara diamond in time for Olaf, pompous little ass and Duke of Kara, to unveil it for his subjects before his coronation ceremony. Olaf, who was the opposite of his popular aunt, the recently deceased Queen Isabella, apparently considered the diamond some sort of Holy Grail.

Olaf thought that getting the diamond back into the royal collection would improve his image. Jeopard smiled grimly. True. Everyone in Kara would then think of Olaf as a pompous little *ingenious* ass.

Jeopard tucked the phone into the crook of his neck and watched Tess come out of the *Lady*'s cabin. It was impossible to look at her without aching to hold her. Even thinking about her put him into hyper-arousal.

She'd changed from her black swimsuit into a peach-colored sundress with a halter top. Her skirt swung fluidly around her bare legs as she moved about the sailboat, polishing bits of its trim with an old rag. Her dark hair fluttered like curtains about her face and neck.

She turned toward the *Irresistible* as if she felt his gaze, though Jeopard knew that she couldn't see into the dark interior of his cabin from where she stood. She smiled, raised a slender, honey-dark hand to her lips, and blew him a kiss.

Then she went back to her chores.

*I could watch you for the rest of my life.*

His phone connection went through, and Kyle answered.

"Hey. Kyle. It's me, the brother you idolize."

Kyle, a colorful talker, began a detailed and bawdy analysis of Jeopard's faults. The point seemed to be that he'd expected a phone call long before.

"How's it going with the seduction of the sea witch?" Kyle finally asked.

Distracted, Jeopard thought for a moment, then said, "She's having me to tea tomorrow." He cleared his throat. "Did you find out where the duke's people got their information on her?"

"They're vague. Kept saying they'd interviewed people who know her, but they wouldn't say who. But I double-checked the background on the diamond, and that's legit. It belonged to Queen Isabella, and it was stolen twenty years ago while she was visiting England.

"It was a hell of an embarrassment for the Brits, Jep. I talked to Edwards at Scotland Yard. He remembers the case. Royce Benedict was the prime suspect, but he had an alibi. They couldn't nail him, though they felt sure he was responsible."

Kyle laughed. "He was cocky. He'd stolen a million dollars in jewelry from Queen Isabella a few years before that. Served time in prison for it. The gems were recovered."

"What was this guy—the royal thief of Kara?"

"Sounds that way."

"Kyle, doesn't it strike you as odd that nobody wanted the Blue Princess back until now?"

"Look, the thing's not worth that much, as royal trinkets go. Apparently the Queen just wanted to forget the whole incident. After she died last year, Olaf decided somebody ought to settle the old score with Benedict. He's the vengeful type, from what I've learned."

"Good work, kid. I'll remember you at Christmas."

"Jep, Olaf's people want the diamond before the end of the week. The duke needs a public-relations victory real bad right now."

"Oh?"

"To put it simply, his future subjects think he's a dirt-sucking scum bag. There's a movement afoot in the parliament to kick him out and make the country a democracy."

"Fine. I'd like that."

"But they can't without rewriting their constitution. It says Kara remains a monarchy as long as there's a royal heir to the throne."

"I hope Olaf is the last of his species."

"He is—unless he finds a woman with no taste who wants to have his kids."

"I'll see what I can do."

"About finding a woman with no taste?"

"About getting the diamond, smart guy. *If* Tess has it. I don't think she does."

"You're getting softhearted or softheaded or both. Kiss Tess Benedict a few times for me," Kyle ordered cheerfully.

"You should get so lucky. And she uses her maiden name. It's Tess Gallatin, not Tess Benedict."

"She couldn't wait to forget Benedict, eh?"

Jeopard started to say something in her defense, then frowned. He still didn't know what had motivated Tess to marry a dying man old enough to be her grandfather.

He glanced out the window and stiffened with concern. The two college boys—the ones from Royce's rugby team—stood on the dock talking to Tess. From their downcast expressions he knew they were upset, and Tess looked distressed too.

They handed her a bulky brown grocery sack. She cradled it in her arms and looked inside at the contents. Slowly she turned her face away, and Jeopard could tell from the boys' awkward, pleading looks that she must be crying.

"I have to go," Jeopard said abruptly. "I'll call back later."

He hung up the phone on Kyle's startled "But—"

Jeopard reached the dock in front of the *Lady* in time to hear one of the boys say, "I swear, Tess, the dog never did anything like this before."

She looked from him to Jeopard, her eyes glistening, her expression sorrowful. "Hi." She introduced them quickly, and the boys shook his hand. They squirmed, disgruntled to have anyone else see their misery.

Jeopard gazed at the bag, then up at Tess. "What's wrong?"

"There was an accident with my scrapbook." She gave the boys a sympathetic look. "It wasn't anyone's fault."

"My dog chewed it up," one of the boys explained.

"Tess, we know how much it meant to you," the other said plaintively.

"Guys, I understand. I really do. Forget it." Her jaw clenched and she blinked rapidly, trying to smile. "If Royce were here he'd say 'Why all the bloody nonsense over a heap of paper?' "

They smiled back wanly. When they left fifteen minutes later they were still apologizing.

Jeopard studied her carefully, torn between a desire to comfort and the need to interrogate her.

"Come on, we'll see what we can do," he murmured. Jeopard put an arm around her shoulders and they went aboard his yacht. Once in his cabin she sank down on the bed and spread out the remnants of the scrapbook. It had been thoroughly mauled.

Looking stricken, she gently arranged pieces of paper containing ripped photographs and newspaper articles. Jeopard sat down near her.

She looked up, her smoky blue eyes miserable. "I don't have much that belonged to Royce. He brought very few mementos with him when he moved here from England. His daughters received the rest—rightly so, of course." She touched the ruined scrapbook tenderly. "But that makes what I have more special."

"I didn't realize how much he meant to you."

She tilted her head to one side and studied him quizzically. "Why do you think I married him?"

*Tess, I can forgive you for being tempted by a five-million-dollar inheritance.*

"My vanity wants to believe that you were lonely and vulnerable after your father died. Royce represented emotional security."

She nodded. "At first. But he was hardly a father figure. He was quite a lady's man—a bit on the retired side in that respect, but a lady's man nonetheless." Tess paused. "Your vanity?"

Jeopard smiled devilishly. *Keep it light*, he warned himself. "I hate competition. Tell me you married him for his money."

She laughed. "Of course. Isn't that why all young women marry older men?"

Jeopard watched her gaze at the destroyed scrapbook again. Tears pooled in her eyes and slid down her cheeks. She wiped them away hurriedly.

"I'm an awful crybaby these days, I fear. Please don't think I'm always such a faucet."

*Royce's money wasn't what made her cry over a whimsical scrapbook.*

"You really loved Royce," Jeopard said simply.

"Yes."

He believed her, and another knot of worry unwound inside him. He was thrilled that she'd adored her husband. Sometime later he'd have to consider the irony of his feelings.

Jeopard paused, planning his next words. "How did his grown daughters feel about having a stepmother younger than they were?"

"They thought their poor dad had gone bonkers, but they weren't surprised by it. He was never a conformist. I only met them once. They were extremely polite to me."

"And after Royce died?"

She smiled grimly. "They took their inheritance and bid me an extremely polite farewell. Don't call us, we'll call you."

"They didn't resent you?"

"Because of the inheritance? Hardly. Royce left everything to them."

Jeopard stared at her. He had just fallen off a cliff, but he was floating. He prayed that everything she'd told him was true. "How did you feel about that?"

"Oh, I knew he wouldn't leave me anything. He told me before we got married."

"But . . . honey, you took care of the man when he was dying. You suffered with him."

"Jep, I represented only four years in his life. Hardly anything in comparison to all of his family obligations. He helped me learn a marvelous profession, and I'm very comfortable financially because of that.

Besides, I wasn't a hired nurse, I was his wife. I didn't resent having to take care of him toward the end."

Jeopard looked at her for so long that she shifted awkwardly and covered her face in mock embarrassment. She peeked through her fingers at him.

"Sundance, rest assured that I'm no saint. Stop looking at me that way."

He pulled her hands to him and kissed each of them. His lips against her warm, smooth skin, he asked gruffly, "Want some help trying to put Royce's scrapbook back together? I'm great with puzzles."

"Yes," she whispered, delighted.

*Except in your case*, he added silently. *I'm more lost than ever.*

THE MORNING FOG had just lifted when Jeopard guided their rental car through the steep San Francisco streets. Tess hunched forward in the passenger seat, hands excitedly bending the sheaf of maps and written directions balanced on the knees of her aqua-colored chinos.

He glanced at her and smiled. She was as eager as a kid on the way to Disneyland, and he enjoyed her enthusiasm. In the past few days he'd absorbed her unsullied view of life until he almost felt lighthearted. It was easy to forget that he had work to do, or that he'd failed to get answers to his most important questions.

Did she have the Kara diamond? Had she been Royce's accomplice?

For today, he'd forget. He wanted to believe that this gentle, classy woman was everything innocent that he was not.

"Drive faster," she ordered, staring out the car window and impatiently tapping her white sandals on the floorboard.

"It's going to be at least an hour, Mario Andretti Gallatin. Sit back and take your gear off."

Her thirty-five-millimeter camera hung from a wide

strap around her neck, indenting the abstract pastels on the chest of the fashionably huge white T-shirt she wore with a wide cloth belt. Also hanging around her neck were her gold medallion and her antler amulet.

Her chocolate-colored hair was pulled back in a French braid. Next to her he felt rather ordinary in a white golf shirt, dusky blue slacks, and Docksiders.

That was all right—in his business, it wasn't wise to draw attention with flamboyant clothes. He bought the best brands, and he had an eye for color, but he kept his style simple.

"You look like a Yuppie Indian," Jeopard said teasingly.

She flashed him a droll smile. "Silence, white eyes."

They left the city behind and headed north toward the wine country. In just over an hour they were deep into some of the most beautiful agricultural land in the world.

The rented sedan slipped through lush valleys filled with sheep grazing in emerald pastures and vineyards backed by tree-tufted mountains. The landscape was as picturesque as anything Jeopard had seen during several excursions in France, and when he rolled his window down he sighed at the heady, ripe scent of early summer greenery.

Tess made a husky sound of appreciation in her throat and slid over to him. She draped an arm around his shoulders and kissed his cheek. A poignant emotion filled Jeopard's chest.

"It's good to be alive," he said abruptly.

Tess laughed. "You sound as if you just realized that fact."

"Maybe."

She kissed his cheek again, and her voice was tender. "Jeopard, what have you done in your life that makes you so sad?"

*Seen too many people die,* he thought. "Spent too much time watching soap operas."

She chuckled but patted his shoulder kindly, her fingers caressing him through the material of his shirt.

Her unquestioning, intuitive sympathy worried him a little. She sensed too much about him, which meant that one day soon she might find his dark side.

What would she think of her lover then?

"That's it!" she said suddenly, bouncing forward in the seat and pointing. "Glen Mary Road. To the winery!"

A minute later they were grinding down a two-lane gravel road between rolling hills striped with long rows of vine-covered redwood stakes.

In the distance an impressive stone mansion rose majestically amidst other stone buildings. The home was square and functional but enhanced by graceful turrets. Dense ivy covered the walls of the lower floor.

A sign at the driveway invited them to tour the Glen Mary vineyards, winery, and museum. Jeopard parked in a nearly deserted lot, and Tess bolted out before he removed the ignition key.

She waited for him impatiently, grasped his hand, and tugged him behind her while he jovially protested the indignity. They passed under a vine-covered arch, pushed open a mahogany door easily ten feet tall, and entered the mansion's foyer, a cool, marble-floored place decorated with Persian rugs and dark, heavy antiques.

An elderly woman in a tweed suit sat behind a desk. She smiled up at them and said, "Welcome to Glen Mary. Ten dollars each, please. Here are your brochures. The upstairs is closed to the public because the current owner lives there. We hope you enjoy our gift shop and museum. The tour of the winery buildings begins in thirty minutes."

Tess did a good imitation of smiling nonchalantly during the woman's spiel, Jeopard thought.

"I'm Tess Gallatin, and I spoke to the manager about visiting an old cemetery on the property."

Thirty years fell away from the receptionist. She leaped up spryly. "Gallatin. Oh, my, yes. Mr. De-Forest wants to meet you. He's the owner. He's so excited about your visit. If he'd gotten to talk to you himself . . ."

The woman motioned exuberantly toward a hallway. "Follow me. I'm Mrs. Johnson. I've worked here for years. You don't know what to expect, I can tell. I'm sure you'll be delighted. Oh, my!"

"Oh, my!" Tess exclaimed as the woman started into the main part of the house, waving for them to follow. She looked at Jeopard in shock. "She must know something about my family."

"Oh, my," Jeopard repeated dryly, smiling. He put a supportive hand under her elbow and propelled her forward.

"Here, look," Mrs. Johnson called, stopping at the oversized entrance to a large room. "Our museum."

Tess and Jeopard followed her into a softly lit, elegant room with tall ceilings and plush carpeting. Old photographs lined the walls; a restored grape press from the early 1800s sat on a shallow platform in the center of the room; various artifacts and memorabilia were displayed in glass cases. Mrs. Johnson hurried toward a corner and began studying the photographs that hung there.

"I understood that there was small Presbyterian church on the grounds back in the 1800s," Tess offered, "and my great-great-grandparents are buried in its cemetery."

"Would you like to see their photograph?"

"*What?*"

"Oh, my," Jeopard interjected on her behalf. But even his cynical heart was thumping hard, and he wasn't sure who broke into a jog first, he or Tess.

Mrs. Johnson stood aside, beaming at Tess like a proud mother. Tess halted in front of a well-preserved daguerreotype portrait inside a Plexiglas display box.

"Justis and Katherine Gallatin," Mrs. Johnson announced.

Tess made a soft keening sound and put her fingertips on the display box.

Jeopard gazed with fascination at the dignified

couple in the portrait. Katlanicha Blue Song Gallatin's beauty was evident even in the stern, drab setting typical of old photographs. She sat in a high-backed chair, her hands folded in the lap of an incredible dress Scarlett O'Hara might have worn to a ball at Tara, but Scarlett had the coloring and features of a full-blooded Cherokee.

Her black hair was parted in the middle and pulled back into fat coils at the back of her neck, giving her a regal appearance. She was smiling slightly, and Jeopard thought her dark, compelling eyes held cheerful determination. He could imagine her issuing exasperated orders to her husband.

Justis Gallatin stood slightly behind her chair, lean and tall, one long leg bent slightly, one hand hooked into a pocket on his vest, the other hand draped over the chair's back so that the fingertips were twirled in a bit of ribbon on his wife's dress, as if he had been playing with it, teasing her, possibly.

His coat and trousers were formal and well cut, but his hair and moustache hinted that he cared for neither barbers nor fashion. He had craggy, handsome features scored with laugh lines around the eyes.

Judging by the challenging look in those eyes, Jeopard concluded that Gallatin also didn't care for photographers.

"They're magnificent," Tess whispered.

"This photograph was made in 1850," Mrs. Johnson told her. "In New York. It was sent to Mr. DeForest by one of their grandsons."

"Benjamin Gallatin!" Tess said, reading information on a placard at the base of the photograph. "This particular grandson of Justis and Katherine's was my grandfather! Do you know anything about him? He and Grandmother Gallatin were killed in a car accident when my father was a child, so I never learned much about them."

"Sorry," Mrs. Johnson said mournfully. "I wish I could tell you more."

"Oh, I'm so greedy! It's enough to see this photograph." Tess made a sniffling sound, then laughed at her own sentimentality. Jeopard slipped a handkerchief out of his trouser pocket and handed it to her.

"You can be proud of them," he told her gruffly. Did this romantic darling of a woman have *anything* of which to be ashamed? Dear God, he hoped not.

She continued reading the placard. Her voice became a low, incredulous rasp. "Justis and Katherine lived here? They started the Glen Mary winery?"

"We don't know a great deal about them," Mrs. Johnson told her, "but it's intriguing. The church you mentioned was built in 1840. We have sections from a diary the first pastor kept. He mentions that Katherine Gallatin came here in 1840 with her baby daughter, Mary. Just the two of them.

"And listen to this," Mrs. Johnson continued. "She was an Indian, but she'd been educated at a Presbyterian academy for women, in Philadelphia. The locals must have been impressed—they hired her, an Indian, to teach school in this area. That wasn't the kind of treatment most Indians received."

Tess pointed to the loving way Justis's hand rested on Katherine's shoulder. "But why would he let her leave him?"

"Maybe he didn't have a choice. We don't know. The first pastor moved away six months after her arrival here, and the next pastor didn't keep a diary. But Justis found her eventually, as you can see. They began this house and the winery. We think that they sold it in 1850. By then they had three sons. The children are listed in the church records."

"Silas, Ross, and Holt," Tess said softly. "But what happened to Mary?"

"She died when she was only a few months old."

Tess made a wistful, sympathetic sound.

"Glen Mary," Jeopard noted. "They must have named the estate in honor of her. That says a lot about their feelings."

"And they made certain that they'd be buried beside her, years later," Mrs. Johnson said reverently.

Now she was becoming tearful too. She wiped her eyes. "I'll get Mr. DeForest. He'll show you the cemetery."

Sniffling, she left the room.

Jeopard idly patted his pocket, thinking that he should have stocked more handkerchiefs.

"Oh, Jep, this is incredible," Tess whispered.

He put his arms around her while she dabbed at her face.

"I wish I could get in touch with my cousins to talk about all this. They're both traveling or on vacation or something. Our lawyer in Georgia says he'll try to find them for me."

Jeopard stroked her hair, and she leaned against him, chuckling. "Did you ever expect to get involved with such a sentimental idiot as me?"

He kissed her forehead, then rested his cheek against her hair and held her tightly. "No, but I can't stop now. There's an old French custom that says once a man offers his handkerchief to a lady, he's pledged to protect her honor."

"Lovely balderdash. You made that up."

"No. As long as you keep my handkerchief, I'm yours."

She tucked the handkerchief into a pocket of her pants and gazed up at him adoringly. "Then I'm never giving it back," she whispered.

Jeopard managed a slight smile and ached from wishing that their future could be settled that easily.


"THERE'S THE CEMETERY!" Tess exclaimed.

She and Jeopard entered a large, grassy clearing at the base of a gently sloping hill. Up the hill Tess saw gnarled old trees in the midst of much younger ones—the site of the old church.

At the bottom of the hill, canopied by ancient oaks scattered among the grave sites, lay a small cemetery.

"Let's go find them," Jeopard murmured.

They walked among the old, weathered stones. Tess

held Jeopard's hand tightly, anticipating the moment when she'd see her own last name spelled out across a gray monument.

Finally, there it was. In a separate plot surrounded by a low stone wall sat a dignified, steeplelike stone at least seven feet tall.

*Gallatin* was carved into it in simple, bold letters.

"Oh, Jep. Jep, I'm shaking."

"Does seeing your last name on the stone make you feel uncomfortable?"

"No. It makes me feel eternal."

A walkway led to the monument from an entrance cut in the wall. Tess halted at the entrance, Jeopard close beside her. She felt as if her chest would burst from the sense that she'd connected with another something that was wonderful and important about herself.

Her Cherokee heritage and Jeopard. She'd found two beautiful new worlds.

"Hello," she said softly.

A bird broke into song somewhere on the hillside. A billowy summer cloud parted to let a streak of golden sunlight fall on the graves.

Jeopard's hand tightened around hers. "If I were a romantic, I'd say you've just been answered."

She turned to him, took his face between her hands, and kissed him tenderly. "You *are* a romantic."

He shrugged lightly, then released her hand and prodded her forward with a gentle touch in the curve of her back. "I'll wait here."

Tess moved down the short walkway, gazing raptly at the three smaller, beveled stones in front of the monument. Tess read the inscriptions easily.

*Our Cherished Daughter.* She blesses the angels with her soul.

*Wife, Beloved, Friend.* All that my spirit holds, she has given.

*Husband, Beloved, Friend.* I shall take his soul to the Sun Land, for he is my home and my heart.

Tess read the inscriptions out loud, her hands

cupped under her chin almost prayerfully. "They loved each other, Jep," she said over her shoulder. "I don't know why Katherine ran away from him and took their first child, but he found her and they stayed together the rest of their lives."

She pointed to Justis's stone. "The Sun Land. The name for the old southern homeland, remember? In Katherine's case, it meant Gold Ridge, Georgia."

"Maybe she thought she'd go back there one day, in spirit if nothing else," Jeopard said.

Tess knelt in front of a gravestone. "Katherine," she whispered. "You and Justis have three great-great-granddaughters." Tess took the gold medallion in her hand and drew her fingertips over its mysterious message. "And we'll make you proud."

All around her, birds sang.

## CHAPTER 6

"WELL, HOW WAS it?" Tess murmured into his ear.

Jeopard lay with his head on her bare shoulder. She arched a little as he drew his hand up and down her torso, pausing to rub her dark, taut nipples each time. Making love had never been a spiritual experience until he met Tess.

He crooked his hand over her hip and pulled her closer to his satiated body, then angled one leg between her thighs. "An eleven on a scale of one to ten. I don't know which I like best, when you seduce me or I seduce you. I'll seduce you in a minute so we can compare results."

Tess chuckled a little as she stroked his shoulders. "Actually, I was asking about dinner. Pardon my vagueness. Your effect on my mind is rather dramatic."

"Dinner. Oh." He traced her collarbones with the tip of his tongue before he answered.

Tess moaned. Her body felt deliciously heavy, and

she sighed at the tingling sensation that scattered downward from his tongue. He slid his hand between her legs and stroked the moist folds there.

"Dinner was terrific," he declared. His mouth closed on the pulse point at the base of her throat, where he sucked gently for a moment. "And dessert was fantastic. I think I'll have seconds."

Soft New Age music, like starlight poured into sound, was playing on the cassette deck of Tess's stereo. The *Lady* shifted in the water from time to time, creaking slightly, soothingly. The wonderful man beside Tess raised his head and kissed her with a tenderness that made her sigh.

She tipped her head back and welcomed him. Life didn't get any better than this; confessions didn't get any easier.

"I'm in love with you," she whispered. "I love you."

He quivered against her. Rising on an elbow, he framed her face with his hand and looked down at her with somber, pain-filled eyes. Tess inhaled sharply.

"Oh, Jep, I said it too soon. . . ."

"I love you too."

She moaned with relief and happiness. Searching his eyes, Tess reveled in the adoration there but couldn't understand the sadness.

"What's wrong?" she asked, taking his face between her hands.

He shook his head in self-rebuke and smiled, easing his troubled look. "I've never said that before and meant it. It's a shocker."

She gasped softly. "Not in thirty-eight years?"

"Oh. I've meant it to my family—Kyle, Millie, my mother when I was about seven, not long before she died. I even told my Dad that I loved him, once. It embarrassed him. But no, I never put any commitment behind the words when I said them in the romantic sense. Until now. I don't ever want to lose you.

That's a different kind of love from anything I've felt before."

"Well," she whispered, her throat burning from emotion, "I'll make sure that you don't regret saying it to me."

He sat up, pulled her into his arms, and held her with an intensity that brought a bittersweet ache to her chest. It was as if he'd found some kind of salvation.

At that moment Tess realized that she couldn't do anything to cheapen this great gift he'd given her. Unless she trusted him with every secret she held dear, she didn't deserve him.

"I love you," she repeated, smiling against his shoulder. "And I have something very important that I want to share with you."

His arms tightened quickly, as if she'd startled him. He drew back and looked at her, his expression wary.

"Jep, relax," she said soothingly. "Wait here and I'll get it."

"Don't." His voice had an odd, strained quality. "Not right now."

Tess stroked his hair and smiled at him. "It won't take long. And then I'd like to make love with you again."

He let go of her reluctantly. She slipped into a cream-colored silk robe and went into the galley. There she opened the top door of the refrigerator, rearranged a stack of ice trays at the back of the freezer compartment, and removed the bottom one.

Standing at the kitchen's tiny sink she dumped an ice cube into her hand. Smiling in anticipation, she folded a kitchen towel and placed the ice cube on top of it. She left the galley with the towel cupped in both hands, like a sacred offering.

Jeopard sat on the edge of the bed, looking oddly tense, the coverlet wound around the lower half of his body.

"Jep, there's no need to be formal," she said teasingly, indicating the cover.

Tess sat down beside him and held her hands out proudly. Frozen in the center of the ice cube was a blue diamond the size of a marble.

"My secret," she said softly. "And now it's your secret too."

Jeopard stared at the melting cube. After a moment he almost laughed at the sick irony of it. The Iceman's hopes had been ruined by a damned ice cube.

Everything shut down inside him. It was a self-protective instinct, the same way he reacted whenever his life was in danger or a delicate situation had just become volatile.

Only this time, he never wanted to feel any emotion again, because he knew the bitterness would eat him up.

"That's some trinket," he told her smoothly. "A present from Royce?"

"No. It belonged to my mother. My grandparents gave it to me on my eighteenth birthday."

*The hell they did. It disappeared twenty years ago. Royce stole it. He left it to you.*

Jeopard took the ice cube in his hand and squeezed it. Tiny rivulets of water ran down his wrist. Tess dabbed at them with the towel.

"Good heavens, Jep, do you have a fever?"

He opened his hand and looked down at the magnificent blue stone emerging from its prison of water. "Your mother must have been an incredibly successful pro skier if she could afford something like this."

*Admit it, Tess. You know this came from the crown jewels of Kara. You know it's the Blue Princess.*

"Oh, the diamond has been in the Kellgren family for three generations. Grandfather says it belonged to his mother."

*Great story, Tess. Your sincere look is perfect.*

"Honey, it must be worth a small fortune."

"Actually, it's not. Royce estimated the value at around thirty thousand dollars. A diamond as large as it ought to be worth a lot more. But it's got some flaws."

"Not to the average eye."

"No, but I can tell. I love it for the sentimental value more than anything else."

Jeopard felt as if some small wild animal were clawing to get out of his chest. "Why isn't it in a setting?"

"Grandfather said the old setting didn't do it justice, so he had it removed. I'll have a new one designed someday."

*Yeah, kid, the setting would have made it easier to identify.* "You aren't anxious to wear it?"

"I'd be too worried. It's valuable enough to make it worth stealing."

*You ought to know, Tess.* "Then why keep it on board the boat?"

She reached out and touched a fingertip to the glittering stone. "I never knew my mother. This makes me feel close to her."

*And you can't risk putting it in a safe-deposit box. A nosy bank official might ask questions about such an unusual stone.*

"Why are you showing it to me?" The last bit of ice melted under the diamond. It lay on Jeopard's palm, a pale blue teardrop that glittered even in the dim light. Disgusted by the feel of it, he dropped it onto the towel in Tess's hand.

She stared at him in confusion, looking a little hurt. "It's a whimsical secret of mine. I wanted to show you how much I trust you." She gave him a tentative smile. "My grandparents are worried that you're up to no good."

He forced himself to smile back as if that were the most unlikely thing he'd ever heard. "Tell them that your secret's safe with me."

Jeopard caught her chin, turned her to face him squarely, and asked in a teasing tone, "Any other secrets?"

*Royce. Tell me again that he was a retired diamond broker. Tell me again that he left everything to his daughters.*

She searched his eyes so long that he knew she was worried about his strange mood. He could almost feel her withdrawing. "No," she said softly, and looked away.

*Dammit, Tess. That hurt worse than anything.*

He felt as if he were being torn inside out. He couldn't touch her, could barely look at her, and yet he knew he couldn't risk leaving. That would make her more wary.

"Honey?" he said in a low voice that aimed for gentleness.

She looked back at him, her eyes troubled. "Yes?"

"I'm a bastard for acting so unexcited. Thank you for sharing the diamond with me. It's just that I'm getting a killer headache. Remember that I mentioned I get migraines occasionally?"

"Oh, yes," she said happily, and exhaled with relief. "I mean, you had me worried there, Sundance. Poor man." She brushed her fingertips across his forehead. "Can I get you anything for it?"

"No. Maybe I can short-circuit it by going to sleep."

He grasped her hand and curled her fingers over the Blue Princess so that he wouldn't have to look at it anymore. "Go put that away. It concerns me that you keep something so valuable in an ice tray."

Her eyes filled with adoration. "You don't have to worry about me. I'm careful." She paused. "But I love you for worrying."

It was all Jeopard could do not to wince openly. What was she trying to do, destroy him? Had he met an equal at the game of deception he played so well?

"Get under the covers and relax," she murmured, stroking his neck. "Your muscles are full of knots! I'll give you a massage."

"No, I—"

"Come on, Jep. You can't tell me it won't help." She kissed him jauntily. "Into bed, Sundance. I'll be right back."

Miserable, he got into bed and lay on his stomach, his head burrowed in a pillow. She returned a few minutes later, turned off the desk lamp, and climbed into bed beside him. The white curtains let in a bit of light from the dock lamps, but still the darkness was blissfully deep.

Jeopard dug his fingers into the pillow as her warm, gentle hands slid over his shoulders. He replayed what he knew of her and realized that she had no reason to tell him that she loved him if it weren't the truth.

He ground his teeth. *Unless she knew what he was after and meant to sidetrack him.*

Jeopard considered that possibility for a long time, while she rubbed his neck and shoulders, occasionally bending forward to caress his back with a kiss. Each time she did, her breasts brushed against him.

"I feel a lot better," he said, lying. "Let's get some sleep."

She lay down close to him and rested one hand in the center of his back. "I love you, Jep," she whispered. "Good night."

"Good night." After a long hesitation, he swallowed hard and gave her the reply she wanted. "I love you too."

Damn, he was glad that she couldn't see his eyes. He hadn't cried in years.

SHE DREAMED GUILTY dreams because she hadn't told Jeopard about Royce's being a jewel thief. She'd intended to tell the story after she showed him the blue diamond, but he'd looked at her so strangely that she'd faltered. And when she'd realized that he had a terrible headache, she'd decided to wait.

Tess woke up anxious to right her wrong. She reached for Jeopard and sat up sharply when she found him gone. Her heart pounding with a puzzling sense of dread, Tess squinted into a stream of early-morning sunshine that had slipped between a curtain and the air conditioner.

He could be out jogging.

But he didn't jog—he hated it. He swam in the ocean every morning.

But he didn't swim this early.

He'd gone to the *Irresistible*, for some reason. He'd be right back.

Tess bounced out of bed, threw her robe around her shoulders, and went to the port window. Oh, how silly, this compulsion to open the curtains and look.

Okay, so she felt silly that morning. Tess raked the curtains back.

The *Irresistible* was gone.

A stunned minute later she gasped out loud and ran to the kitchen.

Her blue diamond was gone too.

JEOPARD ARRIVED IN Los Angeles by 8:00 A.M., less than an hour after he handed the yacht's key to a man who worked for Olaf.

He thought that his driving time from Long Beach was particularly good, considering his unplanned stop beside the freeway, where he'd hunched over a guard rail and regretted the four cups of strong coffee he'd poured into his stomach.

Coffee and misery didn't mix well.

He was met in the lobby of a sleek L.A. hotel by a lanky, well-dressed wolfhound of a man with enormous gray eyes and long blond hair. The man had already registered Jeopard under a false name.

The wolfhound shooed the bellmen away and carried one of Jeopard's suitcases himself. Jeopard carried the other two. He and the wolfhound didn't speak at all as they rode a glass-paneled elevator and walked to the hotel room.

Once inside, Jeopard pulled the blue diamond from the pocket of his sports coat. He tossed it to the man, who exhaled visibly with relief. Jeopard received a check for ten thousand dollars in return. It was the second half of his and Kyle's fee.

"I wish you'd taken another day," the man said wistfully. "I've grown to like Los Angeles while I've been waiting for you. Tomorrow I was going to Burbank to see the Johnny Carson show."

"Sorry."

"She won't contact the police?" the wolfhound asked in a heavy Swedish accent. Swedish was Kara's official language.

Jeopard had always suspected that Olaf's top aide was an idiot. That question confirmed it. "She isn't going to report that someone stole her stolen diamond."

"Ah. Yes."

"And you won't attempt to prosecute her."

"Correct. We have nothing to gain. Plus it would be difficult to prove that she knew the diamond was stolen."

"All right. Then we're done."

The wolfhound smiled slyly. "Tell me, did she live up to her reputation? I have many photographs besides those I gave you in the report. So many pictures of her in swimsuits. What remarkable legs! A man could easily imagine them wrapped around him. . . . Pardon me. I've offended you."

Jeopard never said a word. He simply looked up at the man until all the color drained from the face beneath the fine, flowing hair. The wolfhound bowed slightly and backed toward the door as if he were afraid to turn his back.

"Your work is excellent, Mr. Surprise," he said in a small, strained voice. "And I'm glad we'll have no more need of you."

He slipped out the door and slammed it behind him. Jeopard didn't move until he heard the last faint footfall as the man hurried away.

Then he slumped on the side of the bed and put his head in his hands.

IT WAS JUST as well that she'd loaned the Jaguar to Brandt for the week. Driving would have been dangerous in her current emotional state. Running wasn't much safer.

Tess covered the three miles to her grandparents' duplex in record time. When she fell against the low wall of their terrace, gasping desperately for breath, her heels were blistered and her insteps ached from running in ordinary tennis shoes without benefit of socks.

Her faded UCLA t-shirt was soaked with sweat, and her cut-off jeans bore bloodstains where she'd wiped her scraped palms after she tripped on a curb.

Before she could stagger up the tiled steps to the front door, her grandparents saw her from the living-room window. Their faces contorted with anxiety, Viktoria and Karl met Tess halfway up the steps and practically carried her inside.

She slumped on their couch and stared numbly at the floor while Viktoria hovered over her, dabbing her face with a cool washcloth. Karl sat down and took her hand.

"What is it, *raring?*" he implored.

"He stole the blue diamond," she answered wretchedly. "Jeopard Surprise."

Their audible gasps made her wince with humiliation and sorrow. Tess knew that her pain would worsen as soon as she fully comprehended the words she'd just spoken. Just then nothing seemed real.

"I showed it to him last night. He . . . he took it while I was asleep. His yacht was gone this morning."

Tess looked from Karl to Viktoria, watching their faces as they absorbed her news. Their expressions seemed frantic. "I love . . . loved him," she said in a choked voice. "And I thought he loved me."

"But you knew him only days!" Viktoria exclaimed, wringing her hands.

"Yes." Tess hung her head. She couldn't explain why there'd seemed nothing foolish about loving a man she'd known for such a short time.

"We were having him checked out," Karl muttered. "But now, it's too late."

Tess froze. "Checked out?"

"I have friends at the American embassy in Stockholm. I asked for their help. They know people who can find out anything about American citizens. We haven't heard from them yet."

Tess clenched her fists. "What's going on? Why did you suspect Jeopard from the start?"

Viktoria sank into a chair and covered her face. "Oh, Karl, Karl. We are lost."

Tess rubbed her forehead. Shards of pain shot through her scalp. Nothing made sense. She almost strangled on the next words. "I have to call the police."

Viktoria burst into tears. "No. Oh, Karl. Tell her."

Tess stared at her grandmother in confusion. "What?"

"You can't go to the police," Karl murmured wearily.

Tess straightened, her pulse roaring in her ears. "Why not?"

"The diamond is . . . not safe."

Tess pinched the bridge of her nose and fought the urge to scream. "Why, Grandfather?" she asked patiently.

Viktoria and Karl traded a long, covert look. "Because we stole it from someone twenty years ago," Karl said slowly, his eyes never leaving his wife's. "And now perhaps that someone wants it back."


JEOPARD LAY ON the hotel bed, his hands behind his head. Beyond the room's picture window Los Angeles sweated under a smoggy sky. The late-afternoon sun sifted through the smog and made the room hot.

Jeopard hadn't changed clothes, hadn't unpacked, hadn't even bothered to take off his sports coat. He was sweating, but not from the heat.

This time the Iceman had lost. He couldn't just walk away; he could only admit defeat and surrender.

The following day he'd go back to Long Beach, tell Tess everything, beg, coax, and seduce her into telling him everything in return, then try his best to win her trust again. If she could accept his work he could accept her past.

And they'd both start new, together.

## CHAPTER 7

"Yo, TESS. WANT a doughnut while you stare at the sunrise?"

Tess roused herself from the chair on the *Lady*'s aft deck. She hadn't slept at all, her body felt caved in, and she was certain her shapeless T-shirt and wrinkled shorts qualified her for a slob award.

Brandt stood on the dock, grinning and holding up a box from one of the local doughnut franchises. "I brought the Jag back last night, but you weren't around," he called. "I've got something to show you. You're gonna love it."

Moving like an old woman, Tess met him on the dock. She gazed at Brandt distractedly. Her throat felt rusty, and she was glad he couldn't see her eyes behind the dark sunglasses she wore.

The love of her life was a con artist, and her grandparents were jewel thieves. Sure, she felt like being entertained at that moment.

"Another electronic toy?" she croaked, glancing at

the device Brandt held in the hand not occupied by a doughnut box.

"Yeah. Just finished it this week. It's bitchin', Tess. Politicians in Third World countries use this kind of stuff to protect themselves from terrorists. Watch."

He pointed toward the marina parking lot. Through a haze of disinterest Tess noted that he'd parked the Jaguar in a good spot next to the curb. Brandt was an ultraresponsible teenager, and she didn't worry about loaning him her pride and joy.

Brandt held up his new plaything, which resembled a walkie-talkie. "Press a button, and . . . all right!"

The Jaguar's engine purred to life, and the headlights flashed on. "Ignition by remote control!" he announced happily.

And then the Jaguar exploded.


JEOPARD CAUGHT THE midmorning news update as he was dressing to leave the hotel. He halted in front of the TV and stared at the screen with cold horror. He saw the Sun Cove Marina sign in the background. In the foreground was a television reporter beside the burned, twisted ruins of a car.

". . . again, Los Angeles city attorney Suzanne Burdett, vacationing in Long Beach, was slightly injured by flying metal when a car exploded in a parking lot where she was jogging early this morning.

"She was treated and released from a Long Beach hospital. Luckily the car's owner, Tess Gallatin, wasn't in the car at the time. She told me that she was testing a remote-control ignition device designed by a friend when the car exploded. Experts from the Long Beach Police bomb squad said evidence indicates that the bombing was the work of a professional.

"There are no leads in the case. More details at noon. For Eyewitness News, this is Rena Brown, Long Beach."

Five seconds later Jeopard was on the phone, calling Tess's number at her grandparents' house. Her dulcet voice came to him via the recording on her answering machine.

"This is Jeopard," he said calmly. "Check in to a hotel under my name and lock yourself in a room. Don't come out. I'm in L.A. It's ten A.M. I'm leaving for Long Beach right now. I'll find you."

He prayed that she'd check the answering machine sometime soon. Next he called Kyle. In Florida it was 1:00 P.M. Kyle was barely awake.

"What? Jep?"

"Olaf's people may be trying to kill Tess Gallatin."

That cleared Kyle's fog. The mellow jokester snapped to alert. "You got a tip?"

"Somebody wired her car this morning."

"Was she hurt?"

"No. God help Olaf if she were."

Kyle's stunned silence greeted that remark. Finally he asked, "Personal?"

"Yes."

"She's hiding something else," Kyle said musingly. "They want her quiet."

"Yeah. I know less about her past than I thought. Doesn't matter. If they want her, they'll have to kill me first."

"What?"

"I love her. I'm going back to Long Beach and get her out of there."

"*You love her?*"

"If anything happens to me, make certain she's protected, Kyle."

"You love—all right."

"Call Drake. I'll need him."

Kyle whistled softly. "You *are* serious."

Jeopard slammed the phone down, then grabbed his wallet, the keys to his rental car, and the loaded Magnum .44.


JEOPARD WAS TRYING to kill her.

Tess sat in her grandparents' living room, hugging

herself. Karl paced. Viktoria sat by the telephone, staring at the answering machine as if Jeopard's voice were the essence of evil.

"It's a trick," Karl said grimly. "The man must think we're fools."

Tess shuddered. She wanted to curl up and hibernate until the world made sense again. It might take years.

"He doesn't know that we learned about his background," she said wearily. They knew all about Jeopard Surprise now. Karl had gotten in touch with his sources and demanded whatever information they had.

A dull sense of horror was the only emotion that kept Tess from feeling empty. She'd fallen in love with a cold-blooded assassin.

Jeopard Surprise was a mercenary in the worst sense of the word. He'd made a career out of killing people for pay. His wholesome businessman's image was a complete lie.

Someone wanted the blue diamond and then wanted her dead, and had sent an expert to take care of the job. An expert who knew how to capture her heart and soul to make his task easier. Now Tess realized that the coldness in his eyes had hidden indescribable cruelty.

"I don't understand," she said raggedly. "Why does he have to kill me? He's got the diamond. What did I do?"

"No more time for talk," Karl interjected. "We'll get out of the country. Mama, go pack. We'll go home. In Stockholm I'll find help to fight this monster."

"No! It's all our fault," Viktoria cried. "We'll call the police and tell them everything. Then they can protect Tess."

Tess rose proudly and looked at her grandparents. "No. You wanted to give me something no one else had—a queen's diamond. I've been struggling to understand how grief over my mother's death provoked you to steal the diamond from the Queen of Kara. I'm trying to understand your need for revenge after Mother was killed on a poorly designed ski slope in Kara."

Tess paused, thinking. "I was married to a retired jewel thief, and I loved him. I love you guys, too, and I won't let you martyr yourselves. I guess it's just my destiny to love people who steal diamonds."

*Oh, Jeopard.*

Tess took a deep breath. "I'm half Cherokee Indian. My father's people are survivors. Warriors. I'm not leaving without my medallion and my amulet. I'll go back to the boat and get them right now."

"No!" Karl cried. Viktoria clasped her heart.

"I have time before Jeopard gets here. I'll take your car—we know it's safe. This is something I have to do for my great-great-grandmother. Katherine Gallatin wouldn't be intimidated by *anything*, and neither will I."

Karl and Viktoria looked absolutely stricken. Tess grabbed the keys to their station wagon and left before she could think too much about her fear.


IF THE GUY was a salesman, then Jeopard was Mr. Rogers.

As Jeopard got out of the rental car his attention remained riveted to the neatly dressed man who strolled along the marina's dock carrying a thick satchel with *Ask Me About Happy Suds Cleaning Products!* stenciled on the side.

Jeopard's nerves tingled. Moving gracefully, he walked down a flight of stairs that led from the parking lot to the dock.

The Happy Suds salesman paused by various boats, casually studied a note in his hand, and moved on. When a voluptuous woman wearing a T-shirt over a bikini waved at him, he waved back but kept walking.

The guy was no salesman, Jeopard knew without doubt.

Every muscle poised for action, Jeopard ambled down the dock behind the visitor. A hard, deadly tightness came over him as the man stopped in front of the *Lady*.

Jeopard glanced back. Madam Voluptuous had gone into her boat's cabin. No one else was around on this weekday morning.

The man lifted his satchel and fiddled with something on the handle. Then he crossed the gangplank and stepped onto the *Lady*'s bow.

Tess's security alarm didn't make a sound.

Jeopard realized immediately that the visitor's satchel held something besides samples. He had just counteracted the *Lady*'s alarm system. A thorough professional.

"Hey, pal," Jeopard yelled. He staggered down the dock, weaving dangerously close to the wooden buffers at the edge. "You got a light?"

The man, a short, stocky redhead with a wholesome face straight out of a Norman Rockwell painting, turned and frowned at Jeopard. "You're drunk."

"Hell, you're kiddin'. I thought we were having another earthquake."

"Beat it. I'm busy."

Jeopard reached the *Lady*'s gangplank and staggered aboard, flapping at his coat pockets. "Damn. No cigarettes. Come on, buddy. If you got 'em, share one."

"I'm afraid I don't—"

"Too bad," Jeopard interjected, and rabbit-punched him in the jaw.

The skilled upper cut made the ersatz salesman collapse like a bad soufflé, and he tumbled onto the deck. His coat fell open to reveal a small handgun with a silencer.

Jeopard knelt beside the man, jerked the gun from its holster, and tossed it over the *Lady*'s railing. "Son of a bitch," he whispered to the unconscious man.

Jeopard propped the satchel on his chest. "You're lucky I don't have time to deal with you."

He didn't have *any* time. Jeopard heard a quick creaking sound and looked down the stairwell just as the cabin door banged open. Tess stood there, staring up at him, an expression of fear and horror on her face.

Jeopard could imagine how confused she must be, seeing him crouched over an unconscious salesman who had a small billboard on his chest innocently advising the world to ask him about Happy Suds Cleaning Products.

"Don't be misled," Jeopard told her in a soothing voice. "I'm the guy in the white hat. Relax, honey."

She raised a tiny pistol and pointed it at his chest.

"The Cherokees had a title for a female who was good at fighting," she informed him imperiously. " 'War Woman.' "

Jeopard straightened slowly and held up both hands. "Tess. I know you have a lot of doubts, but I'm your only hope."

"You're a hired killer."

Faltering at that abrupt charge, Jeopard stared at her in stunned silence.

"I know about you," she continued, the lethal little gun trembling in her hands. "You were hired to steal the diamond and get rid of me."

The accusation that he was a paid assassin—paid to kill the brightest hope that had ever come into his life—made him continue to look at her in astonishment.

"Who told you that?"

"My grandfather had you checked out. He has friends in American diplomatic circles."

Jeopard grimaced inwardly. There were no official government records on former high-level agents such as himself. There were only carefully constructed facades designed to alarm and deceive an enemy.

The truth about his former line of work was disturbing enough; the lies she'd been given must have terrified her. But maybe he needed that advantage right now.

"Tess, we haven't got much time. We have to get out of here."

"So you can take care of me without anyone's seeing you?" Her voice cracked. "Who hired you?"

The assassin stirred weakly under Jeopard's feet. Time had run out. Now that this guy had been exposed, someone else would be after her.

Jeopard watched Tess glance downward at the fallen man. He used that unguarded moment to lunge for her. She yelped, lowered the gun, and tried to shove her cabin door shut. Jeopard plowed through and wrapped both arms around her.

The momentum carried them both to her bed, where he fell on top of her. The gun sailed out of her hand and struck her computer with a metallic thud.

Jeopard pinned her arms and legs down. "The gun wasn't loaded," he told her gruffly. "I could see the empty chambers."

Her silver-blue eyes were as fierce as they were frightened. "You cruel, deceiving bastard. Where were you when you called my answering machine? It would have taken you an hour to get here from Los Angeles."

"I came by helicopter."

She inhaled harshly. "My grandparents will look for me."

"By the time they start, you'll be gone. And later you'll call and tell them that you were wrong about me, that you've gone into hiding with me until the danger blows over."

She wiggled under him. "No."

"Yes. I have a recording of your voice. That night we talked at the Zanzi Bar I recorded you for *hours*. My people can copy your speech patterns and tones from that. Someone will call Karl and Viktoria for you. Your grandparents will hear you say that everything's just fine between you and me."

She groaned and gritted her teeth. "What do you want from me?"

"I'm trying to save your life."

"Tell me the truth!"

"Neither of us is interested in the truth. You've made that clear. You're hiding something that makes somebody want to kill you. If you'd told me everything about the diamond, you wouldn't be in this predicament."

"I told you!"

She writhed under him like a trapped cat. Jeopard knew a dozen different techniques that would subdue her, but none that wouldn't hurt like hell.

He squeezed his legs around hers and clasped her wrists in an iron grip above her head. "Stop it. Stop it, Tess, or by God I'll make you sorry."

She froze, then began quivering at the lethal insinuation in his tone. Jeopard gazed down at her coldly, all reconciliation gone from his manner. He watched her eyes widen in alarm at the look on his face. His heart broke.

He'd pay a price for saving her. He could see it in her disgust and terror.

Jeopard rolled her onto her stomach, so he wouldn't have to look at her eyes. He used his belt to bind her hands behind her back, then went to her small dresser and searched until he found two long silk scarves.

He tied her ankles together with one of them, then knotted the other one snugly around her neck. Jeopard turned her over, winced inside at the wretched look on her face, and lifted her toward the head of the bed.

He fastened the end of the neck binding to the bedstead.

"Tied like a dog to a post," she whispered raggedly. "At least give me a fighting chance."

"Be quiet."

He left the cabin before he lost all sense of logic, ripped the bindings off of her, and begged her to understand what he was trying to do.

The hired killer sat up groggily. Jeopard knelt in

front of him, grasped him by the collar, and smiled at him.

"If you'd hurt her, I'd have made you regret it," he told the man in a soft, pleasant voice. "If I had time and privacy, I'd make you regret even *thinking* about hurting her. But you're in luck. As it is, I'll simply describe you in detail to some very ruthless people who like to take justice into their own hands. Now, get up, walk off this boat, and don't look back. I'll be watching."

The man took his satchel and left without a word. Jeopard tracked him with a shrewd gaze, memorizing everything about him, until he got into a small sedan and drove away.

Back in the cabin Tess had turned to lie on her side, and her neck was bent at an awkward angle because of the way she was tied to the bed. "Don't touch me," she said in a low, raspy tone as he slid a pillow under her head.

Her chest moved swiftly. Jeopard groaned with frustration—she was about to attempt screams that a Banshee might envy. He ran to get more scarves, then stuffed one into her mouth and used another to tie it in place. She made muffled protests and tried to twist her head away from him.

Dull despair washed over Jeopard. She'd never believe his reasons for doing this. He grasped her jaw and forced her to look up at him.

"I'm taking the boat out to sea. Someone will meet us there. You might as well stop fighting, because you're trapped."

She jerked her head away and shut her eyes, effectively dismissing him. Jeopard touched a fingertip to the medallion that lay on her right breast, then lifted the antler amulet and looked at it.

A lump rose in his throat. What had she been trying to do, ward him off as though he were an evil spirit? She still had her eyes shut, finding him too loathsome to look at.

Perhaps he was evil, and it was too late to save

himself. But he'd save her, even if it meant putting her through hell to do it.

Jeopard grimly tossed the amulet back on her chest. "You won't need any Cherokee magic," he told her curtly. "As long as you do what I tell you, you won't get hurt."

Feeling sick, he left her to ponder that heartless warning and went above to set sail.

THE NEXT TWO hours were an endless horror. Wherever Jeopard was taking her, it would be far away from anyone who could help her.

First they were met by a small power boat piloted by a middle-aged man who shook Jeopard's hand but never said a word. They were transferred to the boat, and Tess looked back forlornly at the *Swedish Lady*, sitting abandoned.

"The Coast Guard will find her," Jeopard said brusquely, and pulled her around so that she couldn't look anymore.

The power boat took them up the coast to an unused oil platform, where a helicopter waited. There was another man, who shook Jeopard's hand as if they'd done this sort of thing many times—which they must have, Tess thought bitterly.

The helicopter took them inland to a stretch of empty desert, where a small private plane sat alone on a windswept highway. The pilot smiled at her as Jeopard carried her—still bound hand and foot—onto the plane.

Since Jeopard had long since removed the stuffing from her mouth, she told the pilot that he'd go to prison for aiding a kidnapper. He smiled even more broadly.

Jeopard spoke to her with a minimum of cool, brusque words. He put her in a window seat and sat beside her, his side pressed tightly to hers. After the plane settled into its cruising altitude he untied her.

"Rest room is in the back. Now's your chance."

"How kind of you."

She rose and swept past him without a backward glance. When she returned he motioned her back to the window seat.

"Sit down. All right. Hands on your lap."

Then he carefully prepared to bind her wrists and ankles with strips of wide, soft tape. She'd be more comfortable but no less a prisoner.

Tess stared out the window at clouds and blue sky, her teeth clenched. He handled her with a businesslike intimacy that made her face burn with fury and humiliation. Damn the man!

He rubbed her wrists to make certain they weren't chafed, then probbed gently at her scraped palms. He ran his hand down her ankle and lifted one sandaled foot to study the big blister on her heel. Then he sat back and scrutinized the wrinkled shorts and old T-shirt she'd worn for the past twenty-four hours. Finally he put two fingers at the base of her throat and checked her pulse.

"Now I know how a slave girl feels in a harem," she said between gritted teeth. "Do you intend to molest me later?"

He withdrew his hand slowly. "Of course. I'm that kind of man, as you well know. It wouldn't look good for my reputation if I didn't do a little sordid molesting, now would it?"

She flinched but said nothing.

"Your face is gaunt. I want you to eat," he announced.

"A fattened pig for the sacrifice."

He went to an ice chest in the front of the cabin and brought her a carton of milk, a large piece of cheese, two apples, and a package of crackers, all of which he placed on her lap.

He opened the milk carton and wedged it between her hands.

"Eat. If you need help, say so."

"Let's get something straight. You disgust me. I won't ask you for anything."

"You will soon enough," he said softly, and left her shivering as he went forward to sit with the pilot.

TWO HOURS LATER the plane landed on an airstrip set in a valley among dry, barren mountains Tess couldn't identify. She blanched as Jeopard carried her out of the plane and she saw a small private jet on the runway.

"How far are we going?"

His arms tightened around her. "I got a terrific idea from your Cherokee history lessons. We're going to North Carolina. Remember the caves in the mountains there? We're going to hide in one."

"Hide from what?" she asked in a small, stunned voice.

"That's for you to tell me. You know why somebody's trying to kill you. I don't."

Tess shook her head fiercely. "You're the only killer."

"Enough." Jeopard stopped in the middle of the runway. He looked down at her, his blue eyes icy. "When you're ready to tell me the truth, talk to me. Otherwise, keep quiet."

Tess swallowed hard. She didn't understand his frightening game. After he carried her aboard the jet and deposited her in a seat, she looked up at him desperately.

"Do you want money? A ransom? Is this revenge for the diamond?" She gasped. "You wouldn't hurt my grandparents! Please tell me you don't intend to do anything to them!"

He stared down at her with tired, unhappy eyes. "I'm not interested in them. Only in you. And you can make this a helluva lot easier if you'll open up. Tell me how you got the Blue Princess."

"The what?" she asked plaintively. "You mean the blue diamond? I told you, they gave it to me for my eighteenth birthday! I'd never seen it before then! But I forgive them for what they did! They had reasons—''

''Dammit, stop,'' he said, bending over her with menace. His expression was deadly. ''I know that Royce was a jewel thief. The sooner you talk, the sooner this will be over with.''

Tess's head reeled. He had known about Royce all along. *The sooner you talk, the sooner this will be over with.* When he got his information, would he dispose of her? But what information? And what did Royce have to do with the blue diamond that Jeopard called the Blue Princess?

Silence was obviously her best defense.

Tess met his gaze stoically. He scrutinized her for nearly a minute, as if he were trying to force a reaction from her. She barely blinked.

Finally, fatigue and dismay clouded his expression. He chuckled, then told her in a low, tense tone, ''All right, War Woman, if you want war, you've got it.''

THEY LOST THREE hours of daylight flying east, and when they landed, darkness had fallen. Tess couldn't see much beyond the jet's windows, but she glimpsed tall outlines and suspected that they must be in the North Carolina mountains.

Jeopard and the pilot disappeared outside for a long time. Tess caught glimmers from their flashlights and peered into the night. She thought she saw a third man. Yes.

When Jeopard came back on board he was followed by a muscular black-haired giant with a handsome face that might have been carved from a granite block. Tess gaped. The man had to stoop to negotiate the cabin ceiling. He was easily seven feet tall. He wore western boots, faded jeans, and a khaki safari shirt.

A huge knife was strapped to his belt.

Jeopard, his face unreadable, gestured casually from Tess to the giant. ''Drake Lancaster.''

She and the giant shared a speculative look. ''Nice

to meet you," he said politely in a rumbling bass voice. It was as if the mountains themselves had spoken to her.

Tess arched a brow at him and said nothing.

"She's taken a vow of silence," Jeopard noted drolly. "It's nothing personal. As far as I know she still listens, even if she won't answer."

Jeopard leaned against a seat and crossed his arms over his chest. Lancaster sat down in the aisle and rested his hands on his updrawn knees. "Ms. Gallatin, I brought you some clothes and other necessities. In the morning I'll take you and Jeopard into the mountains on horseback. You need to get a good night's sleep. And please relax. You're safe."

When she didn't answer, he shifted awkwardly and looked at Jeopard for help.

"I think she likes you," Jeopard quipped. "She didn't hiss."

The huge man sighed as if he didn't understand these kind of man/woman games very well. He reached into a shirt pocket and retrieved something. "Before I forget. Take a look at this, man. What a gorgeous doll. Rucker and Dinah sent this to me last week."

Tess craned her head as Jeopard reached for what appeared to be a photograph. Gorgeous doll? Some femme fatale, probably.

Jeopard gazed at the photo, and a gentle smile touched his mouth. She watched him with dull intrigue, wondering what woman could draw such tenderness from him.

Sincere tenderness, not the fake kind he'd shown her.

Jeopard glanced over at her. "My goddaughter," he told her, and held out a photograph of a smiling baby in a pink pinafore.

"Mine too," Drake interjected firmly.

Tess studied the photograph, then let her eyes flicker up slowly to Jeopard's with what she hoped was a distinctly uninterested expression.

"You've heard of Rucker McClure, the writer?" he asked.

She nodded.

"Drake and I helped him rescue his wife and daughter last year. The details are classified, but suffice it to say, we were quite proud of ourselves."

Tess lifted her chin and eyed Jeopard coolly. She couldn't resist taunting his inflated ego. "Am I supposed to be impressed because you two professional killers have a soft spot for children? Sorry, I'm not."

She caught Drake Lancaster's look of astonishment. He turned toward Jeopard. "What does she think—"

"She got my official background."

"Oh." Drake frowned.

"It's a little difficult to prove otherwise at this point."

"Right."

"So she thinks I'm worse than I am. And you're guilty by association."

"My mother warned me not to hang around with people like you."

"Yes. Undoubtedly."

Jeopard straightened. Tess found his gaze back on her. It was challenging but somehow extremely sad. She felt bewildered and exhausted. What new con was he trying to pull?

"Time for bed, War Woman." He gestured toward the tape around her wrists and feet. "Drake, get rid of this."

Drake got up, crouched over her, and sliced the tape with careful strokes of his huge knife. Then he left the plane, his head bent awkwardly to avoid denting the roof.

Jeopard grasped her wrist. "Let's go. There's a sleeping bag waiting outside for you."

"Are we sharing, godfather?" she asked tautly.

"No. I wouldn't want to fall asleep while my throat was within reach of your hands."

He led her out of the jet. Tess looked around, smelled the rich, cool night air of the mountains, then glanced down at the concrete under her feet. "Drug trafficking," she said harshly. "That's the only reason you'd have these hidden runways."

"I don't sell, buy, or use drugs. You've watched too many episodes of *Miami Vice*."

He drew her across an open field toward a campfire at the edge of the forest. The pilot lay on a sleeping bag, swigging a soft drink. Drake Lancaster knelt beside the fire, stirring something in a pot set among the embers.

Several horses were tethered to nearby trees. Tess gazed around at the blackness outside the ring of firelight. In the glow of a half-moon the craggy, forested peaks seemed as mysterious to her as the masterful blond man who had hold of her wrist.

"Welcome to the Nantahala Mountains," Jeopard told her.

He guided her to a sleeping bag at the edge of the firelight. It lay near the base of a large dogwood tree.

"Sit down." He looked over his shoulder. "Drake, did you remember the chain?"

Her heart pounding with dread, Tess lowered herself and sat cross-legged. Chain? Drake Lancaster went to a canvas bag and pulled out a long, slender silver chain. He brought it to Jeopard, along with two small padlocks.

"Here's the key," he said, and dropped it into the side pocket of Jeopard's sports coat.

Tess stared at the chain in horror. She shivered inwardly as Jeopard looped it around her waist, beneath her shirt, and fastened it with a padlock. He took the other end to the dogwood tree and locked it around the trunk.

Then he merely glanced at her and walked away to join his friends.

She numbly pushed the chain out of her way, turned to face the mountains, and hugged her knees to her chest. Only the most rigid pride kept her from crying. Tess dug her fingers into her bare legs and stared into the forest.

The medallion and the antler amulet pressed into her breasts, and the feel of them made a bittersweet chill run down her spine.

This was Cherokee land, the Sun Land of the tribe's mythology, and she had ancestral spirits on her side that Jeopard Surprise couldn't begin to battle. She belonged here, and he didn't. She didn't care what he did to her. She was strong.

Tess caught the low murmur of Drake's voice and heard Jeopard's laughter. Despair engulfed her.

Who was she kidding? She was miserable.

There was only one reason why she felt so hurt and betrayed by Jeopard's treatment. She didn't want to love him anymore, and her agony came from knowing that she still did.

THE CHAIN WAS a hard, rattling weight hanging around her waist. Tess looped it over one elbow so that it wouldn't tug so much on her tender flesh. She slid a hand under the steel links and gingerly rubbed her chafed, sweating skin.

Tess shifted in her saddle and thought about the other chafed parts of her body. She glanced over her shoulder and glimpsed Jeopard, whose horse stayed close behind hers. She sensed that he was watching her, as usual. His unwavering attention seemed designed to force her to notice him in return.

Tess faced forward proudly and pretended to study their surroundings. The air was sweet and the scenery spectacular, which made her situation seem even more depressing. Startled insects hummed louder as the horses' feet crunched through the undergrowth.

To her right the land dropped into a beautiful, dramatic gorge. Massive granite boulders overhung the banks of a stream bed at the bottom, and thick, graceful trees draped their limbs toward the rushing water.

*Nantahala* meant "land of the noonday sun" in Cherokee, because the mountains rose so steeply that some of the narrow passes between them stayed in shadow most of the day. The name also belonged to a river in the area that was popular with white-water aficionados.

Drake, trying awkwardly to chat with her that morning, had mentioned that they were on the edge of the Great Smoky Mountains National Forest and that the Nantahala River was no more than five miles from the landing strip. White-water enthusiasts flocked to the area to raft, canoe, and kayak during the summer. There was a small town in the vicinity.

Tess chewed on her lower lip and considered that information. Civilization was within walking distance. A long walk, but she could make it. Of course, for the past two hours Drake had led them farther from civilization and deeper into the national forest along winding, nearly indistinct trails.

Let's see, she thought. She could follow the sun back. No, she could barely see the sun. Wasn't there some rule about moss growing on the north side of a tree? Or was it the south side?

Landmarks. Tess looked around. Yes, there were thousands of them. Trees. Identical trees. She sighed with dismay. Weren't Cherokees instinctively supposed to know their way through the woods?

She ran her fingers under the chain again and winced at the raw prickling sensation on her waist.

"Here. Take this."

Jeopard nudged his horse up beside hers on the narrow mountain trail. He pulled a soft red bandanna from the back pocket of his jeans and handed it to her. "Wrap that around the lock."

Tess eyed him coolly. Drake had supplied them both with basic clothing for this venture: jeans, leather hiking shoes, and loose cotton shirts with short sleeves. But he hadn't known her size, and apparently liked to think everyone was as large as himself.

If the wind caught her just right, her jeans would

inflate and *float* her to safety. At least her shoes and socks fit.

Jeopard, on the other hand, looked like the Esquire Man at a cattle roundup. His tousled blond hair gave him a deceptively boyish charm, his light blue shirt bore no sweat stains, and his jeans maintained a neat crease down the center of each lean, muscular leg. Head 'em up and move 'em out, Calvin Klein, Tess thought sarcastically.

Tess ignored the bandanna as she'd ignored every gesture, word, and look of his all morning. She gazed disdainfully at the chain looped around his saddle horn. He kept her on a leash, but the last thing she'd be was his pet.

"Either tie this bandanna around the lock or I'll tie it for you," he ordered calmly.

"If you're going to kill me, why do you care about my comfort?"

"Drake! Hold up a minute!"

Drake reined his horses in and looked curiously over his shoulder. Jeopard reached out, grabbed the chain, and pulled her toward him with even, firm force.

Her horse felt the off-center shift of her body and halted, sidestepping until it bumped Jeopard's horse to a stop too. Tess clung to the saddle horn and tried not to fall off. When her face was only inches from Jeopard's and her leg was mashed securely against his from knee to hip, he tucked the bandanna around the lock. His warning blue eyes held her defensive ones.

"I've killed people," he told her in a low, controlled tone. "But I'm not a *killer*. I've done some ugly things, but I've done them for good reasons. That doesn't make me a saint, but I'm not a monster, either. I'm not going to hurt you."

His tense, heartfelt words made goose bumps scatter down Tess's arms. She searched his face desperately, not knowing what to believe. She couldn't ignore him any longer. "Then who blew up my car?"

"Possibly the people who hired me. I don't know."

His jaw tightened. "How many people have reason to want revenge against you and Royce?"

She stared at him, open-mouthed. "Me and Royce? I wasn't involved in Royce's profession. He was retired."

"And Royce didn't leave you anything in his will?"

"I told you that he didn't!"

"Except for the Blue Princess."

Tess bit each word off emphatically. "I told you, my grandparents *gave* me the diamond on my eighteenth birthday. They stole it from Queen Isabella of Kara because of some misguided urge for revenge. My mother died in an accident on a ski slope at a Karan resort."

"That's a ridiculous story. I had your grandparents checked out after they came to the marina and spied on me. They wouldn't steal an apple from the corner grocery."

Tess shivered with frustration. On that point she agreed with him. The story still perplexed her.

"I thought *you* weren't capable of stealing from *me*. I thought you were a Florida businessman on vacation. I thought you were someone very special."

"I retrieved your *stolen* diamond for its owner. Don't play games with me. You knew the diamond was hot, and that Royce was the one who stole it."

She shook both fists at him. "I'm telling you the truth, which is more than you ever told me! You were paid to get close to me, and you weren't particular about the way you did it!"

He inhaled sharply. "I love you. Even if you're still determined to lie about your past."

"Oh, stop!" she demanded in disgust and shock. Tess pulled back from him, her eyes full of tears. She held the chain out defiantly. "Is this how you treat someone you love?"

"When it's the only way to make her do what's best for her, yes."

"I don't need that kind of love."

"You need to stay alive, don't you? And I intend

to keep you that way while my brother and Drake try to learn who the hell wants you dead. It would be helpful if you'd give me some clues."

Her shoulders slumped. "I've told you all I know."

"Dammit, I might as well talk to the mountains." He waved curtly to Drake, who started up the trail again.

Tess slanted a look at him. "You'd better learn how, if you want friendly conversation."

Jeopard urged his horse ahead of her and tugged on her chain. "Move it. The sooner you tell me the truth and make friends, the sooner I can let you off this leash."

Tess bit back bitter words that would only antagonize him more and hurried her horse after his. The chain stretched between them like a bond neither could escape.

FOR A CAVE, it was cozy.

It looked as though some giant had scooped a handful of rock from the mountain's side. There was nothing dank or dark about the cave; it had a wide, tall entrance that let in a lot of the afternoon sun. The floor was fairly level and the walls had a whitish limestone surface.

Tess stood at the entrance and gazed outward at a vista of gently rounded blue-green mountains. The ground sloped for a hundred feet in front of the cave, then dropped gradually toward a distant valley.

"It's like looking out a window at the top of the world," Drake observed as he began unloading gear from the pack horse.

"Get used to the view," Jeopard told her. He took his end of her chain to a stout young maple tree growing by the cave's entrance. There he knelt and padlocked the chain into place.

The chain was easily thirty feet long, so Tess could walk to the center of the cave or well outside the entrance. But it was a short tether, considering her humiliation and anger.

She sat down on a rocky outcropping and stared into the distance, her back aching with the attempt to maintain her dignity, her thoughts turbulent. Jeopard refused to believe her story about the blue diamond, he claimed to be on her side, and yet he intended to keep her chained in a cave, at his beck and call.

And he'd said that he loved her.

"Here. Make yourself useful. Blow up these air mattresses."

Jeopard dropped a heap of plastic and a bicycle pump onto the ground in front of her, then walked away. Her mouth clamped tightly shut, Tess went to work.

While she was inflating the first mattress, angrily stamping the foot pump, Drake came over and laid a large canvas bag beside her.

"Things for you," he explained. "Jeopard told me to get them."

Tess stared at the bag, wary of Jeopard's continuing attempts at kindness. She hated the wistful, eager way her pulse jumped.

She started to open the bag, caught Jeopard watching her with a cool, slit-eyed expression, and changed her mind. Curiosity would make her vulnerable. After all, she'd never have gotten into this mess if she hadn't been curious about an enigmatic stranger who had trouble docking his yacht.

She shoved the bag with her foot and went back to pumping up the air mattresses.

When Drake and Jeopard finished setting everything up she had her own territory on the left side of the cave. Tess arranged a pillow and sleeping bag on her air mattress and sat down.

She watched them fiddle with elite camping gear—powerful lanterns, a small kerosene-powered grill, buckets, pots, skillets, and a dozen other items.

"My apartment isn't this well furnished," Jeopard quipped.

He put his mattress on the opposite side of the cave, fixed a campfire site in the center, then came to her and gestured with one finger. "Up. Test time."

She raged inwardly when she realized what he meant. He led her to the end of her chain, then moved gear around to make certain she couldn't reach it.

"Afraid I'll attack you with a spatula?" she asked grimly.

"Frankly, yes, War Woman."

Drake set a CB radio on Jeopard's side of the cave and ran a long cable to an antenna outside. "Six P.M. every day," he called.

"I'll be listening."

Tess went back to her side of the cave and sat down. "Exactly how long are we going to be here?"

"As long as it takes. Look at it as a native cultural experience. Cherokees may have hidden in this cave a hundred and fifty years ago."

"I doubt they had CB radios."

She touched her voluminous jeans and shirt. They were hot and uncomfortable. "What am I supposed to wear?"

"Anything you want. Go naked. I could use the entertainment."

"Perhaps you can amuse yourself by throwing rocks at small animals or pulling the wings off of insects."

"I think I'll leave you two lovebirds alone," Drake interjected. "I'm not a good referee." He mounted his horse and tipped a hand to his forehead in salute to Jeopard. "And you thought the Russians were tough."

Jeopard glanced drolly at Tess. "I know how Custer felt."

*Russians?* Tess was intrigued, but refused to ask for an explanation.

A sense of foreboding filled her as Drake rode away, leading the other three horses. When the forest swallowed him up, it was as if he'd never existed. She and Jeopard were alone, and the cave seemed awfully small and quiet.

His back to her, Jeopard knelt by a bag, unzipped it, and rummaged inside.

"What now?" she asked in a weary voice.

"Drake says there's a big creek not far from here." He stood and turned to face her. He carried towels and a bar of soap. He smiled pleasantly. "I'd say we both need a bath."

IT WASN'T JUST a creek, it was a natural work of art, with a ten-foot waterfall that bubbled over a granite ledge into a shallow pool.

If she hadn't been so upset, she would have sighed with awe. Tess sat down on a flat boulder by the pool and hugged her knees.

"I have no desire to bathe while you watch," she told Jeopard.

He chained her to a nearby tree. "You spent the better part of a week naked in my bed. There's no reason for you to be modest with me now."

She stared into the shimmering pool while a knot of bittersweet pain grew inside her. "That was different," she murmured. "I wasn't ashamed of loving you then."

He slowly sat down beside her. The air seemed to crackle with emotion. "You're ashamed now?" he asked in a husky voice.

"Yes."

Tess looked at him. A muscle flexed in his jaw, and his eyes were shadowed, but he looked more regretful than angry. She could have sworn that he was struggling with deep sorrow.

"Take a bath, Tess," he finally said, his voice tired. "I won't try to make love to you, if that's what you're afraid of."

He turned away and stripped off his clothes. Tess watched, strange emotions gnawing at her as he revealed his body without inhibition.

Jeopard took the bar of soap and stepped into the pool, his back to her. "Are you coming in?"

"Is this the only chance I'll have to wash?"

"Yes."

"All right," she said in a defeated tone. Tess removed her clothes and slid into the water, then turned her back and sank down until the water covered her to the shoulders.

She heard Jeopard splash water on himself and wanted to cry at the memory of running her hands over his body, of touching him everywhere, of pleasing him in every way a woman could please a man.

"Why did you want me to fall in love with you?" she asked in a tear-soaked voice. "Was I so easy and foolish that you couldn't resist?"

"It was the other way around. I couldn't resist you."

She shut her eyes. *Stop lying to me, Jeopard.* "But you stole from me."

"And after I turned the diamond over to its rightful owner, I planned to come back to Long Beach and tell you why I'd done it."

"You did it for money. Someone paid you. How much?"

He hesitated for a second. "Twenty thousand dollars to my brother and me. We work together."

She gasped. "Who wanted the diamond that badly?"

She heard sloshing noises. The water undulated around her. Suddenly Jeopard touched her shoulder. Tess jumped.

"The soap," he said brusquely, and let it slip down her chest.

Trying to control her voice, she asked again, "Who wanted the diamond?"

He told her about Olaf Starheim, the Duke of Kara. "But why would he want to kill me?"

Again Jeopard touched her. She wanted to withdraw, but couldn't make herself do it. He ran his hand back and forth across her shoulders, massaging her.

"You tell me," he murmured. "Tell me, and let's go on with our relationship."

Tess's momentary languor dissolved in anger. She moved away from him and said tautly, "I won't forget what you are and what you really want from me."

"Just the truth."

Tess dropped the soap in the water and buried her face in her hands. "I've told you. You don't believe me. You're hopeless. I don't understand you. I don't really know who you are."

"I'm not sure myself these days," he said bitterly.

"You frighten me. I don't feel safe with you."

"*Tess.* That's the one thing you shouldn't doubt."

"Fine words from a con artist."

His voice was more anguished then angry. "You're awfully arrogant for a jewel thief."

Tess grabbed the soap, twisted around, and threw it at him. He caught it just in time to keep from being hit in the head. Slowly, his eyes taunting her, he smiled.

"I'm definitely keeping the spatula away from you."


IF HE'D COUNTED the times she spoke to him during the next few days, he doubted they'd have come to more than a dozen. She withdrew into a silent, wary world, doing what he told her to do, asking quietly when she needed something, but otherwise ignoring him.

The one time he saw excitement and pleasure in her eyes was when she opened her canvas bag and found all the books and pamphlets he'd instructed Drake to buy for her at the museum on the Cherokee reservation, which wasn't far from the Nantahala area.

"I thought you'd enjoy them," Jeopard told her.

She clasped a book titled *Myths and Sacred Formulas of the Cherokees* to her chest and drew herself up regally. "What do you want in return?"

He glared at her as if she'd just slapped him, then went outside the cave and stayed until nightfall. Had he lost her entirely? She was so bitter that there wasn't

any point in talking to her just then. The knowledge
that she found him repulsive tore at his soul.

When he returned she was poring over the book of
myths and formulas, and he had the disturbing notion
that she was searching for some incantation to do him
harm.

DRAKE CAME BACK a week later, bringing supplies, smaller clothes and more books for Tess, and a
packet from Kyle.

"He's been researching Kara," Drake explained.
"He thought you'd like to see what he found, even
though it's nothing exciting."

That night, as Tess stirred a pot of soup over the
campfire and a gas lantern cast sharp shadows on the
cave's walls, Jeopard opened the packet and began
reading photocopies of articles about Kara.

"Kara is only a short flight from Sweden." Tess
spoke in a rare break from her habitual silence. "I
went there many times on vacation. It's a Scandinavian version of Monaco. Tiny and expensive."

"Lots of ski resorts and casinos, it says here."

"A beautiful little country. It's an island, you know,
between Sweden and Denmark. The royal palace is a
fairy-tale place on a mountaintop that overlooks the
North Sea."

"What I can't understand is how monarchies survive in the modern world."

"The people loved the king and queen. I remember
when the king died—I must have been about twelve—
I was visiting Grandmother and Grandfather in Stockholm. Grandfather, being a member of the Swedish
parliament, went to the funeral as a matter of courtesy. Grandmother and I went with him. I'll never forget the people I met. They were sincerely grief-stricken
over the king's death. And they adored the queen."

"Too bad nobody likes the king and queen's
nephew. Olaf has apparently been waiting all his adult

life for the queen to pop off, so he could take over, and nobody's happy about his claim to the throne.''

''So recapturing my diamond will win him some brownie points?''

''It's not your diamond.''

''And killing me might win him more?'' she continued pertly. ''Tell me, if Olaf had approached you for that job, how much would you have charged?''

Jeopard struggled to keep from beating one fist against the cave floor. ''I don't kill people for pay. That's the last time I'm going to say it.''

''Why *do* you kill people?''

''If they're trying to kill me or someone I'm responsible for protecting. And I'm retired from that line of work. I'm just a plain, ordinary private investigator now.''

''Hmmm. I see. My father had no respect for PIs. He said they spend their time peeking through keyholes.''

''I'm not quite that disgusting,'' Jeopard told her drolly. ''I peek through keyholes, but only for big corporations and governments. I peek through *important* keyholes.''

''And con innocent people out of their possessions.''

Jeopard ground his teeth. She was retaliating for all that he'd put her through, and she obviously wasn't afraid of him anymore, or she wouldn't be so cocky. At least that was good.

''What else would you like to know about Kara?'' she asked innocently, still stirring the soup.

''Why you wanted to keep one of the more mediocre royal diamonds. Why not steal something worth more?''

She didn't say another word to him.


TESS WOKE TO a strange snuffling sound. She propped herself on one elbow and stared into the moonlight outside the cave's entrance. Leaves and twigs crunched under ponderous feet.

She tugged at her chain. Jeopard could run. She couldn't. Tess made a small, fearful sound.

"Sssh, I'm here," Jeopard whispered in the darkness.

Tess realized that he had slipped across the cave to her. He lay down on his stomach beside her. She caught a glimmer of steel in his hand and realized that he held one of the several guns Drake had supplied.

He pressed a tiny piece of metal into her palm. "Open your padlock."

Surprised, she fumbled with it, but finally got the lock undone. The chain fell in a heap on the air mattress.

"Come here." He put an arm around her and pulled her close to his side, shielding her with his body. Tess clutched his warm, hard waist and realized that he wore nothing but briefs.

The night was muggy, and she'd slipped off her T-shirt, so that she wore only her panties. Fear made her ignore that fact as she pressed herself to him and peered over his shoulder.

A huge, dark shape lumbered into view and stopped at the entrance to the cave.

"Bear!" she whispered.

"I know you are," he whispered back in a voice choked with relief and amusement. "I can feel both of your breasts against my side. Your nipples are hard."

The situation was too unsettling to allow her to think straight. She tweaked his back in playful rebuke. "What if it comes into the cave?"

"Know any Cherokee formulas that basically say, 'Get away from me, you big monster'?"

"No! The Cherokees had a lot of affection and respect for bears!"

"Lovely. Just lovely. Cover your ears."

Tess barely had time to clap her hands over her head before Jeopard fired the pistol. A tremendous reverberation rolled through the cave. The bear bolted into the night.

Her chest heaving, Tess grabbed Jeopard's forearm. "You didn't have to shoot him! Damn your cruelty!"

"I just fired a shot over his head! Lord, Tess, do you think I *like* hurting things?"

She inhaled sharply. "I'm sorry, I just assumed—"

"That I like to kill."

She bent her head to his shoulder. "I'm sorry. Sorry."

He rolled to one side, snatched the chain into his hands and put it back around her waist, then fiercely snapped the padlock into place. He took the key back and started to push himself away.

"Jep. Oh, Jep, I misjudged you this time," she said sadly.

The sound of the nickname sent a shudder through him. "This time," he said raspily. "Just this time, you mean."

His hand brushed across her firm, full breasts as he drew back. He cursed darkly and returned to his own side of the cave.

Later he heard her crying in a way that told him she was doing all she could to stifle the sound.

W$_{HEN\ HE\ WOKE}$ up the next morning she was sitting at the end of her chain as close as she could get to him, watching him solemnly, her hands latched around her updrawn knees. Jeopard caught his breath and lay very still, as if she were a wild animal he might frighten away.

She wore a long, colorful cotton skirt that Drake had picked out in a whimsical moment—it looked like something a pioneer woman might wear, he had mumbled—and a white T-shirt with the tail tied in a knot at her waist. The white shirt made her honey-colored skin look more dramatic; her hair was dark silk against the white background.

She was barefoot, and she dug her toes into the earthen floor as if she were scratching the mountain's back. Except for her hypnotizing silver-blue eyes she could have been a Cherokee princess dressed for the wrong century. The picture she presented was earthy, serene, and extremely feminine.

"Good morning," she said. "I apologize for hurting your feelings last night."

"Oh." His chest swelled with pleasure and relief at her simple words. The night before, her crying had upset him more than her accusations. "I didn't know I had feelings to hurt until I met you," he offered gruffly.

She tilted her head in bewilderment.

"Never mind," he said quickly. "What I mean is, apology accepted. Are you all right? I heard you crying."

"Yes. Fine, the, um, the bear upset me."

Sure, the bear was the big problem. Jeopard couldn't resist. "The bare what?"

She looked at him with guarded amusement. "The bare man who flopped onto my mattress carrying a gun."

"I like to be ready for action when I meet a bear."

"A bare what?"

"A bare woman who snuggles close to me for protection."

This conversation was not helping him get out of the sleeping bag. Jeopard idly glanced down at himself, checking to make certain he was covered. He slept with the bag unzipped and sometimes threw the top back when he got warm.

He woke up hard and aching for her every morning, but since he usually woke before she did, he was able to keep his passion from complicating matters. Just then it would have been impossible to hide it.

"I'd like to go into the woods and look for wild roots," she said politely. "Will you take me?"

Jeopard choked back a pained laugh. She could stay right there and find what she wanted. "Sure. What kind of wild roots?"

"I've been reading a book on herbs the Cherokees used. Since we don't have much else to do, I thought we could go on a field trip."

She paused, lifted a hand to caress the medallion and amulet she had taken to wearing all the time, and added, "But I'd like to visit the creek first. It's an old ritual, to 'go to water' every morning. The Cherokees did it for spiritual reasons."

Jeopard gazed at her with bemused admiration. "You're becoming a Cherokee."

"Yes." She touched the thick silver chain and looked a little downcast. "I even feel oppressed now."

THAT REMARK STAYED with him, making him feel terrible. He moved back on the creek bank, holding the end of the chain but trying to let her have some privacy. There was something reverent about the way she stood in the creek watching the sun rise over the distant mountains.

She had her skirt tucked up to her thighs; regardless of what her ritual meant, Jeopard wouldn't have minded standing there every day at dawn watching the water touch her. He envied it that intimacy.

She bent and scooped water into her hands. "There were a number of ceremonies connected to the rivers and creeks," she called over her shoulder. "The basic idea is that the water cleans your spirit."

Jeopard wondered why she felt the need for it that morning. Was she trying to say that she felt guilty for thinking so badly of him?

"Maybe I should go stand under the waterfall," he called back.

She nodded. "Maybe we both should."

"Come on! Let's do it!"

She looked at him in astonishment, then smiled for the first time since he'd kidnapped her. "All right!"

Jeopard made his way along the bank while she waded up the creek. When they neared the waterfall and its pool she stopped just out of the reach of the spray, shivering.

"It's cold enough to make a person feel *very* virtuous," she said between chattering teeth.

"Good. I need that."

Jeopard wore only shorts and hiking shoes. He

climbed onto a rock by the pool, kicked off the shoes, and began tugging at his shorts. She looked up at him wide-eyed.

"Maybe you want to wear wet clothes all morning, but I don't," he explained, squinting at her innocently.

"Hmmmph." She pulled her shirt over her head, revealing a bra so flimsy, it was transparent.

Jeopard did a double-take. "I've never seen that before."

"Drake brought it. I told him that I needed a spare."

"I'd like to have seen the saleswoman's face when seven feet of Drake Lancaster walked into the lingerie department."

"I think Drake has a romantic side."

"No. He's not comfortable around women. They're intimidated by his size and the fact that he's such a loner. It's a shame, because he's a good man."

"Any man who picks out lingerie like this is more comfortable around women than you think."

Tess removed the bra and held it in her hand. It was obvious to Jeopard that she intended to look at the bra and not at him, now that he was naked and she was bare from the waist up.

She has the right idea, he thought as he felt a tightening low in his belly. Carrying the end of her chain as usual, Jeopard quickly stepped under the waterfall and stood with his back to her. He could feel his skin shrinking from the frigid shower.

"Virtue!" he shouted in a strangled voice. "Give me virtue!"

A few seconds later she crept under the fall and stood beside him. He looked at her through the veil of water pouring over their heads. She'd removed the rest of her clothes.

She had her eyes shut and her arms crossed over her chest. She shivered violently and hugged herself, then opened her eyes and gave him a watery smile.

*Progress*, he thought. She was freezing, but she was warming up.

A streak of light slipped through the water, turning it into a shower of pearls. They stood there gazing at the magical sight, then looked at each other.

His heart pounding, Jeopard held out his arms. Sorrow and frustration filled her eyes. She nodded toward the end of her chain, which he still held in one hand.

He dropped it. It disappeared into the water around their legs. She looked as if she were bound to the waterfall and the mountain.

In a way, she was. Her Cherokee ancestors had been part of this land for centuries.

Jeopard groaned inwardly. If she'd let him, he'd cherish that heritage and become part of her life. He continued to hold his hands out to her.

She pointed to the chain. "Promise me that you'll take this off when we get back to the cave. And you'll believe what I've told you about the blue diamond."

After a tormented moment, Jeopard lowered his arms to his side and shook his head wearily. She pressed her hand over her mouth in distress.

With quick, angry movements she pulled the chain out of the pool and gave the end to him. She left him standing under the beautiful water alone, and went to dress.


TESS DIMLY REMEMBERED some rules about decorum and elegance; rules she'd learned at boarding school in England. They belonged to another life, one she didn't miss.

She loved the feel of the dark, damp earth under her knees and hands as she knelt on the forest floor, digging into it with a large spoon. She almost forgot that Jeopard sat at the other end of the chain, watching her with a troubled expression.

She almost forgot that she'd wanted to throw herself into his arms at the waterfall this morning; that she'd been tempted to say that nothing mattered but taking him into her heart and her body again. What was she becoming, a chained pet devoted to her master and ready to do whatever he wanted? *No.*

"Got it," she said excitedly, and held up a dirty root for Jeopard's perusal.

"Oink," he replied.

"A little respect, please. This is ginseng, *atalikuli*, which means, 'It climbs the mountain.' "

"Or 'It needs plastic surgery.' That's pretty obscene-looking."

"Medicine isn't pretty. This is good for headaches, cramps, and ahem, female troubles, the book says."

She tossed it into a bucket, where she'd already collected a variety of roots, leaves, and bark.

"It's getting late," Jeopard noted. He glanced at his wristwatch. "Let's start back to the cave. I have to turn on the CB."

He listened every evening from 6:00 P.M. until ten after. If Drake had any news to report, he'd do it then. And if Jeopard needed to tell him anything, he knew that Drake would be beside his radio at that time.

Jeopard held the end of her chain in one hand and took the bucket in the other. Tess looped the excess over her arm and headed off in front of him, too proud to trail behind or even walk beside him.

She pointed. "I believe that's a maidenhair fern growing in that log over there. *Kaga skutagi*," she added primly. "It means, 'Crow shin.' "

"I didn't know that crows had shins."

"It's good for rheumatism and chills, I think."

"Do you want just the plant, your highness, or should I bring the whole log?"

"The plant alone will do."

He tucked her chain into the waistband of his shorts, put the bucket down, and went to the log. Tess watched with grim amusement as he jerked at the fern without result, whacked the log with his fist, and announced, "I need a blowtorch and a crane."

He thumped the log again. Suddenly a half-dozen red wasps swarmed out of a crumbling hole in the log's side and dive-bombed him. Jeopard didn't make a sound, but he backed up rapidly, with his hands in the air.

Tess ran to him and shooed at the wasps that had followed his retreat. He stood still, his hands still in the air, his face grim and pale. He was trembling.

Tess stared at him in wonder. Had she finally found the one thing that unnerved the Iceman, as Drake sometimes called him?

"You didn't get stung, did you?" she asked in bewilderment, and peered at his bare torso. He'd gone shirtless all day. "Ouch, they got you in three places. This arm, your shoulder, and the back of your hand. Mmmm, I have some rabbit tobacco in the bucket. I'll put it on the welts. You'll be good as new."

"Rabbit tobacco," he said ruefully, and lowered his hands. He took a deep breath, tossed the end of her chain onto the ground, and shook his head. "We have to get back to the cave."

Tess already had a wad of leaves in one hand. She stared at him anxiously. "What's wrong? They're just wasp stings."

"Whatever Cherokee curse you put on me, it worked. All your wishes have come true. You're going to be free of me."

"Jeopard, what are you talking about?"

He looked at her with quiet resignation. "I'm about to have a severe allergic reaction."


BY THE TIME they got to the cave his entire upper body was swelling and turning red. He had a chance of surviving only because he'd undergone a complete series of antivenom shots in the past and regularly took boosters to keep up his resistance.

He explained that one sting wouldn't have hurt him, but three were too much for his system to control. Still, the protective shots gave him a little hope. *But only a little hope.*

Tess spoke as calmly as she could. "I'm still going

to put rabbit tobacco on your welts. At least it'll pull some of the venom out.''

She was so frightened for him that she could barely keep her teeth from chattering. ''Jep, stop gesturing . . . what do you want? Be still, I'll get it after I put this tobacco on you.''

Breathing harshly, he sank onto his mattress. ''Come here. Close.''

Tess grabbed the tobacco from her bucket, spit on it, and began mashing it between her fingers.

''Come here,'' he demanded, wheezing.

She knelt beside him and almost cried at what was happening to his face and torso. His skin looked as if it had been badly burned by the sun.

''What, Jep, for heaven's sake?''

''The key.'' He patted the pocket of his shorts. ''Get rid of . . .'' He panted for breath. ''Your chain.''

''Not right this minute.''

''Listen! Guns, here. Ammo, too. Beside mattress. If I die, wait for Drake to come for you. Pull my body out of the cave and *stay put.*''

Horrified, she grabbed his shoulders. ''I won't let you die!''

He managed to smile, although his face was now so badly swollen that it was a pathetic effort. ''Know some Cherokee . . . magic to save . . . me?''

Tess choked back a sob. ''No, but I know how to broadcast an emergency call for help on the radio.''

''No!''

She ran to the CB. ''My father loved these things. He taught me all about them.''

''No! I don't want anyone to know . . . where you are. Might not be safe. Wait till six. Talk to Drake.''

''Shut up. Lie down.'' She grabbed the microphone.

''Get away from that. Dammit, I'll shoot!''

She looked up and found him pointing a gun at her. No, not at her, at the radio. He could barely sit up now. He leaned heavily on one elbow and had to prop the gun in both hands.

"Jep"—she spoke softly and firmly—"I *am* going to call for help."

The radio made a popping sound and leaped sideways as a bullet crashed into it. Tess fell back, holding the disengaged microphone in her hand.

"No," he answered weakly, "you're not."

He slumped onto the mattress and dropped the gun beside it. Then he shut his eyes and groaned.

Crying with frustration and despair, Tess ran to him and knelt down. "I'll never forgive you for that."

"Save you. Do that . . . good thing. Love . . . you."

"Oh, Jep." She balled her hands into fists and stared down at him in desperate anguish.

The histamines released by the stings were making his blood pressure soar. He had trouble breathing, and he put a horribly swollen hand on the center of his chest.

"Bad," he whispered. "Pain."

Tess jerked the padlock key from his shorts pocket and quickly unfastened the chain. It dropped to the floor, and she kicked both it and the gun aside without a second glance.

She had to do something fast or he was going to die. *He was going to die for her sake.*

"*No!*" she said in a guttural tone. Tess ran to the bucket of medicinal plants and searched through it. She'd collected a bark that was supposed to act as a mild stimulant; from what she knew of insect allergies, the medical treatment sometimes included a shot of adrenaline for that purpose.

Tess bit her lip until it bled. She might overdose Jeopard or fail to help him at all, but it was her only hope.

Tess grabbed a double handful of bark and threw it into a cooking pot, then opened a jug and added drinking water to it. She fired up the camp stove and turned both its burners as high as they'd go. While the brew was heating, she hurried back to Jeopard.

He was panting, and his eyes had swollen shut. Tess grasped his face between her hands and kissed him.

"I love you, Sundance. Don't you dare die," she cried. "I'll wear your chain the rest of my life! I'll do anything! Just hang on!"

He raised his hand weakly, and she sobbed out loud at the state of it. Tess kissed the angry welt mark, then retrieved the rabbit tobacco from where she'd dropped it on her way to the radio. She plastered his hand with the soggy, crushed leaves, then put the same poultice on his forearm and shoulder.

"Yuck," he managed to say.

"Yuck. Good." She glanced down his body and gasped when she saw that his feet and legs were swelling too. Tess frantically undressed him, and when he lay naked she poured cold water over him.

"Virtue," he murmured, his voice so breathless that she could barely understand him.

"I don't know what else to do. It might be the wrong thing."

Tess went to the stove. The simmering bark had turned the water a dark brown color. She wasn't sure if it was ready, but she couldn't wait any longer—he might lose consciousness, and then she'd never get the liquid down him.

Her hands shaking, Tess poured some of the hot tea into a cup and carried it to him. She sat down and struggled until she had his head and shoulders propped on her leg.

"Drink this, Jep," she urged, holding the cup to his mouth.

He could barely open his lips, and his tongue was badly swollen too. After a few seconds of futile struggling, Tess groaned with defeat. She knelt beside him and took a mouthful of bitter bark tea from the cup.

Holding his jaw with one hand and tilting his head back with the other, she put her mouth in his and dribbled the tea down his throat.

He coughed and tried to turn his head away, but he swallowed. "Good! That's it, Sundance! Anything that tastes this bad has got to work!"

She forced the entire cup of tea down him, one

mouthful at a time, then got another cupful and did the same with it.

Tess sat back on her heels and stroked his chest, watching him anxiously. He seemed to be breathing a little more easily. "Better?" she asked.

He nodded weakly. "A little."

She catapulted to her feet. "More tea!"

Cup by cup, he recovered. Tess began to wait for long periods between each new dose, afraid that she'd give him too much. When he could breathe decently and the worst of the swelling was gone, she decided to stop.

Exhausted from fear, she slumped beside him and wiped his perspiring body with a wet cloth. When he didn't move or make a sound, she poked him in the ribs.

"Ouch," he said finally, his eyes shut. "Sleepy."

"Sorry. I have an inclination to worry."

"Love you."

Tears ran down her cheeks. She wiped his swollen, ugly face and whispered, "I love you too."

"Must look like a toad."

"Yes, you do. I love you anyway. In fact, I think I love you more right now than when you look incredibly handsome."

"Strange woman."

"Yes," she whispered, smiling.

"Missed your chance to escape."

"How could I leave a man who shoots CB radios? Such an ornery creature. I had to stay and see what ridiculous thing you'd do next."

"Not ridiculous."

"Not the sort of thing a coldhearted con artist would do, I suppose." Tess lovingly brushed her fingertips over his forehead.

"Think like the enemy too long, you become like him. Can't help it, unless you turn everything off. Machine . . . doesn't feel. No hurt. But no love, either."

"What enemy, Jep? Tell me."

He sighed deeply. "Worked for a government contractor. Agent."

"CIA?"

"No. Free lance. Group of us. Only top people knew about us. Very covert."

"What kind of work was it?"

"Went after specific people. Terrorists. Spies."

"So you worked outside the law?"

"Yes."

"And sometimes you did things—"

"Things that had to be done. No regrets. World's a better place for it. But it gets to you after a while. World seems so ugly. That's why Kyle and I retired."

"Drake too?"

"Yes."

She rested her head on his good shoulder. "My poor Sundance. I understand so much now."

"Tess? Whatever you tell me . . . about the diamond . . . you can trust me with the truth."

"I know that," she whispered. "I know it better than ever."

"I won't ask anymore."

She kissed his dear, puffy face. "Listen to me. There's no way I can prove what I've already told you, but it's the truth. I knew Royce was a jewel thief, but he'd given it up by the time we became involved. He was a lovely man who cared about people, acted honorably toward his friends, and I don't regret marrying him.

"He wouldn't let me take his name—he wanted to protect me from his past. He never did anything that would harm me, and he certainly didn't give me the blue diamond. My grandparents did, and I have no idea how they really came into possession of it.

"I don't know why anyone would want to take revenge on me. My business is totally legitimate. I've never stolen anything from anyone."

She was silent, watching Jeopard's face. He opened bloodshot eyes and looked at her gently for a long moment. "Okay," he whispered. "We start fresh. Go to water. Feel virtuous. Take care of each other."

"Yes." Nodding, crying a little, she smoothed his hair, then lay down beside him. "Now try to sleep."

"What . . . what are you doing?"

"Just holding your wrist. I want to keep track of your pulse for a little while."

"Blood's full of bark juice. Might sprout leaves."

Chuckling, she placed tiny kisses on his face until he fell into a deep, peaceful sleep.

"GET READY," DRAKE said over his shoulder. "The cave's at the top of this rise."

Kyle Surprise, one hand wrapped tightly around his saddle horn because his horse was determined to make him a tree ornament, pulled a semiautomatic machine gun from the sling on his back. He wondered ruefully if Jeopard would appreciate his greenhorn efforts to ride this damned rock-headed horse.

Kyle just hoped that his brother was all right. He'd arrived from Florida that day, planning to accompany Drake into the mountains and meet the fascinating woman who'd turned Jeopard into a romantic. Kyle had news that would shock them both.

If he weren't too late. When Drake couldn't get a response during the six-o'clock radio call, Kyle had feared the worst. Now that he knew why Olaf Starheim wanted Tess dead, he worried more.

Jeopard was a stickler for routine. If he'd said he'd be on the radio at six, only a catastrophe would have prevented it. A catastrophe or capture by Olaf's people.

Kyle drew up on his horse's reins as Drake waved him to a stop. They stepped down from the horses and watched the flickering light of a campfire dance on the outer edges of the cave walls.

"I'll go first," Kyle whispered, and in deference to his relationship to Jeopard, Drake moved aside.

Kyle slipped forward with a grace that belied his

lanky frame. While Jeopard was put together with compact perfection, Kyle was too long in some places and too short in others.

Still, women told him he was just right in the places that counted, and he was certainly no less athletic than his brother. And no less dangerous, when circumstances demanded it.

He crept to the cave entrance, the lethal little machine gun held in front of him. Listening intently, Kyle heard nothing but the crackling of the fire.

Adrenaline pulsed through him. He dived into the cave, tucked one shoulder and rolled neatly into a crouch, the gun aimed at anything that moved.

Not much did. Jeopard, naked except for a towel covering his groin, lay unconscious on an air mattress beyond the fire. He looked as if someone had scalded him with boiling water.

A beautiful woman with lightly bronzed skin and dark hair stood over him, her feet braced on either side of his body.

She was barefoot, and she resembled some sort of gypsy, in a flowery skirt and clinging white T-shirt. A large gold medallion dangled on a chain over her full breasts. She glared at Kyle with fierce silver-blue eyes.

As she pointed her own machine gun at him, she said in a polite British accent, "I am quite capable of shooting you, if you move one inch."

Kyle stared at her, amazed.

So this was the Princess of Kara.

T ESS NEARLY COLLAPSED from relief when Drake hurried inside the cave and ended the confrontation. She explained what had happened to Jeopard and that he was all right, just sound asleep. She'd heard noises outside and had risen to defend him.

As Jeopard stirred groggily and propped himself up on one elbow, Kyle ran to him and knelt by his side. Tess stepped back to give them privacy, and her heart wrenched at the sight of Kyle's ravaged face. What neighbor's dog was capable of this? She knew that there must be more to the story than Jeopard had told her.

What had surely once been handsome was now a patchwork horror outlined by jagged red scars down his cheeks and across the bridge of his battered nose. Scars fronted both of his ears and made pathways through the reddish-blond hair at his temples.

But his eyes, dark blue eyes like Jeopard's, were so loving and kind that after a moment she noticed nothing but them.

"Damn, you look like an overcooked lobster," Kyle said hoarsely. Then he leaned forward and kissed the top of Jeopard's head.

Jeopard grasped his brother's shoulder affectionately. "I never thought I'd be so happy to hear your insults."

Kyle lifted the gold chain Tess had slipped around Jeopard's neck while he slept. He gazed drolly at the antler amulet, then nodded over his shoulder to Drake. "This is the man who refused to be seen with you and me that time in Brazil."

"Yeah," Drake grumbled. "Didn't like our earrings."

"Simple rhinestone hearts worn on one side only," Kyle continued, "and we *had* to wear them so Alvarez's people could find us. But would my brother let us live that down? Noooo. And yet now he's wearing deer parts around his neck. Does this strike you as a sudden change in attitude, Drake?"

"Strikes me," Drake said, nodding.

"Very funny," Jeopard muttered.

"It's been in my family for quite some time," Tess explained. "I believe the Cherokee symbols on it have something to do with my great-great-grandmother's tribal clan. The Blue clan."

Jeopard glanced down at it, then up at her. She blushed, wondering how much she'd embarrassed him with her whimsy. He looked back at his brother.

"It's for spiritual protection," he explained seriously. "I wear it all the time."

Tess thought her chest would burst with adoration.

"Oh." Kyle looked flabbergasted. He put the amulet down carefully.

Jeopard chuckled. "Nice of you to drop by the neighborhood, bro."

Kyle recovered his cockiness, grinned, and gestured toward the towel that was Jeopard's only covering. "Wearing loincloths these days?"

"It's not kind to make fun of lobsters."

Drake, who'd been examining the blasted radio,

came over for a closer look at the angry welts on Jeopard's body. "What kept you from going into shock?"

"Tess saved my life." He explained about the bark tea. When Kyle and Drake looked at her in astonishment and admiration, she bowed grandly.

"Have you learned anything new about Tess's situation?" Jeopard asked.

"Nothing important. It can wait. We have to get some food into that bizarre-looking body of yours."

Tess noticed Jeopard's frown and the sharp scrutiny he gave his younger brother, who seemed adept at ignoring him.


THE NEXT MORNING Jeopard waited impatiently until Tess and Drake went to the creek to fill buckets and pots with water. She'd declared that *someone* in the cave smelled like a spittoon full of rabbit-tobacco juice and therefore needed a bath.

Jeopard knew she was just trying to give him and Kyle time for a private, brotherly powwow.

"What have you found out about Tess?" he asked Kyle as soon as they were alone. Jeopard threw open the sleeping bag and wrapped himself in a big towel, moving gingerly because his welts throbbed and itched.

Kyle brought a large envelope out of a saddlebag and sat down cross-legged beside the mattress. He tossed the envelope to Jeopard and looked intently into his eyes.

"How important is she to you?"

"I love her."

"That's obvious. Does she love you?"

"Yes."

"You've known each other for such a short time."

"We've barely been apart since the day we met. It doesn't have to be rational."

"Those are words I never thought I'd hear from Jeopard Surprise's mouth."

"Oh? Listen to this. I'm going to ask her to marry me."

Jeopard watched closely as his brother's expression turned grim.

Kyle nodded toward the envelope. "Open it."

Jeopard pulled out an old color photograph clipped from *Life* magazine.

"Look at that face. Tell me what you see."

Jeopard frowned at the close-up of a pretty blond woman wearing a tiara. The caption underneath said simply, "Kara's Popular Monarch—Queen Isabella." He saw aristocratic features and silver-blue eyes.

*Tess's eyes.*

Recognition slammed into his stomach and took his breath away. Jeopard held the clipping in one hand and covered the lower half of the queen's face with the other.

"She's Tess's mother," Kyle said softly.

Stunned, Jeopard continued to stare at those haunting eyes. He removed his hand and saw other likenesses—a certain tilt to the mouth, a familiar curve in the jaw.

"Hank Gallatin had an affair with the queen," Kyle explained. "They met twenty-eight years ago when the palace hired him to find the diamonds Royce Benedict stole. The irony was that Royce and Hank were pals.

"Hank got the diamonds back without incriminating his friend, but one of Royce's enemies blew the whistle. Royce went to prison, though he never blamed Hank for that. Anyway, Queen Isabella and Hank Gallatin developed a relationship. She was committed to the king by a polite, socially correct marriage with all the right bloodlines. She and the king had no children.

"The king and the country were her duty; apparently Hank Gallatin was her pleasure. We're not talking a casual affair here, Jep. Their relationship began two years before Tess was born and lasted until Gallatin's death."

A sense of foreboding wound around Jeopard's chest. "Where do Karl and Viktoria Kellgren fit into this?"

"Friends of the queen's. She wanted to stay close to Tess, and she knew Gallatin would need help raising her. The Kellgrens loved Tess like their own blood. It was a perfect arrangement."

"What about the blue diamond? Did Benedict steal it too?"

"No. He had nothing to do with it. The Blue Princess was one of the queen's favorites, and she thought it was ordinary enough that no one would question her if she said that she'd lost it. Of course, she didn't lose it at all—she gave it to the Kellgrens to pass along to Tess."

"But she never acknowledged Tess publicly," Jeopard said with disgust.

"It wasn't because of shame. The Karan people would have welcomed any child of Isabella's, legitimate or not. But Isabella didn't want Tess to lead the kind of regimented, cloistered life she'd had. She was trying to protect her."

Jeopard numbly laid down the magazine clipping. "How'd you learn all of this?"

"From the Kellgrens. I got Brett Sanders from the State Department to convince them that I was on their side; Sanders is an old friend of theirs. They're terrified, Jep. They know now that Olaf won't stop until he eliminates Tess."

Jeopard gave his brother a troubled look. "Even though she's illegitimate, she's the heir to the throne?"

"Yes."

"Can the Kellgrens prove what they told you?"

"Yes. Sanders went over their documentation and said it's indisputable."

Jeopard stared at Queen Isabella's photograph and fought an urge to toss it into the campfire.

"Jep?" Kyle asked gently. "You look pretty damned miserable."

Jeopard raised his gaze dully and said in a gruff,

anguished tone, "How can I ask Tess to give up a king-dom?"

SHE WISHED THAT Kyle hadn't quit joking around her and that Drake had whispered an apology for selecting such a racy bra for her. They were treating her differently now, and she didn't want to be different.

She just wanted Jep to stop looking at her with a guarded, fathomless expression, as if he no longer thought it wise to share his feelings with her.

"It'd be best to meet your grandparents—uh, Karl and Viktoria Kellgren, that is—in Kara," Kyle told her. "Our State Department man has already been in touch with the Karan prime minister. To say that you've caused some excitement is an understatement."

Tess paced back and forth, her fingertips pressed to her temples. Even now, an hour after Jeopard had quietly explained her heritage to her, she felt that her head would burst with the enormity of it all.

"Is this the only way?" she asked, and looked at Jeopard wistfully. "To go there and stake my claim?"

He nodded, his eyes shuttered. Oh, she knew that private, neutral look too well, and it made her ache with loneliness.

"Going public is the only way you can protect yourself from Olaf."

"And that's all I need to do? Then I can come back home?"

There was a strained silence in the cave. Drake, leaning against one wall, shifted awkwardly and looked out at the clouds. Kyle stared at the floor. Only Jeopard met her gaze directly.

"Tess, you're heir to one of the oldest and richest monarchies in Europe. The Karan people revered your mother, and they don't want Olaf to be king. They'll probably welcome you with open arms. Think about the life you'll inherit."

He began to list on his fingers. "Two hundred million dollars—and that's just your mother's personal fortune, Tess. She also had an extraordinary collection of jewelry. A royal yacht that sleeps one hundred and fifty people. Homes all over the world, including two palaces in Kara.''

Jeopard smiled wearily. ''The fastest sports cars in the world. Any car you want, Tess. A whole fleet of Jaguars.''

''Oh, my,'' she said in a weak voice. Tess fingered the gold medallion around her neck and looked down at it numbly. Her voice broke. ''I've discovered *two* wonderful heritages.''

She raised her head and gave Jeopard a beseeching look. ''But I don't know where I belong anymore.''

''You can be a Cherokee and a Scandinavian queen at the same time.''

Her heart thudded with a strange feeling of dread. ''How do you feel about all this?''

He gave her one of his perfect, noncommittal smiles. ''I'm happy for you, of course.''

Tess stared at him with disbelief. She'd thought they'd put those kinds of deceptive games behind them, but he was shutting her out of his real emotions just as he had before. It hurt her more than she could put into words.

Everything was changing, even Jeopard's feelings for her.

Tess drew herself up proudly. ''I'm going to the creek,'' she announced, her voice shaking. ''I need to think.''

Jeopard, who was now dressed in shorts and a T-shirt, rose from his mattress. He was still a little weak, but recovering quickly. ''I'll go with you.''

''No. Since I seem to be something other than a normal human being now, I don't need company.''

''Tess, calm down—''

''I really would like to be alone.'' She felt as if she already were.

''All right,'' he said slowly, his voice grim.

Tess left him standing there, his emotions closed

within a vault that she no longer had the power to open.

HE'D CAUSED HIS own destruction. The aborigine shaman had been right: Jeopard had brought it on himself. And there wasn't a damned thing he could do about it except sit on his side of the campfire and watch with anguish as Tess remained sitting at the cave entrance, where she'd been since supper, staring into the night sky.

Jeopard ground his teeth together. But wasn't he doing the best thing for them both? He couldn't complicate her new life with a commitment to him. She was only twenty-six years old; she was going to have fame and wealth beyond imagination.

How could she tie herself to a private, moody man with a past that would feed the world media's gossip mill? A man who was ready to settle down and have children? A man who wanted nothing more grand than to stay in these mountains alone with her?

Kyle rose from his spot by the fire. "Well, good night," he announced dramatically. "We're going to have a long day tomorrow. Let's leave by dawn. Tonight I'm 'going to water,' myself, Tess. The sound of the creek might make me forget how much I hate camping out."

"Me too," Drake said, and vaulted up. He busied himself grabbing his sleeping bag and a few pieces of gear, just as Kyle was doing. "We'll see you two in the morning. 'Night."

*Cupids*, Jeopard thought darkly. *Two large, bumbling Cupids.*

"There's no need," he told them. *Can't you apes see what I'm trying to avoid here?* "Stay put."

Tess swiveled her head and tortured Jeopard with her wounded gaze. "Are you uncomfortable in my royal presence?" Before he could say anything else she told Kyle and Drake, "Thank you. And good night."

They hurried out, sensing the upcoming battle like

two old war horses, and anxious to get out of harm's way, Jeopard thought ruefully.

Tess rose, went to the lantern that lit the cave, and brusquely turned it off. Star-softened darkness surrounded the campfire like a lover and enhanced its flickering light.

Jeopard's skin tingled with alertness and a sense of anticipation that was blatantly erotic, no matter how much he wanted to ignore it. She walked to the end of his mattress and stood looking down at him.

Then she began to undress.

Given the privacy of the shadows, Jeopard let his mouth drop open. What kind of tactic was this? No. *No.*

"Don't do it, Tess," he warned in a husky voice.

She flung her shirt and shorts onto the ground, followed them with her underwear, and stood there defiantly, a mysterious Cherokee war woman outlined in sensual detail by the firelight.

"I want to see if you can make love to me the way you did that first night on the *Irresistible,*" she said in a haughty tone. "Without emotion."

He groaned inwardly. "It wasn't without emotion. I just couldn't let you see how much you affected me."

"You're awfully good at that. I won't have it, you hear? I won't be shut out now as if I'm some strange, rare beast at the zoo. You can't keep me at a distance."

"Yes, I can," he murmured. "I've spent all of my adult life learning how to do that with people."

She knelt on the mattress and crawled slinkily up to him, a ferocious cat on the prowl. "It won't wash, Sundance. Give up. I've got your number. You can't tell me that you want me less, now that I'm royalty."

"We need to back away from each other. There are going to be a lot of changes in your life, a lot of new opportunities . . ."

He gasped as she ran a hand up the inside of his thigh and caressed him through his shorts. "What does that have to do you and me?" She skimmed her hand over the rock-hard bulge at the apex of his thighs. "Yes, you want me as much as ever. If this is the only way you can show your love for me right now, I'll take it."

Jeopard grasped her wrist with a trembling hand. "Stop."

"I saved your life. You owe me."

He groaned. She had his shorts unzipped now. "That's not fair."

"You force me to play this way, the way you like."

"No. I love your honesty."

"Then give some in return."

She quickly tugged his shorts and briefs down to his thighs and cupped him in both hands. His chest heaving, Jeopard fell back on one elbow and cursed softly.

"This is honest," she murmured hoarsely. "Your body, hard and hot and eager for whatever I do to it. Is this all you're willing to share with the future queen of Kara?"

"Yes," he said in harsh agony.

"So be it." She stripped his clothes off and straddled him, then ran her hands over his chest and stomach with wicked intent. "I shall enjoy ruining your defenses, my fine peasant."

His back arched as she slid herself over him. Her hips moved fluidly while she circled his nipples with her fingernails. "Love me, Jep," she begged. "Love me the way I love you. *Please.*"

His defenses broke apart at the sound of her sweet English voice torn by passion and despair. "Tess, I do." He moaned and dragged her down to his chest.

Jeopard kissed her intimately, sucking the tongue she slipped deep into his mouth and gliding his own tongue between her lips. She cried out and slid her arms around his neck, careful even in her wildness not to hurt his swollen shoulder.

Her body shuddered, driving him to the brink and holding him there as she loved him in a slow, breathless rhythm. He grasped her hips and arched upward, knowing that he'd never get enough of her, either in bed or out of it.

She whispered his name, giving herself to a vortex of emotion that defied him to remain aloof. Lost, lost, he thought as he sank his hands into her hair and kissed her face desperately, licking her skin with the tip of his tongue, making gruff, yearning sounds deep in his throat.

Tess surrounded him with an explosion of pleasure that stroked the last bit of restraint from his body and his mind. He was lifted to a level of loving that merged the physical with the spiritual, until all he could do was float in a dimension where her voice was his only connection with reality.

She called him back, her lips on his face, her hands fervently caressing his hair.

"Did I hurt you?" she implored. "Are you all right?"

*No, he'd never be all right if he lost her.*

He was almost crying, and as much as it horrified him, he couldn't keep his voice from cracking when he said, "Do you want me to go with you to Kara?"

"Yes, *yes*, of course." She made a whimpering sound. "Is *that* what's upset you? I thought perhaps you wanted to get rid of me, that you'd be glad to send me off without you."

"You think I'd stop loving you that easily?"

"No, but you're accustomed to being alone. And we've become so inseparable so quickly. Does it worry you?"

"*No.* You're the best thing that's ever happened to me. But you need to face the fact that your whole perspective on life is about to change. You can have anything or anyone you want."

"I've already got the *anyone.*"

"You may not be free to make that choice."

She speared her fingers into his hair and looked down at him possessively. "Now, you listen to me. Doesn't a princess have special privileges to do what she wants and love who she wants? Certainly! Otherwise, why would anyone take the bloody job?''

Jeopard would have chuckled, but he was afraid it might sound ragged. "I can't imagine," he told her solemnly, and hugged her to him, wishing that their last night in the mountains together would never end.

SHE ABSOLUTELY WOULD not cry, because she didn't want to admit to anyone that she was already homesick for those ancient, blue-green Nantahala mountains and that she was terrified of what waited for her outside them.

The same small jet sat on the same runway, ready this time to take her and Jeopard to New York, where they'd board the Concorde for Europe.

Jeopard clasped his brother's hand, then Drake's. Tess handed Drake her medallion.

"I have a favor to ask."

He looked down at her with gentle, curious eyes. "Anything."

"Will you take it to the reservation and see if anyone can translate it?"

"I'll be glad to." He carefully slipped the medallion into a shirt pocket.

Tess blinked hard and fought a lump in her throat. "I intended to do that myself, but I . . . I'll have to put it off."

Jeopard slid a consoling arm around her shoulders, sensing her distress. "Damn, I haven't got any handkerchiefs."

Tess chuckled hoarsely and kissed his cheek. "Then we'd better leave this instant." She hugged Drake and Kyle, feeling like a sorrowful Dorothy leaving Oz.

She and Jeopard would have to find their way back to this side of the rainbow, somehow.

## CHAPTER 11

D URING THE FOUR days since Jeopard and Tess's arrival, the palace-protocol officers had let him attend every meeting with her—but only because she had insisted. They'd assigned him a servant's room adjoining her luxurious ten-room apartment in the palace, even though Tess had delicately explained that he'd be staying in her suite.

As soon as the maids confirmed that the princess wasn't kidding, that she shared her bed with the *liv-vakt*, the bodyguard—everyone went into quiet hysterics.

Sanders, the U.S. State Department man, explained that Jeopard was a former government agent and now a self-employed businessman, but wild rumors started anyway.

Jeopard sighed. Now they simply pushed him to the sidelines, and when Tess protested he gallantly winked at her as if it were all some silly game that she and he would win eventually. When she wasn't looking he seethed behind his nonchalant facade.

One day he was waiting tensely in a high-backed chair to one side of a conference table in a huge, opulent meeting room. Tess was seated at the head of the enormous table, flanked by the Karan prime minister and his five-member cabinet.

She looked serene and elegant in a white double-breasted dress ornamented by a sapphire broach that had belonged to her mother. But Jeopard knew that the antler amulet was hidden underneath her clothes, and the way she kept glancing at him over her shoulder radiated volumes of anxiety.

Various people got up and made speeches. Since Jeopard didn't understand Swedish, he had no idea what those speeches concerned.

But he knew that Tess was upset. When it was time for her to respond she stood up and clutched the edge of the table, her knuckles white. She spoke at length in fluent Swedish, her demeanor gracious but firm, and his heart twisted with bittersweet pride.

Even if she hadn't had one drop of royal blood, she deserved to be queen; they'd never find another woman with such intelligence and innate class.

Whatever she was saying, it knocked them on their Scandinavian ears. Strained looks and nervous finger-tapping shouted the politicians' discomfort.

She finished, gestured to him to accompany her, and they walked out of the meeting hall.

Back in her suite, he got right to the point. "What went on in that meeting just now?"

"They asked me outright if I want the crown and the responsibility that goes along with it—you know, representing Kara all over the world, lending my support to charities, acting as a proper figurehead. They want me to do it. They say I was *bred* for it by generations of royalty, all the way back to the Vikings, at least on my mother's side of the lineage. And Jep? Olaf Starheim arrives tomorrow. They want to introduce me to him. My second cousin." She added drolly, "Isn't *that* special?"

Jeopard finally had reason to smile, even though it was the kind of smile that might have frozen a fjord in midsummer. "I look forward to tomorrow."

THEY WANTED TO persuade her to take the crown, and they went all out, starting the next morning.

She liked purple irises; when Jeopard strolled out of the bedroom wearing nothing but a sleepy squint, he found several maids and butlers setting a dozen vases full of irises around Tess's suite.

One of the maids saw him, squealed, and dropped her vase. Jeopard stalked back into the bedroom.

"What does *otrolig* mean?" he demanded.

Tess collapsed in the center of the bed, laughing. " 'Incredible.' "

After breakfast a palace aide requested that they come to one of the courtyards. There sat four sleek, shiny Jaguars in assorted colors. The aide handed her four sets of color-coordinated keys, smiled, bowed, and said, "From the royal collection."

Several local designers were waiting for her after lunch with racks of clothes and accessories to suit her everyday needs. Then she met with a renowned Paris couturier to discuss "a few simple gowns for your formal needs, mademoiselle."

What he proposed was a wardrobe worth close to two hundred thousand dollars.

"Not including shoes," she told Jeopard breathlessly.

They escaped for an hour to explore the palace gardens. She wore a very feminine red suit with a blousy bodice, padded shoulders, and white lapels. Jeopard sank his hands into the pockets of yet another black suit and watched her wistfully gaze into a fountain.

She glanced up, tilted her head to one side as if she were seeing him for the first time, and said huskily, "Well, hello, gorgeous. Do you know that you look mysterious and dramatic in those black suits?''

He felt as if he'd just been enchanted by a garden elf. ''Do you know that you're the most beautiful woman I've ever seen?''

Her eyes glowed with devotion. ''We are very much in love with you.''

''We?''

She grinned. ''The royal 'we.' ''

His heart sank. She was enjoying her new status, it was obvious. He couldn't blame her, but he ached to keep her from drifting away from him.

''No one's watching. Go ahead,'' he urged wickedly. ''Enjoy the water.''

She looked from him to the fountain, biting her lower lip. ''All right.''

Tess stripped off her white pumps, then went behind a bush and quickly shucked her panty hose, glancing around with delighted naughtiness. She tossed Jeopard a kiss, climbed over the fountain wall, and stood in knee-deep water.

''Brrrr! Jep, this must have come straight from a glacier!''

But she padded around happily, bending down to scoop water over her hands, holding the water to her nose, and inhaling its scent. ''It's so crisp and pure!''

''It's probably Perrier.''

They both laughed. Tess flung water in the air and watched the silver droplets fall. ''Did I ever tell you about the Cherokee fairies?''

''Is this a bad joke?''

''No. Really. The Cherokees believed in all sorts of spirits. They called the fairies 'Little People.' The Little People were very good-hearted and helpful; they were best known for leading lost hunters back home.

''Then there were the *Nuhnehi*, a race of invisible immortals who looked just like ordinary Cherokees— when they wanted to be seen, that is. They were also good-hearted; sometimes they'd show up and help fight the Cherokees' enemies.

"There were also fairies who lived in the caves and on the mountaintops, and some who lived in the rivers and creeks."

Jeopard peered over the edge of the fountain. "I hope a few followed us here. We can use the help."

"I hope so too."

She delicately flung some water at him, as if christening him. "I'm going to bind you to me forever. This is part of a love charm I read in the book on sacred formulas."

His heart pounded as Tess raised her wet hands to the sky and chanted, "Listen! No one is ever lonely with me. Now he has made the path white for me. It shall never be dreary.

"Let him put his soul in the very center of my soul, never to turn away. Grant that in the midst of women he shall never think of them. I belong to the one clan alone that was alloted to him when the seven clans were established.

"I stand with my face toward the Sun Land. No one is lonely with me." She looked at Jeopard solemnly. "Your soul has come into the very center of my soul, never to turn away. I take your soul."

He gazed at her with a sweet breathlessness inside his chest. "Will you marry me?"

*So much for objectivity.*

Her hands paused in the air. She stared at him, and time seemed to stop under a sky as blue as the Blue Princess, a sky as eternally beautiful as the look in her eyes.

"Yes, Sundance, I will."

He stepped close to the fountain. She cupped his face in her hands and kissed him, happy tears shining in her eyes. Jeopard ignored the self-rebuke that stabbed at him. He'd enjoy this wonderful moment and let the future take care of itself.

"Ahem. *Prinsessa*, pardon."

They looked up to find a stern protocol officer glaring at them.

"The duke, your cousin, is here to meet you."

*   *   *

Olaf starheim was perhaps forty years old, short and very pale, with thinning blond hair and pink cheeks. He wore a gray necktie and a gray suit that made him look even less vibrant.

Tess was shocked to find him so harmless in appearance; then she looked directly into his washed-out blue eyes and saw a sharp slyness that chilled her skin.

This was the man who wanted her dead, though there wasn't any way she could prove it.

With a crowd of officials around them, she could only smile at him and try not to shiver when he smiled back. She wanted Jeopard beside her, but Jeopard had been barred from the room. The look in his eyes had left no doubt that he was frustrated by the exclusion.

"What a remarkable claim," Olaf said softly. "So you say you're the queen's daughter?"

"I *am* Isabella's daughter."

"With such, hmmm, unusual coloring. Your father was an Indian?"

"A nearly full-blooded Cherokee, yes."

"But you grew up in England?"

"In boarding school there."

"And you think someone such as yourself is capable of assuming the queen's duties?"

"Yes, but I may relinquish my claim. I understand that if I did, Parliament could vote to discontinue the monarchy."

"And destroy more than a thousand years' of tradition?"

"It seems to me the best of the tradition died with my mother. Perhaps the world is no longer a place where a few can expect privileges because of their bloodlines."

"You talk nonsense, like an American!"

"I am an American. From the original Americans." She gestured toward the Cherokee angles of her face. "And that heritage is much older than the ruling house of Kara."

He was almost trembling with rage. Tess tried to freeze him with her eyes and hoped that she looked half as deadly as Jeopard could.

Then she turned and walked away.

TESS WENT TO bed with a mournful headache caused by seeing what kind of cousin she had on her mother's side of the family. She made a note to call Georgia and learn whether the lawyer had located Erica and Kat yet.

She needed a dose of good cousins to wipe Olaf from her mind.

Jeopard waited until she was sound asleep, then slipped out of her apartment. He found the palace maid who'd called him "incredible" and thanked her with so much charm that she nearly dissolved inside her uniform.

Then he asked her whether Olaf had an apartment at the palace.

Yes, there were apartments for him and other members of the extended royal family. He was in his suite now—she knew because she'd heard a servant complaining about the duke's demands for liquor. And yes, she could tell him how to find the duke's apartment.

When Jeopard arrived there, he told Olaf's secretary that he had a private message from the *prinsessa*. The secretary ushered him into a sumptuous office, where Olaf sat brooding in a thronelike chair behind a large desk.

When he saw Jeopard his face grew even paler than usual. "My people told me that you'd gone to work for her after finishing my job," he said icily. "She provides benefits I did not, I've heard."

Jeopard stopped at the edge of the desk, pulled a small automatic pistol from one pocket, leaned forward, and pointed it directly at the Duke's forehead.

"I know that you tried to kill her. I can't prove it, but it's true. Listen to this carefully. If she has an accident or develops some sort of suspicious ailment, you're dead. Dead.

"Even if you manage to get rid of me first, I have friends who know everything about you. They'll make sure that the job gets done. Believe me, they can find you anywhere, and it won't matter how much money you have or what royal title you have or how well you try to protect yourself. Understand?"

"Such bizarre fears shouldn't worry you, Mr. Surprise," he managed to get out in a faint voice. "I'm sure no one wants to harm you or the *prinsessa.*"

"You'll return the Blue Princess diamond to me."

"Now, really, your accusations—"

Jeopard pressed the gun's muzzle between Olaf's eyes. "I want that diamond back. Understand?"

The duke shut his eyes and nodded.

"Good." Jeopard stepped away and slipped the gun into a pocket. "One other thing. Your twenty-thousand-dollar fee. I donated it to charity."

Jeopard went to the door, paused with his hand on the latch, and turned for one last look at the duke, who seemed to be wilting behind the enormous desk.

"Don't come near her again; don't talk to her. Ask your people for details about my reputation. Believe what they tell you."

The duke buried his head in his hands as Jeopard left the room.

IT WAS THE most amazing dress. Tess gazed at herself in the mirror. The sleek satin ball gown was meant to look regal, and in truth, it made her feel that way.

The sleeves were long and tight, with puffed shoulders. The V-necked bodice hugged her gracefully to the waist, where it flared into a voluminous and flowing skirt.

One sleeve and half of the bodice were a glossy black; the black ran down the neckline diagonally to her hip, where it disappeared under a wide black-and-white-striped bow. The rest of the dress was a soft, antique-pearl shade of white.

Three maids fussed over her appearance, oohing and aahing, admiring the way the stylist had swept her dark hair into an old-fashioned chignon. They called for the valet, and he entered her dressing room carrying a black, velvet-covered case in both hands.

"What's this?" Tess murmured.

"The prime minister asks that you wear these in honor of your mother."

The valet opened the case and revealed a pearl-and-diamond tiara with a matching bracelet and teardrop-shaped earrings.

Tess trembled as the maids helped her don the exquisite jewelry. Her voice shaky, she asked, "Has Mr. Surprise finished dressing?"

The servants greeted her questions with awkward silence and furtive looks. "He was asked to go ahead of you, Your Highness. The prime minister wished to speak to him in private before the ball began."

Tess whirled around, studying their faces anxiously. "Would you send for him, please? He's supposed to escort me."

"The prime minister intends to do that, Your Highness."

Tess rushed up to Kristian Bjornsen as he entered the anteroom of her suite. The tall, graying prime minister was a Scandinavian Jimmy Stewart; there didn't seem to be anything harsh about him, but his quiet presence was commanding.

"What's going on here?" she asked firmly.

"Mr. Surprise agrees that it would be best if you experience this event alone," Kristian explained gently. "Tonight you'll meet our most important political and social leaders. Mr. Surprise will be in attendance, but he intends to stay in the background."

Kristian Bjornsen paused, looking solemn. "*Prinsessa*, this evening I'd like to announce who you are."

•　•　•

How COULD JEOPARD do this to her? Tess stood beside the prime minister, her hands clasped loosely in front of her, her head up. The magnificent ballroom simmered with excitement and hushed whispers—rumors had been traveling around Kara's inner circles for two weeks, and now they'd been confirmed.

Queen Isabella had given birth to a daughter, and here she was to meet the country's best and brightest; she was Kara's princess and might one day be its queen.

And all Tess could do was stare numbly into the crowd, tormented, searching the room for the man who'd betrayed her.

She answered questions in a daze; she heard her beauty congratulated and her mother complimented; she was told with which men she should waltz and why each one was important.

It finally dawned on her that most of her partners were single, under forty, and members of royal families. With horror Tess realized that she was being presented with acceptable candidates for a husband.

*Had Jeopard known about this too?*

At the end of the long evening she dragged herself to Kristian Bjornsen and in a soft, emphatic tone said, "If you do not find Jeopard Surprise and bring him to me this instant I shall do a war whoop and throw hors-d'oeuvre knives at the orchestra."

Astonished, he stared down at her. "Your Highness, there's only one waltz left for the evening. And we've already scheduled—"

"*Now*, sir."

"We don't want you to be unhappy, Your Highness." He signaled a man and sent him for Jeopard.

Unhappy? Was that a strong enough word? How about miserable? Disappointed? And one waltz with Jeopard wouldn't change the fact that he'd deserted her. Tess went to the center of the ballroom and waited.

The glittering crowd began to part to allow the lone, unfamiliar figure through. People stared at the glorious blond stranger dressed in white tie and black tails. His stunning entrance bespoke a natural ruler and a strength of character that made him a royal presence in his own right.

Women fanned themselves fervently; men traded disgruntled looks of envy.

Tess looked Jeopard in the eye and saw exactly what she'd expected—a cool, perfect mask.

"I believe this will be the last dance," she said with unsmiling aloofness. "Could we share it?"

He bowed slightly. "If Your Highness wishes."

He held out one hand. When she touched the palm, she found it damp and cold, much like her own. She knew then that he shared her anguish, but the fact didn't change what he'd done.

Jeopard took her in his arms as the orchestra began a dreamy, majestic waltz. She'd never danced with him before, but they melded with the same inner rhythm that made them so wonderful together in other ways.

No one else danced; the crowd seemed riveted—upset, perhaps, as word spread that the *prinsessa* was dancing with a common bodyguard.

"Why did you make a mockery of everything I feel for you?" she whispered. "Are you so easily turned away by what other people think of us?"

His hand tightened on her waist, and she saw a muscle flex in his jaw.

"I'm giving you the opportunity you deserve. There's no other way I can make you look at what these people are offering you. As long as you're with me, you won't know how you really feel about all of this."

"You think you're so much wiser than I am. I hate your righteous attitude."

"I feel older, but not wiser. It's killing me to let you go."

"*Let me go?*" She stared at him, while her stomach twisted with dread. "Did you know that tonight they've introduced me to a parade of blueblooded bachelors, each acceptable as the queen's consort? Do you approve of that?''

''Yes.''

Tess would have stumbled had he not held her closer. Rage and grief built inside her like a thunderstorm. ''You asked me to marry you,'' she reminded him. ''And I agreed.''

''I won't hold you to it.''

''Did I indicate that I'd ever let you out of it?''

He shut his eyes for a moment, and when he looked at her again they glistened with despair. ''I'm letting you out of it. I'm leaving for America tonight.''

''*No*,'' she said weakly, almost moaning the word.

''You stay here and look at this life without my interference. I'll be waiting, and you'll know where to find me.''

She started to speak.

''No, Tess, sssh. No vows, no promises that you'll follow me. You've got to be honest with yourself and decide how you feel about the life you could lead here.''

Tears shimmered on her cheeks. ''Your cynicism is breaking my heart. I'll never forgive you for doubting me.''

He winced. ''I'll have to take that chance.''

The waltz ended. She swallowed harshly, and dignity was the only thing that saved her from digging her fingers into his coat in an attempt to hold him.

He lowered his head, brushed his lips over hers, then stepped back and bowed. Tess stood, frozen in unspeakable sorrow, as he walked away.

## CHAPTER 12

MILLIE SURPRISE MCKAY was no lightweight. She may have been small and pretty, with soulful green eyes and chin-length curly hair the color of old gold, but she was, in her husband's adoring words, "a little Tasmanian devil."

She'd mellowed only a bit since becoming the devoted mother of a sturdy baby boy nicknamed Zot because of certain impolite sounds he made.

And now she was standing in Jeopard's office, looking deceptively delicate in a chic blue jumpsuit, while looking undoubtedly upset. She held a gurgling Zot under one arm; the other arm was held akimbo.

"Kyle called me," she said sternly. "I caught the next plane out of Nashville."

Jeopard gave her a hug, kissed Zot's forehead, and led her to a couch. They sat down, with him slouched and her sitting anxiously on the edge of her seat.

Jeopard smiled at her. "How's Brig? Still cutting the new album? I saw the interview in *People* last week."

"Don't change the subject. You've got to get yourself under control."

"I am under control."

"You're wearing a piece of deer antler around your neck! Kyle told me that you rented a sailboat so that you could sit on it for hours every day and stare at the ocean! What is that stubble doing on your face, and why are you wearing shorts and a T-shirt in the office?

"Jep, unlike the rest of us, you were *born* elegant. To sum this up, right now you look like misery on two legs."

"I'm happy to be miserable," he said sincerely.

"*What?*"

"It's good to have feelings again." He cupped the antler amulet in one hand and rubbed it thoughtfully.

"Oh, Jep, I don't know whether to laugh or cry. I've never seen you this way before."

"I've never been this way before."

She sat Zot on the floor. He curled his lips back like a chimpanzee and made an eeking sound.

"My nephew has potential as a politician," Jeopard observed.

"I read about Tess Gallatin in the paper yesterday."

Jeopard looked at his sister dully. "I saw the article. All the wire services carried it. It was the first official announcement about her."

"It sounds as if she's going to accept the crown. At least, she didn't say that she wasn't. Jep, you've been home for three weeks and she hasn't called you once."

"That's the way I wanted it."

"You are one tough *hombre*. What are you going to do now?"

Jeopard cleared his throat, then got up and went to a window. He stood there, squinting narrowly in the bright Florida sun. "Keep waiting."

"Oh, Jep," Millie said sadly. "For how long?"

He lied. "I don't know." *For the rest of my life.*

•    •    •

PEOPLE AT THE Fort Lauderdale marina were beginning to whisper about him, but he didn't care. He knew they thought it strange that he kept renting a sailboat just so he could sit on the aft deck in a lounge chair.

Well, hell. He'd never been whimsical before, and he wanted to practice.

Jeopard stood up, adjusted his sunglasses, and walked to the port railing. He fiddled with the chrome work on a post, polishing it distractedly. The newspaper article from the day before stuck in his mind. He'd read it so many times that he'd memorized it.

Sierdansk, Kara—Officials of the tiny Scandinavian principality of Kara announced today that they have verified the claim of an American woman who says she is the illegitimate daughter of the late Queen Isabella.

Tess Gallatin, a California resident, is the daughter of H. R. Gallatin, author of the well-known Sam Daggett adventure novels. Gallatin, now deceased, was a Cherokee Indian.

"We're delighted that she's come forward," a palace spokesman said. "Everyone who's met her has been thoroughly impressed."

The Karan Parliament issued a resolution officially recognizing Ms. Gallatin's royal titles. As the queen's daughter she becomes Princess of Kara, Duchess of Olnawan, Duchess of Cedmur, and Countess of Arvbrijek.

Speculation is growing that she will succeed her mother as queen. The palace spokesman would not comment, but did confirm that the new princess will be interviewed on national television next week.

JEOPARD STOPPED POLISHING and stood quietly, all his energy and spirit submerged in missing her. He'd encouraged her to stay there; he'd asked for this; he'd once again fostered his own destruction.

But he'd done it unselfishly, and because he loved

her so much that he was a better man than he'd ever
been before. He had no regrets.

The knowledge didn't make his heartache much
easier to bear.

"Captain Sundance, you really *must* leave the dock
more often," a soft English voice called. "Or does the
idea of steering a boat still turn you into a bumbler?"

Jeopard whipped around. Tess stood on the dock,
looking like peach sherbet, in a flowing shirtwaist
dress and matching pumps. Tears streamed down her
face, but she smiled giddily as he ran to the edge of
the bow and looked at her.

"*Tess!*"

Jeopard held out both hands. She took them and
leaped gracefully onto the bow. For a moment she and
he were too emotional to do more than face each other
and share a look of tender greeting. Then she flung
her arms around his neck and held him fiercely.

"Oh, Jep, being away from you was a special kind
of hell."

He groaned and took her in a deep embrace, then
nuzzled his face into her dark hair. "When do you
have to go back? I read about the television interview—"

"It's already done," she whispered, her breath
warm and fast against his ear. "I taped it yesterday."

"But—"

"I suppose you could say it's my hello-and-good-
bye interview."

"What?"

She leaned back in the circle of his arms and gazed
lovingly at him, then glanced at the antler amulet dangling on his T-shirt. Smiling, she slipped a hand inside
the neck of her dress and drew out the chain bearing
her Cherokee medallion.

Now it also bore the Blue Princess, in a delicate setting of gold filigree. "I found this in my room after
you'd left," she murmured, touching the diamond
with a forefinger. "Thank you. I'll consider it a sort of
wedding present."

Jeopard grasped her face between his hands and looked at her in bittersweet agony. "What are you trying to tell me?"

"That I'm here to stay and marry you, of course."

"Tess, don't—"

"I know what I'm giving up in Kara, and I don't care. I only stayed until I'd settled my duties there.

"Jep, listen. Drake finally found someone on the reservation who could decipher the message on my medallion. I honestly believe that my great-great-grandmother wanted to send a message to her family for all the generations to come."

"What does the medallion say?"

"On one side it says, 'Katherine Blue Song, daughter of Jesse and Mary Blue Song, sister of Anna, Elizabeth, and Sallie. I left my family's souls at rest in Blue Song land, Gold Ridge, Georgia, 1838.'

"On the other side it says, 'Katherine Gallatin, wife of Justis Gallatin. A bluebird should follow the sun.' "

Tess kissed him gently. "Jep, it's a prophecy, and old Dove Gallatin must have known that when she passed the medallions on to Erica, Kat, and me. I can't wait to find out what their medallions say."

"But how did you interpret yours to mean—"

"I'm the Blue Princess, and you're from the sun land. I'm the last princess, just as Katherine was the last Blue Song. Don't you understand? It all seems to hint that I'm *supposed* to follow the sun, just as my great-great-grandmother did. I'm *supposed* to marry you. I even call you Sundance. Do you think it's all just whimsical coincidence?"

"Whimsical? No," he said hoarsely. "Besides, what's wrong with being whimsical?"

And then he kissed her until they were both laughing breathlessly.

A WARM GUST of April air swept over the new graves with deceptive innocence, carrying the fragrances of pine, oak, dogwood, and honeysuckle down to the magnificent spring-green valley below. The breeze lifted specks of red-tinted Georgia soil from the graves and dried the tiny spots where tears had fallen. The baked earth hinted that the summer of 1838 would be oppressively hot and tortured by drought.

To the young woman who placed white-blossomed dogwood boughs on the graves the air foretold more death, sorrow, and betrayal.

Because she was a Cherokee, she whispered sacred formulas to guard the graves of her parents and sisters. Because she had graduated only a month earlier from the Philadelphia Presbyterian Academy for Young Ladies, she added prayers.

Because she was Katherine Blue Song, a proud girl of imposing character—but mostly because someone was watching—she didn't cry anymore.

The people of her tribe were being herded away

from their homes like animals, in preparation for removal to the Oklahoma territory. Her family had resisted, much to the delight of the unscrupulous local militia. Now she was the only Blue Song who would have to leave the ancient homeland. Her family would remain here forever.

"I'm finished, Mr. Gallatin," she said in a tired but formal tone, and straightened rigidly inside her plain black dress. "You may do the rest now."

The tall, rough-looking man stopped studying her with his perpetually intense gaze. Justis Gallatin touched a blunt gold spur to the side of his gray stallion. Then he tipped his wide-brimmed felt hat to her and ordered in a deep, drawling voice. "Back off, gal, so you won't get trampled."

She walked down the slope a few feet and stood staring into the distance, anger and grief burning inside her so terribly that she hardly saw the old blue-green mountains that were sacred to her people.

*Gal.* He was so crude, this chestnut-haired young man, with his unfashionable moustache and reputation for brawling, this white man who had been her father's partner until the government decreed that Cherokees could no longer mine gold.

Now he owned everything that had once been Blue Song property—the mine in Gold Ridge, the valley below, even the burned shells of the large frame house and barns on the hill behind her. Tears stinging her eyes, Katherine let her gaze drop to the distant creek where she had played as a child.

She tried to ignore the sound of his horse's hooves destroying the mounds of her family's graves.

He finally reined the big stallion to a halt and sat quietly watching her dignified profile. After a moment he offered, "None of those grave-robbin' bastards from town'll find 'em. You can count on it."

"Thank you."

Katherine was surprised by the gentleness in his voice, and she didn't trust it. She didn't trust him. He had money and power; he was white; the state of

Georgia had given him and other white men the right to take everything that had belonged to her family, to her.

He stepped down from his horse, went to the small mare tethered to a nearby tree, and led her to Katherine. "Up you go, gal. It's not safe for you to stay here long."

Katherine faced him. "Of what concern is my safety to you, sir? You've done your duty."

He stared down at her with astonished gray-green eyes that slowly narrowed. "I'm not gonna let Jesse Blue Song's daughter end up like the rest of the Cherokee women around here. If you don't know what the militia boys are doing to them, I'll tell you."

Katherine's knees went weak, and she almost choked on the pain in her throat. "Are you saying that my mother and sisters . . . ?"

She swayed and raised a hand to her mouth. Suddenly Justis Gallatin stepped close to her and took her in his arms. Her pride failed to keep her from leaning against him.

He cursed softly under his breath. "Forgive me, gal. No. That didn't happen to them."

She didn't believe him, but she was touched by his sympathetic lie. Her eyes shut, tears scalding her cheeks, she finally managed to say, "No one else cares. Why do you, Mr. Gallatin?"

He led her to a shady spot under a maple tree, and they sat down. He kept an arm around her, which offended her sense of propriety, but not enough to make her rebuke him. Her father had liked him and trusted him, which might mean that he was a good man.

But a blunt one. "I've got selfish reasons, gal . . . Miss Blue Song. You're a beautiful woman, a woman with education and culture. I want you for my wife."

Numbed and exhausted by grief, she gazed up at him in dull disbelief. "I won't marry just to have a roof over my head, sir. Besides, you *can't* marry an Indian." Sarcasm tinged her voice. "It would scandalize polite society—and your friends would call you a squaw man."

"Not up north. That's where I'm heading—gonna put some Gallatin gold into New York investments."

"Blue Song gold," she corrected. "Taken from Cherokee land. Stolen from people who were peaceful farmers and merchants."

"Your pa and I went in business together. There was no stealing on my part. I did everything I could to protect him and his, but I couldn't stop what happened. I didn't want to see the Cherokees driven off the land, and I fought many a white man over that difference of opinion." He paused. "Now. If you want to have a say in how the gold's spent, come with me. We don't have to get married until you get accustomed to me."

"How noble of you," she said drolly.

"Not the least bit. And I don't give a damn what polite society thinks of me. Never have. But I'll get you a chaperone—I'll hire you a wagonload of chaperones to keep your reputation up till we say the 'I do's.' How about that?"

"Mr. Gallatin, you're very presumptuous."

He shrugged. "You think on it, gal. You got nobody but me." Standing, he held out a hand and helped her to her feet. He swept an experienced, predatory gaze around the woods while one hand came to rest on the pearl-handled pistol tucked in his belt. "We best get back to town. I've killed my share of the trash roaming these woods. Like to avoid killing any today."

He looked down at her and spoke with another show of gentleness. "I'll walk off a little ways. You say your farewells. Say 'em good—you probably won't come back here."

She watched Justis Gallatin go to the horses, her mind spinning with the idea that this white invader thought he could have her for the asking; that she'd willingly become intimate with his moustache-draped mouth and lean, hard-looking body.

She didn't understand the strange sensation that

thought created inside her, and some warning instinct told her she was better off not contemplating it. Slowly Katherine turned and faced the valley for the last time.

She ached with sorrow. This land of glorious forests, rivers, and rolling, blue-green mountains was part of her family, part of her blood.

As she grieved for all she'd lost she formed a silent, sacred promise to herself. Nothing must ever take this land away from her. There must come a day when the legacy of her family would live again here.

Katherine whispered a phrase in Cherokee. It meant more than a promise. It was a prophecy.

*Someday.*

# TEMPTING
## *the* WOLF

## CHAPTER 1

W HAT THE HELL was he doing there? And what difference did it make?

James Tall Wolf leaned against a wall outside the opulent banquet room, one expensively loafered foot crossed over the other, big-knuckled hands shoved in the pockets of custom-tailored trousers, an unlit cigar clenched between his teeth.

He asked himself the same questions every time he spoke at one of these shindigs, and lately it had been at least once a month. Was he just a curiosity, or did these business types really listen? How could he make them listen? Should he just tell them to go suck a to- tem pole, that Native Americans didn't need their smug patronage?

"Mr. Tall Wolf! I've been looking for you!"

James glanced down the hall. The little blonde was so close that he could see her eyelashes flutter invit- ingly. Her gaze lingered on his face as if she'd never seen such fascinating features. He straightened and put his cigar in his shirt pocket.

"Mr. Tall Wolf," she said sweetly, and held out a hand. "Let me show you to your table. I'm Lisa, the publicity coordinator for the developers' association. We're so glad to have you as a speaker. You're such a credit to your people."

James smiled at her, shook hands, and felt her forefingers stroke his palm. *Credit to your people.* Okay, he wouldn't tell her how insulting that line was. He'd learned long ago that there was no tactful way to explain without coming across as arrogant and oversensitive, neither of which did the tribe's image any good.

"Why, thank you," he said drolly. "It's not true that the only good Indian is a dead Indian."

She laughed. "Oh, it's so nice to see that you have a sense of humor about yourself." She caressed his arm through the sleeves of his dark jacket as they walked into the ballroom of the hotel. "Do you get back to D.C. often, these days?"

"Every few months. I've got some real-estate investments here."

"I'm a big Redskins fan."

*In more ways than one*, James thought wryly. "Thank you."

"I was sorry when you retired."

"I was too. But I like to walk without limping."

"You look very healthy. Very." She led him between banquet tables that were quickly filling with members of the developers' association. "Do you ever see your old teammates?"

"Occasionally. I've been away from pro ball for three years, though."

"Which reservation do you live on? The one in Oklahoma or in North Carolina?"

"Neither. I've got a little piece of land in Virginia."

She looked surprised. "But I thought—"

"That all Indians lived on reservations." He smiled wickedly. "I'm a renegade."

"Yum. I'd love to see your teepee some time."

"It's not called a teepee. And it's not much to see."

"I'm free this weekend."

"Sorry. I've already accepted an invitation to a scalping party."

"You like blond hair?" She pulled a strand of hers over one eye and winked at him. "Think of the delicious contrasts we could make."

They reached the table on the dais and stopped. James shook her hand in farewell. Again he felt the slow, intimate movement of her fingertip in his palm. He sighed. "Lisa, I'm saving myself for marriage."

She jabbed him with her nail. "You're kidding!"

"Nope. There's only so much of me to go around. I have to save my energy every chance I get."

She studied his slitted eyes, frowned, and suddenly seemed grateful to introduce him to the association's president, so that she could end her responsibilities.

James sat down next to the president and distractedly exchanged greetings with him and the other men at the head table. His thoughts churned. Once upon a time he would have encouraged the blonde's attention and heartily enjoyed the result.

Now he understood that he was an exotic pet to many women; through him they could fulfill some harmless Wild West fantasies about noble savages, he guessed. He was good at giving them what they wanted, but he didn't get enough in return anymore.

*I'm getting old and cranky*, he told himself as he ate his salad. His bad knee ached more often than it used to, and he missed his family down in North Carolina more than ever. He hadn't been home in four years, and, homesick as he was now, still he remembered funerals and bitterness.

"The ugly ones always make trouble."

"You think she's ugly?"

"She's six feet tall, for cryin' out loud! Women that big are always insecure. They don't feel feminine, so they end up trying to dominate men."

James forgot his brooding and listened curiously as his dinner partners continued to whisper among themselves.

"You don't know Ricky, or you wouldn't say that."

The heavyset man to James's left snorted derisively. "The broad stole that award from me last year."

"Stole it? Hell. She earned that construction award."

"Well, she sure didn't sleep with anybody to get it. Not unless one of the judges liked big-mouthed, skinny broads."

Intrigued, James looked around for the troublesome Ricky.

"Excuse me. Thank you. Sorry I'm late." The tall woman slipped awkwardly between nearby tables, bumping people with a scuffed brown briefcase.

She was gawky in an endearing sort of way; not clumsy, exactly, but all arms and legs, in a blue skirt and jacket that were too plain and a little too big. Her wavy, shoulder-length chestnut hair was laughably disheveled, but it reflected the overhead lights in glossy coppers and golds that held James's rapt gaze.

No one would ever call this woman pretty, not in the soft, rounded way of most women, but no man in his right mind would call that combination of statuesque body, glorious hair, and beautifully chiseled face *ugly*.

She drew glances from many in the nearly all-male crowd, and the red dots on her cheeks told James that she was painfully uncomfortable with the attention. She scooted into a chair at a table right in front and sat there with rigid dignity. He could see her profile, and in it he read careful reserve. She was a successful woman in a profession dominated by men from the highest management to the lowest laborer, and she probably knew that she was an easy target for jealousy.

James studied the tentative, tight smile she offered her table mates. She was aware that her entrance had elicited everything from compliments to contempt. She was definitely an outsider.

*You and me both, doll,* James told her silently. A tingling sense of arousal came over him, a sudden affec-

tion and protectiveness. His body's response didn't
surprise him, but the sentimentality did. He kept
watching her in the hope she would look in his direction.

The man who'd defended her at James's table
turned around and called, "Hey, Ricky, leave the killer
briefcase at the office next time."

She swiveled, looked relieved to see a friendly face,
and patted the bulky leather rectangle by her ankles.
"I was out at a site, and my truck died. I took a
cab. And I have to go back to the office after dinner."

"All work and no play, Ricky," he said teasingly.

The heavyset man snickered. "She's not exactly a
plaything. I'd rather make it with a construction
crane."

"You know," James told him in a soft, pleasant
tone, "one of the most distinguishing things about
Cherokee culture has always been its respect for
women. Cherokee women could fight in battle and
hold positions of power on the councils. And the family structure was a matriarchy."

The man slapped his thigh and guffawed. "The
squaws were in charge while the braves lay around."

A waiter placed a thick steak in front of James. He
studied it for a moment, wondering idly how it would
look flattened on his table mate's face. "Former Redskin wallops jackass with beef. Details at eleven." No,
it would play too big in the media.

"Some of us don't use those terms," James explained patiently. "Squaw, brave, buck, papoose—
they're considered demeaning stereotypes."

"Don't tell me you people are into all that consciousness raising, affirmative-action stuff. You're a
businessman, just like me. You know that all this mi-
nority bellyaching is ruining us."

James's frayed patience dissolved in one blistering
second of anger. The depth of that anger startled him,
but he knew he had nothing to fear from it. In the old
days, when he was out of control, he would have

thrown a plateful of steak in the man's face, and probably his fist, too.

He glanced up and saw the skinny redhead gazing at him anxiously. The look in her eyes was so worried that he stared back at her, shocked that a stranger had deciphered his mood.

James was a master at returning flirtations, but this was no flirtation. This was compassion. He lost himself in her soulful green eyes.

"What about that issue, James?" the obnoxious questioner asked. "Are you people big on federal handout programs?"

James turned slowly to the man. "We're big on anything that helps us keep what's left of our land and culture." He tossed his napkin on the table and told the association president, "Come get me when you need me. I'll be in the hall."

He stood and walked out of the room. Even in his anger it seemed to James that he could feel the redhead's eyes on him as he left.

THERE HAD TO be a bond between people with Cherokee blood, Erica thought. Why else would James Tall Wolf have returned her gaze so intensely and with such gratitude?

She could barely eat. Where had he gone? What had that jerk, Harold Brumby, said to him? Harold, a hulking Archie Bunker type, as sensitive as a log, was constantly in trouble with some union or other.

James Tall Wolf. The moment she'd learned that he was the guest speaker at the association's spring meeting she'd rearranged her schedule so she could attend. For years she'd heard of the Cherokee Indian who played defense for the Washington Redskins.

The press always made a big joke out of the coincidence—an Indian Redskin—but, not being a football fan, she'd never paid much attention. And after all, James Tall Wolf had left professional football three years ago, owing to a knee problem.

From now on, she'd pay attention.

She tuned in to the conversation at her table.

"He's off the juice, you can tell. I bet he's dropped thirty pounds since he retired."

"You know that stuff turns 'em into monsters. It makes 'em big and mean."

"Wolfman was one of the meanest. I swear, I think his own teammates were afraid of him sometimes. But he was great."

"The coaches like that, when the guys are half crazy. It's a big macho thing. Everybody thought it was funny when the Wolfman used to tear up benches with his bare hands."

The men chuckled among themselves. Erica sat there feeling a little stunned. "What's juice?" she asked. "Alcohol?"

"Steroids," one of the men explained. "Growth hormones." He growled comically. "Testosterone."

"Ah." James Tall Wolf didn't look as though he needed any extra of that. "Aren't steroids dangerous?"

"Sure. But a lot of the guys in pro football take them. Makes 'em play better."

"Defensive linemen are animals anyway," someone added. "Gorillas in helmets."

Erica poked nervously at her food. She'd made eye contact with a dangerous man, then. Funny, he'd looked gentle. There was something exciting about being noticed by a man who tore up benches with his bare hands.

She waited anxiously for him to come back into the room; finally, during dessert, he did. Erica had hoped to study every fascinating detail of him, but as soon as he appeared his gaze went straight to hers.

She clutched the napkin in her lap. What had she done to deserve this scrutiny? Frowning, she turned her attention to a piece of runny lime pie and ate as if it were delicious.

But every time she glanced up, he was still watching her. Her stomach twisted. She knew she'd made a gawky entrance. That must be it—Harold Brumby had probably made fun of her, as she knew he'd done frequently since she'd won the construction award away from him.

Perhaps Harold had told some disgusting lie, and it had made James Tall Wolf find her fascinating, like a bizarre story in a grocery-store tabloid.

"Martian Disguised as Female Housebuilder. Two-Headed Hammers Discovered!"

She made certain her pie lasted until the association's president got up and welcomed James as the guest speaker. Erica kept her attention on the last crumbs as she listened carefully to the introduction. Honors and awards as a star player for North Carolina State—the Wolfman had played for the N.C. State Wolfpack (hah-hah)—then many more as a defensive lineman for the Redskins (hah-hah); and now James Tall Wolf was a successful entrepreneur, with varied investments in real estate.

And to top it all off, as the president pointed out, James was a full-blooded Cherokee, who devoted much of his spare time to telling his inspirational story to groups all over the country.

*Give 'em hell, Tall Wolf,* she thought proudly. As everyone applauded, Erica lifted her gaze to the podium and clapped vigorously.

The Wolfman was looking directly at her.

Erica's hands hesitated in midair. She could do nothing but gaze back at him and wait to see what he'd do next. What he did was start talking in a deep, melodic voice faintly touched by a Southern drawl; a voice so rich that it made her think of chocolate.

Finally he drew his gaze away from her to look at his audience. Erica sagged as if a puppeteer had let go of her strings.

Tall Wolf was perfection molded from bronze, his hair the color of sable, his eyes like dark mahogany. His features were classic—the high cheekbones, deep-set eyes, wide mouth, and blunt nose of a beautiful American original.

He had to be six-feet-four, at least, and his post-football body was big but lean. He knew how to dress and obviously had the money to dress well; he wore a black sports coat, blue-gray pants, a crisp white shirt with a broadly spaced blue stripe, and a blue tie. A thick gold watch gleamed on his wrist.

"I took my grandfather to New York," he was telling the audience, "and we stood on Fifth Avenue during the rush hour. We watched all the people for a while, and finally Grandfather turned to me and said, 'James, I don't think they're leaving.' "

The joke brought warm laughter and a smattering of applause. Erica felt a twinge of dismay. How could he make fun of such a sad subject? His people had lost so much over the years. She paused, thinking of the cousins she'd met two days before. *Our* people, she corrected herself, feeling proud.

"We have a popular bumper sticker down on the reservation," James said. "It reads, 'I'm glad Columbus was looking for India instead of Turkey.' "

People guffawed and thumped the tables. Erica drummed her fingers and tried not to bite her tongue.

"We've made a great living at being mascots and advertising symbols," James told the audience. "Sports writers love us. 'Washington Redskins Scalp Opponents.' 'Cleveland Indians Go on Warpath.' Folks, we do take time out to pose in front of cigar stores, you know."

Erica couldn't stand it. She stood up quickly. "Mr. Tall Wolf, could you tell us a little about some of the fine Indian leaders the Cherokees have had? Men like Sequoyah, who invented the Cherokee syllabary, and John Ross, who sued the federal government in an attempt to save the southern homelands?"

An awkward silence settled in the room. He stared at her for only a second. Then, an exasperated look on his face, he shot back, "I think you just told us."

Erica gritted her teeth as the audience chuckled at his quick reply. She didn't want to annoy him; she wanted to help. She kept her tone pleasant and sincere. "Do you feel that humor is an effective weapon against prejudice? Are the Cherokee people able to laugh about their problems the way you can?"

He bristled. "I'm not laughing at these problems."

"As their spokesman—"

"I'm just a businessman who happens to be Cherokee. I'm not the tribe's official representative."

"But you're treated that way. Is it a burden? Do you resent it?"

"This is a surprise," he said with a strained smile. "When I got here tonight I didn't notice the cameras from *Sixty Minutes*." Everyone laughed. "And you don't look like Mike Wallace."

Harold Brumby lolled back in his chair and said in a stage whisper, "Mike wears better suits."

No one dared laugh at that, but there were a lot of satisfied smiles. Erica felt a dull, sinking feeling at the center of her dignity, but she grinned cheerfully at Harold. "And Mike's a lot shorter."

Now the laughter was on her side. She glanced toward the podium and was surprised to see James Tall Wolf eyeing Harold with disgust. Slowly James swiveled his gaze to her.

"When you make people laugh *with* you about a problem, you gain their attention and respect," he told her. "I think you just proved that."

"Ah. Yes." She sat down, undone more by his subtle compliment than she would ever be by Harold's less-than-subtle insults.

He continued with his speech, but now he cast wary looks at her each time the audience laughed. Erica forced herself to smile and nod, but questions kept sticking in her throat. He wasn't addressing the issues.

At an opportune moment she vaulted to her feet. "Mr. Tall Wolf. Excuse me again."

The cuff of her jacket caught a spoon and sent it clattering loudly into her neighbor's coffee cup, splashing him. Erica grabbed the spoon and thunked it back into place, her face hot.

"In the old days we named people according to

their personalities," James Tall Wolf said in just the
right tone of patronizing amusement. "I think I'll call
you She-Who-Makes-Noise." He paused. "Okay,
Noise, what is it now?"

Erica cleared her throat and waited for the chuckles
to end. Damn him, he knew how to work a crowd.
"Mr. Tall Wolf, what are you and other prominent
Cherokees doing to solve the economic and social
problems facing the tribe today? What are you doing
about poor housing, unemployment, lack of adequate
educational opportunities, and the disintegration of
traditional Cherokee culture? Besides telling jokes, that
is."

The lethal tightening of his facial muscles warned
that she'd finally gone too far. Erica stared up at him
stoically. The issues were too important to ignore.

He smiled, flashing white teeth at her in a predatory
way that iced her blood. "I don't waste my time trying to answer complicated questions in a twenty-
minute speech after dinner."

"Why? Do you feel that most whites really aren't
interested in the plight of Native Americans today?"

He went very still, his bench-breaking hands
clenched on the sides of the podium, his dark eyes
holding hers with a look that made her knees weak.
He seemed to be fighting some monumental decision.
Whatever chord she'd touched, it was a deep one.

He lifted his chin and said in a loud, firm voice,
"*Yes*. I frankly don't think most of you give a damn."

That blunt remark sent a ripple of shock through
the audience. Erica gazed breathlessly at James Tall
Wolf, mesmerized by the challenge and the fury in his
eyes, even though they were directed at her.

"Could you elaborate?" she asked.

"Hell, yes." And he did so nonstop for the next ten
minutes, his voice reaching through the ballroom like
a dark whip. Erica sat down limply in her chair and
watched him in awe. She sensed the crowd's electric
response, and when she glanced at the faces around

her she knew that whether they liked or disliked James Tall Wolf, they'd never forget him.

Neither would she.

He finished abruptly, shot her a cold look that brought her back to reality, and told the audience good night. He strode out of the ballroom without looking back, leaving a patchwork quilt of approval and disdain; areas of bright applause bordered by gray silence.

Erica barely heard the president's closing remarks. When everyone stood to leave she fumbled distractedly for her purse and briefcase.

All right, she'd let him cool off for a few days, and then she'd get his phone number from the association's secretary and give him a call. She'd explain that she was part Cherokee and had only wanted to express a sincere interest in the tribe.

Getting wearily to her feet, she tucked her briefcase under one arm and endured silent frowns from the departing crowd. A few were not so silent.

"Thanks for insulting a guest speaker."

"Didn't know you were so interested in Indians."

"You broads never know when to shut your mouths."

To that remark she replied, "Blow it out your chimney, Harold."

She escaped to a rest room, where she gaped first at her ashen face, then at the disheveled state of her hair. Her dark blue skirt was twisted, and she'd forgotten to pull the jacket lapel over a small mud stain on her blouse.

Damn, she didn't care about her looks ordinarily; she'd never been able to compete with her mother or half sisters on that basis, so she'd stopped paying attention long ago.

"I love you," she told the chestnut-haired Amazon in the mirror, "but you must have looked homely as hell to the Wolfman."

The Wolfman. An appropriate nickname, even if he wasn't hairy.

The hotel hallway was deserted by the time she finished straightening herself up and headed for an elevator. Even the elevator was empty. Good.

Erica put her briefcase down, leaned gratefully against the cool, paneled wall of the elevator, and reached for the ground-floor button.

Her fingers bumped into a big, brawny hand the color of light copper. Erica jerked her hand back and gazed up into James Tall Wolf's dark eyes. Angry, watchful eyes.

He stepped into the elevator and hit the top-floor button. His intense, unwavering gaze never left hers as the door slid shut, closing them in together for a long ride down.

He planted both hands on the wall, trapping her between his arms. Erica gasped. He leaned forward, a muscle throbbing in his jaw, and said grimly, "I've been waiting for you."

## CHAPTER 2

"I WASN'T TRYING to antagonize you."

"The hell you weren't." He leaned closer, his breath hot on her face.

Erica inhaled good cologne and a faint trace of rich cigar smoke; to her it was the essence of threatening masculinity. His hair was blue-black under the elevator lights, and his eyes were so dark that the pupils seemed to merge with their backgrounds.

"I don't need lectures from a knee-jerk liberal"—he spoke between gritted teeth—"who hasn't got one friggin' idea what it's like to be Cherokee."

"I have an imagination."

"Dammit, what did you want from me tonight?"

She hugged herself and glanced at the passing floor numbers. "Nothing." They reached the bottom level and stopped. "Ground floor," she quipped in a mechanical voice. "Sporting goods, appliances, amnesty for women with good intentions."

Without taking his eyes off her he reached over and

hit a button. She made a soft protesting sound as the elevator began to move upward.

"Women with good intentions," he echoed in a sarcastic tone. "Oh, hell, now I get it. The questions were just a come-on, a little bit more dignified than most. Congratulations. Your intentions got my attention."

Erica stared at him in astonishment. "No."

"Next time just shake that skinny behind at me instead. I'd give it a second look."

"You're mistaken. I'm not interested in jocks with egos bigger than their—"

"Oh, come off it."

His arms scooped around her, and he pressed her to the wall. Erica yelped just as his mouth sank onto hers with angry force, twisting, taking, proving a point. He stabbed his tongue between her lips and ran his hands over her rump, squeezing hard.

She stood on tiptoe, trying to escape, but her foot slipped out of its blue pump and she lost her balance. Half-hanging off the floor with her fanny cupped in his hands, she squirmed against him and tried to shut her mouth.

Erica told herself that everything had happened so fast, she didn't have time to be rational. The fact that his touch was much more passionate than angry had a disastrous effect on her resistance.

"Hmmm," he said from deep in his throat.

"Hmmm," she responded hesitantly.

Then he willed her tongue into his mouth and attacked it as if it were a melting Popsicle.

Big Red Riding Hood was definitely about to be eaten by the wolf—and it amazed her that she didn't want to run away. Why? What was wrong with her? She was vibrating with blind, desperate excitement, and he knew it. Dammit, he knew it, and she was beyond caring that he knew.

Erica gave up and wound her arms around his shoulders. The shifting of her body brought her closer to him, and he flexed slightly, nudging her belly with a hard ridge.

James Tall Wolf pulled his mouth away from hers just enough to talk. "Your intentions are even better than I expected," he said hoarsely.

He frowned at her, his expression not so much angry as it was surprised. A painful realization cut into Erica. He hadn't expected her reaction or his own. He was shocked to find her desirable.

Wounded and embarrassed, she shoved him away. He stepped back tensely, watching her with a troubled awareness that made him look fierce. "Yeah, there's plenty under that blouse besides a bleeding heart." His voice was gruff.

She sagged against the wall, one shoe off, her blouse half out of her skirt, her mouth feeling so hot and swollen that she lifted a hand to it. "Touch me again and I'll kick an extra point right between your goal posts."

The elevator reached the top floor, and the doors opened. A sweet-looking elderly couple stood there in the small alcove, holding hands. "Oh, my," the woman said pertly, peering in at Erica's disarray.

"Sorry. Excuse us." Erica pushed the button that closed the door. "No!"

But James Tall Wolf had already pushed the button for the ground floor again. She gave him a lethal look. They were both breathing too fast. "If you wanted revenge, you got it."

He gazed down at her sternly, his arms crossed and his long legs braced apart. "A jackass at my table called you ugly. Are you?"

The question was so bizarre that she sputtered, "N-no!"

"Then get rid of that awful suit and buy something that fits. And pull your hair up so your face shows. And when men look at you, don't hang your head like some sort of wimpy old maid."

His words hit her in the solar plexus, but she drew her chin up and glared at him. "I don't know who you were looking at, but it wasn't me. You've got more money and power and reason for happiness than most people ever do, but all you can do is whine about being misunderstood because you're a Cherokee and then insult me with your stupid-jock notion that any woman who's nice to you wants to crawl into your bed."

She tucked in her shirt and quickly jammed her foot back in the lost pump. "I wanted to be your friend."

"So you stood up and made fun of me in front of people."

"I honestly didn't mean to." Her shoulders slumped. She was so addled at that moment that all she could think about was the feel of his mouth on hers and the damp heat he'd created between her thighs. She shook her head at him wearily. "Thanks for the education, Mr. Tall Wolf. I guess I did think that you'd be more noble than the average sports-celebrity-turned-businessman. But you're just a spoiled jock."

He dismissed her with a fierce wave of one hand. "Fine. I'm not used to desperate, frumpy women who don't have the courage to ask outright for what they want."

*Frumpy.* Erica could stand most insults, but having this man make fun of her looks was too painful. "Take steroids again," she told him. "They couldn't make you any nastier than you are now."

His eyes flared. "Doll, if I were still on the macho juice I'd have torn this elevator apart and chased you down a hall."

The elevator bumped to a stop. She grabbed her briefcase and started toward the door, not caring which floor they were on. He blocked her with one long arm. Erica nearly stumbled, trying to avoid contact with him.

"This is my floor," he told her in a low, challenging tone. "I don't think you want to get off here."

"No. I definitely don't."

He smiled wickedly. "Be honest. I might grant you a favor."

"I've never tried a one-night stand before, and I'd prefer to wait for a friendlier offer."

"You sound like you spend a lot of time waiting for *any* offer."

"And I doubt you have enough morals to turn down any offer. Good night, Rabid Wolf."

"She-Who-Makes-Noise, you're a hard woman to please." He chuckled harshly and walked away without looking back.

"RICKY, YOUR MOTHER'S on the phone."

Erica snapped to attention. "Thanks, Marie. Got it. Right. Is my lunch here yet? Have you typed that contract to send to George Gibson? Where's my new box of floppy discs?"

Marie Stewart, never one to take employer-employee relationships seriously, frowned at her like a scolding nanny. "Are you all right?" The office manager glanced at an air-conditioner vent on a wall painted functional brown. "Too hot?"

"No. Why?"

"You're edgy, and you were fanning yourself a second ago."

"Too much coffee." *Too much James Tall Wolf,* Erica added silently. Too much thinking about the night before. Too much of that lust-in-the-teepee novel she'd bought on the way to work that morning.

"Your mother. Line two."

Erica slapped the phone to one ear. "Hello?"

Patricia Gallatin Monroe said what she always said when she called. "This is the Boston mother phoning her Washington runaway." In eight years the words had rarely varied. "I received your message."

"Hi. Your secretary said you were out of town. Something about catering a party for the Kennedys. Again?"

"Hmmm. They adore my people. I have the best pastry chef in Boston."

"Mother, I'm proud of you."

"I know. I did a marvelous job, as usual. Ask Lucianne. Your sister is still trying to steal my clients."

Erica sighed. Her mother's household ran on pride, propriety, and vigorous competition, even among family members. Erica's half sisters, Lucianne and Noelle, thrived on the system. It was either compete or get out. Erica had gotten out.

Erica the rebel. She looked down at her navy blue tailored dress. Little pieces of lint clung to it. Some rebel.

"I flew down to Georgia, day before yesterday, and met my Gallatin cousins."

There was dead silence on the Boston end of the phone. Finally her mother said, "I asked you not to."

"I'm going to study Dad's family. I want to know about them."

"Your father was white."

"One-eighth Cherokee."

"Why do you care, after all these years? You never cared before."

Erica rubbed her forehead wearily. "I never knew anything about the Gallatins because you refused to discuss them."

"You were so little when your father died in the accident. After I remarried I thought you wanted to feel like a Monroe."

"Not so little—seven years old. I never forgot Dad." That was an understatement. She still had all his navy aviation insignia in her jewelry box.

Marie buzzed her on the intercom. "Boss, T.K. is on line one."

"Mother, I have to go. I just wanted you to know that my cousins are wonderful people. You'd like them. 'Bye."

Her head throbbing with tension, Erica punched the other line. "Are we on for tonight?"

A sinister, chuckling male voice came back. "The

Nemesis Gang sallies forth again. Bring your hammer."

"WE'RE GOIN' ON a raid, my man," Stephen said in his thick Texas drawl as he tossed a basketball at a hoop on his expensively decorated office wall. Beside the hoop hung the annual *Sports Illustrated* swimsuit calendar. Stephen Murray, real-estate tycoon, good friend, and lady-killer, was the most laid-back businessman ever put in pinstripes.

James eyed his partner warily. "Like the time you left me in the girls' dorm with thirty pairs of panties stuffed under my shirt?"

"Hah. We're gonna trap us some carpenter ants of the human variety. And we're gonna put their carpenter-ant butts in the D.C. pokey."

James propped his feet on Stephen's custom-made teakwood desk and sipped a glass of brandy. "Does this have anything to do with the property downtown?"

"Our lovely block of vacant lot, yessir. I got me a tip from an inside source. Gonna have a carpenter-ant problem there tonight."

"Same kind as before?"

"Ants named Nemesis. Yessir."

James frowned into his glass. Nemesis was a coalition of architecture students who sneaked onto downtown property to build huts for homeless people. They had a slick game plan: in twenty minutes they could erect a cozy ten-by-ten hut complete with window and door.

The huts gave shelter and security to the saddest of the homeless cases—chronic outcasts who'd fallen through the cracks of the system—and Nemesis thumbed its collective nose at that system for being so heartless. He'd approved of the gang's tactics as long as it built huts on public property, but when the members grew bold about trespassing on private lots he lost sympathy.

"What's the deal tonight?" he asked.

Stephen chortled. "Gonna hide and wait, pal. Got me some private security boys lined up. I'm goin' along for the excitement. Thought you'd like to come too."

"What the hell. Sure."

James downed his brandy. What the hell. He had a limited amount of sympathy to go around, and he saved it for his own kind.

THE FIRST HUT went up without incident. Twenty well-coordinated gang members, wearing dark clothes and ski masks, hammered and sawed, and christened the tiny dwelling with their victory cry, "Home, Sweet Home!"

Erica tugged at her hot, itchy mask and almost decided to pull it off—after all, Nemesis had been building huts for a year now without ever being caught. It was two A.M. and this part of D.C. wasn't exactly hopping with people.

But caution made her keep the mask in place, so she wiped sweaty palms on the legs of her overalls, rolled up the black sleeves of her work shirt, and helped hoist a prebuilt base into place for the second hut.

Suddenly the group was flooded by blinding light. "Do not move," a voice boomed over a speaker. "You are trespassing on and defacing private property. The police have been called. You are surrounded by security guards from Stephen B. Murray Developers. Do not move."

For a second there was tense stillness. Then T.K. yelled, "Plan B!"

Everyone dropped everything and scattered wildly. Erica raced into the darkness and dodged two uniformed guards of rather tubby proportions. Her heart threatened to knock a dent in her chest.

Erica Alice Gallatin, fugitive. Oh, Lord. First the incident with James Tall Wolf, and now this. Her staid self-image had undergone some bizarre changes in the past two days.

"Get the tall guy!" someone yelled. "He's heading for the street!"

Tall guy heading for the street? Erica faltered. They were after *her*.

She quickly recouped and ran faster, glad that she'd been a distance runner on the women's track team at Georgia Tech. The way adrenaline was pouring into her blood just then, she thought she'd come to a halt somewhere around Vermont.

She hit the two-lane street and aimed for an alley on the opposite side. If she were lucky it wouldn't be a dead end.

But then she heard feet on the pavement behind her, closing fast and taking long, forceful strides that made the patter of her own feet sound childish.

Frantic, Erica zipped into the alley, jumped a low pile of paint cans, and tripped on a soggy cardboard box. Who had they sent after her—the Incredible Hulk? The *thing* was right behind her, and suddenly it pounced.

She thought her back would break as two big hands grabbed her waist. Smashing into another stack of boxes, she fell on her stomach, with the thing on top of her.

Her breath exploded in a pained yelp. Erica imagined two popped balloons where her lungs had been; she figured her breasts looked like fried eggs.

She couldn't move; she couldn't inhale; she gasped like a beached fish as the thing rolled off her and took her wrists in an iron grip.

The thing had a voice. "Sorry it had to be this way," it said, breathing with disgusting ease. "I didn't want to tackle you, but you've got a helluva stride. Get up on your knees, kid, and puke if you need to."

She managed to get her knees under her and crouched amidst the boxes, coughing. He—it—patted her shoulder. "Okay, kid?"

Erica nodded. The thing clamped a hand on the

back of her overalls and helped her up. Her ski mask
was askew, and she weakly tugged it back into place.

The thing snorted. "No need to keep the yarn face,
kid."

He was laughing at her, and she suddenly realized
that she had a lot more aggression in her Boston-bred
soul than she'd realized. Erica lifted her head and
croaked, "Kiss—"

The thing was James Tall Wolf.

SHE SAT IN a circle of her comrades, her arms
locked with theirs, bathed in the lights of the television crews that had just arrived.

Erica's stomach felt like a knotted rope. Someone
had not only squealed on Nemesis to Stephen Murray
and associate—the victorious James Tall Wolf, who
now stood on the perimeter, watching nonchalantly—
but someone had also called the media. She suspected
T.K., who was a known glory hound.

"Keep your masks on," T.K. called. "And go limp
when they try to carry you off the lot! It's an old protest technique."

Erica peered out of her ski mask at Tall Wolf and
was extremely glad that he didn't know whom he'd
captured so easily. Anger tore at her. A man with his
heritage ought to be sensitive to human suffering, yet
he just stood there heartlessly, his expression shuttered.

She heard shouts of anger and jerked her head to
the left. A tall, craggy-faced blond man in chinos and
a sports shirt was moving along the circle of gang
members, grinning merrily and pulling their masks off.
He jauntily tossed each mask over his shoulder.

"Lookee here," he drawled. "Carpenter ants, Lord
have mercy. Boys *and* girls. Right ugly bunch."

"Don't unlock your arms!" T.K. shouted. "Murray, you're an SOB."

"Been called that so much, I had it embossed on
my checks."

Erica and her neighbors locked arms more tightly as Murray continued removing ski masks. She glared at James, whose troubled expression showed that he either had indigestion or didn't like what his partner was doing. Probably had indigestion.

"Whoo, here's a big ol' skinny ant," Murray said when he got to her.

The humiliation was too much for Erica. She was already a criminal, so she might as well go all the way, she decided. When Stephen Murray grabbed her ski mask, she kicked him in the shins with the hard-soled heels of her work boots.

"A fighter!" He grunted in pain and stumbled back, his mouth open in shock, her ski mask hanging in his hand. "A she-fighter!"

Erica glared up at him and shook her matted hair free. "Touch me again and I'll kick you so hard, your knees will bend in the opposite direction."

James ran over and halted by his injured partner. He stared down at her in astonishment. "You."

"You," she muttered back.

He dropped to his heels in front of her, his eyes riveted to her face. Erica felt the color rise in her cheeks as she gazed at him, resenting his easy power and the way the television lights shimmered around him like a silver aura.

He shook his head. "You wasted time and resources tonight. Are you hurt?"

His concern caught her by surprise. "What?"

"Did I hurt you in the alley?"

"Ah. Yes!"

He rammed a hand through his hair. "Dammit, I thought Nemesis was a bunch of young college guys."

"No, we old alumni women take part too."

He gazed at her as if meeting her anew. "You don't look like the type."

She looked at him reproachfully. "*Frumpy* women, unite."

His expression hardened. "Be nice to me and I'll keep you out of jail."

"Forget it."

Police officers moved in then. James rose and stepped back, where Stephen Murray stood eyeing the group balefully, and her in particular.

"Have fun, y'all," Murray said in disgust. He turned and limped past James toward a limousine waiting on the street. "You need a lift back to the hotel, Jim?"

"In a second."

Burly policemen grabbed Erica's neighbors and dragged them away from her. "Passive resistance," T.K. yelled. Erica kept her solemn gaze directly on James Tall Wolf's frowning face.

"Get up, ma'am," an officer told her. Erica glanced around. Members of Nemesis were being forced to their feet.

"No."

"Ma'am, if you don't get up voluntarily I'll have to make you get up."

"Go ahead."

Thick fingers dug into the pressure point on one side of her neck. Sharp pain zigzagged down her back, and she squeezed her eyes shut.

Erica couldn't help biting her lip when the officer twisted her arm behind her and pushed upward. "No," she said raspily.

"Get up, ma'am." He began pulling her up by her twisted arm. The pain made her back arch, but she refused to give in.

Two new hands latched under her armpits and lifted her to her feet. "Stop it," James said in a low, growling tone.

Startled, she stared up into his eyes. "This is my fight."

"I'll handle this, sir," the officer interjected tautly. "Walk, ma'am."

"Don't do it, Ricky!" T.K. called.

Erica cried out without meaning to when the officer pinched her neck harder.

"Let her go," James said abruptly.

She gazed at him in astonishment. "Mr. Tall Wolf—"

"She's in custody," the officer warned him. He twisted her arm. "Walk."

"You're hurting her. That's not necessary."

The officer was angry now. "Back off, sir." He called over his shoulder. "Reece, gimme some help here!" Another officer trotted over. "Grab her legs."

Erica fumed helplessly as the two officers carried her to the van like a human hammock. She looked at James with a mixture of anger and gratitude. She wouldn't have been caught if it hadn't been for him and his superjock speed, but if anything could have made her cry just then, it would have been his unexpected concern.

And she was shocked when an officer pushed him but he refused to move. He stood with his fists clenched, his mouth a grim line, his dark eyes watching her until the door of the police van closed her away from his sight.

THE MEDIA LOVED the colorful, combative Nemesis Gang. Local television stations gave big coverage to the arrests on their early-morning newscasts. Erica only heard about them because she didn't get up until nine. She'd left the D.C. jail at four A.M.

Gritty-eyed, she drove to a residential site to meet with her carpentry crew. Then she called the office to check for messages.

"Call George Gibson," Marie said in a troubled tone. "He's upset about the Nemesis thing."

Erica waited until she got back to the office. Then, her mouth dry, she phoned the developer, one of the most prestigious in the D.C. area. Ten minutes later she walked into the spartan room that served as Marie's office and the company's reception area.

Erica sat down and stared numbly at the floor. "He withdrew the contract."

Marie groaned sympathetically. "Oh, Ricky, no."

"I was supposed to sign it tomorrow. Five hundred thousand dollars' worth of business down the drain. Two houses in the best new development in D.C." Erica swallowed hard. "We would have grossed over a million dollars this year."

"We'll do it next year, boss."

"Gibson detests Nemesis. Of course, he didn't know I was a member until he saw the newspaper this morning."

"And your response was—"

"Sorry you feel that way, Georgie. Go hire a builder who'll let you run her private life."

"Oh, boss, I'm proud of you."

"Work's going to be kind of sparse around here for a month or two."

"Why don't you take a vacation? You haven't had one in years. You've got a good office manager and a good construction foreman. The jobs we're working on now don't need your supervision."

Erica leaned back in the chair and shut her eyes. Idly she fiddled with the gold medallion hanging around her neck. For some reason she'd felt compelled to put Dove Gallatin's gift on a chain and wear it that morning.

Gallatins. Cherokees. James Tall Wolf. If it hadn't been for him she would have escaped last night. It was his fault she'd lost half a million dollars that day.

He'd said she didn't know anything about being a Cherokee. Well, she'd learn, and she'd be a better Cherokee than he was.

Erica stood up, filled with grim resolve. "Marie, get me a plane ticket to North Carolina."

"What's in North Carolina?"

Erica lifted the medallion and looked at it thoughtfully. "My tribe."

ERICA HADN'T HAD a clear-cut mental image of Dove Gallatin's house; she had even wondered if Dove had a house, because Dove's lawyer, T. Lucas Brown, hadn't mentioned a home or personal belongings in the will.

But here it was, perched halfway up a mountain in a little grove of oaks and maples, a small log-and-clapboard structure with a front porch so big that it looked like a jutting chin on an otherwise well-proportioned face.

She left her rental car under an enormous oak in the yard and walked around, eyeing the weedy ground for snakes. There was an old barn nearby, still in good condition; there was a concrete pad where a fuel-oil tank had once sat; there was an overgrown garden plot and a black mound, where decades of household trash had been burned.

The home's windows and doors were boarded over with new two-by-sixes; whoever had done the care-taking had wanted to make certain no one got inside.

But the place looked solid enough to withstand almost anything; and that fact alone made her like it immediately.

Erica discovered a small back porch with a concrete well in one corner. The well was boarded over, but an old electric pump was still in place atop it. Charmed, she studied it with an engineer's interest in quaint gadgets.

Then she returned to the big front porch and stood gazing in awe at a panorama of rounded blue-green mountains so vibrant that a painter might have just finished giving them their spring coat. Delicate white clouds hugged the tops of the taller ones, and low in the valleys a late-afternoon fog was already gathering.

Erica shivered with delight. She understood now why these were called the Smokies: Mists shrouded them as if preserving ancient secrets. These mountains were older than the Rockies, more gentle in their grandeur, more hospitable. And the Cherokees had loved them for hundreds, maybe thousands, of years.

She squinted at a hawk gliding overhead and took a deep breath of air so clean, it made her feel fresh inside. Yes, she understood why people would fight to stay there. A friendly meowing sound caught her ear, and she looked down to find a fat calico cat walking toward her across the porch.

"Hello, kitty." She knelt to pat it. "Are you a Cherokee elf in a cat's body?"

The distant crunch of wheels on gravel made her look up anxiously. Dove's driveway was nearly a quarter-mile long; it occurred to Erica that she was effectively trapped at the end of it.

She stood, watching closely as a police car rounded the last bend, then sighed with relief as she noted that the car belonged to the tribal authorities. She studied the tall man who climbed out, and a puzzling sense of recognition tugged at her.

Dressed in neat slacks and a short-sleeved shirt bearing official emblems, he might have been an officer from any small-town police force, except that he was Cherokee. Suddenly she understood. He looked like an older, more solemn version of James, full of the same controlled power and easy self-confidence.

Nodding to her, he strolled to the foot of the porch steps and stopped. "Ma'am, you lookin' for someone in particular?" he asked in a gravelly drawl.

Erica smiled. "Word travels fast around here."

He nodded again. "I heard at the motel that you'd asked about this place. And the neighbors called when they saw you go up the driveway."

She puzzled over that. "What neighbors? I didn't see another driveway near here."

"Boy was on his way back from a fishing trip. Saw you from the woods."

Erica's spine tingled. The forest suddenly seemed alive with watchful eyes. "I'm a relative of Dove Gallatin's. I just wanted to see her house. I thought I'd talk to the new owners, but I see that there aren't any."

"A relative of Dove's?" His voice showed his surprise.

Erica explained the family history, and as she did, his face took on a pleased expression. He really was a handsome man, and he reminded her more and more of James.

"So I've come down for about a week to learn about my Cherokee history," she said in conclusion. "And I'd like to know what became of Dove Gallatin's possessions—particularly anything that has to do with the family, such as diaries or a Bible."

The officer held out a hand. "Let me introduce myself. I'm the reservation's director of community services—fire, police, and sanitation. And I'm the U.S. deputy marshall around here. Name's Travis Tall Wolf."

Erica clenched his big paw so fiercely that he frowned at her in discomfort. "Do you have a brother named James?"

An odd wariness gleamed in his eyes. "Yes."

"I—well, I know him. We met a couple of days ago at a business dinner in Washington."

Travis Tall Wolf looked relieved. "Then he told you."

"Told me what?"

He stopped looking relieved. "About Dove."

"No." She paused, a sense of dread sinking in her stomach. *We almost ravished each other in an elevator, he tackled me in an alley, but we're strangers.*

"What about Dove?" she asked in an uneasy voice.

Travis looked at her grimly. "James owns her place. And everything she left in it."

JAMES KNEW THERE was trouble the second he heard his brother's voice on the phone. For one thing, Travis never called; he left that social nicety to their sisters. He and Travis hadn't had anything pleasant to say to each other in years.

Travis didn't beat around the bush. "Erica Gallatin has moved into Dove's house," he told James. "I helped her pry the boards off the front door and I got the power hooked up for her."

"What?" James sat speechless and listened to his brother's explanation. When Travis finished, James had almost conquered disbelief. Erica Gallatin was related to Dove. But what in hell was she trying to do about it? "She can't stay in Dove's house."

"Then you come down and make her leave. It's her and her cousins' place by tradition."

"It's my place by law."

"You're a white man now, huh? Always call in the law to settle your personal problems? Or will you just try to solve your problems with money, like always?"

James bit back harsh words. He grieved for the days when he and Travis had been best friends, before tragedy sent them on different missions in life.

Travis had been his idol. Travis could have played college football and probably pro, too, but he'd joined the marines right of high school and had been sent immediately to Vietnam.

Three years later, when James turned eighteen, he'd been determined to join the marines too. Then Travis had come home with a piece of shrapnel buried permanently in one leg, and Travis had vowed to punch him silly if he didn't go to college and play football.

"Be somebody important and make us proud," Travis had told him. "You'll do more for your people that way than I ever did."

James had become somebody important and for a few years he'd made the family and his tribe proud. They'd never know the price he had paid to do that.

Now Travis spoke softly, fiercely. "The old man wants to see you. Becky and Echo want to see you." He paused. "So do I. I don't know if this Gallatin woman is sincere or not, but if she gets you back home, she's worth the trouble."

James gave a humorless chuckle. That was the problem—she *was* worth the trouble. "I'm on my way."

ERICA LEFT THE motel in town and drove back to Dove's place early the next morning, armed with a crowbar, hand tools, and camping gear. She was in her element, wearing cut-off jeans, an old T-shirt, and ratty tennis shoes, her hair pulled up in a ponytail, and thick leather gloves covering her hands. She went to work on the boards barricading the windows, fueled by righteous anger.

How had James dared to buy this place out from under an old woman who needed money? How had he dared to try to put her in a nursing home against her will? The day before she was supposed to leave here. Dove Gallatin had walked into the woods, sat down under a tree, and died. Of grief, the staff at the motel said.

Erica wrenched another board free from its moorings and slammed it to the ground. Travis Tall Wolf hadn't told her the complete story, only that James had bought Dove's home and furnishings.

She walked around behind the house and began jamming the crowbar under the boards on a back window. She'd buy this place back. James Tall Wolf had a lot of explaining to do.

Erica flipped a set of Walkman earphones over her head, attached the tape player to the waistband of her cut-offs, and returned to work listening to the sound track from *Phantom of the Opera*.

The Phantom was singing his solo about revenge, when a hand grasped her arm.

Erica screamed and swung around with the crowbar raised in defense. James intercepted it with his free hand, jerked it out of her grip, and threw it into the weeds behind him.

"What do you think you're doing?" he shouted.

She gaped at him and stood there with her hand in midair. He looked tired and rumpled in loose khaki trousers and a wrinkled blue sport shirt; he must have traveled hard and fast to fly down this early and make the long drive from the nearest airport, at Asheville.

"I'm fixing up my family home," she said between gritted teeth. "I want to buy it from you."

His face was a mask of rigid control as he stared down at her through narrowed eyes that crinkled at the corners, not the least bit merrily.

Erica put the earphones around her neck and snapped off the tape player. The sounds of the spring day pushed eerily into the silence; katydids singing in the rhododendrons, birds chirping, her breath rasping like sandpaper on concrete.

"I said I want to buy this place."

"No."

"No one in town understands why you want it. Mr. Tall Wolf."

"That's none of their business."

"You took advantage of a woman who was almost ninety years old! My grandfather's cousin! I'm not sure what relationship that makes her to me, but Dove Gallatin was my family, just about the *only* family I have on the Gallatin side, and I intend to protect what was hers!''

During the tirade his gaze had gone to the thick gold medallion that lay near the center of her chest. He reached for it boldly, the backs of his fingers brushing across her breasts as he lifted the medallion for inspection.

Erica shivered with anger and frustration over the intimate way he always invaded her personal space. ''That's none of *your* business,'' she told him, and took the medallion out of his hand.

She slipped it under the neck of her T-shirt and frowned at the way his eyes followed its journey.

''Where'd you get it?'' he demanded.

''From Dove. And I want to know what it means. What did you do with her belongings? If she left any personal papers, I want them.''

He smiled sardonically. ''They wouldn't do you any good without an interpreter. Dove only wrote in Cherokee.''

''There *are* papers, then. Where are they?''

''In storage.''

''What did you do with her furniture?''

''I didn't do anything with it,'' he retorted. ''Dove gave most of it away; what she left is in storage too.''

Erica made a sharp gesture at the house and land. ''Why would a man like you want a place like this? Did you con her out of—''

He cut her off with a brow lifted in warning and a look that could have started a fire. ''I never conned her out of anything. We made an honest deal, and I paid her more than the place was worth. I plan to live here someday.''

''You're kidding. Your brother said you haven't been home in four years. And not very often before that.''

His voice never rose, but it became more commanding. ''This land means something to me, more than it will ever mean to you.''

''I'm not the only Gallatin who may want it.'' She

told him about Tess and Kat. "Kat's practically full-blooded, and Tess is half. They look like Cherokees. You wouldn't deny them their heritage."

He turned away, shaking his head, his hands propped jauntily on his hips. "Sounds like they don't know any more about the tribe than you do."

"We can learn."

"It doesn't work that way. You have to live it. You have to grow up with it. You have to see the contrasts between the Cherokee and the white world."

"This is a heritage I'm proud of! Why do you want to keep me away from it? How am I hurting you?"

He swiveled toward her, his eyes glittering with anger. "You want to play at being a Cherokee. The glamour'll wear off as soon as you see that life's not quaint or easy here. You won't fit in."

*You won't fit in.* How many times she'd heard those words in her life. And they always hurt.

Erica went to the back porch and sank down on a step. She propped her arms on her knees and, blinking hard, tried to focus her anger on a solitary clump of grass between her feet.

"I've always been an outsider—in my mother's family after she remarried, in the construction business because I'm a woman, in social situations because I'm too tall, I'm too plain, I'm too aggressive. I don't expect to fit in."

She glanced up as he came to the porch and sat on the step between her feet. Erica leaned back from the sudden closeness when he propped one hand beside her hip. He rested the other hand on his updrawn knee.

He'd lost a lot of his anger, for some reason she couldn't fathom.

"You're sincere," he said gruffly. "And don't ever think I don't admire that."

"Ah." She looked away from the searing scrutiny of his eyes, feeling awkward.

"But you're naïve. I've seen it before. It'll wear off quickly."

"What makes you so sure?"

"I've brought outsiders to visit the reservation. They never wanted to stay."

She propped her chin on one hand and tried to look casual. "Women, huh?"

"Yeah."

"Well, I'm not one of your lady friends, and you didn't bring me. I came on my own. So don't write me off so soon."

She stared at him. "I heard that Dove Gallatin walked out into the woods and willed herself to die because she didn't want to go to a nursing home."

Slowly, he nodded. "She did. She had a way about her. The old people said she had powers."

"Did you . . . what part did you play in the nursing-home thing?"

He frowned. "What do you mean?"

Erica took a deep breath. "I heard that you had something to do with making her go."

His voice was bitter. "Like maybe I conned her out of her place so she had nowhere else?"

Erica nodded.

"Will you believe me or believe people in town?"

"I don't know. You're almost as much of a stranger as they are." She paused. "I want to believe you. I'll try."

He rubbed his forehead in mild exasperation. "I bought this place years ago because she needed money and she wouldn't take a gift. She had to pay back taxes on some piece of land she owned in Georgia, and she was desperate."

Erica wanted to cry. Gallatin land, in Gold Ridge. Oh, Dove. Oh, Wolfman. He'd saved the land from being sold for taxes. She owed him the truth about it. "It's mine now," she murmured sheepishly. "Mine and my cousins'. Dove left it to us."

James gazed at her with an expression of astonishment that quickly turned into a grim smile. "She gave up everything to save that land for you. Why don't you go stay there?"

"My cousins and I will reimburse you for the taxes."

"I bought this place. Dove paid the taxes."

"But—"

"This place is mine, and I'm not giving it to a bunch of five-dollar Indians."

"What?"

"People who get themselves on the tribal roll just to collect benefits."

Erica wanted to scream. "I feel like slapping you for that, but from what I've heard you'd slap me back."

He raised a finger and pointed at her with slow, furious emphasis. "When I was growing up my only goal in life was to be a famous football player, so that my people would be proud of me. I did what I had to do to make that happen.

"I did and said a lot of stupid, humiliating things when I was taking steroids, but I was willing to pay that price. Football's a tough game. I got punished and I punished back. But I never hurt anybody off the football field and I never hit a woman in my whole life."

She had watched his eyes as he talked, and the brutal honesty in them was obvious. Erica hung her head, embarrassed by her accusation. "I'm sorry if I misjudged you."

When she looked up, his blank expression told her that her apology had surprised him. "When I'm wrong I say I'm wrong," she muttered.

His jaw was tight, his gaze thoughtful. A little disconcerted, he fiddled with a blade of grass at his feet. "I intended to let Dove live here as long as she wanted. But finally I did talk her into moving to the nursing home. She had arthritis so bad that she could barely walk. She was half blind. She couldn't stay up here alone any longer."

"But didn't she have family—"

James's expression went grim again. "Obviously not," he muttered, and rose to his feet.

Erica looked up at his ominous expression, the

straight black brows pulled together, the clean-cut angles of his face looking majestic even in anger.

"If we had known," she murmured, "if Tess and Kat and I had known about Dove, we would have come to see her. We would have tried to help."

"But you didn't know because you never cared to find out. I don't really blame you for that. Just don't come up here now and try to take over. It's too late."

He headed toward the front of the house with a long, swinging stride, and Erica trotted after him. "I don't want to take over."

"You can't have the place," he said over his shoulder. "What were you going to do—stay here a week or so and then board it back up when you leave for Washington?"

He grabbed a hammer and a plank. "If you've got anything inside, go get it. I'm closing the place up again."

Erica stepped in front of him, fury scorching her skin, her hands clenched by her sides. "I'll go to the tribal council or the Bureau of Indian Affairs or wherever I have to go, and I'll get myself listed on the tribal roll."

He started at her in dismay. "So you have checked out the system."

"Yeah. I guess that makes me a five-dollar Indian, all right. I found out that anyone who's at least one-sixteenth Cherokee can ask for land on the reservation. The council has to approve all transactions, and I'm going to ask it to take a second look at the way you bought Gallatin land. You're not very well liked around here, so I suspect I can at least get a hearing on my predicament."

"They may think I'm an arrogant bastard, but they won't like an outsider either."

"From what I've heard everyone worshiped Dove Gallatin, and they'll treat any of her relatives with respect."

His silent, frustrated glare told her she'd hit pay dirt. Erica thought about the half-million-dollar contract back in D.C., and smiled. She'd won a measure of revenge.

His voice vibrated with control. "What exactly do you want to do on your little vacation in Injun land?"

"Visit. Go into town and talk to people. Read books about the tribe."

"For how long?"

"I don't know. For once in my life, I'm not going to set a schedule." She eyed him regally. "What about those personal papers of Dove's? How can I get them?"

A dangerous gleam came into his eyes. A slow smile slid across his mouth. "There's only one way you'll ever get those."

Erica's regal confidence faltered. "How?"

"Never say 'How' to an Indian. Oh, excuse me, you *are* an Indian, I forgot. You'll have to prove it."

"How—I mean, in what way?"

He walked to the edge of the yard, his head down in thought, his hands shoved into his pants pockets. After a few seconds he turned around and said loudly, "You have to stay here for two months. At the end of two months I'll hand over all of Dove's papers, and I'll even find someone who reads Cherokee well enough to interpret them for you. And if you still want this place, I'll give it to you."

Erica leaned against a porch support and crossed her arms, not loosely, but with the hands clamped on the elbows to form a stubborn shield. Anyone who knew her well would have recognized the gesture as evidence of desperate inner turmoil. Thankfully, James Tall Wolf didn't know her well.

"Don't get upset," he called. "It's a simple offer."

She almost groaned. How could he be so stern and so insightful at the same time? "Two months? I have a business to run."

"If you could leave it to come down here, you must have a trustworthy foreman. I know the construction business. You don't have to stay on site if you've got a good straw boss."

Erica paced, her hands clasped behind her back.

"Can I fly home for a day or two at a time, if I need to?"

He nodded. "All right, but you live here. This is home. And you'll learn what I tell you to learn."

She halted suddenly. "You're staying on the reservation?"

"For a while."

"You just want to make this difficult for me."

"Yeah."

Erica's shoulders slumped. "Do you disapprove of me that much?"

He didn't answer; he seemed to be struggling for something polite to say. "That's not the point. Because if you make it through two months here, you'll still go back to D.C. It won't matter how I feel about you."

*It matters to me*, she thought sadly. But she'd be sensible and accept the fact that he only thought of her as misguided and aggravating. Erica made a grim correction. When he felt the urge to prove his seduction skills in an elevator, he also thought of her as a lonely, willing old maid.

Well, there were no elevators here. There weren't even any buildings over two stories tall, from what she'd seen thus far, so she'd be safe, she thought drolly. Somehow, that didn't make her happy.

"I'll take you up on your deal," she called. "And I'll win."

He answered with a wolfish smile.

NO ONE HAD warned her that peace and quiet could be so unnerving. Erica sat on her sleeping bag in the middle of Dove's bedroom floor, a tuna-salad sandwich laying uneaten in her lap, her head tilted toward the window screen. Actually there were night sounds—the rustling of tree limbs, the poignant calls of whippoorwills, a chorus of tree frogs.

But she'd been raised in cities, weaned on the unceasing hubbub that formed the background drone of urban life, and there in the mountains the night noises weren't sounds so much as a form of mysterious silence. They weren't human.

And the darkness beyond the window screen was deeper than any city darkness. She understood now why ancient peoples had created all sorts of myths about the night world.

Shivering, Erica squinted at the bare light bulb in an old fixture on the ceiling. More lights, that was what she needed. The next day she'd put up flood lamps outside. Just let the creepies try to get past a two-hundred-watt bulb. She got up and went to fetch the book she'd brought with her, the latest Stephen King novel.

She loved thrillers and suspense novels—they were such fun when read in the cozy confines of her condo bedroom. Suddenly she froze. On second thought, reading Stephen King might not be a good idea that night.

Something very real was growling outside the bedroom window.


JAMES HAD BORROWED his grandfather's truck, and the high-set headlights cast a bright arc of light on Dove's narrow, graveled driveway. They caught the two boys full in the eyes.

The pair, dressed in shorts and dark T-shirts, bolted into the woods that bordered the road. James cursed grimly and floored the accelerator. This was what he'd suspected.

Dove's house was dark, a mere outline against black woods. James leaped onto the porch and pounded on the door with his fist. Quick-running feet crossed the creaking porch as he whipped around, searching the darkness.

He heard an ominous whirring sound just as something sharp jabbed him in the arm. Pain and surprise made him react with automatic reflexes honed by years of competitive sports. He swung powerfully and cuffed the attacker with the heel of his hand. The boy was tall, and the blow hit him in the temple.

With a soft yelp the youngster crashed against the side of the house and slid into a heap at James's feet. The whirring sound stopped.

"Sorry, kid," James muttered anxiously, bending over. "But your game's pretty damned reckless." He latched his hands onto slender shoulders and felt his way up. Horror ran through him when his fingers curled into wavy, shoulder-length hair.

Oh, no. A tall kid. Not again.

She-Who-Makes-Noise was frighteningly silent.

L AND OF THE Giants, that was what this was. Maybe
she was just woozy from being thumped in the
head, but for the first time in her life, Erica didn't feel
too big.

She estimated that Echo Tall Wolf was six two and
Becky Tall Wolf, the puny one of the family, was
maybe five ten. Grandpa Sam Tall Wolf was nearly as
tall as James, which meant about six five. Becky,
Echo, and Grandpa Sam looked majestic even in terry-
cloth robes.

Erica smiled groggily. Robes were the attire many
tall people favored when forced out of bed at this time
of night.

James kept one hand on her forearm and one between her shoulder blades as he guided her into a
rustic den with a decor somewhere between a middle-
class family room and a Cherokee museum. He sat Erica down on an overstuffed sofa and covered her in a
colorful quilt as she squinted around at Indian paint-

ings, woven rugs, a big stone fireplace, and lots of homey clutter.

"She needs some fresh ice," James said. He took the washcloth she held against her temple and dabbed her face with it.

Eric barely noticed the soreness radiating through the spot beside her right eye. No matter what she thought of James most of the time, that night he'd been utterly wonderful—except for knocking her in the head, of course, but she couldn't blame him for that.

She glanced at the angry bruise below the sleeve of his white golf shirt.

"I'm sorry I drilled you," she murmured again. "It was the only weapon I had."

"It's sort of funny. How many women are skilled in hand-to-drill combat?"

"I have to hear this story, but right now I'll get the ice," Becky Tall Wolf said in a soft, musical voice, and left the room.

"James, she needs to be checked by a doctor," Echo Tall Wolf scolded, trading a sympathetic gaze with Erica. Beautiful and majestic, with rump-length hair and a magnificent figure that had to be size sixteen at least, Echo knelt in front of Erica and held up a hand. "How many fingers?"

"Two. And three left over."

Grandpa Tall Wolf chortled. "She's all right."

Erica nodded, feeling uncomfortable under all the scrutiny. "James didn't knock me out. I just couldn't find my eyeballs for a minute."

James rubbed his own face with the washcloth. "I was more upset after it happened than she was."

Erica nodded, and patted his arm gently. "I haven't been carried so many places since I was in diapers. I hope he didn't get a hernia."

Becky came back with a cup of ice. Curvaceous, graceful, her ink-black hair cut in short, feathery layers, Becky looked like a modern earth mother.

Erica watched silently as James held the washcloth

for Becky and Echo to arrange ice in it. "You guys make a great team. If first aid becomes an Olympic sport, you'll take the gold."

The women laughed, and even James smiled. "If there were more of us, we'd start a basketball squad."

He wrapped the ice into a tight bundle. "Lie down, and I'll hold this in place for you."

Grandpa Sam tossed James a pillow from the recliner across the room. James put it next to his leg while Erica gingerly stretched out on her side. She put her head on the pillow and decided that an injured woman couldn't be called a flirt even though the top of her head was mashed cozily against a man's thigh.

So she enjoyed herself thoroughly each time his thick, ropey muscles flexed against her head. Who would have thought that a scalp could be an erogenous zone?

Gently James placed the ice pack on her temple and let his hand rest against her hair. "How's that, Red?"

"Fine." Fantastic. "This is the first time I've stretched out on a couch where my feet didn't hang off the end."

"James built this couch when he was in high school," Echo told her. "He did everything, even the upholstery."

"I build furniture. It's a hobby," James said with a touch of embarrassment.

*He's a builder, like me,* Erica thought happily.

"It was an anniversary gift to our parents," Becky noted.

"Where do your parents live now?"

"They were killed in a car accident a few years ago," James answered in a guarded tone. After a second he added, "Travis's wife and Echo's husband were killed in the same wreck."

Erica winced and raised her head. Echo and Becky sat on the floor, which was carpeted in well-worn deep shag, a pretty fawn color complementing their skin tone. Grandpa Sam sat in the recliner, an unlit pipe in his big, gnarled hands. He had luxurious white hair that hung below his shoulders, and his weathered, craggy face made Erica think of a nice old walnut tree.

His and his granddaughters' expressions were somber, touched by memories that would always be with them.

"I'm sorry about your loss," Erica said softly. She couldn't turn her head to see James, but she felt his fingers brush her cheek in gratitude.

"Be still. Let your brain settle."

She rested her head on the pillow again. "Does Travis live near here?"

"He has a trailer in the woods a few miles off," Becky said. "He's building a house beside it."

"Ummmph," Grandpa Sam offered with disdain. "Some year."

He added more comments in a long string of undecipherable sounds, although he kept repeating Travis's name in a way that said Travis was a source of concern in the family. Erica tingled with excitement as she realized Grandpa Sam was speaking Cherokee.

James answered him in the same language. It was the most intriguing thing Erica had ever heard, full of long vowels and round tones, with emphatic pauses. It came from the back of the throat, and the few consonants she noticed were only languid hints of their English counterparts.

When he finished everyone was silent for a moment, and she sensed old disagreements in the air, "No more," James said.

"We're not trying to shut you out, Erica," Echo added quickly. "We don't usually speak Cherokee in front of guests. I apologize."

Erica waved a hand excitedly. "I love the language. I want to learn it. Would it be difficult?"

"Try this," James offered. *"Gah yo, le sa lon Cha-lag-gee."*

*"Gah yo, le sa lon Cha-lag-gee."*

"There. You said, 'I speak Cherokee a little.' "

She repeated the sentence several times, smiling.

"Good," Becky told her. "Now you're fluent in one

sentence. The rest is easy. Now say, *Do yu nay ga je nah we.*"

Erica dutifully repeated the words. "What's that?"

"I am of white origin."

"Ah. No. My great-great-grandmother was Chero-kee. Katherine Gallatin."

"Don't argue with this woman," James warned his sister. "She packs a mean drill."

That sparked new curiosity. Nothing would satisfy James's family until he recounted the night's lunacy in detail. Then they wanted to know about Erica's Cherokee history, and why she'd decided to visit the reservation. She carefully omitted any mention of her bargain with James.

"James can bring you to the museum tomorrow if you want to buy some books about the tribe," Echo told her. "I teach elementary school, but during the summer I work at the museum store. I'll pick out some good texts for you."

"And when I have time I'll take you to rent some furniture for Dove's house," Becky added. "I run a restaurant on the tourist strip, but I've got a couple of free hours after the lunch rush."

Erica tried to smile her thanks at the Tall Wolf sisters, but couldn't move her head enough without disturbing James's touch. She wanted to lie there forever, her head against his leg, feeling his hand gently rub the ice pack over her temple. The thick, callused pad of his thumb kept brushing her cheekbone.

Of course he was just being polite because he felt guilty for whacking her, but she wouldn't quibble over that. She nudged his leg. "Do you really think that those boys didn't mean any harm?"

"No, not the way they were running from a drill-carrying mountain witch. They weren't exactly tough punks."

"Aw, of course not," Sam added.

"Dove's house is supposed to be haunted," James explained. "Going up there to pester you was an act of courage."

"Uhmmm. Like counting coup in battle?"

"I don't know if Cherokees ever did much coup counting," James answered wryly. "We didn't fight very often after about 1800—not against the whites, at any rate. We did help Andrew Jackson beat the Creek Indians during the War of 1812."

"And see how little good it did us?" Sam said in consternation, as if he'd been there. "Jackson got elected President, and he kicked us off our land! We shoulda helped fight him."

Erica's thoughts were still tuned to her unwelcome visitors. "Did those boys want to scare me because I'm white?"

"Could be," James murmured. "Most of the tribe are mixed-bloods. They're friendlier to tourist types than the full-bloods, as a rule. There's a conservative element that doesn't want much to do with the outside world. Dove's house is in a conservative community."

*Tourist type.* Erica was disappointed James had classified her that way, even though his arrogance shouldn't have surprised her. She phrased her words carefully. "Does the Tall Wolf family fit the conservative description?"

"Moderate," Becky answered. "We want to preserve the old ways and benefit from the new."

"We welcome anybody who wants to fit in," Echo assured her.

Erica smiled. Take that, James. "I'm glad."

"We'll see," he announced grimly. "Time for bed." He got up and held out a hand. "Come on. I'll put you in my old room. The gals and I'll take turns checking on you to make sure you're all right."

"I'm fine," she insisted. She tried to take his hand, but found herself being hoisted into his arms again. He made the effort so nonchalantly that she felt almost little. It was a wonderful discovery.

"Good night. And thank you," she told the others hurriedly as James carried her out of the room. They looked a little shocked by his actions, and she wondered if he'd done something that was unusual for him.

He climbed a short set of stairs and moved sideways down the second-story hall so that her feet wouldn't bump knickknacks and family portraits on the wall. Erica glanced around curiously. Seams showed on the pale green wallpaper, and the carpet had a foot trail in the center, but the ambiance was homey rather than shabby.

"Good floors. Solid construction. Careful attention to detail," she observed.

"Thank you, carpenter ant."

She almost grinned at him. "The spirit is friendly. Where I grew up in Boston, the housekeeper yelled at us all the time."

"My mother never yelled. She just roped off rooms and threatened to set them on fire if we didn't clean up. My father called it slash-and-burn housekeeping. But it worked. When I got my first pro contract I gave them the money to build a new house, but they wanted to keep this one."

He carried her into a small room crammed with storage boxes. James worked his way along a cleared path to a bed that was twin-sized in width but giant-sized in length. "You made this bed frame," she said matter-of-factly.

"Yep. The mattress isn't as long as the frame, so the end is stuffed with pillows."

He put her down on a thin red blanket with a geometric eagle design woven into it. Erica glanced around at walls covered with high-school and college football memorabilia. He cleared his throat awkwardly.

"My parents kept it like a shrine."

"They must have been proud."

"Yeah. There were a lot of things I wanted to give them in return, if they'd lived."

She looked at him in quiet sympathy. He frowned, and gestured toward the long, slender legs sticking out of her cut-offs. "Get rid of those."

Erica chuckled nervously. "My legs?"

"Those shorts. Wear jeans or skirts. You don't want to look like a show-off. The old folks will approve of you quicker if you're a little on the prim side."

"No one has ever accused me of flaunting these knobby knees. And I've always been on the prim side."

"Not in those shorts," he insisted.

She stared at him in bewilderment, and finally decided that her legs were such bean poles that the sight bothered him. "James, in town I saw plenty of homely tourists in short-shorts and halter tops. If nobody is offended by them, they won't give a second glance to my legs in respectable cut-offs."

"If you want to be a tourist, go ahead," he retorted, his face stern. "If you want to get your hands on Dove's papers, do what I tell you to do."

Her friendly thoughts about him faded in a burst of aggravation.

BY THE END of the next day Erica had furniture— funky, lime-green furniture rented from Trader Tom's Motor Lodge. Because Dove's two bedrooms were tiny, Erica put the queen-size bed and the dresser in the living room, along with a couch. She decided wryly that the arrangement looked like a low-rent bordello.

The kitchen now sported a table and four green chairs, plus mix-matched dishes and cookware loaned by the Tall Wolf sisters. The old cupboards were stocked, and a small bookcase in the living room/bedroom held a dozen texts Erica had purchased at the reservation museum.

It was home—at least for now—and she felt content. After she ate dinner Erica donned her cut-offs over a black bathing suit and watched the sunset from a rocking chair also loaned by the Tall Wolf household.

That night she lay in bed reading *Myths and Sacred*

*Formulas of the Cherokees* by the light of a lamp on a lime-green nightstand. There were formulas for everything from doctoring to romance.

Erica found one called "To Fix The Affections" and smiled thoughtfully. Well, what the heck.

"Now the souls have met, never to part. His eyes have come to fasten themselves on one alone. Whither can his soul escape? Let him be sorrowing as he goes along, and not for one night alone."

Erica paused. Good. Perpetual sorrowing on her behalf. "Let him become an aimless wanderer, whose trail may never be followed.

Take *that*, James, she added.

She suddenly felt very free from worry, and in celebration she stripped naked. Erica stretched out on top of the blanket, loving the brisk spring air on her body. She turned out the light and began to doze, lulled by the big new flood lamps she'd installed on each corner of the house. Through an open window she heard the forest moving in the night wind, the trees whispering secrets she badly wanted to learn.

Her last thoughts before sleep were happy. *An aimless wanderer . . . sorrowing as he goes along.*

The next thing she heard was the click of the lamp and a low, masculine groan of dismay.

J AMES THOUGHT LATER that it was like finding an unexpected gift without the gift wrapping.

In the second before Erica gasped and scrambled to the other side of the bed, pulling the blanket up to her chest, he glimpsed a long, svelte torso with beautiful breasts and a taut stomach just made for a man's lips.

He groaned because that kind of temptation was the last thing he needed. Seeing her in shorts and a T-shirt the day before had convinced James that "skinny" was a description he'd never use again. She was a tall, coltish woman, but her angles were soft, and his senses went into high gear whenever he imagined how her body would feel under his.

"What are you trying to do?" she yelled, her eyes like green ice. "Do you want to be drilled in a spot that really hurts?"

No. Particularly not at the moment, he thought.

James sighed and backed away from the bed, his hands up. "I knocked. You didn't wake up. I have a key to the front door. I didn't expect you to be in the living room naked.''

''What are you doing here?''

He nodded grimly toward a heavy leather tote bag on the floor. Then he caught her gaze and held it. ''Moving in.''

Her eyes widened, and she looked like a wild mare about to paw the ground. Lord, he'd liked to have been the man who gentled her to ride.

''Why do you want to stay here?'' she demanded.

''One, I own the place. Two, there's an extra bedroom.'' He looked around drolly. ''Two extra bedrooms, apparently. Three, I hate motels.''

''You have a bedroom with nifty football pennants on the wall and a rock collection glued to the windowsill. Yes, I lifted the curtain and noticed. Why don't you stay with your rocks?''

James wasn't about to explain how much it hurt to visit a home filled with photographs of his parents, Echo's husband, and Travis's wife. He wasn't going to explain that he wanted to cry when he overheard Grandpa Sam solemnly reading the newspaper aloud to them, so they wouldn't miss out on tribal happenings.

And he wasn't going to tell her that the day's fishing trip with Travis had been a bitter fiasco of grief and anger that had ended with Travis telling him quietly that they were no longer brothers.

''I'm moving in,'' he repeated fiercely. ''I won't bother you, so don't sit there like a spinster-on-the-half-shell, looking as if you're afraid I might take a bite.''

He tracked the rise of fury in her fair complexion. With her face flushed and her hair tangled like a chestnut mane she looked not only wild, but violent.

''I'm not afraid. I know what to do and how to do it right,'' she said in a seething tone. ''I know where to put what and what happens if I put it there.''

''Now if you could only get somebody to put it there for you.''

She twisted the blanket in one fist and pounded the bed with the other, all control gone. "I was married for eight years! It's not my fault that I'm a virgin!"

They stared at each other in shock, she looking as surprised as he felt. Then her head drooped, and she covered her face with one hand.

"I'm joking. What a dumb joke. You didn't even smile."

"You're not joking. Too late for a recall."

James looked for a place to sit down. All this time when he'd teased her about her attitudes he'd never dreamed she was a virgin. He'd never encountered a virgin before, much less one over thirty.

He went to the ugliest green couch he'd ever seen, sat on the edge of a cushion, and waited until Erica lifted a troubled gaze to his.

He watched her shiver visibly.

"I should have gone into journalism." She moaned. "I know how to broadcast news without thinking first. Congratulations. You're the only stranger I've ever told my sexual history to."

"Well, Erica Alice," he said numbly. "Well."

She shook her head in defeat. "When I tell people I'm an old maid, they believe I'm kidding. I'm not. There. Think what you want."

"Doll, you've gotta explain how you could be married for eight years and still qualify for volcano sacrifices."

"Catch my story on *Oprah Winfrey* next week. The 'Oddities of Nature' show."

"Look, we're going to be housemates. I'm not a stranger. And I'm great at keeping secrets."

"We're not going to live in this house together. If this community is so traditional and conservative, what will people say?"

He arched one brow. "Relax. If they say anything at all, they'll blame the big bad wolf for corrupting you. You'll get sympathy."

"Why didn't you tell me up front that you intended to stay here?"

James pretended to study his watch. "Can we discuss this tomorrow? I can't wait to get a good night's sleep on this comfortable couch."

Her voice was ragged. "This is just another way to antagonize me into leaving. Dammit, you're really cruel."

James stood ominously. "If I were cruel I'd lock your butt out of my house and say to hell with the consequences."

"You wouldn't like the consequences, I promise."

The day's frustration and fatigue boiled over. James strode to the bed, snatched the blanket with both hands, and jerked it away from her. She backed off the bed like a cornered animal, hugging her arms over her breasts.

"Out," he commanded, and pointed toward the front door. He figured he'd let her sit on the porch for five minutes, then toss her the blanket and apologize.

She gaped at him as if he'd lost his mind. *"No!"*

"You want me to carry you out?"

She heard the determination in his voice and edged warily toward the short hallway that went to the kitchen and bedrooms. "Let me get my things," she said between gritted teeth. "And I'll go to a motel."

"No." He waved a hand at her nakedness. "You want to be a native, then go outside like a native."

"You're despicable!"

He smiled with malevolent pleasure. "I don't use my seat belt. I drop cigar ashes in houseplants, and I thought *E.T.* was a so-so movie." He pointed. "Out."

She had nothing left but dignity, and she used it. His heart twisted with admiration and self-rebuke as she straightened imperiously, lowered her arms, and walked past him to the door.

He caught the unadorned, squeaky-clean scent of her hair and skin. He saw the pride outlined in every inch of her backbone, though muscles quivered around it. She had to know that he was looking at everything below her backbone, too, but he suspected that she didn't know how perfect that part of her was.

She didn't have much padding, but it had found the right places.

Without looking back she slung the door open. James cursed under his breath. "Forget it," he said gruffly. "It was a dumb joke. I'm entitled to one myself."

She paused for a moment, glanced over her shoulder, and said with icy disdain, "I'm going to prove something to you. I may be an old maid, but I'm a hell of a tough old maid, and I don't need your patronage."

Then she stepped onto the porch and slammed the door behind her.

James followed her to the porch. She descended the steps and walked across the yard, looking incredibly majestic even in the harsh lights of the flood lamps. His mouth opened in dismay. How the hell could a man deal with a woman like her?

James watched in disbelief as she strolled into the darkness. "You'll get bitten by gnats, and the nights are cool up here even in the summertime," he called.

"Cold gnats are preferable to staying in the same house with you," she called back.

Then he heard only the silence of the night; it had captured her, taking her away for who knew what purposes. He'd either have to go after her and drag her back, strip naked and go sit with her, or let her suffer nobly.

He didn't think she'd appreciate any of the options.

James paced the porch, unwillingly thinking about *Utluhtu*, the spear-fingered monster who haunted the forests, stealing people's livers; and *Uktena*, a giant, dragonlike creature so dangerous that just looking at it could be fatal.

He chuckled harshly. And those two were just the tip of the arrow, where Cherokee monsters and evil spirits were concerned. No matter how modern and questioning and cynical he became, a part of him would never forget the stories he'd learned as a boy.

And Erica was out there thinking gnats would be her worst problem.

When he heard her scream he flung himself off the porch and hit the yard at a dead run. James pushed blindly into the woods, his shoulders scraping against the dark shadows of trees, feeling thorny vines tear at his jeans and golf shirt.

He heard a commotion that sounded like devils with giant wings trying to escape from the trees. Ahead of him in faint starlight he saw the ground drop away in a deep gully. The top of a small pine tree showed over the rim, and the branches were swaying wildly.

Erica screamed from somewhere in the gully.

James dived over the rim and landed hard on the exposed roots of a nearby oak. He flung out a hand and caught Erica's arm. She was huddled on the gully floor, and when he grabbed her she jumped like a rabbit.

Then she hit him across the stomach with a tree limb the size of a baseball bat.

He groaned. "Thanks."

"James!"

"No kidding."

He pushed her onto her side and curled around her spoon-style, one arm protectively flung across her head. They lay there panting and listened to the unknown terror in the pine tree.

Finally it got free of the limbs, emitted a ridiculous gobbling sound, and flew away on ponderous wings. James groaned again, this time in disgust.

"A damned turkey."

"A bird?" Erica asked in an apologetic tone.

The adrenaline surge ended, and pain rushed through James's bad knee. He bit his lip and rolled onto his back, then drew the knee up gingerly and described turkeys in terms that had nothing to do with Thanksgiving. He got to his feet and threw his shirt to her. "Follow me back to the damned house and don't give me any more grief."

He started climbing the gully wall, his movements

slow and painful. He had to stop halfway up the gully to catch his breath.

Erica chuckled fiendishly. "I think I'm going to enjoy this."

"RED! BRING ME a glass of water!"

"In a minute."

"Now."

"When I finish this chapter."

Sitting at the kitchen table, Erica lifted her gaze from a history book and smiled. For three days it had been that way—James in bed, bawling orders, her in the kitchen, ignoring them as long as possible.

She heard furious rustling in the living room, then uneven clumping. Alarmed, Erica put the book down and looked toward the kitchen door. James appeared in its whitewashed frame, his swollen knee half-bent, his hair disheveled, his eyes black with aggravation.

And he was naked.

Erica felt the pulse throb in her neck. She folded her hands in her lap to hide their trembling and said calmly. "Nice crutch."

He emphasized each word slowly. "From now on, every time you ignore me I'm going to get up, find you, and wave this thing until I get attention."

"You think I'm so mousey that I'll faint? Just because I've never had personal contact with one of those doesn't mean it terrifies me. It's just another part of the male body."

Her stomach shrank under his evil, slit-eyed smile. "Oh? Then you won't mind if it moves closer."

He hobbled toward her with a great deal more menace than she'd expected. Erica jumped up and sidled around the table, using it as a barricade.

To her chagrin, he began to laugh. He braced both hands on the tabletop and chortled heartily, his deep-set eyes squeezed almost shut, his teeth flashing white in an uninhibited show of victory.

Erica walked to the battered old metal sink, picked

up a big glass from the drain rack, and filled it with water. She held her hand under the faucet for a moment. Mmmm, well water was so wonderfully cold. She turned gracefully, her chin up, and tossed the whole glass on him.

He jumped, knocked his bad knee on the table edge, and shot her a look of pain and exasperated shock. Water dripped from his eyebrows and nose; rivulets of water ran down the center of his sleek chest in a southward journey that ended in hair even blacker than that on his head.

To her amazement, the anger faded from his eyes. He sighed and shook his head. "This would have been a hell of a lot simpler two hundred years ago. I could have just kidnapped you."

They gazed at each other while golden afternoon sunshine poured through a tiny window over the sink. It cascaded onto the table between them as if marking a common ground for friendship.

Erica was amazed at herself. She was calmly grinning at the most enticing man in the world, he was stark naked, and he was grinning back at her. Her life had certainly gotten more interesting in the course of one week.

"What are those marks on your chest?" she asked.

He glanced down. "Under my pecs?"

Somehow she hadn't expected to get this detailed. Erica thought he made "pecs" sound very sensual. "Under them, yes."

"Stretch marks. You get 'em from taking steroids. The steroids make your muscles grow faster than normal when you lift weights, and the skin can't take the stress." He paused, looking troubled. "In college we were proud of them."

"You can be proud of them now," she assured him gently. "Because you went through a lot of hell to do what you thought was right."

There was a vigorous change in attitude low on James's body. She couldn't help staring. Really, it was impossible not to. Erica's legs went weak, while a languid heat made her belly feel hollow and ready to be filled.

Would his body have reacted to any woman who stared at him? Erica shoved that worry aside.

James glanced down at himself and murmured distractedly, "Looks like I've got my own *Uktena*." Then he was silent, studying her reaction.

She whimpered silently as heat scorched the skin below her navel and moved higher, tightening her breasts until they ached, then finally warming her face with passion. Erica turned toward the sink and fumbled with some dishes there.

"Sorry about this," he said softly.

"I'm not embarrassed. I'm a normal woman with a normal reaction to a man in your . . . condition."

"I understand that. I'm just sorry, that's all."

She glanced back at him. He was scowling—if not at her, precisely, then in her general direction. He pursed his lips as if thinking, then turned and quickly limped out of the room.

"Would you mind bringing me some water when you get a chance, Red?"

"No problem."

"Thanks, doll."

Erica slumped in a chair and put her head in her hands. He didn't want her, even when she couldn't hide the fact that she was ready, able, and extremely willing.

Erica wiped tears from her eyes. "Water," she said in a ragged, angry whisper. "There's your water, Mr. Tall Wolf."


WRAPPED IN A thin blanket, she sat cross-legged on the foot of the bed and listened to James tell stories. The bedside lamp cast cozy light on him, softening the planes of his face and making his hair look like polished onyx. He kept the bedcovers pulled up to his chest, which told her that he was politely avoiding another scene like that afternoon's.

Erica sighed. He had a lot of kindness in him, and that made her want him even more.

Beyond the living room windows owls "Whoo'd" in the June night, and inside, the house still smelled delicious from the steak dinner she'd fixed.

Erica pulled her blanket more tightly around herself. They'd had a wonderful dinner, and he was wonderful company. She should be content with that.

"How did the Tall Wolf family end up in North Carolina?" she asked. "How did they avoid the Trail of Tears?"

"My great-great-grandfather lived in Tennessee. When the soldiers began rounding up the Cherokees, he escaped and hid in North Carolina. Here in the Smokies." James smiled. "The *Tsacona-ge.* Place of the Blue Smoke."

"So most of the North Carolina band came from refugees?"

"Some. Others had lived here a long time, and the mountains were so rugged that it was too much trouble for the soldiers to hunt them down."

"Do you think your ancestor survived like the other refugees did, by hiding in caves?"

He nodded. "We have records made by a Quaker missionary."

"What kind of records?"

"Aw, that's not important. People nearly starved, hiding from the soldiers the first year, but then—"

"James, what kind of records?"

He looked annoyed at her persistence. "A family Bible."

"But why would the missionary record anything about your ancestor in his *family* Bible? Unless—" Erica whooped. "Did the big red wolf marry a little white lamb in the missionary's family?"

"Yeah, but—"

"Then you're part white. All right! We have something in common."

James crossed reddish-brown arms over his chest

and feigned dismay. "Funny, I don't feel like a Quaker."

She rocked nonchalantly, smiling. "I understand that after you move back here for good you're going to find yourself a nice Cherokee wife."

"Hmmm. That's always been my plan."

"Keep the bloodline pure."

His gaze was riveted to hers; she wasn't certain what was going on behind those dark eyes, but she doubted it had anything to do with Erica Alice Gallatin's bloodlines.

"Travis's wife was white. Born and raised in Chicago. She left him five times. He always took her back. She made him miserable."

Erica looked at James wearily. The bitterness in his eyes defeated her. "I'm sorry. I like Travis, and it's too bad that his marriage didn't work. But maybe it had nothing to do with his wife's being white."

"You're right. It only had to do with her being an outsider."

Erica tried to sound flippant. "So you're just having fun with the palefaces until you find the right woman here at home. Hmmm, a practical attitude." She looked around as if searching for a clock. "Well, heavens, it's getting late. I must be off to my new bed. I'm so glad Tom's Trader Inn had one more lime-green beauty to spare."

Erica uncurled her legs and started to get up. James's broad hand latched on to her ankle.

"Not so fast. You owe me a story in return."

She had to get out of that room before her smile broke. Not only wasn't she sexy enough for him, she wasn't Cherokee enough.

"Well, let's see, I know a story about the great Boston Harbor sewage monster, but I don't think it's as charming as your stories about *Uktenas* and *Utluhtus* and other native things that go bump in the night."

"I want to know about your marriage."

"Ah. No way. You might have a tendency toward

diabetes, and the story's too darned sweet to be safe."

"Red, quit stalling," he said softly. "I can keep a secret. Come on. Give."

"Really, it's a ridiculous story and I don't want to—"

"Erica Alice, I'm not letting go of your ankle until you talk."

"I was a nerd; he was a nerd. We dated all through high school. It was a terrific nerd romance. Then I went to Georgia Tech to study civil engineering and he went to UCLA to study world arts and cultures.

"We hardly saw each other for four years, but he wrote lots of long letters full of deathless prose about making the world into a better place. Then he got a chance to visit the Middle East on a year-long study program. On his way out of the States he met me up in Boston. He made me feel as if no one would ever love me more in my life. We were married an hour before he got on an airplane."

She picked at the blanket for a second. "And that was the last time I ever saw him in person."

James stroked her ankle. "What happened?"

"He disappeared. The State Department confirmed that he'd been kidnapped by some political faction. I saw photographs of him over the years, so I knew he was still alive."

"So you waited," James murmured. "For eight years before you found out that he was dead. My God, you're incredible."

"I'm a dolt," she retorted, and chuckled harshly. "He wasn't dead. He wasn't even kidnapped. He'd joined a terrorist group and married a Lebanese woman. At last count, they had three kids."

She sat in awkward silence, toying with a string on the blanket. James's hand tightened around her ankle as if he wanted to stamp his fingerprints permanently on her skin. Erica avoided looking at him even when he shook her foot lightly.

"What'd you do when you found out?" he asked

in a husky voice that played havoc with her emotions. This forceful giant of a man might growl and snap at her sometimes, but he could be as sweet as a puppy, too. A wolf puppy, but a puppy, nonetheless.

Blinking back tears, Erica could only manage to repeat, "I was a damned dolt. What a boob. Eight years."

"Sssh. You ought to get a medal."

"An idiot award."

"Hush. When did you find out about him?"

"About two years ago. I got an annulment and tried to think of myself as a free person, but it hasn't worked real well. I guess eight years of martyrdom turned me into a creature of habit. And I'm not exactly self-confident around men . . . except in business."

"Dammit, you can't waste any more time." He cursed again, this time less politely. "What a story. The guy ought to be barbecued."

She almost smiled. "I've often thought about which parts I'd like to roast first."

James looked at her shrewdly. "So what are you going to do? Let that bastard ruin the rest of your life?"

"No, but—"

"What are you waiting for?"

"I—I guess it's a who, not a what."

"No, no, no. You can't sit around waiting for Mr. Perfect and ignoring everyone else. You'll never get anywhere that way."

Erica looked at him hopefully, her heart filling her throat. Was he making an offer?

"I don't need romance," she said eagerly. "I mean, I know I'm not the type that men get mushy over. Guys just don't pamper big women. We don't look delicate. If I could find someone who's experienced but not too cynical, someone who could be a good friend, someone who, you know, would teach me things, I'd be happy."

James frowned at her. "You need a lot more than sex education. You need a new self-image. Don't worry about being too tall to attract men. Take me, for example. I'm such a hulk that you look delicate to me.''

Happiness bubbled up inside her. He *was* making her an offer. ''You're good for my ego,'' she said, and laughed merrily. ''I feel like Eliza in *My Fair Lady*. Make me a new woman, Henry Tall Wolf Higgins.''

''Let's see, let's see.'' He squinted thoughtfully, his fingers tapping on her ankle.

''Tell me what to do, and I'll give it a try.''

''Hmmm. Okay, I've got it.'' He didn't look particularly happy, but he did seem satisfied.

Erica leaned forward, waiting breathlessly. ''Anything.''

He patted her ankle. ''I know a great guy up in D.C. Used to play for the 'Skins. He's divorced, but it was nothing ugly. He's real clean-cut, a little shy, not nearly as bookish or smart as you are, but he does read a lot. He's a liberal Republican. I think you'd like him.''

For a second Erica could only stare at James, her mouth open in disbelief. Her chest constricted with stunned bitterness. After years of idiotic martyrdom and self-denial she'd been forced into close company with this man, this incredibly provocative man, and all he wanted to do was get rid of her.

She clambered off the bed and stood at the foot of it, her hands clenched around her blanket, her feet braced apart in a stance of pure defiance. ''I don't need you to pimp for me!'' She turned and marched from the room, her dignity in tatters around her.

## CHAPTER 6

T HE NEXT MORNING at six A.M. he pounded on her bedroom door and called, "Wake up, *kamama egwa.*"

Erica refused to ask what the name meant. She sat up wearily, still angry and tense. "Yes?"

"I'm going out. Meet me at the museum at twelve."

"Why?"

"We're going on a hike. Wear comfortable shoes."

"Where are we going?"

"And don't eat lunch. We'll go native in the woods."

Frustrated, Erica sank both hands into her hair and groaned softly. Native. "I'm not taking my clothes off to eat lunch. *Where are we going?*"

"Be there," he said firmly, and she listened to him leave the house. He still had a slight limp, so they couldn't be hiking far.

Erica fell back on the bed and stared at a ceiling made of thick boards painted pale blue. Dove had certainly loved blue; most of the colors in the house were some variety of the color. It was soothing, and she needed soothing just then.

She suspected she was going to need it more as the day went on.


ERICA DROVE OVER to Asheville after breakfast and turned in her rental car, then went to a used-truck dealer and drolly leased a Jeep Cherokee. As she drove back along a winding road perched on the sides of mountains, she blessed the Jeep's oversized tires and four-wheel drive.

She rolled down her window, let the fragrant spring breeze wash over her, and slipped a Cherokee-language cassette into the Jeep's tape player. She'd mail-ordered the tape from the reservation in Oklahoma, and the dialect differed significantly from that used in North Carolina, but she could still benefit from it.

She smiled as she went through the tape, feeling very Cherokee as she repeated phrases and words. *"Egwa.* Big." Erica gritted her teeth. James had called her *kamama egwa.* Something big. Whatever it was, it couldn't be good.

After that she didn't smile.

Eventually she reached the sign that marked the reservation's eastern border. *"Qualla Boundary,* she read aloud. She didn't know what *Qualla* meant, but it sounded homey. A few minutes later Erica slowed the Jeep as woodland gave way to billboards and the road became crowded with tourist traffic.

She turned off the tape as she entered Cherokee. Gazing out at the tourist district, Erica cataloged the offerings—the Sequoyah Cafeteria, the Papoose Motel, the Pow Wow Gift Shop, an amusement park called Santa's Land, and dozens of other attractions.

In contrast, Becky Tall Wolf's little restaurant was simply called Mama's Best Meal and, judging by the early lunch crowd, it was a success. Erica had to stop at crosswalks to let hordes of camera-toting families pass.

As she sat waiting she glanced at the storefronts.

Before one stood a middle-aged Cherokee man in full chief's costume—beaded moccasins, fringed buckskins, and a huge feathered war bonnet. A large sign was propped on a porch post beside him.

"Take a photograph with Chief Running Bear. And don't forget to tip!"

She sighed. On the reservation this occupation was called "chiefing." The costumes were strictly Plains Indian style, and more Hollywood than authentic, at that. But still, it was a job, and from what she'd heard the men who did it worked long, hard hours. Even when the public was obnoxious they demonstrated an incredible amount of courtesy and showmanship.

Farther down Erica stopped at another crosswalk. This time when she looked over at the shops she gasped in surprise.

Grandpa Sam was chiefing.

She pulled into one of the slanted parking spaces that fronted the stores and hurried over to Sam's spot. He held a squalling toddler in one arm while the mother stood beside him uncertainly and the father snapped pictures with an expensive-looking camera.

Erica winced. Grandpa Sam had braided his long white hair into two plaits that hung down over his shoulders, onto his chest, and decorated them with orange feathers.

Still, dressed in a headdress that hung to his heels and wearing a beaded buckskin outfit made by an obviously loving hand, he brought dignity to the costume.

As the family walked away Sam called cheerfully, "Have a good stay in Cherokee!" He turned, saw Erica watching, and grinned. "Howdy do, *Eh-lee-ga.*"

She smiled with fascination. "Is that how you say my name in Cherokee?"

He nodded. "Eh-lee-ga. We got no 'r' sound."

"Mr. Tall Wolf—"

"Call me Grandpa Sam. You're one of us, the *Ani-Yun-Wiya*, the Real People, and all of them call me Grandpa."

Erica thought her chest would burst with affection.

"Thank you, Grandpa Sam," she said around a knot in her throat.

"What you doin' today?"

She told him about going to the museum to meet James. As she did, his gaze strayed across the street. Suddenly he muttered, "I'll be damned. Quicker than flies after a dead horse."

Erica glanced over. A competing chief, this one short and plump, with a face like a Cherokee Buddha, was holding a toddler in *his* arms. He gave Sam a thumbs-up.

"Copies me 'cause he's too dumb to think up things on his own," Sam grumbled.

Erica bit her lip to keep from laughing. "Do you do this every day?"

The majestic war bonnet nodded solemnly. "Make good money at it, most days. Mainly do it 'cause I like to keep busy and meet people." He thumped his chest. "I've had my picture made with people from all over the world, and some of 'em write me letters when they get home. I'm on ten different postcards, too." Sam cupped a hand beside his mouth and said in a low voice, "Don't mention I said so, but Germans tip better than Americans."

Erica clasped her hands behind her back and asked casually, "Grandpa Sam, what does *kamama* mean?"

"Hmmm. It means butterfly."

Erica gazed up at him in surprise. "If somebody called me a big butterfly, would it be a compliment?"

He looked mischievous. "Yes. Who called you that?" When she shifted a little and smiled ruefully, he clucked his tongue. "That James," Sam murmured. "He's a caution."

Erica nodded, a dull lump in her stomach. *Caution* was the appropriate word.


OUT OF THE corner of one eye Erica spotted James crossing the museum floor toward her. He was waylaid by an elderly museum worker who apparently knew him. She squealed and grabbed his hand, then began to talk.

The giant standing near Erica took that moment to speak to her for the first time. "Pardon me," he said politely in a voice as deep as mountain thunder. "May I ask you a question?"

Erica turned toward him, tilted her head far back, and looked at a rugged, attractive face topped by black hair. But it wasn't Indian-black, and neither his features nor his coloring indicated any Cherokee blood. Her neck ached from looking up. Lord, he was seven feet tall. Was there some sort of magic-growth elixir around there?

"Yes?"

"I saw you in the bookstore talking to the cashier. Is she a friend of yours?"

That was Echo. Hmmm. What did this black-haired Atlas want with James's sister? "Yes, she's a friend."

"Is she married?"

"Uhmm, no." Erica squinted at him shrewdly. There was a worldliness about his dark eyes that made her feel he was much more sophisticated than his questions made him sound. She glanced at his tan corduroy trousers, short-sleeved khaki safari shirt, and well-used hiking shoes.

"Who are you, and why do you want to know about her?"

He thought for a moment, then leaned close to her ear and murmured, "I noticed in the guest book that your name is Erica Gallatin. Do you have a relative named Tess?"

Erica drew back in astonishment. "Yes."

"I'm a neighbor of hers. Drake Lancaster. Call her in California and check me out."

That sounded legitimate. Erica gestured vaguely around them. "But how—"

"I work for the forestry service, and I'm based in Los Angeles. I'm doing some pollution research over in the Nantahala area, a few miles west of here."

"But how—"

"I keep a sailboat at the marina where Tess lives. At Long Beach."

"Ah!" Well, amazing as this coincidence was, he *did* know indisputable details about her cousin. Erica was still stunned, but she held out a hand. "Hello, then."

He shook gently so his large paw wouldn't crush her fingers. "Now, about the cashier. I want to buy some books, and then I want her to go to lunch with me. Will you help me out?"

Erica had been glancing at James, and she enjoyed the way he kept glancing at her and the giant. She took Drake Lancaster's hand again. "If you'll do me a favor I'll introduce you to the cashier and tell her you're a friend of my cousin's."

His dark eyes gleamed with pleasure at the intrigue. "All right."

"Put your arm around me. Pretend we're old pals from college. This won't get you in trouble, I promise."

He smiled slowly. "That's all right. Trouble doesn't bother me."

He might have been shy, but he wasn't awkward. Gracefully he slipped a massive arm around her waist and pulled her close to his side. "Just old friends?"

"Right." Erica smiled at James. He arched one brow but continued talking to the museum worker. She lifted a hand and waved casually. Drake Lancaster followed the direction. He smiled and nodded to James before looking down at her again. "Now what?"

"You went to Georgia Tech. Studied . . . hmmm, biology. Yeah, that ties in with your job. I was a little sister in your fraternity—"

"Whoa," he said, chuckling. "When you make up an identity, keep it simple. It works better that way."

She looked at him quizzically, wondering how a biologist would have experience with such things. James's appearance beside her made her forget that thought. Erica grinned at him and pointed to Drake. "An old college friend."

She patted Drake's chest and smiled up at him. "I can't believe it's been so many years."

He squeezed her waist companionably. "We had some good times. I've never forgotten."

Lord, this man was a wonderful accomplice. Erica smiled at James, who was doing a good job of looking inscrutable.

"Drake Lancaster, meet James Tall Wolf. James is helping me do some research on a relative of mine."

James shook the giant's hand and smiled pleasantly at him. "You went to Georgia Tech with Erica?"

"Sure did."

"He studied biology," Erica chimed in. "And now he works for the forestry service."

James arched a brow. "Did you play football?"

"Oh, yes," Erica interjected. She looked up hopefully at Drake Lancaster.

There was a hint of exasperation in his eyes, but he chuckled. "Sure did."

"What position?"

Drake never missed a beat. "Defensive end."

"Hmmm. Well, glad to meet you." James looked from Drake to her and smiled with a nonchalance that made her heart sink. He didn't care if she knew a dozen giant, good-looking men. "Ready for lunch?"

Erica shrugged. "Sure. But I want to introduce Drake to Echo first. Umm, Drake knows my cousin Tess, by the way. Tess, from California."

"Go ahead. I'll be waiting." He shook Drake's hand again, then sat down on a cushioned bench and yawned.

Erica grimly led Drake Lancaster to the museum bookstore. "Thank you," she told him. "You did all you could."

The bookstore was empty of customers; Echo had her back to the door, and she was rearranging books on a big display rack, one that rotated.

Erica glanced at Drake Lancaster and was fascinated by the intense way he studied a woman to whom he hadn't yet spoken. But of course Echo was beautiful, in addition to being six two and having an incredible mane of black hair. She wore deerskin ankle boots, soft cotton pants, and a ruffled blouse that made her look very feminine.

Wonderfully feminine, but not delicate. Erica recalled that Echo, in her spare time, was a blacksmith.

Echo grabbed the rotating rack, hoisted the whole thing off the floor and easily carried it to a spot in one corner. Drake Lancaster leaped forward to help her but arrived just as she plopped the rack into place.

He grasped her elbow. "That was impressive," he said with utter sincerity. "You must have strong hands."

Echo jumped, looked up, and simply stared at Drake in open-mouthed wonder. Erica stopped a few feet away and watched wistfully as an almost visible form of energy passed between the two of them.

She sighed, thinking of James waiting for her in the museum without an ounce of jealousy or interest. Well, if she couldn't find romance for herself, at least she'd find it for other people.

"Echo," she said softly, watching the hypnotized look in her eyes, "this gentleman wants to talk to you."

JAMES GUIDED HER to Grandpa Sam's old pickup truck. He kept a benevolent silence as he drove along a pleasant, almost suburban street paralleled by a tree-shadowed river. He pointed to it. "Oconaluftee," he noted.

"Gesundheit."

He chuckled. They passed the ceremonial grounds, the tribal council house, and a small, neatly kept building that housed the Bureau of Indian Affairs. James cut across the river and turned down another road.

Erica gazed out the passenger window as they

passed a large, impressive brick building. A fire truck and other official vehicles sat out front. "How's Travis?" she asked abruptly. "You don't say much about him."

"We don't have much to say to each other."

Erica looked at James quickly. His wide, firm mouth had thinned a little, and the pain around his eyes couldn't be hidden. She'd spent several days watching this man try to ignore the pain in his knee, and so she recognized the different type of pain in him now.

"Anything you want to talk about?" she asked.

"I told his wife I'd set her up in a house in Chicago if she'd divorce Travis and stay away for good."

"Oh, James," Erica said sadly.

"I guess I sound like a real SOB."

"I don't know. Were you doing it for Travis?"

"Yeah. After she left him the fifth time. Father and Grandfather tracked Travis up to the top of Rattlesnake Mountain—it's a sacred place in the old legends—and they found him sitting there with a gun in his hands. I don't know what he would have done to himself if they hadn't brought him back home. When I heard what almost happened, I knew I couldn't let my brother get to that point again."

Erica let her breath out. "You're a good brother, not an SOB."

"Don't ask Travis for an opinion."

"I doubt that he's stopped loving you. He sounds like a man who loves with great loyalty."

"I hope so. It's a tradition with us wolves."

Erica turned her face so he couldn't see her expression. "So once you take a mate, it's for life, eh?"

"We try to work it out that way."

"Good plan." She was silent as he drove out of town and into the steep hills. "Where are we going?"

His voice was wicked. "To a wolf's cave."


THEY ENTERED THE shadowy coolness and gazed at walls etched with Cherokee letters. "This is where

my great-great-great-grandfather hid from the soldiers," James said softly. "Over one hundred and fifty
years ago."

Erica went to a wall, knelt, and reverently touched
letters of a more familiar kind. "Amanda and James,"
she read. When she looked up at James urgently, he
knew he had to explain.

"I was named after him."

"And Amanda was the Quaker missionary's
daughter?"

"Yes."

"She came up here and hid with him?"

"That's what we think. Nobody's sure. Grandpa
says he remembers old stories that say she ran away
from home to be with James against her parents'
wishes."

Erica looked around sympathetically. "She must
have suffered up here in the wintertime. They both
must have." She gazed at him with a jaunty tilt to her
head. "So the only other James Tall Wolf in the family
loved a proper but strong-willed white woman."

James cast a troubled frown at her. Why had he
brought her there? He'd simply wanted to show her
how rough life had been for his ancestors, to give her
a feeling for the past. Or was that all?

Suddenly he felt that he'd tricked himself into a
dangerous situation, that forces beyond his conscious
will were making him do reckless things.

James resisted the urge to look around for Little
People.

"Why did you bring me here?" she asked.

He gave her the safe explanation he'd given himself.

"Thank you for sharing this with me," she murmured softly. "It means a lot to me."

James looked at her and felt a disastrous urge
simply to surrender to the affection in those green eyes.
He'd make love to her right there in that lonely, beautiful cave where the Tall Wolf family had begun so

long ago. He'd bond her to him with her love for Cherokee history and her need for his touch.

And when she left him, he might be as Travis had been, lost and self-destructive with grief over a woman who'd never been destined to stay with him.

James said gruffly, "So your good buddy Drake was a defensive end at Tech, huh?"

He saw the light fade from her eyes. She smiled innocently and shrugged. "Yep."

James leaned forward, scrutinized her hard enough to make her blink a few times, and said softly, "Doll, I'd have heard about a monster like him if he'd played defense at a college as important as Tech. Drake Lancaster sure as hell never did."

Her shoulders slumped. "Right," she said grimly. "I made it up."

"The whole thing?"

"The whole thing. I met him about a minute before you walked in the room." She lifted her chin and looked haughty. "You're not the only one who can play games."

Lord, how he loved this woman's spirit. If she botched things up, she simply admitted it and took the consequences. And what were the consequences? She'd been trying to make him jealous, and he'd never tell her how well it had been working before she'd made that revealing comment about Lancaster's playing football.

"Why did you do it?" James demanded. He knew the real reason, but he had to hear the official one.

"To show you that I'm no wimp around men," she retorted. "Now, go ahead and be annoyed, if you want to. I'm annoyed at myself. I'm not accustomed to stooping to such childish pranks."

James opened the bag and pulled out a shelled acorn. "Any woman who attacks me with a hand drill, hits me with a stick, then throws cold water on me when I'm naked is no wimp."

She looked startled by his good humor; then the affection came flooding back into her eyes. "You and I are friends. Nope, you can't deny it anymore. You want it too. Pals. And because we know it's never going to be any more than that, we can relax, okay?''

He felt bittersweet sorrow gather inside his chest like an empty mountain valley filling with blue mist.

"Okay," he agreed solemnly, and sat back wondering why victory had never tasted less sweet.

E RICA ROCKED SLOWLY in her chair and peered at an article in the quarterly history journal published by the tribe.

James lay on the porch near her feet, his head propped on a pillow. He was a very languid-looking wolf as he studied her medallion and awkwardly tried to copy the symbols onto a note pad that lay on his chest. Erica glanced at him, then glanced away, sighing at his effect on her heart rate.

They'd had a lovely friendship for three days; except for her constant state of lovesickness she thought the arrangement worked well.

More than ever he wanted to keep it platonic, judging by his sudden decision to dress like a character from Li'l Abner. He wore faded overalls sans shirt or shoes, he ruffled his hair and let its straight black strands do what they wanted, he smoked a long cigar every night after dinner, and he tromped around with grass stains on his feet.

Erica smiled ruefully. He thought he looked ugly to her that way.

Didn't he know that overalls exposed a tantalizing expanse of his chest and shoulders and that there was something wonderfully indecent about the way they pulled tightly across his muscular rump? He also didn't realize that she loved the scent of cigars, because her father had smoked them, and the fragrance brought back warm feelings of happiness.

Erica smiled helplessly. James's hair shagged over his forehead in a handsome way when he didn't brush it, and his bare feet were big, knotty, cute-ugly things.

"I wonder if my great-great-grandmother had to go on the Trail of Tears. It was worse than I ever imagined. Listen to this, Wolfman."

"Hmmm?" he mumbled, and looked up at her. Erica snapped her mouth shut—half the time she felt like a slack-jawed trout around him—and went back to reading.

"Here's the reprint of a letter written by an elderly lady who was a teenager at the time the Cherokees were removed to Oklahoma.

There was a woman of the Blue Clan who knew white people's medicine. Her name was Katlan-icha. She doctored people on the trail, but could not help so many who died from hunger and fever.

We called her *Ghighau*, Beloved Woman. A white man came and stole the Beloved Woman one night. Our people chased him, but his horse was too fast. There was great sadness in the camp. I don't know what happened to the Beloved Woman. She was very pretty, and the man probably sold her. Sometimes that happened to pretty Cherokee women.

Erica put the journal down and stared into space, thinking. "What an awful fate. Sold into some kind of bondage, I bet. Maybe to a bordello."

"Think positive. Maybe she escaped."

"I hope so. Poor woman."

The sound of a car made them both look toward the driveway. Echo's deluxe station wagon rolled into sight.

"Nice wheels," Erica said. "Wonder what ex-football player with lots of money gave it to her for her birthday last year?" She gazed up at James as he came to stand beside her chair. "You're a sweet guy, even if you do talk dirty to old maids."

He tried to resist, but finally he smiled at her nonsense. "You love it."

Echo parked and got out, moving wearily. Her hair was carelessly braided down her back, and she wore a rumpled sundress with old tennis shoes. Erica studied her anxiously, and when she glanced up at James, he looked worried too.

"Hi," Echo said as she walked to the porch. "I need to talk."

"Here, sit down." Erica moved to the floor.

James hugged his sister and looked shrewdly at her pinched face. "It's about Lancaster," he said grimly.

She lifted her chin and frowned at James in warning. "I love him. I know he's an outsider and we haven't known each other long, but don't say it's a mistake."

To Erica's surprise James only squeezed her shoulders and said, "I understand. It happens that way sometimes."

Erica buried her anguish behind a stoic mask. He spoke with such experience. Whom had he loved so deeply and so quickly?

He guided Echo to the chair and sat down at her feet, his legs crossed. "What is it, sis?"

But Echo had turned her attention to Erica. "What else do you know about Drake Lancaster? Anything besides what he told you the other day?"

Erica shook her head. "Do you suspect that he's not telling the truth? I know what he said about my cousin Tess is true."

Echo rubbed tired eyes. "All I know is that yesterday he took a pack horse and rode up into the national
forest. And when he came back the pack horse had
been unloaded. He goes off by himself for about fifteen
minutes every afternoon at six. He's renting a room
over near the Nantahala outfitters—one of those places
where people stay while they kayak on the Nantahala
River. But he won't let me visit it. Says it's too cheap,
too messy."

James looked a little perturbed at the idea of his
little sister, though full grown and previously married,
visiting a man's room. But he said without rebuke,
"So where do you go?"

Echo looked just as perturbed. She cleared her
throat. "He took a better room over at one of the inns.
But he kept the other room. It doesn't make sense.
And he won't talk about his research at all. Says it's
dull. Doesn't that strike you as odd?"

Erica sighed with resignation. "Yes, and I'm afraid
something else is odd." She told Echo about Drake's
confident way of handling false identities.

Echo put her head in her hands and made a soft
sound of despair. "I'm afraid he's into something illegal," she said wretchedly. "Maybe drug running? I
don't know." When she looked up there were tears
on her face. "And he says he loves me, but I think
he's got someone else."

James vaulted to his feet and began to pace. "What
makes you say that, sis?" he asked in a lethal tone.

"He . . ." Echo swallowed hard and looked at Erica
for moral support. Erica reached out and took her
hand. "In one of his tote bags I found a brand-new
bra. One of those really racy, see-through things. Not
my size. It was a gift for someone. It had a pink bow
tied to one strap. And I found a box of condoms with
a blue bow tied around it."

"Maybe he's invited to a, ummm, coed bachelor
party," Erica said lamely.

Echo shook her head. "He's a loner. He says he

doesn't need to know anyone around here except me.''

James stopped by the chair and looked down at her, a muscle flexing in his jaw. ''Tell me what you want me to do, and I'll do it. That's what big brothers are for. I'll go talk to this character—''

Echo gasped. ''James, I love you dearly, but I don't want you to fight my battles. I just hoped that you and Erica would have some advice. I mean, you two are from the outside. You've both had a lot of experience with relationships.''

James pursed his lips and gazed at Erica solemnly. ''Red? What kind of advice do you have?''

Erica thought she'd enjoy taking the drill to him after Echo left. ''Well, I believe in honesty. You should just go to Drake and tell him you want the truth.''

''Or your brothers will help him reenact Custer's Last Mistake,'' James added. ''With the obvious ending.''

Echo wiped her eyes and managed to smile. ''At least you and Travis finally agree on something. He said the same thing.''

Erica watched quiet pleasure darken James's eyes. ''Good,'' he said gruffly.

Echo looked from him to Erica. ''I think you should know. People are talking about you two. Of course, Becky and Grandpa and I just ignore it, but we'd like to know what the, ummm, arrangement is here.''

Erica smiled brightly. ''We have a very modern relationship. We're just housemates and friends.''

''Ah-hah.'' Echo looked at her askance, as if James had never had such a rare animal in his possession before.

''What are people saying?'' James asked, his eyes troubled.

''Gossip.'' Echo exhaled as if the word were a burden. ''The most interesting rumor is that Erica's pregnant and she's hiding here until she has the baby, because you don't want to marry her. But James, you remember how it is around here. People gossip just to have something to do. And you're big news. It'll pass. Becky and I'll work on it.''

Erica's heart sank as she saw even more dismay on James's face.

''Well, that's the end of that,'' he said gruffly. ''I'll move out. I was wrong to stay here in the first place.''

Erica clenched her hands in her lap and fought to keep from making a sound of despair. ''Hey, I don't mind what people say,'' she assured him. ''You know, up in D.C., I'm used to Harold Brumby's calling me things like 'that big Amazon witch who stole my award.' I'm certainly not offended by rumors of being pregnant.'' She paused impishly. ''Even by you.''

James shook his head. ''You've only been here a couple of weeks. I won't let gossip ruin your chances of making friends with people.''

Echo stood up, and it was obvious from her tactful smile that she thought it best to leave. ''I'll let you know how things go with my mysterious giant. Bye.''

After Echo's station wagon disappeared down the driveway, Erica followed James into the house. Misery was a cold lump in her stomach.

''Hey, Wolfman, are you sure I'll be safe here alone, with violent turkeys flapping around at night?''

He slipped his feet into a pair of jogging shoes and began stuffing clothes into his leather tote. ''You'll be fine, Red.''

Erica shut her eyes for a moment, then quoted to herself: ''Let him be sorrowing as he goes along, and not for one night alone. Let him become an aimless wanderer, whose trail may never be followed. His eyes have come to fasten themselves on one alone.''

''There's a draft in here,'' James said abruptly. Frowning, he looked around.

Erica gazed at the goose bumps on his arms and hoped that he'd just been zapped by her lovespell. There was something else in the formula, something about wiping your spit on the intended. What the heck.

''You've got a spot of dirt on your arm,'' she told

him. Erica licked her fingertips and dabbed quickly. "There."

He looked at her quizzically for several long seconds, then said, "Thank you, Erica Alice."

She pulled an imaginary skirt out from her jeans and curtsied. "Come back any time. I have lots of spit." Erica wanted to die at what her mouth had just said, *I have lots of spit?* No wonder he didn't find her sexy.

"I'll be just a few miles away. There's so much you still need to see and do. Don't worry, I won't desert you."

"I know. Sure." Erica smiled widely, using muscles that would never recover from the strain, she figured. "You've been great. Thanks for giving me a chance to fit in."

He started to speak, seemed to have trouble, waited another second, then said finally, "I know you can fit in, but I also know that you can't stay."

Erica nodded. She had a successful business in Washington, and what kind of work could she possibly do here full time? But she wanted desperately to tell him that she'd gladly earn a million frequent-flyer points shuttling between her world and his, if he'd only ask.

She said in a playful, tear-soaked voice, "But I'm going to keep our bargain, Wolfman, and then I'll always have Dove's place if I want to visit."

He nodded. "I hope you do that."

That was it. She couldn't talk to him for another second without losing her dignity. Erica nodded jerkily. "Bye." She thought her voice did a great imitation of a laryngitis victim's. "The *kamama egwa* says see you later. *Do-na-da-go-huh.*"

"*Do-na-da-go-huh,*" he murmured, his eyes so still and dark that she could see herself in their reflection.

Erica stepped out of his way and went inside. As soon as she shut the door she pressed both hands to her mouth and walked quickly to the back room.

Erica knew she'd be sore from crying so hard, but

she cried anyway, her knees drawn up, her breath coming in big gulps that obliterated all outside sound.

So by the time she realized that there were noises in the house, James was already halfway across the bedroom to her. Erica bolted upright and covered her face. "No!" she wailed in humiliation.

"I can't take this anymore!" he shouted fiercely, grabbing her by both arms and pulling her off the bed. "I don't care what might happen later! I can't stand seeing you like this and I can't stand myself like this! Do you want me, Red? Do you want me to stay here? Do you want me to be your lover until you go back to Washington?"

She looked up at him in stark amazement. "W-what?"

"Oh, Red," he said hoarsely, and grasped her face between his big hands. "Look what I did to you. I'm sorry, Red."

"I d-don't need a m-mercy—"

"I'm the one who needs mercy, because I'm half out of my mind from wanting you." He pulled her closer and searched her eyes. "No promises, no regrets. Just you and me. You need a teacher, and I promise you that I'll be the best." His voice dropped to a graveled whisper, and he repeated, "Do you want me to be your lover?"

Dreams came true, magic was real, and for the first time in her life she belonged.

"Oh, *yes*."


DARKNESS WAS A gentle cloak around the house, and the open windows let in just enough air to stir the flames on the big candles James had placed on the bedside stand.

Erica smoothed trembling hands over her hair and robe as she stood there in the flickering brightness watching him light more candles on the dresser. Her skin felt deliciously warm and receptive, as though the bath she'd just finished had cleaned away old sorrows.

James glanced up and saw her in the doorway. He straightened slowly, smiling at the way she eyed the white towel wrapped around his hips.

"Have a nice soak?" he asked. "You were only gone five minutes."

"I was lonely." Her heart beat a thready rhythm as she watched the candlelight dance on his body, polishing his skin to burnished copper.

He held out a hand. "That's the last bath you'll take alone here."

Somehow she made her rubbery legs cross the floor to him. Erica slipped her hands into his and smiled from the inside out, emotion rushing through her. "You made the room look beautiful," she murmured. "Even the furniture."

She watched his breath quicken as he looked down at her. Knowing that he wanted her, that he found her extremely desirable, gave Erica a confidence she'd never had before. "Let's go take a bath together," she told him.

He chuckled. "Easy, Red, easy. This is a very special occasion, and everything has to be done just so. That's why I wanted to wait until nighttime. Important ceremonies should be performed slowly and at night."

Erica realized that she was squeezing his big, warm hands and that his fingertips were making suggestive movements against her palms. "It's going to be a ceremony?" she murmured with a crooked smile. "Will I have to make a speech?"

He cradled her hands against the center of his chest. His dark eyes glittered with amusement and unmistakable anticipation. "No speech, but you'll probably want to say a few words in appreciation."

"Oh? Will I get some sort of award?"

He smiled wickedly. "You might call it that."

Erica placed her hands flat on his chest and smoothed them slowly over his sleek skin. "I've never touched a man this way before," she murmured, her face flushed more from excitement than uncertainty.

He inhaled sharply as she brushed her fingertips over him. "You missed out on a lot of awards, then, 'cause you're great at it."

Erica grasped his shoulders and looked up at him wistfully. "I read how-to books for fun. Ask me any clinical question. Go ahead. I know exactly how things are supposed to be done."

He put his hands on her waist and pulled her closer, until their torsos were almost touching. "Reading about it is like trying to learn football by correspondence course. Can't be done. You've got to get out there and really play."

"Make passes," she added, nodding sagely.

He winked at her. "And complete them."

"Without fumbling."

"Or rushing."

Erica slipped her arms around his neck. "And certainly without roughing the passer."

"Never." He gripped her sides and slid his hands down her hips. "But it's important to take possession any way you can."

Her voice throaty, Erica murmured, "Intercepting the pass is one way." She lifted her mouth to brush his.

James gripped her rump hard and teased her lips with quick, flirtatious kisses. "I like your offense."

"I like your defense."

"It's not working very well," he said huskily, and lifted her slightly, so that their mouths could merge.

The gentle invasion of his tongue made her moan and press upward for more. She quickly found herself exploring his mouth while he kept still, enjoying it.

"That's a very unusual defense you've got," Erica whispered.

"It's all part of a winning game plan," he said with a soft growl, then nibbled her lower lip.

Erica arched against him. Her spine felt loose and pliable; she could bend with him, wrap herself around him, easily become a part of him. "James. Oh, James. This was worth waiting thirty-three years for."

He stepped back, holding her gently by the shoulders as he studied her with quiet determination. "That's the way I hope you'll feel tomorrow morning too."

"You made me wait all afternoon," she said teasingly. "Now you're telling me I'll have to wait until morning?"

He jerked her to him with playful roughness. "You've got a smart mouth, doll."

Erica tilted her head back and inhaled the blended scent of masculine and feminine arousal. This was an essence no book could capture, no fantasy imagine. She looked at James through heavy, half-shut eyes. "It's actually a very uneducated mouth. Waiting for you to train it."

"*Erica*," he said in a helpless, rebuking tone, and kissed her so deeply that her knees buckled a little and she clutched his arms for support. Then he wound a hand into her hair and turned her head to one side. His lips brushing her ear, he murmured the details of his training techniques and how he hoped she would respond. His towel fell to the floor.

Leaning against him in perfect relaxation, her senses tuned to every nuance of his voice and scent and touch, she floated in a blissfully hypnotized state. When he stepped back and took her hands again, she gazed at him in speechless surrender.

He led her to the bed and stood looking at her, his dark eyes burning with affection and desire. "Take off your robe for me, Erica Alice."

Erica pushed the soft material from her shoulders and let it fall to the floor. Feeling a little shy, she studied his reaction stoically. "All six feet of me is happy you like tall women."

His gaze roamed down her body with uninhibited admiration. "So you thought you weren't sexy to me?"

"Yes. Skinny. Plain. Average. That's my self-image.

Actually, I didn't think too much about the way I looked, until I met you. Then I wanted to be beautiful."

Trying to put her at ease, he gestured grandly toward his arousal. "Does this look like you're not beautiful to me? I have this reaction every time I get near you."

Erica stepped closer and caressed him. He made a throaty sound and roughly pulled her against him. She caught her breath as her belly cushioned the hard ridge of his body and her nipples touched his chest. Sliding her hands over his lean hips and thighs, Erica explored his taut contours.

Happiness burst inside her. "I'll never forget this night."

"I'll make sure of it," he whispered, and kissed her.

Erica put her arms around him and reveled in the power and possession of his embrace. The erotic sounds of their kiss were enough to make her body open with silky anticipation.

James drew her down on the shadowy bed and lay on his back with her half on top of him. Erica rubbed her thigh over his, feeling deliciously astonished at each new experience.

James molded one hand to her hip and seared a trail of sensation down the back of her leg, his fingertips brushing her intimately in passing. Erica realized that both she and he were panting lightly.

No fantasy could do justice to this, either—this breathless delight in sharing pleasure, this knowledge that they were partners even though he had so much experience and she had so little.

Erica cupped his face in the golden candlelight. "You are an incredible teacher." She spoke slowly, her voice husky. *And I love you*, she added silently.

He gave her a slight smile and inhaled sharply as she stroked his stomach. "Keep doing that and you'll graduate with honors."

A minute later he switched their positions, so that she lay looking up at him. Erica trembled as he

brushed the back of his fingers down her torso, stroking her breasts and belly with long, slow movements.

She burrowed her face against his shoulder and
kissed the hot, smooth skin. After a hesitant second
she licked it with the tip of her tongue.

"More," he urged gruffly. "Don't hold anything
back."

*As if I could resist you,* she thought. Erica tried to
laugh, but the sound was more like a primitive begging for his touch. When he caressed her thighs her
hips rose instinctively. Deep in a still-reasoning corner
of her mind she was intrigued by the basic forces that
had taken hold of her.

"This is the most natural thing in the world," she
told him, startled. "I don't even have to think about
what to do."

James made a strangled sound, and she looked up
to find his face ruddy with passion and amusement.
"That's the way it's supposed to be. You learn
quickly."

Against her hip his aroused body was wonderfully
mobile and eager. He prodded her gently, and the slow
flexing of his hips brought explicit images to her mind.

He searched her half-shut eyes and saw the images
there. "That's right," he murmured. "That's what I
wanted you to think about."

Her back arched as his hand dipped between her
thighs. "I feel so heavy and relaxed and *ripe*," she
whispered in awe.

James drew the hand up, circled one of her breasts,
and squeezed it sensually as his mouth covered the
nipple. White-hot desire shot through her body, and
Erica speared her fingers into his hair.

He tantalized her as if she were a rich fruit he
wanted to take whole into his mouth. The uninhibited
loving left her breasts wet from his lips and tongue.

Erica made a high-pitched keening sound. She was
lost in a haze of pleasure; nothing had ever felt so good
in her whole life. She could have died happy, feeling
James's lips on her this way.

He whispered earthy compliments against her skin during those brief moments when his tongue wasn't involved otherwise. They were the crude kind of words Erica heard construction workers bandy when good-looking women walked by a work site. If the workers had ever used such language about her, they'd been careful to make sure she didn't hear.

"Oh, thank you," she told James in rapt gratitude. "I needed that."

He lifted his head to smile at her, and the half-wild look of arousal in his expression excited her even more. He kissed her. "Later I want you to talk to me that way."

"Now," she said eagerly.

James chuckled deep in his chest and put a hand over her mouth. "It wouldn't be a good idea."

She knew her eyes must have looked huge with understanding, because he chuckled again. "Your voice is too sexy."

He moved down her body, kissing, nibbling, sucking her skin roughly. Erica forgot about talking when James coaxed her legs apart and grasped her gently. "Easy, now," he murmured in a soothing way, as his fingers became part of her.

With a ragged gasp of pleasure she pushed against his hand, aching for release. His mouth sank onto her, and he groaned happily at the taste and feel of her readiness. Erica lost all control and tugged at his hair, urging him to come to her and make this magnificent ceremony complete.

He whispered against her swollen flesh, "That's it, Red. Want me as much as I want you."

Half-crying with the fervor of emotion and sensation, she grasped the item he'd arranged on the bedside stand. It lay on top of its package, waiting grandly. Erica thought no other man in the world would have gone to so much trouble to make her feel safe and uninhibited at the same time.

She was beyond words; the best she could do was a hoarse mewling sound as she stroked the offering against his shoulder. He felt the odd texture against his skin and looked up, his eyes gleaming.

"Yeees?" he asked, his voice a coy rasp. But when he saw the look on her face he quickly knelt beside her and cupped his hand under her shoulders.

He pulled her upwards and watched as she prepared him with shaking hands. "Are you afraid?" he asked hoarsely, stroking the disheveled hair back from her forehead. "It won't hurt. I swear I won't let it hurt."

Devotion surged through her as she looked up at him. "Not afraid," she whispered raggedly. "I want you so much that I don't care if it hurts."

"Oh, Red." He put his hands on her shoulders and eased her back. Gently he caressed her face as he lowered himself on top of her.

"Like this?" she asked as she gripped him with her thighs.

"Perfect," he said, and it sounded like an understatement.

Their eyes met and held. Erica was lost in so many new experiences—the feel of his body nudging her patiently, the weight of him pushing her down into the mattress, the almost fierce look of controlled desire in his face.

The air seemed to hum with intensity, as if it might shatter into crystal fragments just from the swift harmony of their breaths.

Erica lifted her head and kissed him. "No more old maid, please." Then she added in a voice too sensual for him to resist, "Do it quickly, James."

He bowed his head to her shoulder and thrust into her with one smooth, sure movement that filled her completely. She felt her body stretching to accommodate him, but there was only that tightness, no pain.

Erica smiled, and tears came to her eyes. He drew back and looked at her anxiously. As her hips began to move in slow, erotic circles, he sighed with relief.

"No more volcano candidate," he murmured tenderly.

She shook her head, and somewhere in the midst of it she realized that the ache inside her was exploding. Erica shut her eyes and whimpered.

He felt the gathering of sensation and moved carefully, bending his head close to hers so that he could whisper delicious promises in her ear; promises of slower times, of many times, of all night and everything she ever wanted from a man.

Erica slid her feet over the backs of his thighs and rose wildly, her hands digging into his shoulders, her lips moving soundlessly against his jaw.

Caught in her abandoned writhing, he moaned her name and, trembling violently, managed to thrust only once more before he joined her in a trance of sensation.

They rode the cloud down together, looking into each other's eyes, hands moving in gratitude over damp, hot skin, mouths meeting to promise more.

Erica made herself admit that he didn't think of this as anything serious, that he wanted her out of friendship and desire, not love. But she knew also that they had given each other something special, and there would always be a bond between them because of it.

The candlelight made yellow flecks in his eyes, like golden stars gleaming in a night sky. *"Da-nitaka,"* he murmured.

Erica stroked a fingertip along his cheekbone and asked tenderly, "What does it mean, Wolfman?"

"They are together." He put his arms under her and lifted her slightly. Erica was lost in his gaze.

James arched gently inside her. "Their spirits are so close that they share one body," he explained. *"Danitaka."*

Forever, she added silently. Some day she hoped he'd want that too.

E RICA QUICKLY DISCOVERED that James had a marvelous way of turning everything into foreplay or afterplay.

Such as at that moment. He sincerely wanted to know about her construction company, but he had his head pillowed on her naked rump and he kept dawdling a finger down her spine.

"Why'd you decide to study civil engineering in college?"

Erica hugged a pillow under her chin and tried to think despite the fact that he was nibbling her right hip. "I was good in math and science, and I thought I'd make the world a better place by learning to build highways. After I graduated I decided that the last thing the world needed was more strips of concrete covered with oil slicks and flat animals."

Now he politely kissed the spot he'd bitten. "So where'd you learn about building houses?"

"When I was at school I worked summers for a residential contractor, a woman. She wanted to give women a chance in the business, and half her crew was female. You wouldn't believe the looks we'd get when we'd show up at a construction site with our tool belts and hard hats. We had T-shirts printed up that said 'Yes, we've heard the one about the lady carpenter.' ''

"So that's where you learned to use a drill," he said ruefully, and began nuzzling the small of her back.

Erica chuckled, and slumped lazily onto the pillow. His nuzzling destroyed coherent thought. Finally she twisted around and grabbed his bad knee. "Poor baby," she said in a crooning voice, and began kissing the surgical scars that framed the kneecap.

"Sympathy. Ah. Hmmm."

She placed kisses up his leg and scrutinized several tiny white dots on the top of his thigh. "I'd thought that these were just reverse freckles. But they're scars."

He cleared his throat and said softly. "That's where I used to give myself steroid injections. But mostly I put them here." James slapped his rump. "Hurt like hell."

Erica rested her cheek against the scars on his thigh and curled one hand protectively over his leg. "Was it worth it?"

His voice was gruff. "At the time, yes. But I'll never let a kid of mine do it."

"How do steroids help a player, besides making him bigger and stronger?"

"They make you so aggressive that you want to rip people apart. That's a good attitude for football; not so good for anything else. The last season I played, I tore up my locker before every game. Pulled it off the wall and beat the hell out of it. And I wasn't the only player doing crazy things like that."

"Oh, James." She stroked his leg tenderly. "Is that why you didn't come home very often? Because you were so messed up while you played ball?"

"Yes." He ran his hand over her hair, caressed it back from her face, then sank his fingers into it as if the texture were comforting. "I wasn't a good person to be around. The money and the fame didn't change me, but when my knee started to give me problems and I took steroids to compensate, I turned into a real touchy SOB. At least I recognized the change. So I stayed away from my family as much as I could.''

After a second, he added, ''And there was another reason. Travis's wife.''

Erica listened in stunned silence as he told her about times when Danna Tall Wolf had tried to corner him, and the Christmas eve she'd slipped into his old bedroom while Travis slept in the room across the hall. James had firmly set her out and locked his bedroom door.

''That was the last time I came home for a holiday,'' he said.

''Does Travis know any of this?''

''No. And he never will. He can think what he wants to about me. I won't hurt him with the truth about Danna.''

''Thank you for sharing that with me.''

James turned her face toward him and cupped her chin. ''I trust you with it.''

Between kisses she asked softly, ''What are you going to do when you move down to the reservation for good? I mean, what kind of business?''

''I'm going to build furniture. Custom pieces. I've already sold a few things to friends.''

''That's great, James.'' She grasped one of his brawny hands and studied the callouses. ''Yep. You have the hands to be a builder.''

''That's not wood stain, that's my skin color.''

''Strong, tough hands, but not clumsy.'' Erica gave him a solemn look. ''Though you do have knuckles like a gorilla.''

James tugged his hand away and tweaked her nipple. ''I've played football since I was five. Plus my father ran a logging business, and we boys spent all our spare time cutting timber. These hands have been through a lot.''

He wasn't angry, but she raised his hands and nuzzled them in apology, anyway. "I know, Wolfman, I know. I think they're wonderful hands. Very sexy."

That made his eyes gleam. "They look good against your skin."

"Hmmm. Show me." Grinning, she stretched out and put her head on his stomach.

"A lap cat. That's what you are."

"What's 'cat' in Cherokee?"

"*Wis-sah.*" James walked his fingers down her belly. "Here, *wis-sah*, here, *wis-sah* . . ."

They both jumped a little as they heard a car coming up the driveway. They'd been alone for two days, and naked virtually all of that time. The outside world had creased to exist.

James got up quickly and dressed in jeans and a T-shirt. He parted a window curtain and glanced out. "Lancaster. Alone."

Erica hopped out of bed and grabbed her clothes. She didn't know what James might say or do in Echo's defense.

By the time she went outside James and Drake Lancaster were standing in the yard, embroiled in a tense discussion. James had his arms crossed over his chest, and Lancaster lounged against a muddy, dented pickup truck. Both he and the truck looked as if they'd been through hell.

Drake's dark, frowning gaze swiveled gratefully toward Erica as she stopped beside James. "Do you know where Echo is?" Drake asked, his voice gruff.

"No." Erica couldn't decide what to think about this bewildering man, but she did know that Echo seemed to be the kind of woman who loved carefully and for good reason. "What's wrong?"

"I have to leave. I don't have time to say good-bye, and there are things she doesn't understand, that she's worried about—"

"We know," James interjected grimly.

"I love her. There's no other woman. My work is unusual, but it's not illegal. Or immoral. At least not by most people's standards."

*By most people's standards?* Erica gazed at Drake Lancaster quizzically, and was touched by the quiet brand of anguish in his eyes. "We'll tell her what you said," she assured him. "James?"

James glanced at her, saw her beseeching gaze, and sighed. "All right."

Drake reached into a shirt pocket. "Erica, you need to take care of this. I know you have one similar to it." He held out a familiar-looking gold medallion. "It belongs to Tess."

Erica gasped and took the medallion from him. "What are you doing with it?"

"I promised her that I'd have it translated. Can you do that for me? I'll send for it later."

Erica gaped at him in utter astonishment. "What's going on with Tess? Is she all right?"

"Your cousin is fine. She's on her way out of the country. There was a misunderstanding about a diamond she owned. She was in trouble. It wasn't her fault, but she's under protection now."

James took the medallion and looked at Drake carefully. "You had her hidden up in the caves near Bryson."

Drake nodded. "I wasn't in charge; a friend of mine was. She's under his protection. There's no need to worry about her." He gazed at Erica in apology. "I promise that all of this will be explained to you eventually."

"What about my sister?" James asked with quiet authority.

"I'll be back."

"When?" Erica asked.

"I don't know. Tell her to wait. Tell her . . ." He paused, searching for words, a private man who didn't feel comfortable discussing his emotions. "Tell her this is just the beginning for us."

"All right," Erica said softly.

"Good-bye." He shook hands with her, then held out a hand to James. "Trust me. I'm on the level."

After a second James returned the shake. "If you're

not, don't ever let me catch you inside the Qualla boundary again."

"Good enough," Drake agreed pleasantly. He went to his truck and climbed inside. "Oh. For your information, Erica, your great-great-grandparents are buried in California, near San Francisco. Tess found their graves.

"They lived there until sometime in the eighteen-fifties. They started a big vineyard and named it Glen Mary, after a daughter who died when she was still a baby. Tess never learned where Justis and Katherine went after they left California, but they eventually came back there to die. They're buried next to their daughter."

"Thank you," Erica said numbly, stunned.

She and James watched Drake Lancaster drive away. Erica took her cousin's medallion and stared at it in consternation. "Mystery," she said plaintively. "More mystery. What now?"

JAMES CAME TO a disturbing realization: He'd never been happier. The more he learned about Erica, the more there was to know. They shared many interests, and her fascination with the Cherokee language and lore was inexhaustible, much like her fascination with making love.

He tried not to wonder if that fascination had little to do with him personally, and he kept reminding himself that she was an eager listener when he talked about his plans for creating a co-op where local furniture craftsmen could design and sell their work.

After a week of enjoying each other, they took the medallions to show to Grandpa Sam.

Becky had a date, but on her way out she presented Erica with a pair of beautiful deerskin ankle boots she'd made. They had elaborate beadwork across the toes.

In the shape of big butterflies.

"For bringing my brother back home," Becky announced.

James's heart sank at the guarded way Erica smiled, and he wondered what she was thinking.

But she laughed at the butterflies and seemed mesmerized by the workmanship in the boots. "Why don't you make these to sell?" she asked Becky.

"Aw, it's just a hobby. The restaurant keeps me busy."

"If you ever want to market them, I'd be glad to help. I have a friend who works for Neiman-Marcus. I could show these to him."

Becky looked pleased, but James only thought, When you go back to D.C.

After Becky left, Erica changed her tennis shoes for the boots and padded proudly around the Tall Wolf kitchen. Grandpa Sam, seated at the kitchen table rolling bean dumplings, chortled at her.

"You got Cherokee feet now," he proclaimed.

James went to Echo, who stood at the stove, and put his arm around her. "Have you heard from Drake?"

Echo stirred a pot of thick stew and shook her head. "But he'll be back."

"No man can resist a woman of the wolf clan," James teased gently. "And I think Lancaster's trustworthy."

Erica came over and patted her arm. "I agree."

Echo gave them both a meaningful look, then smiled up at her brother. "You've mellowed since you came home this time, I wonder why?"

James glanced over her head and met Erica's eyes. She winked at him as if his sister's innuendo were a cute joke. He winced inwardly. Now was as good a time as any to break the news. "I'm here to stay this time."

"James!" Echo dropped the spoon and hugged him.

Erica gave him a smile that cut him to the heart. She wasn't upset about his announcement, that was certain.

Sam trotted over and threw his arms around both of his grandchildren. Then he grabbed Erica and hugged her. "I knew the first night I saw you that you were good for James! I said to the girls, 'That's the one! That's the one he's been waitin' for.' "

"Grandpa, Erica and I are just friends," James interjected quickly, trying to keep her from feeling more uncomfortable.

She shot him a strained look but made a joke; she didn't want anyone to make permanent plans for the two of them, that was obvious.

Echo, sensing the tension, shooed Grandpa to the table with Erica in tow, ordering them both to finish the dumplings. In Erica's honor, dinner was to be old-time Cherokee fare—dumplings made from brown beans and cornmeal, squirrel stew, baked cucumbers, and sweet-potato cakes.

James made some vague excuse about going upstairs to get the box of Civil War memorabilia left by his great-great-grandfather William. At the top of the stairs he sat down and lit a cigar, but held it limply in his hands and sat frowning into space.

He couldn't call off his bargain with Erica; that wouldn't be fair. But if they had no future together how could he go on like this for another five weeks, needing her more each day, living so close to her thoughts and feelings that he was *da-nitaka* with her, standing in her soul?

Well, there was only one way to help this situation— spend as little time with her as possible until she went home. James got to his feet and moved wearily down the hallway, missing her already.

From the corner of his eye he caught sight of a photograph, and stopped to study it. The beautiful smiling brunette was Danna, Travis's dead wife. James could barely stomach the sight of her even now.

She'd taken malicious pleasure in skewering him after he offered her the house in Chicago. She'd come home and told Travis that his brother had asked her to be his mistress.

Travis hadn't believed that nonsense, but he'd been furious about James's intervention in his marriage. And thus the bitterness had begun between them.

James continued down the hall, his teeth gritted. Erica was no Danna—he hated even thinking Erica's name so soon after looking at Danna's photograph. No, she wouldn't ruin him the way Danna had ruined Travis.

Erica would ruin him through decency, kindness, and her honest need for a temporary teacher and companion. Erica would ruin him because he knew that falling in love with her was right, and good, and hopeless.

IT WAS HARD to concentrate on history after James's disgruntled reaction to his family's match-making comments. Erica kept hearing his grim voice saying that he and she were just friends. He certainly wanted *that* point made clear.

She faked her appetite during dinner, and was glad when they adjourned to a card table Echo had set up in the den. Erica sat stiffly in a folding chair and watched Grandpa Sam spread out photocopied letters, photographs, Confederate money, and other memorabilia.

"Got a present for you, Eh-lee-ga." Sam picked out a tinted contemporary portrait and handed it to her. "Guess that was made sometime around the big war."

"World War II," James explained.

Erica gazed at a studio portrait of a mature, attractive Cherokee woman wearing a black dress with big white lapels. A fat braid of graying black hair wound around her head like a crown, and there was enough imperial strength in her eyes to make the crown seem appropriate.

Her eyes. Gallatin green eyes. Erica gasped softly. "Is this Dove?"

Grandpa Sam grinned. "Yep. She gave me that a

few years ago. Said she wanted to tell folks that a good-looking man was carrying her picture around."

Erica felt James's fingertips on her chin. "Gimme a look, Red," he murmured gruffly. He held the photo beside her face and studied the similarity in eye color. "I wonder if the green eyes started with old Justis Gallatin?"

"They must have, because I'm not directly related to Dove. My cousin Kat is." She glanced at Sam. "Thank you. This picture means a lot to me."

"Dove was a good friend," he answered solemnly. "But you know, there was a lot of mystery about her. She didn't come here until after the war. Never would talk about the years before, but I think she must have had a husband, maybe even some children. Don't know what happened to 'em."

James handed the two medallions to him. "Can you make sense of these, Grandpa?"

Sam hummed and squinted as he ran one knotty, olive-brown finger under the symbols. "This is old style—different ways of saying things, words I don't recognize. Tribe has more than one way of talking. Oklahoma way, North Carolina way. Back before the removal, there were even more ways."

"Different dialects," Becky explained.

"Can you make out anything?" Erica asked anxiously.

Sam pointed to one side of Tess's medallion. "Katlanicha Blue Song, daughter of Jesse and Mary Blue Song, sister of Anna, Elizabeth, and Sallie. Then . . . something about a place in Georgia, 1838."

"Katlanicha." Her heart racing, Erica looked at James.

"The journal," he said, nodding, his eyes black with fascination. "The woman on the Trail of Tears."

"Of the Blue clan." Erica pressed trembling hands together and tried not to squeal with delight. "That was my great-great-grandmother!"

"Blue clan," Echo murmured, smiling. "Good.

Now you know your clan. That was the most important connection a Cherokee had.''

"Still is," Sam said firmly. He studied her medallion. "Can't make this one out much. Only thing I recognize is this." He pointed to a long row of symbols on one side. "The trail where they cried. That's the Cherokee word for the Trail of Tears. She was sent off with the rest of the tribe, I guess."

"But she obviously escaped from the man who kidnapped her," Erica said softly. James explained to Echo and Sam about the journal article.

"Let me keep these a while and I'll figure 'em out," Sam told her, looking at the medallions.

"Thank you, Grandpa Sam!"

"You're welcome, Eh-lee-ga of the Blue clan."

Erica was so proud that she forgot James's earlier coolness and grabbed his hand. He smiled pensively but bent over and kissed her fingers like an old-world gallant.

"Now I can call you Red Blue."

She laughed, and Echo pointed out, "In the old days you couldn't marry inside your own clan. Remember that. If you stick with tradition you have to marry a man from one of the others. Bird, Long Hair, Paint, Potato, Deer, or Wolf."

James let go of her hand and said drolly, "I think Erica needs to find someone from the Democrat clan."

"Independent," she corrected, smiling while his impersonal words knifed through her.

Erica tried to concentrate as Grandpa Sam began talking about James's great-great-grandfather. William Tall Wolf had joined a Cherokee infantry regiment during the Civil War.

William, the half-Cherokee son of the first James Tall Wolf and Amanda, his Quaker wife, had apparently been a well-educated young man. Sam read from his voluminous letters William had written home, letters filled with emotion and colorful details.

"William's regiment even caught itself a Cherokee Yankee," Grandpa Sam said proudly, thumping a letter. "Up in Tennessee. A mixed-blood, like William. But a *Yankee* spy. William says here the fellow was about his own age. Maybe twenty-one, twenty-two."

Grandpa Sam fished around in the clutter on the table and picked up a tarnished locket. "That spy told William to take this to his wife and son up in New York. Wanted her to have it after the war."

"What happened to the spy?" Erica asked.

"They shot him."

"They shot one of their own tribe?"

"He was a Yankee spy. The way William wrote about him, he musta been a nice feller, and I guess they felt bad about shooting him, but it was wartime."

Erica took the locket and gently examined it. More than a century's passing couldn't keep her from feeling sorry for the young man who'd died. "Why didn't William take this to the spy's family?"

"Tried to, I reckon. Probably just couldn't find them after the war. People got so scattered."

Erica opened the badly aged locket and peered inside. "Hmmm. There's an inscription. It's almost worn off." She added wistfully, "Maybe the spy rubbed his fingers over it for good luck."

James took the locket and went to a lamp beside Grandpa Sam's recliner. He squinted at the engraving and read slowly, "There's part of a date—I can only make out the year. I think it's 1860. And there are initials. R.T.—I can't make out the third one—to E.A.R."

Erica gazed at him in shock. "E.A.R.?"

James nodded. "Ear."

She vaulted up and hurried to his side. "Let me see." Erica grasped the locket in quivering hands and read and reread the initials in disbelief. "My great-grandmother's maiden name was Ear! I mean, her initials were E.A.R. It's always been a family joke. Erica Alfonza Rutherford. I'm named after her!"

With a yelp of excitement Echo joined them, staring

at the unimportant-looking little locket in awe. "What do you know about her?"

"Wait," James said, shaking his head. "Red, how could this be your great-grandmother? If she had a son, he'd be your grandfather. Your grandfather couldn't have been born during the Civil War. It'd make him too old."

Erica shook her head raggedly, still studying the locket. "Grandpa Gallatin was almost seventy when my father was born. He never had any children by his first three wives. One divorced him, and two died. His fourth wife—my grandmother—was a twenty-year-old actress."

"Get 'em as kittens, train 'em right," James offered wryly. "Good idea."

Erica punched his arm. "Grandpa Gallatin was a third-rate stage actor in New York and a first-rate lecherous old coot, or so my mother claims. My dad was born two days after his sixty-ninth birthday."

Echo patted her arm enthusiastically. "Then maybe this was your great-grandmother's locket! What do you know about your great-grandfather?"

"His first name was Ross—that's all I've ever been told. I know that he was half-Cherokee and had two brothers—and a sister who died as a baby." She handed the locket to James so that his steady hands could hold it under the light.

"R.T.," he repeated softly, looking at the first set of initials. "Could be that the last initial used to be a *G* for Gallatin."

Erica collapsed weakly into Grandpa Sam's recliner. "That would mean that my great-grandfather was shot by his own tribesmen for being a spy from the Union army."

"A Yankee," Grandpa Sam said in a tone of regret, as if that were the only sad part of it. "Oh, well."

Feeling very defeated, Erica murmured, "I'd hoped that he'd be an . . . Indian."

Echo nodded. "Traditional, you mean. A Cherokee,

not a white man who happened to have Cherokee blood."

"Yes. I thought I'd feel closer to my Cherokee heritage once I knew more about him."

"Ross must have been a hero to the Union forces," James told her gently. He thought for a second, then snapped his fingers. "And if he was, then his name ought to be listed in the records at the National Archives."

Erica nodded. "Maybe I can check over the phone."

James's silence made her look at him closely. His expression was guarded. "I'll check for you. I'm going to be in Washington for the next two weeks."

Somehow she managed to hide the fact that she'd just been knocked down. Erica gave him a quizzical frown. "Oh? Business?"

He nodded. "If I'm moving back here, I have arrangements to make."

"I need to check in at my office, so I'll go—"

"Nope, you stay here and learn about life on the reservation. That was the deal."

Erica clutched the arms of her chair. Had he grown bored with her so soon? He'd hardly let her out of his sight for a week, and now, suddenly, he was anxious to leave. Had he simply done his duty in bed and then felt he could move on? "You agreed that I could take care of my business," she reminded him.

"Later. You can go to Washington after I come back."

So she'd be out of his way around Dove's house, Erica thought in despair. He'd realized that she was in love with him, and this trip was his way of reminding her not to take their arrangement too seriously.

"Okay. Sure," Erica told him affably, and shrugged. She was aware that Echo and Grandpa Sam were watching the scene with quiet interest.

The look she got from James was so intense that she knew he'd been concerned about her reaction to his trip. Erica kept her face composed.

If there was any way of winning him over, it certainly wasn't by acting possessive.

"You don't mind?" he asked.

"No. I've got plenty to keep me busy. Becky's going to teach me how to do beadwork."

"Beadwork, huh?"

The tone of his voice suggested that he didn't see how beadwork could fill up all her time, and the thought bothered him, somehow.

"And I'm going to get out and meet people," she added.

"People?"

"You know, those two-legged creatures who cause so much trouble."

"So you want trouble?"

She smiled jauntily. "Depends on what kind of people I meet."

"Be careful. The men around here are afraid of drills."

"I'll just have to figure out other ways of getting their attention."

He hooked a thumb in the waistband of his faded jeans and said lightly, "There are no elevators here."

Grandpa Sam, who looked confused by the conversation and exasperated by the change of subject, said, "Eh-lee-ga, you keep the locket. If you find out it's not your great-grandma's, give it back to me. Now y'all come sit down. I've got more letters to read."

Erica got up from the recliner, awkwardly trying not to touch James, who was standing in front of it, doing a good impression of an immovable object.

She couldn't avoid brushing against him. Erica raised her eyes and looked at his unfathomable expression, feeling miserable and hoping that it didn't show. She held out her hand for the locket.

He calmly put her family heirloom in his jeans pocket. "I might need to study it some more."

"I don't see why," she said just as the phone rang and Echo went into the kitchen to take the call.

"You be a good little girl," James said to Erica,

"and I'll give it to you when I get back from Washington." He smiled, his arched brow conveying an innuendo that only she could see.

Erica's misery turned to quiet anger. He had that squint-eyed appearance of determination on his face, that smug masculine look he'd had after he'd trapped her in the elevator and after he'd tackled her in an alley.

"Maybe I won't want it anymore," she said pleasantly.

"Oh, you'll want—"

"Grandpa! James!" Echo ran into the den, her eyes frantic. "Travis's house trailer is on fire!"

T HICK, ACRID SMOKE floated through the June night, and Erica's stomach recoiled as soon as she leaped from the back of Grandpa Sam's pickup truck. There was something particularly noxious about the burning scent of man-made building materials. The fake woods and space-age plastics that made up a modern house trailer tended to burn quickly and emit suffocating chemical fumes.

And James was already running toward the door of the trailer.

Erica raced after him, leaving Echo to grip Grandpa Sam's arm in an attempt to keep him from following James. One of the reservation's fire trucks was already on the scene, and Erica saw James grab a volunteer fire fighter by the sleeve of his overcoat.

She reached the two men in time to hear the volunteer yell something about Travis. James bolted inside the trailer.

The volunteer started after him, then glanced around and saw Erica heading full-tilt in the same direction. She dodged his outflung hands and leaped to the trailer steps two seconds after James had disappeared in a hell of black smoke.

Erica took one last breath of fresh air and vaulted into a roasting darkness that smelled like a coal furnace. She stumbled against furniture and pawed the air with both hands, as if she could clear a path in it.

No one could remain conscious more than a minute or two in that suffocating prison of smoke. Dear Lord, where were Travis and James?

Erica struggled forward blindly, the roar of nearby flames filling her ears, her lungs aching with the effort to find oxygen. She slammed into a wall, fell back against another, and realized that she was in some sort of hallway.

When she heard the sound of ragged coughing, she lunged forward and collided with someone. ''James!''

''Get out of here!''

He was hunched forward, pulling Travis slowly along the floor. Erica anchored her hands under Travis's arm and threw herself backward. She and James were both coughing violently now.

''Get out!'' he yelled again.

''Save your breath!''

They got Travis to the end of the hallway and angled him toward the outer door. Travis moved weakly, trying to help himself, and by then Erica was so light-headed that she was ready to crawl beside him.

When she fell down she felt James's big hand sink into her shirt. He was staggering, but he managed to jerk her back to her feet. Together they used their last few seconds of strength to drag Travis to the trailer door.

Suddenly the air wasn't quite so hot, and light shone through the smoke. Someone grabbed Erica and carried her outside. She lifted her head groggily and looked back to see other men pulling out James and Travis.

James was safe. Good. Now she could breathe again. It was time to pass out.

· · ·

THERE WAS A whole pack of fidgeting Tall Wolfs in the medical clinic of the reservation, and one lone butterfly of the Blue clan who wasn't allowed to sit up or even flutter a wing.

"Keep still," James ordered. He sat beside her on the gurney and held a cold compress to her forehead.

Erica eyed him in dismay. His face was haggard, his eyes were bloodshot, his golf shirt and jeans were filthy, and he had a red burn welt across one forearm. All she'd done was faint, and she felt fine by then, but he wouldn't let her get up.

"You're the one who needs to be lying here," she told him.

He bent over and kissed her—not for the first time since she'd come to, with her head in his lap—and then he whispered gently, "Keep still or I'll tie you down."

Travis was already sitting up on the gurney across the room, looking disgruntled because the doctor kept pressing a cold stethoscope to his bare chest. Echo and Grandpa Sam went from one gurney to another with the regularity of mother wolves checking their cubs.

Becky arrived, terrified because she'd heard vague details about a fire at Travis's place that involved injuries, and she made a round of the gurneys twice before she was satisfied enough to calm down.

"What happened?" she asked tearfully.

"I drove up and saw smoke coming out of the windows," Travis told her. "I radioed for help and then I went inside to save what I could."

Becky hugged him fiercely. "You dumb brother, you almost got killed. There's not anything worth that much."

Travis looked across the room and met James's eyes. "I wanted my pictures of Danna."

James nodded. "I would have gotten them for you if I could have."

Both men glanced away. Travis looked at Erica. "What you did was special. I'll never forget it."

Erica winced inwardly. He could compliment her, but not James. She watched the muscles tighten in James's jaw. He took her hand and occupied himself by stroking the back of it.

In the awkward silence that followed, Erica decided it was time to build more bridges, even at the risk of being a meddler. "Travis," she said softly. "James loves you very much, and I wish you'd say that you love him. This is a wonderful family; I envy you all. You don't know how lucky you are." She paused, fighting a knot of emotions in her throat.

"In my family everybody is too busy making career statements to notice one another. We never talk about our feelings." She looked at Grandpa Sam. "My mother put her parents in a nursing home before they needed to go." She looked from Becky to Echo. "My half sisters have always believed that being in the same family meant we had to compete with one another—at school, at our jobs, in terms of the clothes we wore, the number of men we had."

Erica smiled wryly. "I didn't fare very well in two out of those four areas." She looked into James's eyes and felt his hand close tightly around hers. "Nobody would do for me what you did for your brother tonight." Then she looked at Travis. "Nobody would get involved in my problems and try to help the way James tried to help you."

Grandpa Sam made a gruff noise and crossed his arms over his chest. "I'm an old man, and I might die any day," he said bluntly. "I want to know that my grandsons are at peace with each other."

Travis looked at James for a moment. Frowning, he got off the gurney, took his blackened uniform shirt, and started for the door. When he got there he stopped, turned around, and told James hoarsely, "I don't know if I can make peace with you, but I do love you."

"I love you too," James answered. "And I understand how you could love Danna so much that nothing else mattered."

The look on Travis's face told Erica that he had never expected to hear those words from James. Slowly his gaze slid thoughtfully to her, then after a moment returned to James.

"Welcome home, little brother," he murmured, then turned and left the room.

JAMES AWOKE WITH a painful ache in his bad knee and a delicious ache in other areas. He had slept lightly, dreaming about the long bath he and Erica had taken together, the way she'd licked the burn mark on his arm, the way she'd risked drowning to do incredible things to him while he lay in the tub smiling helplessly.

Later, in bed, he'd curled on his side and snuggled her against his body, with her legs draped lazily over his hips. He put his mouth next to her ear and told her more of the ancient Cherokee stories, while he kept one hand moving patiently between her thighs.

When he finished, the praises she moaned with such breathless emotion had nothing to do with his story-telling ability.

What now? Could he bring himself to leave for Washington? *No.* He'd simply tell her the truth—that he loved her and hoped that she was willing to love him too. If she wanted to try, somehow they'd make the situation work even if they lived apart.

James sighed with anticipation and reached out to draw her to him. When he couldn't locate her he sat up quickly and looked around. Morning sunlight filtered through the living-room curtains; he heard birds singing outside, but the house was terribly silent.

James rolled to the edge of the bed and reached for his watch on the nightstand. He wasn't human until he knew the time, an old discipline from all the years when he'd had to get up early every morning for football practice. When he moved back to the reservation for good he intended to quit wearing a watch.

Under the timepiece was a slip of notebook paper. James squinted, then grabbed it and read the uncaring lines bitterly. "I've gone exploring for the day. Have a good flight to D.C. See you in two weeks. *Kamama egwa.*"

ERICA WAS IN the kitchen making construction estimates on a house for Travis when she heard a car door slam. Thinking that one of the Tall Wolfs had dropped by to visit, she kept working.

But when she heard the thump, ka-thump of someone hobbling up the porch steps she thought, *James! And he's hurt his knee again.*

Erica ran to the front door. Lord, had he really been gone only six days? She didn't care why he'd come back, she was just glad—

Kat Gallatin stood there, looking like a little Cherokee princess except for the fact that she wore baggy hiking shorts and a T-shirt that read "*WOW*. Women Of Wrestling."

Above a pink Reebok her right ankle was wrapped in tape, and she held a crutch up as if she'd been about to rap on the door with it.

Kat took one look at Erica's startled expression, clasped her chest dramatically, and said, "Don't open your door so quickly! I've heard there are Indians around here!"

Erica gave a sputtering laugh and grabbed her arm. "Come in! What are you doing here? How did you get hurt?" As she guided her cousin to the couch she glanced out the window at Kat's car, a souped-up old Mustang with mag wheels. It was appropriate.

"I got squashed defending a guy from the audience!" Kat settled on the couch, flipped back her waist-length hair, and propped her foot on the end of her crutch. "I was wrestling a monster named Lady Savage over in South Carolina two nights ago, and I got thrown out of the ring—but it was planned, you dig?

"But I landed in this guy's lap and he thought I was really hurt. So when Lady Savage comes after me, he gets between us, and she doesn't like men, 'cause her husband just ran off with her sister, so she *tries to kill this guy.*"

Erica stared at her cousin in amazement. "What did he do?"

"He wouldn't hit back! I guess he didn't want to hit a woman, even a big hulk like Lady Savage. So I had to punch her in the chops before she brained him, and she kicked me in the ankle!"

Kat sighed. "So now I have a fracture and I can't work for two months. I'd like to find that guy and twist his moustache off." She paused, looking pensive. "But he had a great moustache. And he tried to protect me."

"Oh, Kat. Do you need money?"

She shook her head. "No, I'm not broke yet. I heard from the lawyer that you were hanging out over here in Cherokee land, so I thought I'd hop by and okay my plan with you. I'm going back to Gold Ridge to camp on our property for a while. You know, back to nature, and all that."

"Of course I don't mind. And I'm sure Tess won't, either."

"I tried to call Tess, but she's vamoosed somewhere."

Erica explained what she knew about Tess's situation. When she finished Kat was wide-eyed.

"Nothing that exciting ever happens to me!"

"Somebody named Lady Savage throws you out of the ring and a spectator risks a beating to rescue you? That's not exciting?"

Kat laughed, and the two of them started a companionable conversation about all the things Erica had learned regarding her branch of the Gallatin family and Dove. Kat gave her the third medallion to show to Grandpa Sam, and by the time Kat left for Gold Ridge she had an armload of history books and was calling herself *Wis-sah*, for cat.

She roared away in the Mustang, spinning gravel, one small hand brandishing a rubber tomahawk out the window. She'd brought it at one of the tourist shops in Cherokee town.

Erica laughed in affectionate disbelief and wondered if Gold Ridge was ready for Wis-sah Gallatin.

ONE OF THE tribe's councilmen came to the door of the Tall Wolf house that night as everyone was finishing dinner. Travis looked surprised to see him, but made no comment about the visit. He introduced the man to Erica as Jack Brown and gave him a beer.

Everyone gathered in the den. Brown, who was one-quarter Cherokee, ran a hand through a head of thinning red hair and told Travis bluntly, "James hired me to build you a house. He's already paid me."

Becky gasped. Grandpa nodded with satisfaction. Echo wiped tears from her eyes. Erica knotted her hands together and hoped that Travis would accept.

"I can't take it," Travis said. "I already told him that Erica was going over my old blueprints to see how much the house would cost now. I can pay for it myself."

Erica found the councilman looking at her curiously. "I've heard about you," he said. "You fixed the roof on Sally Turtlehead's cabin the other day."

"She brought me some apples. It was a fair trade."

That wasn't true, and he knew it. The roof had taken all day and cost fifty dollars in new materials. But he just smiled politely and looked at her with approval.

"I can't take James's offer," Travis repeated grimly.

There was no arguing with him. Brown shrugged, finished his beer, and told Travis to call him if he changed his mind. After Brown left Echo said in soft rebuke. "Oh, Trav. You know it's not a handout. This is a family thing. Take it."

"No. All those years when he wouldn't come home, he sent money. I never took it then, and I'm not takin' it now. He's not proud of being one of us, and this is how he buys off his guilt."

"You're wrong," Erica replied. "You're still his idol. And all he's ever wanted was to make his family and his people proud of him. Do you know that he took steroids for years, just to be able to keep playing football, because he thought he had to be a symbol of what Indians could accomplish?"

Everyone looked at her blankly. No, they hadn't known, it was obvious. Travis's eyes narrowed in distress, and he cursed softly.

"Steroids?" Grandpa Sam asked, bewildered. As Becky explained what they were, Sam grew mournful. "He didn't have to do that."

"Yes, he did," Erica said gently. "Because he has so much pride in being a Cherokee that he wanted to represent the tribe the best way he knew how." She went on in a low voice, telling them some of the horror stories from James's football career.

When she finished, Travis was sitting with his head in his hands. Becky and Echo were crying. Grandpa Sam was fumbling with his pipe, his hands shaking.

"I'm telling you these private things because he won't say them himself," Erica murmured. "He doesn't want anyone to feel sorry for him." She looked at Travis. "Travis, let him build a house for you. Nothing would make him happier."

Becky went over and stroked her brother's hair. "Go call him. Tell him you'll accept his gift."

Travis got up and went to the phone on the kitchen wall. There weren't many private conversations in the Tall Wolf family, Erica had learned. So everyone followed him, including her.

She sat at the kitchen table between Grandpa and Echo, while Becky sat on the counter by the sink. Travis called a hotel number James had left.

When the hotel operator put him through Travis

said, "James? Hmmm, sorry. Is James Tall Wolf there?"

Erica straightened slowly, her breath shallow. Who was in James's room? Travis frowned, glanced at her, then glanced away, frowning harder. His reaction alarmed her more.

"It's Travis. So you want to build me a house? Hmmm, yes. All right. Then I accept." Suddenly Travis grew very still and calm, as if having made a decision. "James, is there a woman in your room?" he asked sternly. "Stephen's friend. Where's Stephen?"

Travis looked at Erica and nodded solemnly. "When's Stephen coming back? Oh? Oh? Say, little brother, any messages for Erica? Yes, she's *right here.*" Travis held out the phone to her.

James had a woman in his room, and his whole family knew it. Dammit, it wasn't fair. Now they felt sorry for her.

Erica was determined to sound normal. She got up, took the phone, and asked cheerfully, "Hi, Wolfman. Are you being naughty?"

He must have been embarrassed and annoyed by the whole situation, because it was a second before he managed to say anything. "I'm doing my best."

In the background Erica heard a television playing. Something with lots of car chases and guns, apparently. A woman laughed—one of those high-pitched, girlish, cute laughs.

This woman was definitely not part of the sound track.

Erica shut her eyes. If she got through this conversation without crying it would be because the shock hadn't worn off yet. "Well, I'm staying busy too. Sally Turtlehead is going to teach me how to make baskets."

"Good."

The woman laughed again. Erica dug her fingernails into her palms. To hell with being polite.

"You should have just told me about her, James.

You didn't have to make up an excuse for going to Washington.''

"She's my partner's friend," he said in a low, taut voice. "She's drunk. They stopped by here after a concert because she was threatening to throw up in his Porsche. He's gone downstairs to get a room for her.''

"Ah. Okay.'' She simply didn't know what else to say. He was probably telling the truth. *No promises, no regrets,* he'd offered, and she'd accepted. So she didn't have the right to pry.

"Listen," he said, his voice hard. "You've got your deal back. The deal with George Gibson. I was going to tell you tomorrow, but I might as well do it now.''

Erica grasped the countertop for support. "How did you know about that?''

"Stephen told me a few days ago. I talked to Gibson. He hired your old pal to take your place. Harold Brumby. But Brumby's in hot water with one of the unions, and Gibson doesn't like controversy, as you know.''

James paused. "Stephen and I have some business deals with Gibson. We pressured him to take you back. If you want to accuse me of pimping for you, go ahead.''

"No.'' Erica's shoulder slumped. He was simply trying to get her out of North Carolina as quickly and as honorably as possible.

"So take the job, okay? I've seen your work—I checked out the project that won the award for you. You won't have any trouble with Gibson, now that he's going to give you a chance. You're good. Damned good.''

"Thank you.'' She couldn't have cared less about her work at that moment. "So I need to haul my fanny back to D.C. right away?''

"You got it.''

"This ruins our bargain.''

"No. You win. I'll get Dove's papers for you, and you can have her place.''

"No. Only the papers. Not the home.''

"Erica," he warned, the word full of tension.

But she was furious and heartbroken. She'd at least wanted to end their relationship in person, with kind, thoughtful words and a final kiss. Instead it was ending over a long-distance telephone connection, while some bimbo chortled in the background in sync with a cops-and-robbers show.

"Thank you for helping me with the Gibson deal," she said, and wondered how her straining throat could produce such calm tones. "When you get home to North Carolina just ask Grandpa Sam to interpret Dove's papers for me. We'll be square then."

There was a long pause on his end of the line. "Sounds like you're not coming back."

"Not for a while. The Gibson deal will take a lot of supervision. That shouldn't surprise you."

"No," he said softly. "Nothing surprises me anymore."

"Well, I've gotta go. Stop by my office in D.C. sometime before you leave for home. I'll buy you lunch."

"Lunch." He sounded bored, or exhausted, or both.

"Well, here's Travis again." Erica planted the phone in Travis's surprised hands and walked stiffly out of the room without looking back.

She went out the front door, crossed the yard, and leaned against the trunk of an old oak tree. Echo and Becky traipsed after her without the least bit of hesitation.

"What in the world was that all about?"

"You can't tell us that you don't love James."

Erica stared into the darkness of the mountains around them, thinking. "Let him be sorrowing as he goes along, and not for one night alone. Let him become an aimless wanderer, whose trail may never be followed."

She'd made a mistake by meddling with a Cherokee love formula, because it had worked only on her.

⊗⊗⊗⊗⊗⊗⊗⊗ **CHAPTER 10** ⊗⊗⊗⊗⊗⊗⊗⊗

T HE TALL WOLFS came from a proud people who'd
 always fought to protect what was theirs. If he let
Erica Gallatin walk away without a battle, he ought
to have his name changed to Worthless Wolf.

James got out of a taxi on the back street of a suburban office park and strode quickly into a two-story
office building. He found the correct suite number on
a list in the lobby, took the fire stairs in his hurry to
reach the second floor, and went straight to a door
with a neat little brass sign on it.

Gallatin Construction Company.

Let the war party begin.

A sturdy dark-haired woman rose from a desk in a
small, plainly furnished reception area. She was
plainly furnished in a beige suit, and she eyeballed
him like a drill sergeant with a troublesome recruit.

"You must be Mr. Tall Wolf."

"You must be Marie." He smiled jauntily at her
and sat down. "Is Erica busy?"

"She just got back from a meeting."

"With Mr. Gibson. I know. I arranged it."

The office manager glared at him. "I'll tell her that you're here. She may need a minute to call for the cavalry."

"Um. White woman speak with forked tongue."

Marie's eyebrows shot up and her lips clamped shut. She picked up the phone. "Erica? Mr. Tall Wolf is here to see you. Have you got a minute?"

Marie put the phone down and said primly, "She has just a minute."

James blew Marie a kiss and headed for a door across the room. Erica opened the door and stood there gazing at him, looking calm except for the bright blush her fair skin could never hide.

Wait. It wasn't a natural blush. She had on makeup, and her hair was pulled up in a soft but classic style, and she was wearing a beautifully tailored white suit with onyx jewelry and a black handkerchief peeking from the breast pocket. She was even taller than usual, in high-heeled black pumps that made her legs look about two miles long and worth every inch of the journey.

"I took your advice," she said simply, and waved a hand at her outfit. "I went shopping."

"Good Lord."

"No. Lord and Taylor. Come in."

He stepped inside and glanced around at functional colors and spartan furnishings that would have done justice to any finely decorated government office.

"Oh, don't worry, I'm having it redone," she said crisply. She settled behind her desk as James shut the door. His fingers moved so carefully that he knew she didn't hear him lock it.

"No more frumpy," she announced, gesturing at the room. "I'll change it all. Have a seat. What can I do for you?"

James took a seat on the corner of her desk, the corner nearest her chair. He drew one leg up, let the other dangle near her knees, and in general made himself provocatively comfortable while he watched a real blush creep slowly up her cheeks.

He loosened his blue tie a little, unbuttoned his blue-gray jacket, and flecked a piece of lint off the knee of dusky blue trousers.

"Blue," he said cheerfully, pulling his jacket open so she'd get a good, close look at everything he had to offer. "In honor of your clan."

She blinked rapidly and made a great show of clasping her hands just so on her desk. Very impressive and businesslike, he thought with pride, except that she bumped a file folder and it slid to one side, revealing a very unbusinesslike paperback book.

James flicked a hand out and stole it just as her mouth popped open and her fingers reached anxiously for it. She pursed her lips and rapped newly manicured nails on the desk. "Do you mind?"

"*Savage Endearments*," James read solemnly. "He was a fierce Sioux chief, determined to take revenge on the settlers who had killed his people. She was a strong-willed schoolteacher from back east, determined to civilize a brutal land. But when he kidnapped her, she fell under the spell of his"—James paused dramatically—"*Savage Endearments.*"

"There's a lot of history in that book," she said between clenched teeth.

James looked at her silently, sorting out his feelings. She was caught up in the Indian fantasy, then, like other women he'd known, and that was one reason she was attracted to him.

But it wasn't the only reason she liked him; he was certain of that, and so he could still hope. The best offense was a teasing defense.

James pointed to the book cover, where the chief embraced a schoolteacher so voluptuous that she was bursting from her low-cut gown. "What I want to know is, how come you never wore a dress like that to provoke my savage endearments?"

She took the book away and put it in a desk drawer. When she faced him again he saw a sheen of humiliation in her eyes, and it made his stomach twist with regret. The last thing he'd wanted to do was hurt her feelings.

"I brought you something," he said gruffly. James reached into his jacket and handed her a sheaf of folded papers. "I checked on your great-grandfather. Here are some copies of what I found."

Her eyes brightened until she looked through the material. "It's true, then. Ross Gallatin was shot for being a spy."

"Erica, he must have been a very brave man. It was no dishonor to die that way."

"I know. I just wish my family had stayed closer to our Indian heritage. I mean, my great-grandfather Ross was a soldier, my grandfather was an actor, and my father flew fighter planes for the navy. I guess I don't have a very ethnic Cherokee background."

"Look what I got from the records in Oklahoma," James told her patiently. "Ross grew up on the reservation—no, I'm forgetting. It wasn't a damned reservation at that time, it was still the Cherokee Nation. A separate nation."

James pointed to a list. "See there? By the mid-1850s the whole Gallatin family was living in the Cherokee Nation in the Oklahoma territory. Justis, Katherine—Katlanicha must have been her Cherokee name—Silas, Holt, and Ross. He was raised Cherokee."

James added gently, "And when he died, at least he was killed by my great-grandfather and other Cherokee soldiers who knew he was a brave man and didn't look down on him for being an Indian or even a Union soldier." He touched her cheek. "You've got a lot to be feel proud of, *kamama egwa.*"

Tears rose in her eyes as she gazed at him. James had to struggle not to reach for her. Patience, he told himself. In a good game plan, timing was everything.

"How did you get this material from Oklahoma?" she asked.

"Oh, I had somebody do a little research and send it to me."

She shook her head in disbelief. "Did you go to Oklahoma last week?"

"Well, I've always wanted to visit my mother's relatives out there—"

"Oh, James." She got up and started to touch him, then wavered, smiled wistfully, and sat back down. "Thank you," she said, her eyes brimming with tears.

James tried not to look disappointed. After the intimacies they'd shared, after all the long, lazy conversations and all the laughter, couldn't she even bring herself to hug him in gratitude?

"I wish you could have stayed in North Carolina a few more weeks," he said as casually as he could. "You really ought to consider coming back after this Gibson project gets under way."

She chuckled and swiped at the tears on her bottom lashes. "I have an aversion to lime-green motel furniture when it's in a—what?"

James had taken a handkerchief from one pocket and now dabbed mascara off her bottom lids. "You forgot that you have on makeup."

"Oh, hell." Looking embarrassed, she sat rigidly still and stared at his hand.

"That could make you cross-eyed. Why not look at me?" He arched a teasing brow. "Or do you still act wimpy when men admire you?"

Her gaze snapped up. "Is that what you're doing?" she asked softly, but with anger. "I don't understand why you came here today."

He put his handkerchief away slowly, as if thinking very hard. "I still don't understand why you lost interest in North Carolina so quickly."

"I didn't. You set up a deal for me. I have work to do."

"Once the project gets going you won't be needed on the site. Why don't you come back to the reservation for a few more weeks?"

She held up her hands in exasperation. "If you

wanted me to stay longer, why did you go to so much trouble to get the Gibson contract reinstated?''

"I owed it to you. I was responsible.''

"Responsibility!'' Her tone was sardonic. "All you had to say was, 'I'm through being your teacher,' and I would have moved out of Dove's house.''

"I'm not through.''

She shook her head wearily. "Look, you're moving into Dove's house permanently, with all your personal possessions. You'll be making it a real home. So I can't stay there—''

"Why not?''

"Do you plan to stay somewhere else?''

James grimaced. What had happened? Why in the hell didn't she need him anymore, even for sex?

Frustration and distress boiled over suddenly. He stood up, planted a hand on each arm of her chair, and stared grimly into her eyes. "You wanted to learn everything,'' he said in a low, seductive voice. "Do you think I've already taught you everything I know?''

"I don't want to play your games anymore,'' she whispered.

"You don't like this anymore?'' He lifted one hand and trailed a fingertip down the silky off-white blouse showing between the lapels of her suit. When the breath soughed out of her, James slipped his hand under the jacket and stroked her breast.

The subtle forward movement of her body, needy for his touch, the immediate reaction under his fingertips, the shivering way her breath touched his face, made James sigh with relief.

"You'll always need me, at least in this way,'' he told her grimly, pulling her out of the chair and into a possessive embrace.

"James,'' she protested, then searched his eyes and whimpered, "*James,*'' in a yearning tone. "When you said you were coming up here and you didn't want me to come with you I thought you were tired of being involved with me.''

"No, Red, Lord, no. I was only trying to do what

was best for you. You've got me for whatever you need, for as long as you need it."

She made a tearful sound of surprise and raised her mouth to his, covering it with quick, tugging kisses as she stroked her fingertips over his jaw.

James bent her backward and licked her lips with the tip of his tongue, then savored them with a long, deep kiss that made her knees buckle. She sat down on the edge of her desk and he stepped closer, pushing her knees apart.

He'd known all along how he wanted this meeting to go; he was going to seduce her, court her, turn her inside out, until she wanted to be with him no matter what.

"I'm going to show you a new way to use your desk," he warned her.

"James!"

He pressed her down atop stacks of paperwork and blueprints, his body covering hers. Her long legs dangled off the end of the desk, hugging his thighs as she struggled awkwardly for someplace to put her feet.

James parted her jacket and began unfastening the little pearl buttons down the center of her blouse, stopping every second or so to squeeze the incredibly soft hills on either side. She turned her head away and covered her mouth with both hands to muffle a soft moan.

The heat inside his body made caution difficult. James arched against her and asked wickedly, "How soundproof are your office walls, doll?"

Her chest moved swiftly. She was vibrating under him, her legs moving back and forth against his thighs, and it made him crazy with the need to satisfy his own wants, and hers too.

"I don't know," she finally managed to say, sounding breathless and distracted. "I've never had a business meeting . . . like this . . . before." She gripped his shoulders and looked at him with gleaming, startled eyes. "The door—"

"Is already locked," he said in a lecherous tone, and smiled.

Her lips parted in astonishment but quickly edged up at the corners. She yipped as he cupped both hands around her wriggling thighs and pulled them up to his hips.

James jerked open his trousers.

Erica yipped again. "You're not wearing any briefs!"

"I *knew* I forgot something this morning. We wolves are like that."

She laughed helplessly. The sound broke off in a soft squeal of delight when he shoved her skirt up. His hands touched garters and, a little higher, sheer, lacy panties. She'd always favored plain cotton before. "More shopping," he murmured, with a hoarse chuckle.

"They're pretty flimsy," she whispered, and gave him a meaningful look. James sank his teeth into the shoulder of her jacket and hid his laughter there. With one quick motion of his hand he tore the silk barrier from her body.

"I'll replace them," he promised, and groaned softly when he saw the glow his impatience had brought to her eyes.

She gasped and moved underneath him, biting her lower lip to keep from making more sounds as he touched her.

"Just wrap those gorgeous legs around me and don't let go," James whispered, moving against her, then moving inside her, while her hands feathered over him and she lifted her mouth to take his in a long, sweet kiss.

He clasped her face between his hands and looked into her eyes. *Love me*, he ordered silently.

"*Da-nitaka*," she whispered in a voice torn by bittersweet passion. "Oh, Wolfman, I'm so glad to be standing in your soul again."

ERICA NOW UNDERSTOOD exactly where she stood in James's soul, and it brought her a stoical sense of hope. Her lack of possessiveness had reassured him. He thought that he didn't have to worry about hurting her when he moved to North Carolina, where he'd turn his attention to building a cozy, quiet life with some lucky Cherokee woman.

In the meantime, he gave her the kind of whole-hearted masculine attention that she'd only dreamed about. Washington was just a big playground to him, a playground filled with toys she'd always ignored in the past because she'd been too busy at work, and too self-conscious about going places alone.

But now she had James, who cheerfully sat through the touring production of *Cats* even though he said he'd listened to more interesting *wis-sah* music outside his bedroom window when the moon was full; James, who introduced her to the joys of Sunday brunch, striptease checkers, *Sports Illustrated*, and the subtleties of the four-man defense as compared to the three-man defense with a designated nose-guard.

Sometimes they sat in her living room late at night eating popcorn and watching reruns of *The Lone Ranger*, and they broke each other up ad-libbing rude dialogue that made "Kemosabe" the only polite word Tonto said. Sometimes they watched old westerns and spent half the time yelling things like "Call off the war party! They've sent for John Wayne!" and "Watch out, Running Buffalo, that white man's from Washington!"

Among other delicious secrets, they developed a game that when strangers came up to James in public and asked if he was Indian he feigned a blank look and Erica spoke to him in Spanish.

No, James would answer in horrible high-school Spanish that he faked considerably, he was Rodriguez y Montasantonio, a diplomat from a small island country off the coast of Surador, in South America. He was in town to see the President.

She'd translate for the strangers, and they were always suitably impressed.

Because James wanted to know more about the way she'd grown up, she resurrected talents she thought she'd forgotten. She taught him how to fold dinner napkins into artistic designs, how to choose a good chablis, and how to do a respectable imitation of a Boston accent.

And finally, after he'd lived at her condominium for three weeks, he offered to show her his home in Virginia. She'd almost given up hope of seeing where he lived, because he seemed reluctant even to talk about it.

In honor of the trip he retrieved his car from storage at a Washington garage. She'd begun to wonder if he had an aversion to owning a car, since he always rented cars or took taxis.

Now Erica knew it was simply that he didn't need to own more than one car, not when he had the perfect car already. He drove her through the Virginia mountains in a mint-condition, cherry-red Chevrolet convertible, circa 1957. It was a lovely dinosaur that gleamed from the fins in back to the big chromed grill in front.

The car confirmed her suspicions. James liked a flashy lifestyle more than he wanted to admit, and he was going to have a hard time readjusting to the quiet simplicity of the reservation.

Then they arrived at his home. It was only a ninety-minute drive from Washington, but it belonged in another century.

"I told you it wasn't modern," James said solemnly, after they traversed the two-mile gravel road through dense woods, across a creek via a wooden bridge, to the top of a ridge, where Erica saw a small cabin built of hand-hewn logs.

She got out of the car and began to laugh. Even though she wanted him to be too cosmopolitan to leave Washington and her, she was so proud of him that she couldn't help chuckling at her misconceptions.

"A caveman," she announced, "would have found this a bit primitive."

James held out a hand. "Come see."

There were no modern utilities of any kind; just a well with a hand crank to draw water, a fireplace for heating and cooking, and oil lamps for light.

Inside, among crowded bookcases, animal skins, woodworking tools, and photographs of the family, Erica gazed in awe at magnificent oversized furniture ruggedly designed but impeccably crafted.

She stroked the sleek maple of a dresser and ran her fingers over the Cherokee symbols that he'd etched into one corner. "I know these. *Wa-ya.* Wolf. Is that your signature?"

James slid his arms around her from behind and looked over her shoulder. "Yeah. What do you think?"

"I think you could make a great reputation for yourself, selling this kind of furniture throughout the Southeast."

He chuckled. "You plan big. You think Becky can sell her beaded boots to Neiman-Marcus."

Erica nodded. Now seemed an appropriate time to mention her idea. "And I think if you were my partner we could buy up some of these shops in Cherokee and turn them into places the tribe could use as a craft co-ops."

She rushed on, feeling anxious about James's reaction. "The two of us have the money to take a risk— we could bring in really topnotch native arts and crafts from all over the country. And why should the shops just sell native items? Art is art. We could bring in white artists too. You know, give them a classy place to show their work to an incredible number of tourists.

"You want to sell furniture? Sell it in one of your own shops. With a little luck and the support of the tribe I bet we could start something important."

James's hands tightened on her stomach. "And

you'd want to supervise that project?'' he asked in a soft, unfathomable voice.

Oh, damn. The thought of having her around that much made him nervous. He was afraid she'd want to stay permanently. ''Well, no. You could supervise it. I'd be your long-distance partner, I suppose.''

''Forget it.''

He let go of her and walked to a window, where he stood looking out, with his hands shoved in the back pockets of his jeans. Erica swallowed tears of sorrow that had more to do with herself than the proposed shops.

''Why not, James?''

''It's a good idea, but you're the key promoter. I'm not a businessman—not really. I just want to build furniture. You're the wheeler-dealer. You're the one who would need to be in North Carolina all the time.''

*Where I can watch you pick out a nice Cherokee wife and start a family? No, thanks.*

''I don't think I could live on the reservation,'' she murmured, thinking of the one home she wanted but couldn't have. She loved Dove's place; she'd missed it more than she'd ever let James know. She could live there if she had work . . . and James.

He turned around, his face shuttered. There was no anger in him, or if there was, it was carefully submerged. ''Maybe I can find someone to help you with this idea. Travis has a lot of friends on the tribe council. He'd know who to ask. But you really ought to think about getting a place on the reservation and living there at least part of the year.''

''I'll think about it,'' she said cheerfully.

They stood there in awkward silence, as if neither of them had any idea what to do next. ''Well,'' James said abruptly. ''I didn't just bring you here to brighten up the place. Help me pack.''

IT WAS ALL over in a week's time. He was home, his stuff neatly arranged in Dove's house, *his* house,

and Erica was still in Washington. She'd tenderly
made love to him one last time and cried a little when
he left.

He was miserable.

He was miserable, and on his first day home he was
the guest of honor at a barbecue that seemed to have
drawn half the Cherokee tribe.

"My grandson has come back to his people,"
Grandpa Sam said solemnly, gazing down at James
from where he stood atop a chair in the front yard of
the Tall Wolf home. In honor of the occasion he'd put
on an outfit Becky had made for him—buckskin leg-
gings held up by leather garters, a long buckskin loin-
cloth, a colorfully striped thigh-length shirt belted with
a braided sash, and a matching turban wound around
his head.

That was the way Cherokee men had dressed in the
early 1800s, and it had not only a certain nobility to
it, it had sex appeal, James thought. When Grandpa
Sam moved just right, he flashed a bit of brown thigh
from under the hem of his shirt. The women in the
crowd applauded and whistled. Grandpa bowed.

Travis braced an arm against Grandpa on one side
to keep him from toppling over; Echo braced him on
the other side. Grandpa Sam had had a few snorts of
his favorite vodka.

"My other grandson has come home," he repeated,
holding out his arms toward James. "Now I have all
my grandchildren around me." Grandpa Sam grasped
his heart. "As soon as they all marry and give me
great-grandchildren, I can die happy."

With that announcement he climbed down and
went off arm in arm with a small army of his cronies.
Travis got up next. "My brother is an inspiration to
me," he said, his gaze holding James's. "He's always
tried to make his family proud. He's always loved his
family and his tribe, and now he's come home, where
we can take care of him, the way he deserves."

Travis got down, walked through the crowd, and
hugged James silently, which was Travis's way of say-

ing a great deal. After he turned and walked away, James stood without moving, his throat closed with emotion. If only Erica had been there to see that miracle. She'd helped make it happen.

He returned the tentative smiles and handshakes of people who'd never thought they'd see him and Travis as true brothers again. James was kissed on the cheek by a pretty young woman whom he remembered vaguely as one of Becky's classmates, and he was faintly aware of interested smiles from other women.

"Where is your friend from Washington?" one of them asked. "Are you going to marry her?"

"I'm never going to get married," he said with a devilish grin, and winked at her as he walked away. She giggled.

Two pairs of female hands latched on to his arms. "Now," Echo said sternly.

"Yes, *now*," Becky added. "Come with us."

They pulled him into the house and shut the door. Both of them put their hands on their hips and eyed him like angry chickens studying a fox.

"You can't ignore us any longer. Why didn't Erica come with you?" Becky asked.

"When is she coming back?" Echo demanded.

James was in no mood to explain that their big brother had fallen desperately in love with a woman who didn't love him. But if he didn't explain he felt reasonably certain that Echo and Becky would enlist Travis and Grandpa Sam and that together they would make him more miserable than he already was.

"She doesn't belong here. She knows that she wouldn't be happy here, and she's honest about it. But I'm sure she'll visit again."

Becky said something in Cherokee. He believed it was some sort of womanly insult aimed at him. "Did you ask her to come back?"

"In a way."

"Did you tell her that you loved her?"

"No. I don't recall telling either of you that I loved her either."

Echo tossed up her hands. "Are we blind?"

Becky jabbed a finger at him. "Are *you* blind?"

"No, but I wish I were deaf."

"Of course she won't come back if she thinks you don't love her," Echo protested.

James held up both hands patiently. "Now, sisters, I know neither of you has had a lot of experience with these kinds of relationships—"

"Arrrrgh," they said, more or less in unison.

Becky tapped his arm vigorously to emphasize her words. "Erica has too much dignity to chase a man who keeps saying that when he gets married he's going to pick a nice safe Cherokee woman who'll be sure not to run off and leave him."

"It's not like that," James insisted, frowning. "Has she ever told you that she loves me?"

Echo eyed him proudly. "She has too much dignity to talk about her feelings for you. I think she knew how much trouble there was between you and the family, and she didn't want to make any more. But we don't have to hear the words to know how much she cares. She told us about the steroids you took."

James stared at his sisters in dismay. "Why?"

"So we'd understand how hard you tried to make us proud all those years when we just thought you were a jerk."

Becky shook her finger at him. "Now, don't change our new opinion. Go get Erica."

About that time the front door opened. Grandpa Sam and Travis came in. "What's going on?" Travis asked.

"I'm being bullied by misguided sisters," James said wearily.

Grandpa Sam grasped his arm and looked down at him seriously. "Why didn't Eh-lee-ga come home with you?"

James shook his head in defeat. Surrounded by angry warriors. Now he knew how Custer had felt. He looked at Travis for support.

Travis crossed his arms and smiled pleasantly. "You're one dumb jock if you let her get away."

James groaned. "Look, she's headed for Boston right now to go to a party for her stepfather. He's just been appointed to the President's cabinet. As in President of the United States. You see what kind of life Erica leads? She's my best friend, but she doesn't love me, and she'd never move down here even if she *did* love me."

"I figured out some of that writing of Dove's you sent me," Grandpa Sam informed him. "And two of those Gallatin medals." He put a hand on James's shoulder and said solemnly, "I think you need to hear what I've learned." He smiled patiently. "And then I think you'll want to go to Boston and bring Eh-lee-ga home."

T HERE WAS NO doubt about it. James had taught
her a self-confidence that went beyond the appeal
of makeup, a new hairstyle, and a shimmering blue
dress that left one shoulder bare and hugged her body
from chest to ankle.

Something was different about her, whatever it was.
Because for the first time in her life, Erica Alice Gallatin was surrounded by flirting men.

"Your mother tells me that you build houses. Perhaps we could have dinner and discuss an addition to
my cottage at Cape Cod. You really ought to come out
and see the place."

"Now you've given me proof—tall women are sex-
ier than short women."

"I never knew Dorland Monroe had a beautiful
stepdaughter living in Washington. Why don't you
come up to Capitol Hill and have lunch with me?"

"The Boston Symphony's having a tea next week
to honor a violinist from Surador who just won a big

international competition. Care to attend as my guest?''

The attention had depressed her all evening, and the last invitation nearly dissolved her party smile.

Surador. The home of the great Cherokee diplomat Rodriguez y Montasantonio, alias James Tall Wolf. Erica blinked rapidly, made a polite excuse, and moved leadenly through the glittering crowd of gowns and tuxedos, feeling like a dark cloud surrounded by painfully bright sunshine.

She gave her empty champagne glass to one of the liveried waiters who was roaming the ballroom. The waiter had the terrified look all employees of her mother's wore.

Her beautiful, petite sisters breezed by, husbands in tow like cheerful penguins, all quite comfortably in their element.

Erica eased her way through the crowd to a distinguished, dapper little man who was holding court at one of the flower-decked cocktail tables.

"Pop," she murmured, and kissed his cheek. "It's a wonderful celebration."

Her stepfather looked up and smiled. "Your mother outdid herself." Dorland Monroe took her hand and frowned. "Are you having a good time? The Portuguese ambassador says you have an, ahem, 'alluring air of sorrow.' I suggested that you might have indigestion from the airplane food on the flight from Washington."

Erica chuckled. "I'm fine, Pop. Don't worry about me. Just enjoy your night."

She wandered outside, where the beauty of a star-canopied sky shone on guests who were dancing to elevator music provided by a small orchestra.

Elevators. Where were a private elevator and a big wolf when a big butterfly needed them? Erica bit her lip and felt the familiar anguish deep in her chest. She had a plan for learning to live without James. She'd simply move about in a daze and hope that no one noticed.

"There you are." She was grabbed low around the waist by a lanky man who seemed intent on jiggling her with one hand and his martini with the other.

Erica leaned tactfully away from his campaign-promise smile. "Senator, I—"

"You're just what a politician needs. Big, strong, healthy, Republican—"

"Independent."

He was trying to dance, but his martini olive was the only thing keeping rhythm. "I like independence in a woman."

"Not that kind of independent. The political kind."

"Baby, I can be very persuasive—"

"Not with my daughter, you can't. Excuse me, Erica. Senator, please help yourself to the buffet. Immediately."

Tall, commanding Patricia Gallatin Monroe swept between them, a brusque referee uniformed in an Adolfo original. She sent the senator scurrying and faced Erica with a grandly annoyed expression. "A man wishes to speak to you."

Erica groaned. "Not another one."

"You should have told me you'd invited a guest."

"I didn't invite anyone."

"Then Mr. Tall Wolf invited himself, and I'll tell him you're not available."

Energy shot through Erica like a tonic. "Where is he?" She was already on her way inside.

"In the front hall," her mother called. "We really don't have space for another guest."

*Like a dead horse doesn't have room for more flies,* Erica thought ruefully, to quote Grandpa Sam. She hitched up her dress and ran as best she could despite spike heels.

James waited in the foyer, smiling with sly satisfaction because people were openly staring at him. His midnight hair and bronzed skin seemed more exotic than ever in the light of the foyer chandelier, and his big, powerful body was perfectly packaged in a sophisticated black tuxedo.

Erica met his dark eyes as she tottered through the crowd, and he wasted no time cataloging every curve outlined by her gown. The smile that slid across his mouth said that wolves liked such goodies.

Breathless, Erica stopped at the foyer entrance and gazed at him in amazement. Happiness and bewilderment bubbled up inside her. *"Si yo, wa-ya egwa."*

*"Si yo, kamama egwa,"* he answered solemnly.

"I think he's from the Middle East," she heard someone whisper behind her. "They're speaking Arabic."

As Erica crossed the foyer to him she pressed her fingertips to her lips to hold back a smile that could too easily have accommodated tears.

Dangling over the lapels of his jacket was a necklace of wolf teeth that had been left to his family by his great-great-grandfather William. In one hand James casually held a leather bag covered with Becky's beadwork, and his feet were clad in mocassins.

"I'm the ambassador from North Carolina," he said gruffly, just before she kissed him lightly on the mouth. "I have a gift for you."

James presented the bag to her and said gruffly, "These are yours and Tess's medallions. Grandpa hasn't translated Kat's yet. It's giving him some problems."

Erica tenderly clasped the gift to herself. "Oh, James. You didn't have to come up here just to bring these to me."

He frowned again. "Well, it's my responsibility. I'm trying to tie up loose ends before I get too busy with things at home."

"Oh." Hope crashed inside her. He had an extraordinary sense of responsibility. Perhaps he just felt guilty for keeping Dove's papers from her all these weeks.

Erica straightened formally. "Well, did you just get here from the airport?"

"Yeah."

"Then come and have a drink, and something to eat."

"No." He nodded toward the bag. "Grandpa hasn't finished with Dove's papers, but he made some notes on what he's translated so far. She wrote some poetry that will, well, sort of surprise you. I can see that you're busy right now. Read the notes and call me tomorrow." He gave her the name of his hotel.

"Is that all?" Erica asked softly, her throat on fire. "You don't want to stay and visit?"

He glanced through the foyer and smiled at the finery and the crowd. James shook his head. "Not my style, Red."

"Not mine, either."

They traded a quiet, intense gaze. She searched his eyes desperately. "James, I—"

"Ms. Gallatin. Pardon me. Uh, pardon me, sir." A nervous waiter nodded to her, then James, then her again. "The senator asks if you'll meet him outside for the next dance."

Erica groaned inwardly. "Tell the senator that—"

"He can go stuff his ballot."

"James!"

Erica gaped at him as he strode to her. His teasing facade was gone.

"What senator?" he asked, glaring down at her.

Sorrow and confusion made a dangerous mixture. Erica retorted, "If you don't want to stay and dance with me, why do you care if someone else does?"

James grabbed her by one hand. "I've had enough politeness to last me my whole damned life. We're not getting anywhere this way. Come with me."

"James?" She teetered after him, clutching the leather bag and trying to kick her shoes off so that she could keep up with his long, impatient strides. "What's wrong?"

He halted, looked around, and finally trained his

gaze on the winding staircase to the second level. "There."

"Let me . . ." She tried to get her high heels off before she broke an ankle. "I can't—"

He scooped her up over one shoulder and started climbing the stairs. Erica's undignified yelp brought guests running into the foyer. Hanging head down with her free hand braced on James's rump, she raised her gaze awkwardly and saw her mother gaping at her in disbelief.

"It's all right," Erica called. "It's a game."

James reached the second-floor landing and walked down a wide hallway, where the solemn furnishings whispered money and decorum. "It's not a game," he told her fiercely. "Not any longer."

He looked for an open door, found one, and carried her into her stepfather's private library. Erica watched him speechlessly after he plopped her on a massive antique reading table. "Open that bag," he ordered. He shoved the library door shut and locked it.

Erica fumbled distractedly with the leather sack. "Is it that important?"

He stood in front of her, scowling, his arms crossed, his legs apart. He looked like a modern war chief. "It's that important to me."

Her hands shaking, she laid hers and Tess's medallions on the table, then reached into the bag again. Erica cried out softly as she pulled her great-grandmother Erica's locket from the bag. It gleamed with a new covering of gold.

"Oh, James." She opened the locket and found the inscription restored. " 'Wed June 21, 1860. R.T.G. to E.A.R.' "

"I took it to a jeweler after I went back to Washington," James explained.

Erica pressed it to her lips and looked at him tearfully. "I'll never forget this moment."

"Look at Grandpa's notes about the medallions."

She put the locket aside and pulled a sheaf of typewritten pages from the bag.

"Echo typed them for him," James explained. "His handwriting's not too steady."

Her heart racing, Erica gazed down at the first page.

Eh-lee-ga, when I finish with Dove's papers I think you and your cousins will have a good history of the Gallatin family as it was told to Dove by her father, Holt.

Some folks said Dove had powers to see the future. She wrote down her dreams in poems. I have figured out one that you will want to know.

But first, tell your cousin Tess that her medallion says on one side that Katherine Blue Song's parents and sisters are buried on the land in Gold Ridge. On the other side it says, "Katherine Gallatin, wife of Justis Gallatin. A bluebird should follow the sun."

Feeling awed, Erica raised her head and looked at James. "Then my Cherokee relatives are buried on the land in Gold Ridge. Katherine's family."

James nodded. "You don't want any mining company to come in and tear up that land."

"No." Trembling, Erica shook her head fervently. "Absolutely not. I'm sure Tess and Kat will agree that we don't want to lease it for mining."

He came to her and took the notes. After shuffling through them for a moment, he handed her back one page. When his hand brushed hers she felt the tremor in it. "James? Are you all right?"

"Read that," he murmured. "It's a poem Dove wrote."

Erica bent her head and read:

*I see the white butterfly surrounded by blue,*
*I see her bring light to the darkness,*
*I see her welcome the cat who has a broken foot,*
*I see her gentle the wolf,*

*I see her fold her wings with contentment,*
*And love what I have loved,*
*Because this is where Eh-lee-ga the butterfly belongs.*


Erica slid off the table and sat weakly in a chair. She couldn't describe the feeling of awe that shimmered in her veins. "It's amazing."

James knelt beside the chair. "A white *kamama* of the blue clan inside a house with blue walls," he whispered, his hand on her arm. "A house with rooms painted blue, like Dove's house. You put up floodlights so you wouldn't be afraid of the darkness. Your cousin Kat came to visit you with a fractured ankle." He paused, then added gruffly, "And you certainly gentled the wolf."

She looked at him through a haze of tears. She was crying from the wonder of it—the beauty of Dove Gallatin's gift. She finally felt like a Cherokee. "She even said my name. Eh-lee-ga."

James nodded. "And she said you'd be contented, because you'd be where you belonged."

Erica glanced away, swallowing hard. "I did feel that I belonged there."

He put the other pages in her lap. "Here," he said gruffly. "Read about your medallion."

She looked down, heedless of the tears slipping from her eyes. " 'I left my footprints on the trail where they cried, but I left my heart with Justis Gallatin'. On the other side of the medallion it says—"

Erica halted as James covered her lips with one finger. His gaze held hers desperately. "It says," he whispered, " 'A wolf will find his mate, no matter how far she roams.' "

She made a soft sound full of bittersweet emotion and said in a barely audible voice, "Do you think Justis rescued Katherine from the trail?"

James nodded. He gripped her arms tightly and, without ever taking his eyes from hers, added, "I hope it means something else, too. I think that's why Dove gave it to you."

Old prophecies were a fragile bridge between them, waiting for her to send them crashing or strengthen them. Erica took a deep breath. She would always be a builder.

"Is that why you've come here tonight? To . . . to find your mate?"

Past and future were suspended as James searched her eyes. *"Yes."*

She took his face between her hands. "Then you've found her," Erica answered softly.

THE BUTTERFLY WAS content again, and the wolf was more gentle than ever. He lay on his back in a mountain meadow, sighing peacefully from time to time.

"James?"

"Hmmm?"

"Don't you think we'll get sunburned if we do this very often?"

"Cherokee skin doesn't get sunburned," he answered, pulling her closer to his side.

"Not even in delicate places?" Smiling, she caressed the areas in question. "Not even on the *wautoli* or the *tse-le-ne-eh?*"

He chuckled. "I love it when you talk dirty." Then he reached over and stroked her breasts. "Not even on the *ganuhdi-i.*"

"Ah. If you say so, then I won't worry."

He opened one eye and squinted at her in the summer sun. "But you're a different sort of Cherokee, so I think we'd better go back inside before you turn into a redskin the painful way."

Erica kissed him. "Thank you, Wolfman, for understanding."

"No problem. I love your skin just the way it is."

She arched one brow. "Freckled?"

"Naked."

He chased her into the forest and tickled her while she tried to get dressed. When her T-shirt and cut-offs were finally back in place she attacked in revenge, biting his chest and stomach while he hopped on one foot, pulling a pair of jogging shorts up his legs.

"Butterflies don't bite," he protested.

"When they're going to marry wolves, they have to learn how to bite," she explained, laughing while she nipped at his shoulder.

He wrestled her to a truce, and they walked the rest of the way home holding hands companionably. They found a note from Echo tacked to the front door. "The lawyer from Gold Ridge wants Erica to call him right away."                              .

James stretched lazily. "I guess it's time we put in a telephone."

Still looking at the note, Erica chuckled. "Now, why do I suspect that cousin Kat has stirred up some sort of trouble?"

"Trouble? Red, if you want trouble, c'm'ere." He sat down in the rocking chair on the porch and pulled her into his lap.

Erica put her arms around his neck. "I've grown to love trouble," she whispered.

He looked at her gently. "Trouble loves you." James touched the medallion she wore. "You stood in my soul even before I knew you."

Erica nodded. "Katherine and Dove knew that you and I belonged together."

"Katherine knew?"

"A woman who'd go to so much trouble to preserve her family's heritage must have known that it would be cherished again someday. Maybe she was predicting our future when she wrote about wolves finding their mates." Erica nodded solemnly. "I bet she and Dove were in spiritual cahoots."

"Spiritual cahoots?" James repeated in a droll voice. "For a practical woman you've sure got some wild ideas."

"Look, if you can believe in Little People and invisible people who live underground and *Uktenas* and—"

"Then you can believe in prophecies stamped on gold medallions," James finished.

"Right." She touched her lips to his.

James leaned back and studied her for a moment. "Why, Eh-lee-ga Tall Wolf," he whispered happily, "I believe I can tell the future by looking in your eyes. And I love everything I see."

K ATHERINE BLUE SONG made her way out of the huge Cherokee camp, dimly aware of the glances of the soldiers stationed around the perimeter. She knew they didn't care if one less scrawny, sick woman survived the march to the Western territory.

She staggered when her worn moccasins let frozen clumps of snow torment feet that were already chapped raw, but the fever kept her from shivering. Physical discomfort faded along with her hope for survival, and she wished for only two things—that she could tell Justis Gallatin how much she loved him, and that she could be buried beside her family in Georgia.

*Someday I'll go back there.* The promise had kept her spirits up for months, but it was folly to believe it now.

Disoriented from sickness and hunger, Katherine wasn't certain how far she walked along the high bluffs overlooking the Mississippi River. She dropped her frayed blanket on a snowy knoll, then sank down on it and draped her hair around her shoulders as a little protection from the cold. The thin linsey-woolsey dress she wore was a far cry from the fine gowns Justis had admired so much.

Tears filled her eyes as she gazed at the broad, ice-filled river. Under a full moon, the ice shimmered like the crystal chandelier her mother had hung in the dining room back home. Too fancy for a farmhouse, her father had said teasingly, but the Blue Songs were prosperous, proud farmers, like many of their Cherokee relatives.

The chandelier hadn't survived the robbers who attacked after the state militia came.

*I'll buy you a dozen chandeliers,* Justis had told her later, gruffly trying to be kind.

*Justis.* Katherine lifted her face to the moon and gazed woozily into its pale light. "I wish he had loved me," she whispered.


"HER NAME IS Katlanicha Blue Song," Justis Gallatin told the grim-faced Cherokee matron. "But she goes by the name Katherine, too. I just want to find her. I don't mean the gal no harm."

He squatted by the campfire and pushed a wide-brimmed hat back from his face so that the woman could study the honesty in his eyes.

She stared hard into their green depths, then studied his chestnut hair and frowned at his moustache. Finally she scowled at the luxury of his heavy fur coat and warm wool scarf. Without hesitation he pulled the scarf off and handed it to her. She ignored the gift.

"You call her 'Beloved Woman,' " Justis said, speaking slowly so that she'd understand his poor Cherokee. "Everyone on the trail has heard of her. She knows white medicine and white ways."

"I hear nothing of such a one." The old woman stirred hominy gruel in a chipped kettle set on the embers at the fire's edge. "Go away."

No one was talking. They didn't trust him, and so they protected Katherine. He understood why they loved her—Lord, how he understood. If only Katie had believed that no one, Cherokee or white, could love her more than he did.

Justis stood wearily, his shoulders slumped. He was a strong, no-nonsense man, used to hardship and self-denial, but tonight he was nearly beaten by the fear and fatigue that had swallowed him during the months since Katherine's disappearance. Dully he noticed a lanky young Cherokee man hurrying toward the campfire.

"Mother!" he exclaimed in Cherokee. "The Beloved Woman won't eat! And she's gone to walk beside the river alone!"

The woman gasped. "Be quiet!"

Justis ran for his horses. Behind him he heard the woman yelling for help.


KATHERINE SWAYED AS a gust of wind hit her. She leaned forward, placed both hands on the blanket, and braced her arms. Five-foot-long strands of thick black hair floated behind her as she tilted her face up even more toward the high, cold moon. She could feel its silver fingers running over her.

This same moon was shining on Georgia, blessing the graves of the parents and sisters who kept watch over Blue Song land. Katherine's head swam, and she shook it groggily. Somehow, some way, that land would always belong to her family, even if Justis produced a thousand deeds bearing his title to it.

She cried out sadly. Justis Gallatin had become part of her soul, but he'd never own her, any more than he owned the land in Gold Ridge. Some things had to be won through love, and love alone.

At first she didn't hear the repetitive thudding of horses' hooves racing up the slope to her sitting place. When she did, she lurched to her feet. Katherine staggered, then caught her balance and looked wildly toward the sound.

The moon silhouetted the dark figures of a tall rider

and two big horses. The horses were only a few strides away, and they were charging directly toward her. The rider reached out in her direction.

The horse's shoulder bumped her, and she nearly fell down. When Katherine felt the rider's hand winding into the neck of her dress, she began to claw at him and struggle.

"Katie, girl, calm down!"

*Justis.* Stunned, she stopped fighting, and he pulled her onto the saddle in front of him. His long arm went around her waist like an iron band.

She sagged groggily against him, her hands digging into the wide, furry wall of his coat, her face burrowed in his shoulder. Her feverish mind knew only that hope had come back into the world, and she couldn't understand the distant sounds of men shouting and horses' hooves racing in muffled rhythms. Justis held her tighter and clucked to his horses. They went into a smooth, rocking lope following the riverbank north.

Katherine tilted her head back and tried to look at Justis in the moonlit darkness. Love overwhelmed her, until all she could manage to say was a plaintive, "Home?"

He bent his head close to hers, brushed a kiss over her forehead, and whispered, "Someday."

# KAT'S TALE

NATHAN CHATHAM HAD lived in places so remote that even the *National Geographic* wouldn't visit them. He was an adopted member of primitive tribes in various regions of the world, including one in South America whose witch doctor had tattooed his right buttock while the whole village watched gleefully.

A few years later he'd added to his ornaments by getting the top of one ear pierced. The African chieftain had given him a choice—either have the ear pierced or have it cut off. Being a practical man, Nathan had chosen to get it pierced.

As a kid growing up just over the Arkansas border from the Cherokee reservation, he'd assisted Cherokee shamans in ceremonies held for many purposes—from curing arthritis to conjuring up ghosts and talking wild birds down from their roosts.

Once as a very young man he'd shaved off his mustache and sprinkled the hair on a rose bed, just to see if it would really make the roses grow faster, as a shaman had said it would. The shaman had been right, much to Nathan's delight.

In short, Nathan had an abiding love and respect for other people's customs. But he'd never seen anything half so bizarre as this female wrestling match in the civilized environs of South Carolina.

"Ladies and gentlemen," the announcer bellowed into his microphone, "get ready for . . . four hundred pounds of Lady Savage, the Valkyrie!"

A huge, mean-looking woman shoved the entrance curtains aside and came marching down the aisle, giant metal cones thrust forward on her chest, a horned helmet perched atop her short, punk-cut blond hair.

The announcer said in solemn tones, "Only one woman in professional wrestling has the talent, the heart, and the sheer *raw courage* to face Lady Savage!"

The loudspeakers sent hokey tom-tom music reverberating through the room. "Fans, put your hands together for that fabulous Indian, that pride of the Cherokee people, the incredible Princess Talana!"

Kat Gallatin, alias Princess Talana, bounded through the curtains and scampered up the aisle with the lithe, graceful stride of a gymnast. A colorful warbonnet covered her head and fluttered all the way to her moccasined heels. Her face was streaked with gaudy war paint.

Nathan simply stared at her. She couldn't have been much more than five feet tall, with a lovely little face despite the goo, and a body that was curvaceous and slender. Every curve knew its place, he thought. Man, did it know.

All she wore was a buckskin miniskirt and a fringed buckskin halter top. Her skin was a beautiful honey color and she'd oiled her legs so that their movements produced a symphony of delicate, gleaming muscle.

She leaped to the edge of the ring and perched there holding the top rope, one arm raised to salute the crowd. Cheers rocked the ceiling when she blew kisses and gave everyone a dazzling smile which crinkled her deep-set eyes impishly.

"Me heap happy to see you! How!" she yelled, and held up one hand, palm forward in a gesture no one outside a bad B-rated Western had ever used.

"I know how, just give me a chance!" someone shouted.

Nathan felt grim disgust settle in his stomach. What kind of woman would willingly make a mockery out of her heritage for the entertainment of a bunch of drooling rednecks?

Five generations of Chathams had lived close to the Cherokees, starting when great-great-grandfather Nathaniel settled his family near Indian Territory before the Civil War. The Chathams had a lot of grudges against the Gallatins, but they'd always respected the Cherokee culture.

Obviously, Kat Gallatin did not.

Men and boys were going berserk around Nathan, stomping their feet, shouting her name, calling out blue remarks.

"Whip the Valkyrie's butt, squaw!"

"Tickle me with those feathers!"

"Let me be an Injun lover!"

"Take me to your wigwam, baby, oh, take me to your wigwam!"

This joke of hers wasn't funny at all.

Nathan hadn't expected Kat Gallatin to use her heritage like a bawdy gimmick. He hadn't counted on her being so lovely and graceful that he wanted to haul her away from these damned gawking men and warn her about the snickering comments they made in low voices that she couldn't hear.

She climbed into the ring, took her warbonnet off, and shook free two black braids that fell all the way to her hips. Then she grinned and gave the crowd a cheerful thumbs-up. She managed to look adorable and mischievous rather than tacky.

Nathan sat down, frowning. He hadn't counted on feeling this guilt either. He'd just wanted to see one of the Gallatin cousins up close before he took revenge on them and their land.

SOMEONE HAD ONCE told Kat that wrestling was really a simple morality play—good versus evil, right versus wrong. Having gotten no more than a very basic high school education from tutors hired by the circus, Kat wasn't too sure what a morality play was.

But she knew that Lady Savage was definitely evil, wrong, and just plain ticked off.

"Jeez, Muffie, calm down. You're the winner tonight," Kat choked out at a private moment while Lady Savage had her down on the mat in a pretzellike contortion. "I know you've had a bad day, but don't try to kill me."

"Sorry," Muffie grunted. "I hate men and this is a good outlet for my aggression."

She let Kat thump her in the neck and fell backward, flailing her beefy arms dramatically. Kat staggered to her feet, feeling so pummeled that she didn't have to fake it as she usually did.

Rent. Car payment. Those were her silent mantras as she wavered to the ropes and slumped over them. This was a heck of a way to make a living, but the money was decent.

The crowd yelled at her to watch out, that Lady Savage was coming up behind her. Kat took a reviving breath. Okay, so she'd struggle pathetically to get off the ropes, then turn around and kick Muffie in the stomach, just like in rehearsal.

"Arrrrgh! Svine! Indian svine!" Muffie clamped a hand to the back of Kat's neck, then wound the other hand into her leather skirt. Kat grimaced with discomfort as Muffie jerked her off the ropes. The leather skirt had built-in leather panties.

Lord, she hated getting a wedgie.

But the men in the audience loved it, of course, because they paid to see good bodies as well as good

body slams. Kat had spent most of her life wearing
revealing costumes of some kind or other, so like any
other professional athlete, she barely noticed the
ogling.

She just wished she knew what Muffie had in mind.

Muffie hoisted her overhead and walked around the
ring, snarling. Kat tightened her torso so that her back
wouldn't get hurt, then hung there looking desperate
and trapped.

Kat bit her lip to keep from smiling as the audience
immediately began to chant insults at Muffie. This was
a very effective change in the routine.

But then Muffie bellowed, "Men!" and launched
Kat at the front row.

There was no warning and no time to coordinate
her fall. She broadsided a hard masculine chest and
bounced her forehead off the victim's chin. His folding
chair skidded backward and collapsed, dumping both
him and her on the auditorium's concrete floor.

Wincing from the pain in her forehead, Kat was only
dimly aware of his grunt of discomfort as she sank an
elbow into his thigh. He grabbed her hands, pulled
them around his neck, and slid his arms under her.

"This means he gets to keep her!" someone shouted.

Kat heard other, more bawdy observations on the
victim's luck, and she began to get embarrassed.

"Sorry, man, sorry," she whispered between gasps
for breath. "The routine doesn't usually get this
crazy."

"I want combat pay."

The deep, slightly drawling voice made her tilt her
head back and look at him. And the sight of him was
more of a jolt than having been tossed by Muffie.

Gunmetal-gray eyes looked back at her with an intensity that belied the lazy, sensual droop of the lids.
They were part of a weathered face with a hand-
somely battered nose and a dark brown mustache over
a wide, strong mouth.

His face looked as if it had visited a lot of places
where life was interesting but not easy. His nose

looked as though the visits hadn't always been welcome.

His chocolate-colored hair was neat but rakishly long, and he wore a gold stud in the top of his left ear. *Ouch.* He had either been very stupid or very macho when he had got his ear pierced right in the thickest part of the cartilage.

*Danger, girl, danger,* she thought.

"Just let go of me," she whispered.

"You look like you're in pain."

*I always look this way when I'm hypnotized.*

"It's part of the act," she said softly.

"Oh." His eyes narrowed in dismay and he loosened his grip. "You have to let go of me, too."

Kat realized that she'd wound her hands into his V-necked sweater. Its soft blue material had an expensive feel to it, as if it might be cashmere, and she had twisted it into wads.

"Sorry, dude."

With that blithe reply she let go and rolled away from him. Once she was out of his startling embrace, she connected with the world again and realized that the crowd was in a frenzy and Muffie was headed straight for her.

Muffie had a wild look in her eyes.

"Oh Lord," Kat said plaintively.

She decided to act terrified—since that wouldn't take much effort at the moment—and covered her head with her arms. Peeking out, Kat saw Muffie grab a folding chair and raise it menacingly.

Oh no. If Muffie didn't do the chair bit just right, it would be curtains—hospital curtains—for Princess Talana. Muffie didn't look too interested in technique at the moment.

"She's not pretending," Mr. Pierced Ear observed grimly.

"You got that right," Kat told him. She leaped to her feet. One of the cardinal rules of wrestling was to keep the mayhem out of the audience. Promoters didn't like lawsuits from injured fans.

''Just stay on the floor,'' Kat ordered. ''I'll head her off.''

But this fan didn't want protection. In a flash he was on his feet, too, pushing her aside with an out-stretched arm. Kat bumped into the arm and stopped, gazing at him in shock as he stepped in front of her.

He wasn't overly tall or overly big, but there was a powerful, long-legged body inside that cashmere sweater, those faded jeans and—how odd, she thought—those leather moccasins.

And Muffie was going to kill him.

Kat grabbed his shoulder. ''Her sister ran off with her husband today,'' she hissed into the stranger's unpierced ear. ''She hates men right now. Get out of her way.''

Instead he held up both hands to Muffie in a pla-cating gesture. Muffie raised the chair higher and ad-vanced like a runaway bulldozer. The announcer was calling for the security guards. The audience was call-ing for blood.

''Put the chair down,'' that deep, resonant voice told Muffie calmly.

''I'll put it down your throat if you don't move!'' she retorted.

She swung the chair and he caught one leg of it with a deft twisting motion of his hand. Muffie lost her hold and the chair fell to the floor.

She balled her fists and took a swing at him. He stepped back and the punch missed him by a bare inch. Kat felt the wind of it on her face.

Kat groaned inwardly. Pierced Ear was a gentle-man. He wouldn't fight back. She admired that, but she couldn't let him get stomped because of it.

She ducked around him and charged Muffie, who kicked her in the ankle. Kat gasped as a pain like hot needles stabbed through her leg. She didn't have much time to wonder what the snapping sensation meant, though, because she had to save this fascinating man who wouldn't save himself.

Raising one fist, she cuffed Muffie on the jaw. Muffie pressed both hands to her face and staggered back, looking pitifully shocked. Kat ran up to her and said sadly, "I had to do it, kid. You can't trash members of the audience."

"You hit me on my abscessed tooth!"

"I know. I'll do it again if you don't behave."

By then the security guards and a bunch of the other wrestlers were on the scene. They grabbed Muffie and tugged her toward the exit amidst frenzied booing.

Kat's pulse felt thready and a sick prickling sensation ran over her shoulders. Her ankle was on fire.

The stranger grabbed her elbow. "You're limping." His voice held concern, but then he added sarcastically, "Or is it just part of this stupid routine?"

Kat turned to look at the rebuking expression on his face, and her admiration was replaced by dull fury.

She knew that look, that aura of disgust from men who thought she was a low-rent joke, maybe not much different from women who mud-wrestled naked in a strip joint.

"It's part of the routine," she told him, and pulled her arm away. "Thanks for playing along."

"The routine stinks."

"Hey, sweetcakes, when I want a lecture, I'll go to college."

"Do that. Get a real job. And stop selling yourself as a Cherokee. It's an insult."

Her stomach churned queasily from embarrassment and pain. What did he know about the way she'd grown up? Nothing! Who was he to act arrogant? "I should have let Muf—Lady Savage beat your brains out," Kat replied. "It would have been a small job."

She whipped around and hobbled toward the exit, blushing with humiliation and anger. Thanks to her skin tone, she knew Pierced Ear hadn't noticed the blush.

Agonizing jolts shot up her leg as she tried not to limp on it. *He* was responsible for this. If he hadn't tried to be a nice guy when he really didn't want to be . . .

The audience was cheering wildly. People reached out to slap her on the back and tug playfully at her braided hair. One of the other wrestlers, Maniac Mary, trotted up and put a supportive arm under her shoulders.

"Lean on me, Kat. Think something's broken?" she whispered.

"Yes."

"Don't be so tough. Stop trying to walk on it or you'll make it worse. Go for the sympathy shtick."

Kat sighed with defeat and leaned heavily against her friend. She blew kisses to the audience and wanted to cry because she knew what the stranger thought of her now.

IT WAS ONE of the most beautiful places she'd ever seen, this hilly forested land with its wide valley and lazy, gurgling stream. And the amazing thing was, it was part hers.

Hers. Kat Gallatin—the nomad, a woman who'd spent a great part of her twenty-eight years on the road or in cheap apartments, now owned a one-third interest in two hundred acres in Gold Ridge, Georgia. She felt very important.

She limped along a trail through wild honeysuckle and rhododendron, using her crutch to push low-hanging dogwood branches aside. At the edge of the stream she stopped and inhaled the cool, earthy scent.

Her great-great-grandmother Katlanicha Blue Song had been born on this land, and she'd made certain that it would stay in the family forever. The medallions had something to do with that, but they were still a big mystery to her and her cousins.

Lord, it was so secluded here, the June day was sticky, and her ankle throbbed from too much walking. Kat eyed the stream for a moment, then sat down and removed everything but her bra and panties. She took the elastic tape off her ankle and waded into the stream.

Kat sat down in a shallow part and leaned back on her elbows so that the water rushed over her lower body. Finally she lay down completely, with just her face protruding from the icy water and her hair floating around her like a black cloud.

It felt so right to be here; she felt so close to something, to *someone* she'd never known, that her chest constricted with happiness and homesickness and the odd notion that she'd lain here like this before.

Hah. *Déjà vu.* A chemical quirk in the brain. She'd heard it explained on a talk show once. There were no surprises in the modern world.

Kat sighed, stretched, then reached behind her and unhooked her bra. She wound it into a ball and shot it to the grassy bank with an expert overhand pitch.

It hit Pierced Ear right in the face.

THIS WAS WHAT it felt like to burn up from the inside out, to die from embarrassment. She wanted to dissolve into the water and float away.

He knelt on one knee, wearing nothing but khaki shorts and jogging shoes, his arm propped nonchalantly on his updrawn leg, her bra dangling coyly from his brawny hand. He looked like the kind of man who was used to having women throw their underwear at him.

Even though her breasts were underwater, Kat draped an arm across them. He tracked her actions with a rueful gaze. She stared at him speechlessly.

"Hello again," he said without smiling, although there was a hint of victorious humor in his gray eyes.

Finally her brain cleared. Had this man been following her since the other night? Had he followed her all the way from South Carolina? What did he want? Had he protected her before with the intention of harming her in some way now?

"I have friends with me," she lied through clenched

teeth. "They're at the end of the old trail, with my car, but they'll be here any minute."

He gave her a rebuking look. "No they won't. I saw you drive in. You're alone."

Dread filled her stomach. "Why are you following me? What do you want?"

He tossed her bra onto a holly bush, then sat down and crossed his legs. His chest and arms were darkly tanned. Even at a distance she could see sun-lightened brown hair on his chest and patches of freckles on his shoulders.

"Relax, Princess Talana. I'm not here to body-slam you."

He idly stroked a gold nugget that hung from a slender gold chain around his neck. The nugget nestled seductively in a patch of brown-blond hair at the center of his chest. Ropy muscles flexed around it when he shifted his position.

"Why'd you follow me?" she demanded again.

Kat would have bet money that this man hadn't gotten his physique or his tan at a health club, and that the gold nugget hadn't come from a jewelry store. Considering his attitude, the longish hair, and the pierced ear, he was probably a Hell's Angel looking for a girlfriend.

"I'm not following you," he assured her. "I was here first." He pointed over his right shoulder. "I have a camp in the bend of the stream back that way."

"This is private property. Did you know that?"

"Yep."

"In fact, this is my property."

"Yep. I know."

"How do you know?"

"You're Kat Gallatin. You have two distantly related cousins. The three of you just inherited this land from a nearly full-blooded Cherokee woman named Dove Gallatin, up in North Carolina. This land has been in the Gallatin family for at least a hundred and fifty years—probably a lot longer than that, since it belonged to your great-great-grandmother's people, and they were Cherokees of the Blue clan."

Kat gaped at him. She couldn't help it. He knew almost as much about her family history as she did. "Who *are* you?"

"Does the name Chatham mean anything to you?" She shook her head. "Should it?"

He stared at her hard for several seconds. "I'm with Tri-State Mining."

"Oh. Oh!" Still, she frowned at him in bewilderment. "What are you doing here? We haven't signed any agreement to lease the mining rights."

"Not yet, anyway."

"I don't think we're going to, either. At least not until we learn more about our different branches of the family."

"Hmmm. Well, I'm just a geologist. Doing some studies for the company. Harmless stuff. Soil samples, nothing to worry about."

Kat looked down at the icy water rushing over her body. She was beginning to shiver, both from the water and his provocative stare. The man was used to looking at naked women through those droopy bedroom eyes of his. He didn't seem the least bit eager to stop enjoying her situation.

"This is ridiculous. I'd like to get out of the water."

"Go ahead. I didn't think you were the modest type."

"I'm not the immodest type, either," she said grimly. "Look, you're confirming my suspicion that you're a stuck-up jerk. And a dirty-minded jerk, too. And whatever your name is, Chat-ham, I want you off this land."

"Nope. You'll need your cousins' agreement to kick me off, and I heard that your cousin Tess is out of the country."

"Jeez, you're a regular fountain of information about us Gallatins. Did Tri-State have us investigated?"

"Yep. I know that you and your cousins were all

born on the same day, different years. Very interesting. Some people might say it means something. You're twenty-eight, Erica's thirty-three, and Tess's twenty-six. Erica lives in Washington, D.C. Tess lives in Long Beach, California."

He smiled wickedly, enjoying himself. "They've got money; you don't. You drive an old Mustang which you bought used five years ago, and you have a cheap apartment in Miami. If you're late with next month's rent, you're going to be evicted. I'd say you need the deal Tri-State's offering."

Kat shook with anger. She felt invaded, violated, and more naked than ever. How dare a man who owned cashmere sweaters and wore a gold nugget poke fun at her poverty!

"Get the hell away from me."

He stood up. "The name's Nathan Chatham. Geologist. In the mining business I'm called a gunslinger."

"In my business you're called a pain in the backside."

"Speaking of pain," he said sweetly, "you're a great actress. That limp was perfect the other night. Pitiful. You really looked pitiful. The injured Indian maiden. What a hoot."

Her eyes burned. "Don't be surprised if I *don't* visit your camp."

"So what are you doing here? Studying nature?" He drew himself up and looked around solemnly, as if imitating her. "Hmmm. Heap pretty. Trees. Water. Where fast-food restaurant?"

She understood why her people had once gone around scalping white men. It must have been great fun.

"I'm camping here, too," she told him.

That brought the first honest look of surprise to his face. "You're camping? Can't afford a motel?"

*That's right, wise guy,* she told him silently. "I was born in a circus tent, sweetcakes. I've spent most of my life on the road. I can outcamp you any day."

He laughed richly. "I doubt it. Where are you setting up?"

Kat thought if she didn't get out of the water soon her smaller body parts would freeze and fall off. Fingers, toes, nipples—the only thing saving them now was the heat generated by anger at Nathan Chatham.

She tilted her head and smiled widely, without any trace of sincerity. "Naaah, I don't want you to tell the cavalry where to find me after I loot and pillage you."

"It's *ravish*, loot, and pillage. Don't forget that part of the attack. I'll be disappointed if you don't ravish me."

Smiling, he strode off through the woods—*her* woods, dammit—as if he owned them.

KAT LOVED THE dawn, with its magical light, its stillness, its slow slide into sunshine. She'd always had to keep night owl hours because of the circus routines—most days started with an afternoon show and ended after midnight—and wrestling schedules were just as bad.

But after she moved here for good she was never going to miss another dawn. When she settled down. *Some day.* The story of her life. *Some day.*

But today she was going to take another shot at enjoying the stream. Kat trudged along wearing a Wild Women of Wrestling T-shirt over a black swimsuit. Across her shoulder she carried a cloth tote filled with a towel, soap, and shampoo.

She managed without the aid of her crutch, catching low tree branches for support. Finding a spot where the stream bank was flat and sandy, she kicked her Reeboks off and carefully set them in the fork of a tree.

Good running shoes were her one indulgence, and for all she knew, wild critters might like the taste of them.

A deep, musical voice cascaded through the quiet. Kat gasped, looked around, saw nothing, then stood

rock-still, listening intently. The voice was Nathan's
. . . but he wasn't speaking English.

The words were soft and rolling, the vocal equivalent of water bubbling over rocks in the stream. It was
the most ethereal sound she'd ever heard, and it made
her shiver with emotion.

Was it some native language? And if it was, where
had he learned it? And where the heck *was* he?

She edged onto the sandy bank and craned her head
around a huge laurel bush which hung over the water.
Peeking through the small, oblong leaves, she saw Nathan upstream, his back turned toward her, his hands
raised to the sky, his body newborn naked.

If he was some sort of nature worshipper, he certainly had a head start on being natural.

Kat stepped back from the stream, her heart pounding. Whatever he was saying, it appealed to her on a
subconscious level that wouldn't let her walk away.
Listening to it there in the midst of the land her Cherokee ancestors had loved for centuries, she felt as if
she'd slipped through a gateway in time.

A bird sang sweetly nearby. For a second Kat was
certain that she had only to look around to find her
great-great-grandmother smiling at her.

She trembled and didn't look. Kat shook her head,
a little frightened by the intensity of her imagination.
Abruptly Nathan stopped talking, and the morning returned to normal.

Kat stood there, wide-eyed, and debated her next
move. Oh hell, she might get in trouble, but she
couldn't leave without taking another look at him. She
inched forward.

He was washing, legs braced apart, arms lifted as
he scrubbed each armpit with cheerful vigor. He threw
the soap into the air, then whooped as he leaped up
and caught it before splashing back down.

Next he bent over and dunked his whole head in
the icy stream. Slinging his dark brown hair lustily, he
whooped again. Good heavens, he made washing an
athletic event.

And she was certainly ready to cheer.

Ordinarily Kat thought naked men looked too vulnerable, like newly hatched chickens who'd been happier before they left their shells. Growing up, she'd glimpse a few bare male essentials, but they belonged to circus performers who were hurrying from one costume into another without caring who watched.

Naked men with names like Blinko the Clown had not exactly been heart-stopping.

Of course, she'd seen her husband naked, but he'd never seemed comfortable either. Without clothes he always seemed to be tiptoeing, even when he wasn't moving. He didn't feel important without his designer underwear and custom-made suits, she'd decided.

But Nathan Chatham looked not only important, he looked positively thrilled to be stark naked in the middle of a stream. Speaking of which—what was that on his right cheek? Some sort of tattoo? Yes!

Kat leaned forward, peering intently. She couldn't make it out, but it was at least three inches long. Wasn't putting a decoration on that fantastic male fanny a lot like gilding a lily?

She'd give anything to know what the tattoo said. Then he turned around and she made a soft squeaking sound of admiration.

All men were not created equal, and the tattoo probably said, "Satisfaction guaranteed."

He was now lathering his hair forcefully, with great white suds falling on his chest and slithering downward, until all Kat could think of was a tree in the middle of a snowbank. A giant sequoia.

She pressed her hands to her mouth to keep from grinning ridiculously. It was only fair that she enjoy this show, after the show he'd had yesterday. Oh, she'd pay for this later in unfulfilled fantasies, but at least her fantasies would be a heck of a lot more exciting than usual.

Nathan bent forward, doused his head so long that she was afraid he might drown, splashed water all over himself, then stood up and looked straight at her laurel bush.

"Good morrrning, Kiiitty Kat," he called in a quaint voice.

She almost lost her balance and fell into the laurel. There was no point in pretending that she wasn't there, so she confronted this humiliation head-on, the way she handled most problems.

"Hi." She stepped into the stream and waved. "Turn on the hot water, would you?" He put his hands on his hips and confirmed her impression that he was totally comfortable being naked. In fact, he was a lot more comfortable naked than she was in her T-shirt and swimsuit, at the moment.

And he'd accused *her* of being an exhibitionist!

"It's not nice to spy on Mother Nature," he called sternly. "Next time either walk away or join me."

Kat wished she knew some obscene Cherokee sign language. "This is my stream and my woods and if you want to act like a waterbug, I guess I can stand anywhere I want to and watch you."

"Peeking through leaves is not the most mature thing to do."

"Any man with a lick of sense wouldn't expose himself like some sort of pervert when he *knows* a stranger might be watching."

The dark brows shot up. "Pervert?" he echoed grimly. "You put on a leather bikini and wrestle women in front of an audience and then call *me* a pervert?"

He waded to the bank, snatched a big white towel off a tree branch, slung it around his waist, and started downstream with long, purposeful strides. "If you really think I'm a pervert, then *run.*"

Kat stared at him in horror. Old memories stirred an irrational amount of fear inside her suddenly. What did she know about this man? Practically nothing.

He was at least a head taller than she, and that body had much more than an average share of muscle, stamina, and quickness. Plus, she could barely walk, much less run to save herself. If he weren't trustworthy, if he took her banter as an invitation . . .

She dived for the sandy bank with a force that sent tremors of agony through her ankle. Kat scrambled upright and pushed into the undergrowth blindly, overcome by a panic that numbed her senses.

She didn't know where Nathan Chatham was; she hardly knew where she was, and she didn't care what she might be doing to her fractured ankle. She grabbed a spindly tree for support and went down in a heap when the sapling snapped.

A hand latched on to her shirt. She screamed, twisted onto her back, and looked up into Nathan's severe frown. He held the towel around his waist with one hand; the other let go of her T-shirt and grasped her wrist firmly.

She realized that she was holding both hands up in a desperate and pathetic attempt to ward him off. Stars burst in front of her eyes because she was hyperventilating badly. "Don't," she gasped out, "Please, don't."

He got down on his knees, still holding her wrist, still frowning. She scrambled backward, digging her heels and elbows into prickly vines that a small part of her mind recognized as briars. He wouldn't let go of her wrist.

"Don't, okay? Please?" Kat begged, and burst into tears. That release of energy cleared her head a little, and she finally realized that he was talking to her.

"Dear God. It's all right, Kat, it's all right," he was crooning. "I'm not going to do anything to you. Sssh. I'm not going to attack you. I swear."

She was breathing so raggedly that air barely seemed to be getting past her throat. "Really?"

"Really," he said in a gruff voice. "I never thought you'd suspect me of—Katie, relax. Relax, gal, it's me. You know I wouldn't hurt you."

*Katie.* What was so calming about that nickname? And about the way he said *It's me*, as if she'd known all along but simply forgotten?

Kat cried harder. What was happening to her? Was she so stressed out from the odd turn her life had taken lately that she was imagining things?

"Kat, calm down," he murmured. He let go of her wrist and held his hand up in a soothing gesture. "Breathe. Breeeathe. Slowly. Slooowly. There. Breathe."

He coached her for at least a minute, his hand poised over her as if he were pressing air into her lungs with gentle insistence. The world came back to life. She stopped crying and her chest no longer felt like a bellows being pumped by a maniac.

Her ankle was a ball of throbbing pain, and the rest of her felt like a pin cushion from her mad dash into a patch of briars. "J—jeez," she managed shakily. "You m-must think I'm a n-nut."

But he was looking at her only with sympathy. He cleared his throat and said hoarsely, "No, I think something pretty awful happened to you once and you thought it was about to happen again."

Oh Lord, he was too perceptive. She nodded weakly, and embarrassment made her skin burn.

"Kat, I'm so sorry for scaring you," he said raspily. "I just wanted to see you squirm."

"Squirm." She managed a small smile. "And I *scrammed*."

He sat back on his heels and she finally noticed that beneath the towel his legs were covered in bloody scratches. The man had run not only bare-legged but barefoot into a patch of briars to stop her self-destructive stampede.

"Damn, Nathan, I'm sorry. This is awful."

But his attention was focused on her badly swollen ankle. "You really were hurt the other night. Why didn't you say so?"

"Pride," she murmured, and sat up. Briars clung to her. "You made fun of me."

He looked at her from under his brows, conveying so much anguish and regret in his gray eyes that she reached out and patted his jaw. He had a long briar scratch on it.

"You got hurt because you defended me," he noted.

"Uhmmm, we're not supposed to let the audience get beaten up."

He pointed to her ankle. "Did you lose your job because of this?"

"Nah. I can go back when it heals. It's just a fracture. It doesn't even need a cast."

He knelt there looking more and more upset. Kat shifted awkwardly and began pulling briars out of her hair.

"Easy. Be still." He knotted the towel tighter around his waist and went to work on the briars, gently freeing her. "I'm not going to hurt you."

He said it several more times, until finally she assured him softly, "I know that now, Nathan. I just freaked out for a minute. I'm okay. I'm not afraid of you anymore."

"When did someone attack you?" he asked grimly, tugging a briar away from her arm.

"A long time ago. I was twenty. It was somebody I knew, somebody my parents knew. I'd grown up with him. He worked for the circus."

"Circus?"

"I thought you had a line on everything about me and my cousins."

He shook his head. "Only your recent history."

"I was born and raised with the Sheffield Brothers Circus."

"This guy . . ."

"He liked to brag that he turned girls into women. Only I wasn't ready to turn, at least not with him."

"Did you report him to the police?"

She shook her head. "Local cops don't care what happens among circus people. They wouldn't have believed I was raped. I couldn't tell my family, either. They'd have killed the guy."

Nathan sighed heavily, dropped his hands against his thighs, and looked at her with distress in his sweet, lazy eyes. "It must have been worse than you're making it sound if it still affects you like this."

"It doesn't haunt me anymore. No, I just—" She really didn't want to hurt Nathan's feelings, so she searched for the right words. "I've never been in a situation like this one before. Alone with somebody sort of unpredictable . . . like you."

"Great," he said in weary self-rebuke. "I love knowing that I'm the only man who's terrorized you into hysteria."

His reaction made her catch her breath for new reasons. This man might be dangerous in some ways, but he was a gentleman in the best sense of the word. Kat punched his shoulder playfully. "I'm okay. And, hey, now I'm not afraid of you at all. I trust you. You could run naked around my tent and I wouldn't worry."

He raised a finger and wagged it in mock reproach. "You know, I'm not sure I like this other extreme, either."

As he continued to pull briars away, Kat moved her injured leg tentatively. She was vaguely aware of Nathan Chatham's eyes catching her attempts not to wince with pain. "I'll pay for freaking out," she muttered. "I bet I added about a week to my recuperation."

"Katie, you're a hell of a gal." He stroked his fingertips over the swollen ankle, and she tensed up, expecting the touch to aggravate her pain. Instead the throbbing eased a little.

*Katie. Gal.* She liked his touch and she liked the way he talked. Again she got the odd notion that she'd always liked these things. Kat gazed at him in awe. "A minute ago why did you say, 'It's me. You know I wouldn't hurt you.' I mean, we're strangers."

He stopped, frowned thoughtfully, and shook his head. "Hmmm. I don't know why I put it that way. I guess I don't think of you as a stranger."

They shared a puzzled look. Kat exhaled slowly and glanced around at huge, gnarled oaks and early morning shadows. "This is a weird place. Good weird. It makes weird things happen."

"How weird," he said drolly.

She cut her eyes at him. "I've got a better vocabulary inside my head. I just don't always use it."

Nathan smiled and carefully picked the last briar from her leg. "Let's see if we can get you out of here." He helped her up, then lifted her into his arms.

Kat's heart rate accelerated with a pleasant kind of excitement when she found herself nestled against his hard, sweaty chest. She latched her hands behind his neck and tried to look everywhere but into his eyes.

He stepped out of the briar patch and started in the opposite direction from her camp. "I live that way," she said, pointing over his shoulder.

Nathan halted and gazed at her worriedly. "I have some ice left in a cooler. I'm going to put it on your ankle and make you some breakfast."

"Ah." She felt guilty. He looked as if she'd accused him of evil designs again. Kat smiled at him. "Okay."

After he started forward she searched for neutral conversation. "That stuff you were saying before you took your bath. Was that some kind of Indian language?"

"Yep." He hesitated a moment. "Cherokee."

"It was?" Kat forgot any awkwardness and studied him curiously. "Are you part Cherokee?"

"Nope. But I grew up in Arkansas, right next door to the reservation in Oklahoma. I was like a grandson to an old medicine man. He adopted me."

"Is that why Tri-State sent you down here? 'Cause you're interested in Cherokee stuff?"

He didn't answer for a minute. "I know a lot about the Oklahoma Gallatins, yeah."

Kat squirmed with excitement and craned her head so that she could gaze directly into his eyes. "You do? See, my cousins and I only know that our great-great-grandma lived here in Georgia. Granny was a Cherokee named Katlanicha Blue Song and Grandpa was a white gold miner named Justis Gallatin."

She gripped Nathan's shoulders. "You mean they ended up in Oklahoma? Like they went on the Trail of Tears or something? Have you ever heard of Holt Gallatin? He was their son and my great-grandfather. I think he was a bandit. That's all anybody ever told me."

Overwhelmed by her torrent of words, Nathan stopped. His silver gaze held hers without flinching. Finally he sighed as if resigned and said, "I know about him. He killed two of my relatives."

H E WALKED ON calmly, as if he hadn't just announced that her great-grandfather was a killer.

"He did *what*?" Kat asked, stunned.

"Holt Gallatin ambushed my great-great-grandfather outside a saloon and shot him in the back. Gallatin went into hiding and never came back. It was decades before my great-grandfather caught up with him, and then they killed each other in a gunfight."

Kat clung to Nathan's neck, feeling dazed. He chuckled grimly. "You're digging your claws into me, Kitty Kat."

"Sorry. I'm just in shock. Are you sure that my great-grandpa went around blasting people?"

Nathan nodded. His arms tightened under her as he hopped gingerly from one foot to the other. "Ouch. Dammit."

Kat realized with a pang of guilt that he hadn't bothered to get his shoes before carrying her through the forest. "Let me down. I can walk."

"Nope."

"I don't think you like me anymore. I don't want to be a lot of trouble."

He rolled his eyes at her accusation and kept going. "You weren't responsible for our families' feud."

"It was a feud? Over what?"

"An old grudge that started during the Civil War. My great-great-grandpa Nathaniel was a Union officer; your great-great-grandpa Justis was Confederate. Mine caught yours, yours escaped, and mine got demoted because of it. He was disgraced. He resigned from a career in the army because of the scandal."

"But that didn't have anything to do with Holt Gallatin. That escape was his father's doing. Besides, why would the Gallatins want revenge on the Chathams if Justis Gallatin *got away?*"

"We never figured that out. Holt was just the type to pick fights without much reason, according to historical accounts."

"You mean somebody wrote this story down?"

He nodded. "One of my great-uncles researched it for a book. It was published about twenty years ago by the University of Oklahoma Press."

"What's it called? Can I get a copy?"

"Sure. The title's *Blue Fox, Cherokee Renegade.*"

Kat drew back and looked at him askance. "That doesn't sound very fair-minded, especially if a Chatham wrote it. Who's Blue Fox?"

"That was the Cherokee name Holt Gallatin took during the Civil War. He was just a kid, but he killed a Union soldier so that his father—Justis—could escape from my great-great-grandfather."

"Now wait a minute. There was a war goin' on. Justis was supposed to escape if he got a chance. Holt was only doing what everybody else was doing—protecting his family. You can't blame my relatives for disgracing ol'Nath—you're named after him?"

"Yeah."

"Hmmm. This is a real personal thing with you, then, right?"

"I'm not a fanatic about it. I'm just a history buff."

"Uh-huh," she answered in a dubious tone.

They reached a small clearing about a dozen yards from the stream. Kat gaped at the large majestic structure that sat there. "A teepee!"

"Let me guess. You saw one once on television."

"Don't lecture me," she said, raising her chin. "I know that the Cherokees lived in little huts. Later on they learned to build cabins and houses."

"Why, you've been reading up a frenzy. You might even learn something."

She glared mildly at him. Smiling a little, he set her down on a folded blanket beside the circle of rock that held the dead embers from his campfire. Kat was too distracted to pay much attention to anything around her; while he went inside his teepee she stared at the charred wood and mulled over everything he'd told her.

Was she really the great-granddaughter of a murderer? The thought depressed her; she'd been so excited when she finally started studying her Cherokee legacy, and now, to find out that Holt Gallatin had been some awful character who went around calling himself Blue Fox and shooting Chathams, well, it made her remember ugly things her husband had said, things about her being low-class.

"Here. The last of the ice from my cooler."

Nathan had traded the towel for his khaki hiking shorts, Kat noted thankfully. Lean and bronzed and too sexy for her to feel at ease, he sat down by her feet, holding ice wrapped in something white. The gold stud gleamed at the top of his ear. Wait a minute. It was no ordinary stud, it was a tiny rough nugget, sort of a miniature of the nugget he wore on the chain.

He pushed a hand through his dark brown hair to guide the drying strands into a vague imitation of obedience, then gently pressed the ice pack to her ankle. Kat watched his face in profile, studying the handsome, crooked nose, the provocative mouth, the thick mustache.

What in the world was she doing anywhere *near*

this man? One second he made her want to hold him like a long-lost lover; the next he told her that her family was no-good from way back. Considering what he thought of her work and her lack of sophistication, he must figure that she was worthless.

"I wish you could meet my cousins," she said coolly. "Tess is a diamond broker. She lives on a sailboat. She graduated from college and she has an English accent. Her mother was an Olympic skier from Sweden."

Nathan looked at her with one brow arched, as if she'd lost a few marbles. "That's nice."

"And my cousin Erica owns her own construction company up in Washington. She was born in *Boston.*"

"Uh-huh." He turned his attention back to her ankle, patting the ice bag more firmly into place and then cupping his hands around it.

Kat frowned at his lack of response. "So why'd Tri-State send you here if you don't like us Gallatins?"

"Because I'm their best gunslinger. Who said I don't like Gallatins? I just take a lot of pride in my family and I wanted to meet Holt Gallatin's descendants."

"Now wait a minute. Erica's great-granddaddy was Ross Gallatin: Tess's was Silas Gallatin. Ol' Justis and Katherine had three sons. I'm the only one related directly to Holt."

He sighed dramatically. "You've got my sympathy."

Kat jerked her foot away. The ice pack fell off and unrolled before he could catch it. She gazed at it in consternation. It was made from a pair of white briefs. *His underwear.*

"I don't let many woman wear my underwear on their feet," he quipped. "Don't pass up the thrill of a lifetime."

"Look, sweetcakes, you and me don't do so well together. I'm going back to my own camp."

"Nope. You can't walk." He deftly grabbed her big toe. "Stretch that leg out again."

"Let go of my toe!"

"Did anyone ever tell you that you're moody?"

"I don't know what kind of revenge you want to take on us Gallatins, but you can't bully me."

He looked at her through half-shut, guarded eyes. "Revenge? What makes you think I'm not simply doing my job for Tri-State?"

"Oh, sure, you hate my family, so you just happen to wrangle an assignment to do tests on our land." She shook a finger at him. "You'll go to your boss and tell him that there's no gold here. Well, me and my cousins think there is, okay? Lots of it. We've got medallions that were probably made from gold that came from here. I showed mine to somebody who makes jewelry and he said it was the highest-quality gold he'd ever seen."

Nathan stroked his mustache and smiled at her patiently. "I thought you weren't interested in leasing the land to be mined."

"Well, we probably won't. But don't you lie about what you find!"

His smile hardened. "I wouldn't do that. We already suspect that there's industrial-grade gold here. If there's something better, I'll find it and write an honest report."

"Good!"

This didn't make any sense, which was an indication of how much Nathan Chatham rattled her mind. She didn't want to see this land torn up by a mining company, but she was hotly accusing him of intending to ruin a mining deal.

"Let go of my toe," she ordered.

"Nope." He curved his fingers toward her instep. "Ticklish?"

When he smiled wider, she knew he'd read the answer on her face. "I don't know whether you're a devil or a saint, you pierced-ear white savage," she said lethally. "But don't you mess with me."

"You sit still, you wild-eyed Kat Woman, and let this ice do some good on your ankle. You may not like my company, but you don't want to risk making your ankle any worse. Right?"

She gritted her teeth. "Right."

"Good. Now I'll make breakfast, and you behave."

Smiling benignly, he released her toe and began stirring the embers of his campfire. Suddenly he reached over and smeared a handful of cold ashes on her scratched shins.

She yelped. "What are you doing?"

"Savage medicine," Nathan said solemnly. He scooped up more ashes and held them out to her. "Want to do your thighs without my help?"

Kat sighed with defeat and put her hands out for the ashes. "My thighs don't need your help."

"Think of me as a doctor."

"A witch doctor."

He poured the ashes into her cupped palms. "We're doing a good job of carrying on the Chatham-Gallatin feud. It ought to make you feel proud."

"You bet." Kat's determination flared, and she suddenly felt protective of her family history, no matter how many lawless Blue Foxes it contained. *No Chatham was going to have the last victory.*


SHE WOKE UP to the feel of a hand stroking her hair. It dawned on her slowly that the hand belonged to Nathan, but she didn't open her eyes or rebuke him. Instead she curled cozily on her side and pretended to snooze for another second.

Kat refused to consider that she'd fallen asleep as soon as she lay down on the air mattress he'd put beside his campfire for her, or that she'd smiled groggily when he'd covered her in one of his blankets as protection against the cool morning. She was injured, scratched, and emotionally exhausted; she was also wonderfully stuffed from breakfast. She deserved to be helpless for a little while.

But if this was the way he intended to fight the feud, she'd already lost.

He kept stroking her hair, cupping his hand over the top of her forehead and drawing it slowly downward. Kat felt him lift her hair and knew that he was smoothing it out behind her. Then he returned to caressing it.

She was glad he didn't know that he was petting a woman who relaxed like a boneless chicken whenever anyone fiddled with her hair.

Kat supposed that the weight of it made her scalp more sensitive than most people's, more receptive to touch. At any rate, the few times she'd had her hair done in salons she'd dozed blissfully through the wash, trim, and blow-dry, much to the amusement of the stylists.

"Wake up, Kat Woman," he said softly.

Kat sighed and yawned. "I can't. I was drugged with fried trout and biscuits covered in gravy."

"I think you ought to go put your foot in the stream. Cold running water would do it good."

"I can't think of anything I'd like better than to stick my foot in ice water. Go away."

"Kat, it's for your own good."

Suddenly she had no blanket. Suddenly two brawny hands were under her arms, helping her sit up. Her hair fell across her face and got sucked into her mouth when she inhaled. She sputtered and pawed at it.

Nathan Chatham's low chuckle only added to her problems. If he combined that rumbling sound with a scalp massage, she'd probably just dissolve into his arms like melted butter.

"Here. Let me." He pushed her hair aside and cupped her face between his hands.

The feel of his calloused fingers and palms made her eyes open wide, banishing sleep. He gazed down at her with quiet, intense scrutiny. "Where'd you get those green eyes?"

"I guess from my great-great-grandpa. He was the only white man in my branch of the family. I've heard that my father had green eyes."

"Didn't you know your father?"

"Nope. He and my mother were killed in a train wreck during a circus tour. I was only four. I was adopted by the Flying Campanellis."

"The what?"

"The Flying Campanellis. Italian trapeze artists."

He groaned. "No wonder you don't know anything about your Cherokee background. You're Italian."

She grinned. *"Si. Capisce?"*

Nathan looked at her sadly. "I apologize for making fun of your cultural ignorance."

"Thank you," she murmured softly.

*"Wado,"* he answered.

"Hmmm? Wad what?"

"It means 'thank you' in Cherokee. Say it."

*"Wado."*

"Now say this." He reeled off a short, musical sentence.

She echoed it carefully. "What did I say?"

He smiled. "Something on a par with 'You're the best-looking man I've ever seen.' "

Kat's lips parted in a soft sigh, and his gaze dropped to them. She couldn't think straight yet, and he was taking advantage. "I was duped. I meant to say, 'Which way to the stream?' "

He helped her to her feet, then scooped her into his arms again. Kat was very aware of his forearm nestling under her bare thighs. Her T-shirt had ridden up on her stomach to show her pelvis covered in a clingy black swimsuit cut high on the sides.

At the risk of revealing her dismay, she tugged the bottom of her T-shirt down as far as it would go.

He pursed his lips coyly. "An attack of modesty, Princess Talana?"

"You were looking at my thighs like Colonel Sanders eyeing a chicken dinner."

"Make that a Cajun dinner. You're covered in so much soot that you look like a blackened redfish." He paused. "A blackened redskin, I mean."

She chortled and covered her lips, disgusted with

his easy control over her humor. "You carry squaw to water," she ordered.

Nathan headed toward the stream a few yards away. "Don't use words like that. 'Squaw' is insulting. Back in the old days Cherokee women were a powerful force in the tribe. They had complete control over the children and the households. They had a say on the councils. A Beloved Woman could free prisoners taken in battle. All she had to do was step forward and touch them with a swan feather."

"What's a Beloved Woman?"

"Someone special, someone the tribe respected. A wise counselor."

"So I shouldn't say 'squaw' anymore, huh?"

"Not if you want to show people that you respect your heritage."

"Okay. No more squaw."

He sat her down on the stream bank so that her feet dangled in the cold, rushing water. Kat shivered. "I feel the fracture healing in self-defense."

"Say this." Nathan smiled ruefully. "We'll use English so you won't suspect me of being bad. 'Listen!' "

"Okay."

"No, say it. 'Listen!' "

"Listen!"

"You have drawn near to me, Grandfather Moon." She repeated the sentence obediently.

"My name is Katlanicha. I am of the Blue clan."

"Look, I was named after my great-great-grandmother *Katherine*—"

"Who's the doctor here, you or me? Her Cherokee name was Katlanicha, so *your* name is Katlanicha."

Kat huffed with mock disgust. "My name is Katlanicha. I am of the Blue clan."

"You have come to carry my pain away, Grandfather Moon. And now relief is here. Listen!"

She repeated everything he'd told her.

Nathan nodded with approval. "Say that formula each time you soak your foot in the stream."

"Oh, I see. You're just like every other doctor. 'Take two formulas and call me in the morning.' "

Nathan shot her an amused, exasperated look. "Are you going to be difficult to teach?"

"Who said you're teaching me?"

"You want to feel that you belong on this Cherokee land?"

"Yeah." Her teasing attitude faded. "More than anything," she whispered.

He took her hand and kissed it jauntily. "Then hang around with me, Katlanicha Gallatin."

Kat smiled. That was the best invitation she'd ever heard. Shrugging, she said, "Sure. I guess I can put up with a Chatham."

THEY SAT SIDE by side on the stream bank, not talking, but not uncomfortable with the silence. It was an amazing thing, Kat thought, for two people who'd known each other only a few days to be able to do this.

He fished, and she read one of her history books. At least, she tried to read. She kept a large part of her mind tuned to him since he was only a foot away and wearing only his hiking shorts.

"Says here," she murmured softly, "that the Indian Territory was a pretty wild place."

He flicked a hook baited with corn into a new spot and said something in Cherokee. When she looked at him quizzically he winked and explained, "You're supposed to apologize to the fish for trying to catch them. That way they won't get mad and leave."

"I've known men who tried to get dates that way."

"Did they?"

"Nope. I swim pretty fast." She cleared her throat. "About the Indian Territory."

"Yeah, it was rough, especially on the border between the Nation and Arkansas. Lots of bandit gangs, not much law. But then there were real nice places in the Nation, too—big farms, towns, schools."

"The Nation?"

"Sure. You call it Indian Territory, but it was made up of separate nations—Cherokee, Creek, Choctaw, Chickasaw, Seminole. The Cherokees had their own government, their own courts."

"Then my great-grandpa should have been caught and tried by his own people, if he was so bad."

"Well," Nathan said in a skeptical tone, "it wasn't that neat. For one thing, he was a Keetowah, and the Cherokees had a lot of respect for them."

"What's a Keetowah?" she asked, fascinated.

"Traditionalist. Secret society. Cherokees who wanted to keep strictly to the old ways. They refused to speak English or go by English names. They wanted all whites kicked out of the Nation."

"But wouldn't that have made Holt an enemy of his own family, since his father was white?"

"Nope. Not unless his father was against Indian ways. Ol' Justis wasn't like that."

"How do you know?"

"Well, I . . ." he paused, thinking as his skilled hands slowly cranked the fishing reel. "I figure any man who married a Cherokee, raised his children in Cherokee ways, and led Cherokee troops in the war must have been Cherokee at heart."

"You know a lot about him."

"Not really. Only what I read in the book my great-uncle wrote. Justis and Katherine had a big farm before the war. Didn't own slaves though, and most of the biggest Cherokee farmers did."

"But Justis was a Confederate officer during the war?"

"Hmmm. A major. Got wounded in the arm when my great-great-grandpa caught him. He got away, but I'd bet gold that he was permanently crippled in that arm. The ammo they used in those days did a nasty job."

Kat slammed her book shut. "Well, no wonder Holt had something against your family!"

"Now look, Kat Woman, my great-great-granddaddy

lost two sons who fought for the Union—killed by
Confederate troops made up of Cherokees. My relatives got *scalped*, so don't turn self-righteous on me,
okay?"

"You hate my family and I'm trying to defend
them."

He shook his head, the chocolate-brown hair shag-
ging forward over his forehead. "I don't hate people I
never knew."

"You know me!"

"Well, I sure don't hate you."

The fervent way he said that, as if hate weren't even
in his vocabulary where she was concerned, made Kat
stare at him wistfully. "I don't hate you, either."

An electric silence settled between them as he met
her gaze and held it. "Katie," he said in a soft, gruff
tone. "I don't think we could ever hate each other."

In her rational mind Kat knew that two people
who'd met less than a week ago shouldn't use such
certain words, but with his somber gray eyes pouring
affection into her all she could think was, *He's right.*

"Would you—" she began.

His fishing rod jerked wildly and he faced forward,
struggling with it.

*Kiss me*, she added silently.

"Got a big one, Kat Woman," he shouted. "Sharpen
your claws!"

Sighing, Kat reached for the net behind her. She
made a great pal for Nathan, but not much of anything
else.

SHE PEERED OUT of her tent the next morning to
find the fire burning and a covered pot sitting in the
center of it. Sniffing at an unidentifiable but delicious
smell, Kat peered around but saw no sign of Nathan.
She gazed at his teepee, trying to see inside the dark
triangle where the flap was pulled back, and concluded that he wasn't there, either.

Quickly she tugged her sleeping bag outside and sat

down on it to do some stretching exercises. Her discipline, developed during years of work with the trapeze performers, had now become a form of meditation. It was difficult to meditate when Nathan was around.

She felt decently covered in a long, loose T-shirt and panties. If Nathan came back from wherever he was, he wouldn't see anything compared to what her Princess Talana getup had revealed. She wasn't certain what he thought of her, but she didn't want to look like a tease, especially when the teasing didn't seem to do any good.

With a low sigh of delight, Kat spread her legs in a wide split and leaned forward from the waist, feeling well-trained muscles loosen and slide as she flattened herself to the ground. She rested the side of her face on the edge of the sleeping bag and extended both arms in front of her.

She was still in that position several minutes later when she heard the rustling sound of footsteps. Kat propped her chin on one hand and watched as Nathan strode into the clearing, water dripping from his body, his dark hair slicked back, a towel wrapped low around his waist.

All her muscles went on alert. He really knew how to ruin a good meditation.

He halted the second he saw her in her strange contortion on the sleeping bag, and one end of his mustache lifted under a lopsided, devilish smile. She had the notion that he might growl lecherously and head straight for her. The man was full of mischief.

"I have to stretch," she explained firmly. "Or I get cricks."

"Let me see what I can do to help."

Before she could protest he was beside her, kneeling on the sleeping bag, his hands pushing her hair off her back so that he could massage her shoulders. Kat was very aware of how she must look from his angle—her legs spread almost straight out from her body, her rump sticking up a little, covered only by panties and the tail of her T-shirt.

"I didn't figure on this," she muttered.

"Relax, I'm not gawking," he said cheerfully. "I saw more when Lady Savage was holding you over her head."

"Gee, thanks. Hope you got your money's worth."

He patted her shoulder. "You don't have to worry about me, kid. I'm not gonna scare you again."

"Thanks," Kat said grimly. What he really meant was, he wasn't interested in tangling with her.

He molded his hands to her back and stroked them down both sides, kneading her with the tips of his fingers, rubbing small circles on her spine with his thumbs. "You know," he said calmly, "a lot of times our society calls other people primitive because they run around without any clothes. But it seems a hell of a lot more primitive to go around covered up on a pretty summer day like this."

"What did Cherokees wear, before they turned white?"

He chuckled, his fingers still working their magic through the cotton of her T-shirt. "They never turned white. They took up a lot of white ways, but underneath it they were always different."

"Which way?"

"Well, like your great-grandfather. If his own people had arrested him, they wouldn't have put him in jail to wait for trial. He'd just go on about his business and come into court the day he was due. The old ways were based on personal honor."

He rubbed her lower back, pushing down with the palms of his hands, brushing the curve of her hips with his fingertips before he retreated up her spine again. Kat quivered as her body loosened in a way that wanted to welcome him inside.

"You okay?" he asked.

"Hmmm. Yeah, no problem. The, uhmm, the personal honor. More."

*Oh, yes. More, Nathan, more.*

"Cherokees didn't like to order other people around. Everybody was supposed to know the basic rules of the tribe, but then do their own thing. Not a bad way to live—share what you have, do what you want as long as you don't break the important taboos, respect your elders, be polite to your family."

"What taboos?" Kat asked languidly. She was liquid with heat inside and so mesmerized by his voice and hands that she could barely think.

"Marrying into your own clan, murder, ignoring the mourning rituals after a relative died. And a man, for instance, could get into deep trouble if he abused a woman or child."

"What happened to him?"

"Women from the victim's clan would beat him up."

Kat laughed softly. Oh Lord, Nathan was rubbing the back of her head now. "Cherokee women must have had a lot of power."

"Sure did. They weren't second-class citizens." His voice dropped to a teasing rumble. "But then, women who run around half-dressed can get just about anything they ask for."

This was her chance. Kat raised her head. "Then I'd like—"

"Dammit, my frogs are boiling over!"

He leaped up and ran to the fire. Dazed, Kat pushed herself into a sitting position and stared as he plucked the lid off the pot and stirred the contents with his bowie knife.

"Frogs?"

"Yeah. Bullfrogs. I caught 'em this morning. See, you parboil 'em, then roast 'em. Best frogs legs you've ever tasted."

Kat groaned softly and went back in her tent. Between frogs and fish, she'd never get anywhere with Nathan.

They'd been alone together, not having seen another human soul for over a week now. They'd watched hawks, deer, possums, raccoons, rabbits, squirrels, and owls, and they'd discussed most of them in detail as to Cherokee name and legends. They were happy without other company.

At least she was happy, Kat corrected herself. And she guessed Nathan was—he never got very far away from her, and he was always concerned about her ankle, and he asked lots of polite questions about her hobbies and ideas. But he didn't flirt very much, and that was making her more miserable with each passing day.

Did she want to get herself in deep water with this man? Yes, deep water in the stream, *nekkid*, and she wanted him to run his hands through her hair and later on show her exactly what was tattooed on his rump.

She sat one afternoon and watched him draw the Cherokee alphabet in the sand for her, with the sunlight glinting on his hair, his body clothed only in those damned sexy buckskin breeches, his muscles flexing under the freckled, richly tanned skin of his back.

His voice was smooth as warm liniment. He was kind and patient, the best teacher in the world. When she asked questions or offered some comment he sat very still and listened, really listened, without making fun of her for being uneducated.

Oh Lord. This was terrible. She was falling in love with him.

H E HAD HIMSELF a neighbor, a student, a patient, and a very big problem since he didn't think of Kat as the enemy anymore. In fact, after knowing her for only a week, he wanted to run up the white flag, sign a peace treaty, and give her any territorial right her sweet little heart wanted.

She might talk like a wisecracking truckstop waitress and act as if she didn't care to be sophisticated, but there was a sharp lady under all that fast talk. Her grasp of national and world events would put most people to shame.

Her mind was very quick and as inquisitive as a child's, as a result, he believed, of growing up in the circus. She always had been traveling, always meeting new people and living in new places. Unlike most adults, she'd never fully lost a child's fascination with the world.

She was sincere about learning Cherokee lore, and they spent a lot of their time sitting at the campfire while he talked and she listened, her head tilted to one side, her chin propped on one hand.

She listened the same way whenever he played one of his six harmonicas or his flute or the small guitarlike instrument he'd gotten in South America. They traded stories about his travels as a geologist and her circus experiences and the wrestling tour.

On the other hand, they spent many silent hours together, usually by the stream.

He fished and she read her history books. Periodically she stuck her injured foot in the water and solemnly repeated the formula he'd given her. Now she knew how to say it in Cherokee.

After he'd had time to think about the upsetting scene in the briar patch, he'd continued to keep his flirting lighthearted. Despite her nonchalant assurances that she wasn't afraid of him, she seemed to feel uncomfortable every time he got close.

Lord, he couldn't blame her. The little doll had been through hell—raped at twenty, too scared to fool with men for years after that, then so lonely that she married the first man who made her feel loved and safe.

Nathan had learned enough to know that she'd been married for three years to an ambitious car salesman in Miami. How had she described him? *He just wanted to marry a housekeeper until he could afford to hire one.*

During her marriage the Flying Campanellis had flown back to Italy and joined a circus there, so her divorce two years ago had left her jobless. With no skills outside the circus, she'd decided that professional wrestling was her best opportunity to make a living.

Nathan emptied his pipe into the fire and got up wearily. It wasn't wise for him to get to know Kat so well. He'd been happier thinking of her as a sexy clown with bad taste and no brains. Now he was in a dilemma about the Gallatin land, a dilemma built on promises he'd made to his grandfather. Nothing was ever to happen to the land as long as Dove Gallatin was alive, Grandpa Micah had told him, but after she passed on, the family debt needed to be paid. Grandpa had been an old bastard in some ways—part of the feud was his fault—but in this case he had had a point.

Nathan picked up a bucket and doused the campfire. He stood in darkness lit only by a new moon, gazing at Kat's tent. That activity seemed to be his only hobby these nights. He'd insisted that she keep his air mattress. Injured foot and all that.

Hell, he really just wanted to know that she was lying where he'd lain. Did she sleep naked? He had a disturbing vision of himself affectionately nuzzling his air mattress after she gave it back.

This kind of nonsense had to stop.

He should be discouraging her interest in her Cherokee past and this land. He ought to tell her the ugly details not only about Holt Gallatin but also about Holt's daughter, Dove. Kat's grandfather Joshua had been Dove's brother, so what did that make Dove? Kat's great-aunt?

But Joshua Gallatin had had nothing to do with the Chatham-Gallatin feud. He'd joined the Sheffield Brothers Circus as a kid and left home for good. He'd raised Kat's father in the business, and after her father married a full-blooded Cherokee woman from the reservation up in North Carolina, he'd taken her back to the circus with him.

Kat was born in a circus dressing room, a Cherokee in name only, a damned Gallatin in name only. Kat was innocent. Kat ought not to suffer because of old feuds and old promises.

Nathan rammed his hands through his hair. All right, he had ways to make it up to her—lots of money, more money than she'd ever dreamed possible, and luxuries she couldn't imagine.

After she learned the truth about him and what he intended, he'd show her how generously he could apologize and how effectively he could change her track record with men.

SHE COULDN'T GO on this way, and yet she never wanted to leave. Kat peeked out of her tent, watching Nathan heat a pot of coffee over the fire. He wore his fringed buckskin breeches, leather hiking boots, and a T-shirt he'd gotten at the Olympics in Korea.

Before going to work for Tri-State the man had hunted for gold all over the world. Now that she knew where and why he'd acquired the tattoo and the pierced ear, she was more fascinated than ever. Kat felt a familiar ache of sadness.

He was friendly, helpful, and very, very kind. He really put her at ease. But then, so did a Boy Scout.

Kat sighed. She didn't want a Boy Scout, she wanted the wicked man from their first encounters. She wanted him to make her forget good sense and indulge the reckless sensations that seethed inside her so much of the time.

She plopped down and slipped her feet into her pink Reeboks, leaving the laces on the one on the bad foot untied. She could walk pretty well now, dammit. There were no excuses for him to carry her anymore.

Leaving her tent, she put on a bright smile. "Morning, harmonica man."

He was already watching her intently from his seat by the fire. Kat shivered inside. If he wasn't interested, why did he study her like some new kind of native each morning when she came out?

"Sleep good, Kitty Kat?"

She smiled at the teasing nickname. It had grown so familiar that she cherished it. "Yeah. But I got a crick in my neck." She rotated her head, making sure her hair slipped forward like a silky black wave. "Would you mind braiding my hair for me? Until my neck loosens up, it would really hurt for me to do it myself."

He hesitated, and Kat's hopes fell. But he cleared

his throat, fiddled with the blackened coffeepot, and said lightly, "No problem. Have a cup of tar."

Using a towel, he lifted the steaming metal pot and poured thick black coffee into a metal cup that, thank goodness, had an insulated handle. Kat sat down beside him, put an elastic hair band and brush on the ground, and took the cup carefully.

"Ya know, Nathan, this stuff would make great paint remover."

"It's good for cleaning carburetors, too." He took a swallow from his own cup and made a deep, half-growling sound of satisfaction. "Puts hair on my hair."

"Hair." She smiled sweetly, turned her back to him, and waited.

After a moment his hands slipped over her shoulders and pulled the thick mane back. Kat's eyelids became heavy with a languor that had nothing to do with sleep. Good grief, he'd barely touched her and already a warm, tickling wave of pleasure had begun in her belly.

"Don't ever get this cut," he said gruffly.

"I haven't had it more than trimmed since I was ten years old. It looked real dramatic in the circus act— this little bitty girl with hair longer than she was. 'Course, it really gets attention when I wrestle. Everybody loves it."

"The men in the audience, huh?"

"Well, yeah. It's pretty sexy-looking. I wouldn't be honest if I said I didn't know that."

"How do you feel about the things they yell?"

"I don't much hear 'em." She hesitated for a second. "I guess there are a lot of ugly things I don't want to hear."

He slid his hands down her hair, parting it, lifting it, winding his fingers through it, and then letting go. Nathan's technique told her a lot about his nature— this was a man who loved to touch. He worshipped her hair, and she suspected that he'd treat the rest of her with the same slow attention.

Kat sighed with pleasure. Asking him to braid her hair was one of the best decisions of her life.

"You don't deserve to have men treat you like a piece of meat," he said grimly.

"Well, long as they're in the audience and I'm in the ring, I just look at it as harmless show biz. They're not drooling at me, they're drooling at Princess Talana."

"You can really separate yourself from it that way?"

"Most of the time," she said softly. "But some nights I feel embarrassed."

"What would you do if you could do anything in the world besides wrestle for a living?"

"I'd teach school," she said immediately. "To me that's the best of both worlds. It's show biz, sort of like wrestling, but it's respectable. And you have to go to college to do it,"

When he finished laughing he said, "Kat, I want to be in your class some day."

She grinned. "Teacher's pet."

He ran his fingers through her hair from the crown of her head to the curve of her back, skimming her spine with his fingertips as he did. Kat fought a desire to earn her name by purring.

"You'd make a great hairdresser," she said. "You're awful familiar with the client, though."

His hands halted. "Want me to stop?"

"Not on your life."

"You're one honest woman," he murmured. "I like that."

Kat pursed her lips ruefully. She hadn't been honest about the crick in her neck. With his fingers woven into her hair, she couldn't feel much remorse. "Yeah, I try to tell it like it is."

"So what do you do when people aren't honest back?"

"I drop 'em like hot rocks."

"Hmmm." He kept running his fingers down her hair, slowly, tugging just a little, touching her back just a little, delighting her in ways he probably never suspected. "You don't give people the benefit of the

doubt?'' he asked softly, stroking the back of her head.
"A second chance? Even if they apologize?''

Kat had her eyes shut. Her body hummed with the
kind of delicious alertness that made it feel too heavy
to move. She had to think hard to get her mouth in
gear. "Well, okay, I'm not hard-nosed if somebody
really apologizes. Hmmm.''

"Nothing hard about you,'' he agreed. His fingers
pressed into her shoulder, massaging. "Where's the
crick?''

"Hmmm. That feels good.''

Any second now she'd curl around his legs with her
back arched.

He picked up the brush and put it at the top of her
forehead. Slowly he pulled it back, letting each bristle
caress her scalp. Kat's head tilted back loosely.

"What's that?'' he asked. "Did I hurt you? You
made a noise.''

She forced her head forward and tried to control
herself. "Nah.''

He divided her hair and began to braid it down the
center of her back, his fingers skillful and unhurried.
Obviously concerned about doing a good job, he
stopped frequently to smooth his hand over her head,
tickling her earlobes, brushing the edges of her face.

Kat pressed her palms together and found them hot.
She had to transfer this heat to Nathan, had to tell him
that she adored him and would love to show how
much. Surely he found her desirable; he had seemed
to at first, before she'd frightened him with the briar
incident.

She began to turn her head. "Nath—''

"All done,'' he said abruptly. With a quick pat on
her shoulder, he got up and walked toward the food
supplies hanging in a nearby tree. "Let's eat something simple for breakfast. Now that your ankle's better, we ought to start exploring the land.''

Kat sagged like a rag doll and braced both hands
on the ground beside her. She watched him blankly,
a groan of dismay trapped in her throat.

He had to have felt her quivering; he had to have known that she was helplessly desperate for his touch. He was either biding his time to make her crazy, or he was politely ignoring her interest.

Lord, she hoped it was the first one. Kat drank her coffee in several huge gulps. Jolt. Caffeine. Reality. She tried to connect her muscles to her bones again.

Hunched over the net full of supplies, his back to her, Nathan fumbled with various items, his hands trembling. In about five minutes he might be able to walk back to the campfire without revealing how he'd made a new sort of camping tent in the front of his buckskins.

*Her hair, that was the key. When she was ready to be seduced, he'd start with her hair.*

HE FROWNED AT her dedicated attempt at walking, dropped his canvas knapsack, backed up to her, and pointed over his shoulder. "Climb aboard."

"The top of the ridge is just up there."

"Never turn down a free pony ride. Come on."

Kat grinned. What was she, an idiot? "Never." She grasped his shoulders as he reached behind him and scooped his hands around her thighs. Oh yes, she thought, this pony ride was a wonderful idea.

She straddled his lower back, clamped her arms around his neck, and leaned forward just enough to let her breasts brush his shoulders. He groaned loudly as he bent over to pick up the knapsack.

*Good. He'd noticed that she had a bosom.*

"You're getting heavier," he said in a strained voice. "Here. Take the knapsack."

Kat thought about biting his ear, but decided against it. She had no place to put the knapsack except in front of her chest. She sighed with resignation and wedged it there. "Hike on, mule."

Despite his jovial complaints he easily carried her up the last part of the steep hillside. When they reached the top, sheltered by huge oaks and maples, he turned around. Kat peered over his shoulder at the magnificent valley. She could make out the stream winding across the far side.

"It's so beautiful it makes me kind of hurt inside," she whispered. "I want to hug it."

"Your great-great-grandmother and her family must have hated to leave here."

"When was it that all the Cherokees got kicked out? I forgot."

"Eighteen thirty-eight. Soldiers and state militia rounded 'em up like animals, and mobs of settlers came along behind taking over the farms and stealing everything that wasn't nailed down."

"Katherine, I mean Katlanicha, met Justis and married him, so we know she survived the Trail of Tears," Kat said softly. "But we figure her family didn't. We don't know anything about them."

Nathan turned around, gazing at the forest. "This timber probably hasn't been touched since the family left. Some of these trees have got to be nearly two hundred years old."

"Dove's will didn't say anything about any of the Gallatins coming back here to live—not in four generations."

"Well, for a long time they wouldn't have been welcome. You know, the only thing that saved this land from being claimed by a white settler was the fact that it was in Justis Gallatin's name. The law said Cherokees couldn't own property in the state of Georgia."

She exhaled heavily. "The world's a crazy place, Nathan."

"Better than it used to be, in some ways." He bounced her a little. "Hang on. I'm going to my truck."

"I still haven't figure how I missed it when I drove in."

"You'll see."

He piggybacked her to the end of a narrow trail just wide enough to drive a car along. He walked past her Mustang and down into a deep hollow on the other side of the trail. There sat a shiny black 4X4 with massive wheels and a black camper hood over the bed.

"Oooh. Lots of chrome. And a gun rack!" Kat noted coyly. "Why, men who drive these kinds of fancy toys are the type who *love* wrestling."

"Hey, only party girls drive Mustangs with bad paint jobs and rusty mag wheels. Party girls with names like "Beulah Ann' or "Fanny Mae.' They cruise into town with their beehive hairdos sprayed stiff and they—*yow*. Get your teeth off my ear!"

She eased her teeth from the gold nugget and chuckled victoriously.

Nathan set her down by the truck and glared at her, though his mouth quirked under the mustache. "Hellion."

"Thank you." She blew him a kiss.

The truck had a plush red interior and more gadgets than a gourmet kitchen. He lifted her into the driver's seat so that she could study the cellular phone, state-of-the-art stereo system, and CB radio.

"Where are the flight controls?"

"I love my truck," he said solemnly, and went around back to retrieve something from the camper.

When he returned he held a small shovel and a long contraption that looked like a Geiger counter on a microphone stand with a dinner plate at the other end. "Metal detector," he told her.

"You use that to find gold? I thought those things found metal only near the top of the ground."

"That's right." He clicked a switch and pointed the plate end toward his truck. Inside a panel on the control box a needle bounced crazily.

"You found it, Nathan. It's a truck all right."

He eyed her with amusement. "I'm not looking for gold with this, I'm looking for evidence of people. Find where the people were and maybe you'll find the sites of old mines. Get it, Kitty Kat?"

"Got it."

"Besides, it's fun to hunt for things in the dirt."

She nodded. "I lost a baby tooth once. I went

through a pile of dried elephant manure to get it back. It was worth a quarter from the tooth fairy.''

He slid one arm around her waist and pulled her out of the truck, then held her against him and growled with mock lechery, ''I could really go for a woman who plays in pachyderm poop.''

Kat laughed so hard that she didn't get a chance to protest when he stepped away sooner than she liked. Smiling weakly, she took the shovel and followed him out of the hollow.

Back on top of the ridge he stopped and looked around, squinting his eyes as he thought. ''The trees,'' he said in a soft, fascinated tone. ''Hmmm.''

Kat gazed at the huge hardwoods with a feeling of awe. ''This would be a great place to build a house. With the valley in front and a big, flat ridge in back. There's room for barns and stuff up here, too.''

''Exactly.'' Nathan pointed toward the valley. ''The trees down there are younger than these. I bet that whole valley used to be farmland. And up here—'' He looked around, his gray gaze searching, excited.

''Turn on the metal detector,'' Kat urged.

''Easy, gal. There are dozens of places on this land where the Blue Song family might have built. And they most likely didn't have anything fancy.''

''But this is where the trail comes in from the road,'' she pointed out. *Gal.* It was a good sign when he said *gal.* ''Let's look around.''

He switched the metal detector on and they started across the ridge. Nathan swung the detector in a slow arc as they walked, while Kat hobbled along with the shovel poised for digging.

''How's your ankle?'' he murmured, his eyes on the ground.

''Fine. Everything's nice and flat up here.''

''Put your shovel at ease, soldier. Save your energy.''

''I *know* we're going to find something.''

But an hour later they were still crisscrossing the

ridge without success. The plan didn't seem nearly so easy to Kat now. Her ankle had started to throb.

"Want to call it a day?" Nathan asked.

"Just a few minutes more. Let's go back toward the front."

They ambled along. She began using the shovel like a cane. Nathan stopped, frowning. "Time to quit. You need to go soak that foot."

"Relax, Mommy, I'm fine." She pointed the shovel toward a little clearing a few yards away. "Let's go over there."

"Nope. This is like eating popcorn. At some point you just have to say, 'I'm stopping for now' and then—Kat, come on back. Kat, give it up for today."

"Nope." She limped toward the clearing.

"I'm not following."

"Yeah, you are too."

His voice rose. *"Katlanicha."*

The way he said her full name made an odd feeling wash over her. She kept walking and called, "Sir, you need to indulge me on this."

*Sir, you need to indulge me on this?*

Where had that come from? She'd never said anything so formal-sounding in her whole life.

Well, it worked, at any rate. She turned around and found Nathan striding toward her, looking very exasperated, the metal detector gripped tightly in one hand. He raised the other hand and shook his finger at her.

*"Katie Blue Song, I've told you before that—"*

He stopped, frowning deeply. They stared at each other. "Told me what?" Kat asked, while the odd feeling grew more potent inside her. "Katie Blue Song?"

Nathan shook his head. "I don't know what I was going to say." He glanced down at the metal detector and his mouth opened in shock.

Kat almost fell down hurrying to cover the yard of leafy ground that separated them. Her heart racing, she looked at the detector's needle.

It was going wild.

K AT JABBED THE shovel into the ground, barely missing the toe of his hiking boot. He jumped.

"Take it easy," Nathan urged. "We have a lot of work to do. Go slow and steady."

"I can't!" She tried to balance on her good foot and push the shovel with her injured one; the pain was too great. She levered all her upper-body weight on the shovel and managed to sink it only a few inches into the soft humus. "Arrrgh."

Chuckling, Nathan took the shovel away. "You look like a little brown hen trying to scratch a hole in concrete. Take the metal detector and let me dig."

She grabbed the detector and circled him, watching the needle. Kat was so excited she wasn't sure which was shaking harder—she or the indicator. "There's something. And there. And there. More. Yes! Oh, Nathan. Yes! More!"

"Yes, more, oh, Nathan, more," he muttered. "Women are never satisfied." Shaking his head in mock disgust, he shoveled leaves and dirt aside.

Kat laughed giddily and ranged farther, yipping each time the needle danced. "What do you think we've found?"

"Who knows? Keep track of your area. Try to find the perimeter."

*Whump.* "Ouch! Dammit!"

"What'd you do?"

"Ran into a tree." Smiling sheepishly, she rubbed her forehead and kept walking.

He choked back laughter. "Kitty Kat, look up every once in a while."

Now she hurt at both ends, but she hardly noticed. With adrenaline firing her energy, she swung the metal detector and watched the needle carefully.

Fifteen minutes later she made her way back to Nathan. He'd dug a square hole about five feet wide and a foot deep.

"Why aren't you finding anything?" she asked plaintively.

"Patience, gal, patience."

*Gal.* Yes, a very good sign. He'd probably find something any minute. Kat pointed at the surrounding woods. "The needle stops moving when I get past that big oak over there, that maple over there, and the whatever-it-is . . ."

"Walnut tree."

"Walnut tree over there."

"Good. Now all we have to do is dig."

Kat got down on her knees and vigorously scratched leaves out of the way. If she had to paw through this soil with her bare hands she was going to find evidence that the Blue Songs had lived here.

Nathan laughed. "Cluuuck, cluck-cluck."

"Quiet. If I'm a hen, you're a big ol' gopher."

"I've got another shovel in the back of the truck."

"Can't wait that long," she said, puffing excited little breaths while she dug.

"Kat Woman, you're not going to find any—"

"I found a piece of metal!"

Nathan knelt beside her and looked. Just a few inches beneath the humus her fingers had scratched something flat and rusty. "Let me," he told her, easing her hands aside and edging the shovel under the discovery.

Kat clasped her dirty hands to her mouth and watched raptly as Nathan pried a large door hinge out of the ground.

To her it might have been a bar of gold. "A door hinge," she said in awe. "Oh, Nathan, we found their house!"

"Maybe." He brushed dirt from the corroded metal. It was spread open, the axis rusted solid. "Made of iron, I think. Handmade by a blacksmith, probably. Looks like it even might have had some fancy scrollwork on it."

"That'd mean they had something nicer than a cabin?"

"Maybe."

"Look!" She scratched into the ground and held up something else. "Nails!"

Nathan took them. "Handmade." He smiled at her with an explorer's gleam of discovery in his eyes. "That'd be right for the time period, Kat. Early eighteen hundreds. I think we're on to something."

Kat whooped with glee, grasped his face between her hands, and planted a smacking kiss on his mouth. Then she drew back, laughing and pleasantly delirious. In a more deliberate spirit he slid both arms around her waist, curved himself over her possessively, and lowered his mouth on hers.

Kat felt his arms bending her, letting her drape backward as he brushed her lips gently, then took full command with a poignantly controlled tenderness that hinted at less patient intentions.

It wasn't a lingering kiss, but it was a thorough one, covering every inch of her lips, imprinting her with the complete taste and feel of him as he turned it into a series of teasing movements. Over and over he paused, lifted, almost broke contact, then pressed downward again.

Kat moaned softly and lifted her mouth to seek more. She thought she knew how to kiss, she thought she'd been kissed well before; now she realized that Nathan Chatham had just raised her standard to a level no other man was likely to satisfy.

He lapped his tongue forward just a little and she touched hers to it wetly. With that brief, very intimate ending, like a dramatic coda for a sweet piece of music, he sat back and let go of her.

Kat saw the ruddy desire in his face and the troubled remorse in his half-shut eyes. It confused and depressed her. Why would kissing her make him feel bad?

"I always get excited when I find rusty metal," he quipped, his voice gruff.

"Sure. Me, too." Kat gestured awkwardly toward the ground. "Are you going to do that every time I find a nail?" *I'll dig faster, if that's the case.*

"Nah. You're safe." He scrubbed a hand over his face, as if making sure he hadn't lost something in the exchange.

Kat bit her lip. "I, uhmmm, I got dirt on your mouth."

He laughed hoarsely. "I didn't notice."

"Sorry."

"I *like* the taste of topsoil."

"Here, let me wipe it off." Embarrassed, Kat licked her fingers in preparation, and got dirt on her tongue. "Yaaah!" She covered her mouth and turned away from Nathan, spitting and trying to be delicate about it.

If his roaring laughter was any indication, he'd just seen the funniest sight of his life. Kat reached back and flailed at him. When she finally looked up again, wiping her mouth with the back of her hand, he was smoothing tears from the corners of his eyes.

Well, at least she'd changed the awkward, heated mood.

"Dig, gopher," she ordered, her mouth quirking with humor.

He smiled. "Scratch, hen."

BY EARLY AFTERNOON they'd assembled a small pile of nails, three door hinges, something that looked like the handle of a cooking pot, and various pieces of iron that had been part of implements they couldn't identify.

Nathan watched Kat work and marveled at her tenacity. Her T-shirt clung to her like a wet rag—which gave him an even better reason to watch. She had sweaty streaks of grime on her arms and legs, loose strands of inky-black hair clung to her face, and her hands were covered in dirt.

But she was smiling.

He thrust his shovel into the soil and ripped out another piece of Blue Song land. The symbolism of what he was doing stabbed him with anger and frustration. The scars he made in her land today were a faint scratch compared to what he planned to do later.

Again he thrust the shovel downward, feeling disgusted and letting the aggression leap into his work. With a dull clang the blade hit something large and very solid.

"Kat!"

She limped over quickly. "What?"

They both knelt down. Nathan dug his hands into the soil and grunted with the effort of dislodging the heavy piece. "What the hell?"

"It looks like a big bar of iron."

"Not a bar—a, ummmph, rod." The thick, rusty object came loose and Nathan lifted it up. "Must be fifteen, twenty pounds."

They both looked at it curiously. The corrosion had left its surface pitted and lumpy. It was about a foot and a half long and nearly as thick as a man's wrist.

"Something to fight with?" Kat asked. "Look, there's a hanger on one end."

Nathan turned the rod upright and studied the crude eyelet forged to it. Understanding dawned quickly. "It's a window sash weight!"

Kat touched the strange device curiously. "You mean to make a window stay open when you raise it?"

"Yeah. There were two for each window—four if you wanted both halves of the window to move. Do you know what this means?"

"No." She gazed up at him with wide green eyes.

"It means the Blue Songs had a really nice house. A house with expensive glass-paned windows that only people with money could afford."

He studied the sash weight intensely. "When the Cherokees were kicked out of north Georgia there wasn't much more here than crude gold mines and one-mule farms. The Blue Songs may have owned one of the nicest places around, Cherokee or white."

Kat grabbed his arm. The yearning look in her eyes nearly tore him apart. "Do you think we could find the foundation of the house?"

Nathan nodded. *If she asked him with that childlike eagerness, he'd search for ice water in hell.* "And if we find most of these sash weights, we can get an idea of how many windows there were." He angled his head toward the forest beyond. "I bet we can even get some idea of where the outbuildings were—barns, smokehouse, stuff like that."

She sank down and gave him a teary smile. "Thank you, sweetcakes, thank you. I would never have found this place if you hadn't been here."

His heart thudding with pleasure, he told her, "We need help with this. Somebody trustworthy, somebody who won't go over to Gold Ridge and talk. The last thing we want are souvenir hunters coming out here from town."

He paused, thinking. "Got it. I'll call a friend who works for . . . with me."

She didn't notice his slip of the tongue, and she stroked his arm with her small, gentle hand. "Nathan," she asked softly, "why are you doing all this for me?"

*Because I want you to have something from this old home-place to remember. Because I don't want you to feel so hurt later. Because I'm crazy about you.*

Nathan offered her a jaunty grin. "I told you, finding rusty metal is exciting."

SHE WAS BLISSFULLY exhausted, and so happy she didn't care if she looked like a dirt dauber. Riding in the plush comfort of Nathan's truck, listening to a tape of music made by Cujimo Indians in some little South American country called Surador, she watched mountainside farms give way to the small-town charm of Gold Ridge.

What had once been a bawdy gold boomtown full of saloons, brothels, and gambling houses had become in modern times a cozy place of bed-and-breakfast inns, shops, and restaurants. There was a picturesque college campus right off a courthouse square crowded with big oak trees, and places a short walk from the main street where tourists paid five dollars an hour to pan for gold dust. Mountains rose like an exquisitely hand-painted backdrop in the distance.

"I could really be happy in a little place like this," Kat noted.

Nathan turned the tape player off and tapped the steering wheel rhythmically, thinking. "I've got a great idea. Let's get a couple of rooms at one of the inns and celebrate by staying in town tonight."

"We couldn't get service at a drive-through window, the way we look."

"We'll go shopping. We'll get the rooms and take a bath . . . baths."

Kat squirmed inwardly. She had no money for such things. "Nah."

"You shouldn't go back to the campsite today. You've already been on your bad foot too long."

"I'm okay."

"I'll pay."

"Nope."

Nathan slipped a hand under the seat and withdrew a sturdy plastic box. He handed it to her. "Open it."

Inside Kat found a half dozen major credit cards and a wad of money as big as her fist. The top bill was a fifty. Were all the others fifties?

"Nathan, is it too late for me to learn geology? I want to be rich, too."

He smiled. "Then you'll let me pay."

"No—"

"You wouldn't be out of work right now if you hadn't rescued me from Lady Savage. You're losing money, and I'm responsible. I owe ya, kid, I owe ya."

She was still staring at the money and cards. What did he do—carry his life savings around with him? Maybe it wasn't all he had, but it was undoubtedly a lot more than *her* life savings.

"Okay. But nothing fancy."

She didn't trust the mischievous sound of his laughter.

NATHAN SLID BACK into the truck with a big smile on his face. "All set. A great place. I see why you and your cousins liked it."

Kat peered around him at the Kirkland Inn, a noble old house with an upper gallery, lots of rocking chairs, and a yard filled with azaleas and dogwoods under an umbrella of stately beech trees.

"Well, we only stayed here a little while when we came to see Dove's lawyer about the will. But Tess said it has the *ambience* of an English farmhouse, and Erica said it has strong floor joists."

Nathan pursed his mouth and looked away, smiling. "You and your cousins have got to be an interesting trio."

She punched him lightly on the shoulder. "Now what?"

He cranked the truck. "Clothes."

Fifteen minutes later she stood in the aisle of a boutique, being eyed by a saleswoman who obviously thought she was an ethnic hobo of some sort. Kat went to Nathan, who sat on a wooden bench by the door, looking as happy as a clam—a dirt-covered clam in grimy buckskins, hiking boots, and a sweaty, stained T-shirt.

Kat bent over and whispered. "That walrus acts like we're scum. She's afraid I'm gonna steal something. Let's leave."

He flipped the stem of his empty pipe into his mouth and grinned rakishly around it. "Whatd'ya care? She'll jump when she sees money."

Kat frowned at him. "I hate it when salespeople look at me this way. Circus people aren't trusted, especially in little towns. I grew up with women like that making me feel like a thief."

His smile faded and he pressed her hand gently. "You know, if you'd stop checking all the price tags she might relax."

Kat lowered her voice even more. "Stuff here costs too much, Nathan."

"We're not leaving until you buy everything you need. No more looking at price tags. Hurry up. I've got to get some clean clothes too, you know. And a bath. And I'm hungry. And I want to smoke my pipe."

"All right!"

He counted on his fingers. "A dress, shoes, underwear, and whatever else females need. I want to see it all on the counter. Don't hold back."

She smiled at him with clenched teeth. "The only thing I'm holding back is my fist."

Kat felt a mixture of horror and victorious thrill fifteen minutes later when Nathan calmly handed the saleswoman two hundred dollars plus change. With two hundred dollars Kat could have bought a whole year's wardrobe.

The woman's eyes bugged a little and her attitude became a great deal more pleasant. Kat gripped the counter. She'd never spent that much money on one outfit before.

"I'm sorry, Nathan," she said fervently, as they walked to the truck. "Lord, I'm so sorry. I should have looked at the prices."

"Kat, quit yowling." He tossed her shopping bags into the back of the truck. "It's all right."

"No, it's not. It's not right for you to spend this much money."

"Think I expect something in return?" he asked coolly, one dark brow arched in warning.

"If you do, I sure feel obligated!"

The color drained out of his face. "I didn't realize that you trade sex for clothes. I should have bought you more."

She shook her head angrily. "You know what I mean!"

He gripped her shoulders hard and looked down at her with eyes gone the cold pewter color that meant he was angry. He said softly, "If I want anything from you, I'll just ask. I won't bribe you for it."

She was so flustered that she almost said, *So ask.* Instead, she nodded numbly. "Sorry. I'm not used to gentlemen."

"Well, *get* used."

*I'd love to, Nathan. Especially a gentleman with a cute tattooed behind and a sexy pierced ear.* Kat limped to her side of the truck but didn't get a chance to touch the door. Nathan leaped in front of her, pulled it open, and bowed, his expression droll but still a little angry.

"Hah," she said imperiously, and got inside.


SHE HAD A lovely room full of antiques. It opened on to the inn's back gallery, and when she walked to the railing she could touch the limb of a beech tree close by.

The beech tree was the only thing close by. Nathan had asked for a room on the other side of the house.

Why did he make it clear that he liked her, wanted

her as a woman, but intended to avoid her? Kat stood in the shower and scrubbed her hair fiercely, trying to wash him out of it, as the old song said.

Okay, so she was a nobody, a nomad with no immediate future outside of the weird show biz world of wrestling. She wasn't cut out to get an ordinary job. It would drive her nuts, seeing the same office or store every day, sitting still most of the time.

Nathan had a good job, not a normal job, but an entirely respectable, even sort of glamorous one. He had money. He certainly had no trouble attracting women—she'd watched a salesgirl nearly drool over him. And he even had a regular family back in Arkansas, had grown up on the homeplace Nathaniel Chatham had acquired before the Civil War. He had *roots*.

In short, Nathan didn't need a female wrestler with no education, no decent clothes, a credit rating that made loan officers laugh, and a personal history that included rape plus a failed marriage.

She could just imagine how his family would freak if he brought home an ex-circus performer who was also a Gallatin. They'd be conjuring up General Custer inside of twenty-four hours.

Nathan liked her, he was her friend, and he even wanted to make love to her. But he wasn't going to do it, because he was a gentleman, and he knew she'd be hurt when he left.

And on that point he was very, very right.


NATHAN STOOD ON the back balcony, waiting anxiously. He hadn't seen her in an hour. He rocked in a rocking chair. He walked. Finally he shoved his hands through his hair and muttered oaths. Would this get worse? Would he get to the point where he couldn't stand to be away from her for thirty minutes, then fifteen, then five, until eventually he'd become her constant shadow?

At the other end of the gallery her door opened. Nathan glanced at his scrubbed hiking boots, brushed a tiny piece of tobacco off the tan trousers he'd purchased, fiddled with his suspenders, and checked the rolled-up sleeves of a striped shirt that still smelled like a menswear shop despite all the pipe smoke he'd blown on it.

God, he hadn't been this antsy the night he'd had to explain to a Zambinawee chief that he didn't want to get married, even if it meant he'd own all four of the chief's daughters.

Kat stepped onto the gallery, fluffing her hair as if it weren't quite dry. Nathan gripped the gallery railing and stared at her.

She'd chosen a white dress of some crinkly white material. The short-sleeved bodice knew what to do over her curves and the full skirt knew how to swirl gracefully around her legs.

The white material heightened the honey of her skin and made her hair look blue-black. The dress's neckline was decorated with white fringe and brightly colored beads, giving it a boutique-native look that would have been too cute on anyone but a real native. With the dress she wore plain white sandals and absolutely no jewelry or makeup. Nathan wanted to eat her alive. In Cherokee love formulas, that was the ultimate compliment.

She saw him and abruptly stopped stroking her hair. Her hands framed her face, making a lovely picture which imprinted itself forever in Nathan's mind.

Kat lowered her arms, tilted her head to one side, looked him up and down with unmistakable distress, then quickly adjusted her expression and smiled widely.

"Hi ya, sweetcakes."

She was still edgy around him, he realized, and she wasn't going to take him seriously, no matter how much money he had. *It was time to do a little work on the hair.*

Nathan walked toward her calmly, putting what he hoped was a cocky smile on his face. "That outfit's great, Katlanicha."

"Two hundred bucks' worth?"

"Two thousand."

"That's what my car cost."

He reached her and halted, noting the darkening of her cheeks. Her complexion didn't show a blush, but it took on a richer color, as if someone were mixing strawberries with the honey.

Her eyes flickered with tension but held his gaze. "Ready for dinner?"

"Is your hair dry?" he said softly.

"Oh, yeah . . ."

Nathan slid his hands into it, lifted it on both sides, and studied it as if truly concerned about dryness. "A little damp. Sit down and let me air it for you."

He took one look at her sloe-eyed expression and knew he'd scored a direct hit. "Sure," she squeaked, then cleared her throat and said, *"Sure."*

She went to a cushioned bench by the gallery railing and sat down stiffly, tucking her skirt around her in a defensive way.

"Lean forward," Nathan crooned. "Lean on the railing."

Slowly, glancing over her shoulder with doleful wariness which reminded him of a worried puppy, she rested her forearms on the rail. Finally she faced forward and lowered her chin on her hands.

The mane of hair flowed down her back like a beautiful black river. Nathan didn't think he had a hair fetish, but his body reacted that way.

He stroked his fingers through her hair, gathered it in one hand, then put the other hand underneath, palm up, at the base of her head. Nathan wove his fingers up into the black silk and pulled them along the underside, letting strands slip free until he was holding only a single lock when he reached the end.

Tugging it playfully, he brushed the feathery tip along one of her arms.

Kat trembled. "I don't think you're *airing,* I think you're *daring,"* she murmured hoarsely. "And it's not funny, okay?"

Nathan dropped the strand of hair, smoothed it into place, and silently cursed himself for pushing her too far, too soon. "I was just teasing," he assured her. "Relax."

"Just teasing." She lifted her head, brushed a hand across her eyes, and sighed. "Jeez, I'm tired and crabby. Sure you want to go to dinner with me?"

"We'll be tired and crabby together. Come on."

When she turned to look up at him her eyes seemed ancient and sad and familiar in a way that made him feel desperate.

"Aw, Katie," he whispered, the nickname coming to his lips so easily. "I've been waiting a long time, too."

She erased her strange expression, stood up, and patted his shoulder like a pal. "Yeah, I made you wait while I primped. You must be starving for some dinner. Let's go. We can cut through my room to the hall."

Smiling crookedly, she breezed past him and into the house. Nathan frowned in bewilderment. He wasn't certain what he'd been talking about, but he knew it had nothing to do with dinner.

NATHAN KEPT BROODING about his strange words, and he was still puzzling over them as he lay in bed that night. The inn's wide, soft four-poster was hard on his back, accustomed as he was to sleeping on the ground. So sleep eluded him.

Lost in deep thought, he lifted a hand to a streak of moonlight on his coverlet. Some things were eternal—moonlight, sunlight, souls. He couldn't shake the feeling that there was more between him and Kat than their brief relationship warranted.

There'd been no shortage of women in his life; he'd broken hearts and had his broken in return, more than once. But he'd never felt anything like this before. Was it just a special brand of man-woman chemistry, wonderful but nothing mysterious? If so, then why did he keep saying things to her that he didn't understand, as if they'd been buried inside him long before he met her, just waiting to be said to her alone?

*Listen, O Ancient White Fire! This woman's soul has come to rest with me, and I will never let it go.*

Nathan was a very spiritual man, and he believed many things were possible. But as much as he was drawn to Kat, he wasn't certain he believed that he'd known her before.

He groaned in dismay, laughed wearily, and sat up in bed, holding his head in both hands. If he'd been through this torment in another life, he damned sure wouldn't have forgotten it. Nathan cursed in jovial disgust and got up, pulling the bedcovers with him. He'd sleep on the floor and pretend he'd once been a rug.

As he dropped the covers his ears picked up the sound of hurrying feet. Listening intently, Nathan gazed at the door that led from his room on to the gallery.

It was glass-paned and curtained with diaphanous white material that let him immediately identify the small, shadowy form that halted there. He had the door open before Kat knocked.

"What's the matter?" he asked quickly.

She stood there half-hidden in moonlight, barefoot, still wearing her new dress because it was the only clean clothing she had. In one hand she held a book of local history they'd bought at a store on the town square.

"I'm sorry, I had to talk to you," she said in a tear-soaked voice.

"Katie, what is it?" He drew her inside and shut the door.

She held the book up, her hand trembling. "My great-great-grandfather Justis never married Katlani-cha. He couldn't have. He had a white wife and family here."

NATHAN WENT TO a bedside table and fumbled with the switch on an old-fashioned globe lamp. When he finally had it working he pivoted to find Kat wiping her eyes and trying desperately to look calm.

"Katie," he whispered sadly, and went to her with his arms held out. "It couldn't be that bad."

She leaned against him, her face burrowed into his shoulder, and he held her snugly, stroking her disheveled hair.

"I was in bed reading this d-damned book." she said, her chest rising and falling in a shallow, swift rhythm. "I had to come tell you about it."

The book was entitled *Gold Ridge—The Early Years, A Newspaper History.* It contained the complete texts of the town's first paper, a crudely typeset weekly called the *Gold Ridge Gazette.*

Nathan took the thick hardcover and tossed it on the floor, then hugged her sympathetically. "What'd you find, gal?"

"Well, the paper started about three years before the Cherokees left, 'cause it talks about how Gold Ridge was being built on land owned by the Cherokee Nation but how that was okay 'cause the government was negotiating a treaty to make the Indians leave."

Nathan kept caressing her hair and hoped she wouldn't notice that he was wearing nothing but white briefs. He didn't want her to move away.

He didn't have to worry. She put her free arm around his bare waist and held him as if he were a life buoy in a stormy sea.

"Justis must have been a VIP around here," she continued. "There was a list of big mines, and two of 'em were owned by the Gallatin Company. There was a Gallatin General Store, and a Gallatin Hotel, and even a Gallatin saloon. Justis was a gold miner. He came here to take gold out of Cherokee land, just like all the other settlers. I bet he was only interested in Katlanicha because he thought there was gold on her farm."

Nathan kissed her forehead and tried to ignore the ugly pang of guilt about his own intentions. "There's too much we'll never know. It could've been different from how it sounds. I mean, if all he wanted was gold, then he didn't have to stay with her out in Oklahoma and raise children with her, right?"

New tears slid over Kat's black lashes. "I was givin' him the benefit of the doubt until I came to the m-marriage part. The year after the Cherokees got kicked out, the year after great-great-grandmother and her family had to leave"—she exhaled raggedly— "Justis married a judge's daughter named Amarintha Parnell."

Her voice became bitter. "The judge was a VIP too. He owned a mine here. I guess Justis wanted to have a proper wife from a real good *white* family."

Nathan felt so bad for her that he hardly knew what to say. "But ol' Justis didn't stay with Amarintha. You *know* that." He tried to joke. "He couldn't have loved some babe with a prissy name like Amarintha."

Kat laughed. "Well, he might not have loved her,

but he sure did sleep with her a time or two, 'cause six months later the paper ran a birth announcement. She and Justis had a baby girl.''

Nathan made an inarticulate sound of distress and then a soothing one. ''It's all right. Sssh. He must have divorced her later and married your great-great-grandmother.''

''Divorce? Back then? No.'' She jabbed a finger toward the offending book. ''The society column mentions two times *during the next fifteen years* when he came back to take care of his businesses and visit his wife. Course, the paper makes it sound respectable—like there's nothing strange about a husband and wife not living together.''

She sighed. ''Then Amarintha and the daughter died from some sort of fever that was going around. The paper listed their names in the obituaries.''

''Well, let's see,'' Nathan said hopefully. ''Fifteen years later, that'd be 1853. Hmmm, Justis could have married Katlanicha *then*.''

''Yeah, after they already had three sons.''

''Who says they did? I only know about Holt, and he was just a kid during the Civil War. He could have been born in 1853.''

Kat patted his cheek in gratitude. ''Harmonica man, you're playing a happy tune, but it's not workin'. Erica's and Tess's great-grandpas were old enough to fight in the Civil War. Erica says hers was shot as a spy—and he was old enough to leave behind a wife and a son.''

She shook her head. ''So ol' Justis had himself two families going at the same time—one nice and legal and white, the other one . . . the other one . . .''

Nathan ached with sorrow as she looked up at him in anguish. ''Oh, Nathan, my great-great-grandmother was just his *Indian* wife, and back then that meant she wasn't anything. People didn't just think of my great-grandpa Holt as a killer, they thought of him as a bastard.''

Nathan swallowed a lump in his throat as she clung

to him, crying softly. "Kat, don't set so much store by niceties. A lot of men—white and Cherokee—had more than one wife. Some Cherokee women had more than one husband, or several husbands one right after the other.

"Things weren't real legal and neat, and nobody cared. Most likely nobody thought anything about Justis and Katlanicha's arrangement. They were probably married in a Cherokee ceremony. That's just as good."

"But he used her," Kat insisted. "He didn't make her a legal wife under white law, under *his* law." She clenched her hands against Nathan's chest. "And I bet I know why he stayed with her.

"I read in one of my other books that out in the Indian Territory a white man could claim Cherokee land if he had a Cherokee wife."

Nathan grimaced. She was right on that point. "Yeah, that's the way it was. And here in Georgia, too, when this town was still part of the Cherokee Nation."

"Justis had the best of both worlds—a respectable white wife and a profitable Indian one."

"It doesn't matter."

"Yes, it does!" Her eyes glittered with anger. "You don't know what it's like to want to have something to be proud of. I do! You wanna know why I never talk about my mother? She was from the reservation in North Carolina. *Her* people sold moonshine and stole cars!"

"So who cares?"

"I care!" She began to thump his chest for emphasis. "Growing up, I was snubbed by regular people who figure circus performers are scum, and now I'm snubbed by people who think lady wrestlers are tramps! And, hey, I'm a multiminority representative when it comes to getting insulted by confused bigots! Name your choice—I'm not only Indian, I'm Cuban, Mexican, Oriental, and Iranian—and once some jerk even called me a 'whale-sucking Eskimo'!"

"Kat, you're denting my rib cage. Calm down."

She grasped his face between her hands and searched his eyes for answers, for help. "Is it too much to want respect and love just for *me*, for what I am, no matter how different I am from everybody else?" Her voice was low and choked. "I don't want to go through the rest of my life bein' raped and used and laughed at."

Nathan inhaled sharply. Oh God, she hurt so much. "Katie, I'll make it up to you, I swear," he said hoarsely, caught in a blinding need to right every wrong that had ever been done to her. "We can have it *all* this time."

"*This* time?"

Nathan shut his eyes and grimaced. "I don't know what I'm saying, but I know what I mean." She was stroking his face with quick, possessive little caresses, her hands trembling.

"Katie," he said again, without thinking. *That nickname was part of his soul.* Nathan shuddered with emotion. "Forget what you read tonight. Trust me."

That was stranger than what he'd already said. Nathan looked at her anxiously. "I don't make sense around you. I want you too much to make sense. Don't run scared because I'm this way."

She moaned softly. "I'm not scared. I haven't been scared since the first time you called me 'Katie.' Oh, Nathan, what's going on between us?"

"I don't understand it either," he whispered, lifting her onto her toes. His voice dropped even lower. "I don't have to understand it."

She slid her arms around his neck. "Make love to me, she begged. "I won't ask for too much."

"You won't have to ask. Everything—everything you want, or need—it's yours."

"You, I need you," she cried as he covered her mouth with his.

They were quick, almost rough, fired by needs and emotions that swept the whole world away to leave only the two of them touching, loving, seeking to give pleasure.

Her dress barely survived. Nathan no sooner jerked the bodice open in back than she was fiercely struggling to get her arms out of it. Underneath she wore absolutely nothing. He pulled the dress down to her waist and she tugged him to her, her eyes flaring when her naked breasts flattened against his chest. He reached between their bodies to squeeze her nipples, pulling them forward, rubbing the peaks, wrapping his fingers around first one breast and then the other in an almost frantic desire to make her back arch again and again.

The dress fell off her hips, leaving only one barrier between them. Nathan thought he would burn up from the pure, lovely bawdiness in her as she slid her hands under the waistband of his briefs.

"I couldn't walk away when I saw you taking a bath that day," she told him. "I never saw a man enjoy being naked so much. I wanted to be naked with you."

"Now you are." His briefs fell to his ankles and he stepped out of them.

Immediately he curved both hands down her spine, underneath the mane of hair, along her rump, then beneath it, so he could pull her to his hardness.

She gasped with delight as the ridge nestled into her belly, and he thought there would never be a more exquisite sensation in his life than the feel of her soft mound fitted to the tops of his thighs.

"Nice," she whispered. "And remember, I'm not real good with words."

"You're great with body language."

He picked her up. Her thighs wrapped around his waist and her arms circled his neck in a deep embrace. With his face near enough for her mobile, sweet little mouth to enjoy, she kissed whatever she could reach.

Nathan staggered from sensation, dimly aware that he was flexing against her and that she was answering the primitive, erotic invitation with movements of her own. She dug the necklace from between them and kissed the nugget.

"I want to kiss everything on you and everything that ever touched you," she explained.

Nathan heard the breath slide from his mouth in a sigh of helpless surrender. The spontaneous movements of their bodies joined them suddenly. Kat made a high-pitched keening sound and, panting, looked at him through half-shut eyes.

He knew from her silkiness that he hadn't hurt her. He had surprised her, though.

"You're so strong," she murmured breathlessly, and the devotion in her eyes told him that she loved his surprise.

"I can hold you," he promised, and squeezed his hands into her thighs to lift her higher on his body.

"Hold me," she begged, kissing him deeply, slipping her tongue in and out of his mouth and filling him with a hunger that poured extraordinary strength into him.

She was no heavier than a dream, and he moved inside her easily, nuzzling his face along her shoulder, kissing her, biting her, licking her throat when her head fell back and she cried out to him.

Nathan's knees buckled a little at the feel of her pulsing with release. Her wail of pleasure held surprise and fierce happiness.

He found himself laughing and almost crying and on the verge of filling her with everything he could give. "It's like this with you and me, Katie," he shouted with delight. "Didn't you always know it would be like this?"

Her head fell forward and she sank her mouth onto his for a long moment, which brought him into a realm he'd never known before. "*Yes*," she said against his mouth. "Always."

Nathan dropped to his knees and arched into her in one final, explosive moment that made his head sag back even as his fingers dug into her and she gave him more—more of her body, more of her fire, more of her soul.

They collapsed onto the floor together, still joined, their skin slick with sweat, their breaths mingling in a turbulent search for the center of the storm.

All Nathan could manage to do was hold on to her with the same exhausted grip she had on him. "Now, Katie," he whispered, "we can start again."

Whatever he meant, she stroked his face and hair and smiled down at him with joyful tears in her eyes. "I know."

SHE HAD TO learn everything about him, everything that those handsome, droopy eyes had seen and everything that weathered, work-hardened body had done, everything that had made him into the man she now loved.

Nathan protested that he felt like her private playground, but the smile he gave her said that he didn't mind a bit. She made him lie on the bed while she nuzzled her face over his torso, licking and kissing the sweaty, sexy essence until he swore she was trying to eat him alive.

Kat lifted his hands to study the scars and calluses from rough work and dangerous encounters. She traced the lines in his palms, thinking how his past and future seemed to merge with the blemishes; this man had never avoided a challenge, and it showed in his hands.

Now he'd brought that challenge into her life, and she would read his body like a map, trying to understand him so well that she could find his heart, and keep it.

Kat stroked a fingertip over the fine white lines on his right knuckles. "You used to fight?"

"Just enough to keep my hide in one piece so you'd enjoy it one day." Oh, he knew how to make an electric jolt of pleasure slide through her, and he recognized it in her eyes. "I like your hide, too," he promised softly, brushing his scarred knuckle over her breasts and smiling when the peaks grew harder.

"You're plain *wicked*, Nathan Chatham." She arched one black brow at him. "You ever fight over a woman?"

"Yep." He waited just long enough for her to thump his chest in exasperation. "I punched a water buffalo that was about to do a tap dance on an old Australian lady."

"Oh." She took his hand again and kissed the knuckles. "Other fights?"

"I had a run-in with boys in Surador last year. Just helping out an acquaintance of mine."

When Kat looked at him quizzically he explained, "Fellow I met while I was studying sites. Said he was an anthropologist, but I suspect he was in government work. Nice guy, but a funny name—Surprise. Kyle Surprise. He hung around with me for a few weeks, then moved on.

"I heard later that he'd gotten into some trouble. One of the nationalist *patróns* didn't like Kyle's brand of anthropology, I think. Had him locked up on a banana plantation." Nathan shrugged. "I just organized a few of the rebel troops and got him out."

Pride swept over Kat, making her bend forward quickly and kiss him. "You're a wonder."

"Wonder all right. Wonder what you're gonna do to me next."

She sat back, stroked the hard plane of his belly, and said in a husky tone, "I'm gonna turn you over and see that tattoo. I want to know all about it."

"Got it on the Amazon."

"That's not where *I* saw it."

Chuckling, he rolled onto his stomach without the least hint of shyness and propped his chin on crossed arms.

Kat smiled in delight. "It looks like a clown face!"

Nathan huffed loudly. "That's Numanchuko, the god of earth. The natives said Numanchuko must like me if he let me know his secrets."

"Secrets?"

"Gold."

"Oh." Kat molded her hands to Nathan's back and drew them down to his thighs, watching the muscles flex in response. "Numanchuko's lively," she noted.

"I think he expects an earthquake."

"I expect he's right. I'm gonna get real friendly with him."

Wanting to be close to Nathan in ways she'd never wanted with any other man, she draped herself on top of him like a blanket, smiling a little at the thought of the colorful tattoo face flattened under her stomach.

"Ol' Numanchuko's never had it so good," Nathan said with a soft groan.

Kat nibbled the back of his neck, stroked a small patch of hair between his shoulder blades, then slowly slid her hands down his sides.

"Nathan? I want another pony ride."

He slipped a hand into her hair and guided her upward so that her head was next to his. Kat curled over him, giggling when their mouths met awkwardly, losing the breath to giggle when he rebuked her with a deliciously rough tongue. She moved and lay in his arms, pulled chest to chest with him, her thighs hugging the leg he angled between them.

He drew her lower lip between his teeth, nibbled it, then let go slowly and licked the swollen skin like a wild animal tasting his mate. Kat shut her eyes and still saw him, imagined the primal glitter in his eyes, the ruffled hair of his desperado mustache a little damp from the wet kiss they'd just shared.

As he rose over her she locked her gaze on his face, trying to see inside him, hoping she could pour all of her love into him until he had no choice but to love her back.

He cared for the earth, wore its offering on his body, took from it as her great-great-grandfather had done, but Nathan had honesty and honor; he gave respect in return. On her land, her ancestors' land, she and

Nathan had formed a very special bond that went beyond explanation.

And she believed that the land would keep them together.


NATHAN NUZZLED HIS face into her neck and sighed with contentment. "How's your ankle?"

She lifted it from the water. "Real good. I like your form of doctoring. Lots of rest, with plenty of company. It's working. Even when my ankle hurts, I don't notice."

"You'll go back on the tour right away?"

"Have to. Got bills to pay."

"Nope."

Kat turned her head toward his and kissed him gently. "Yep."

"Nope. I already paid 'em."

She twisted quickly and looked him straight in the eyes. "When?"

"When we were in town eating lunch the other day. You went to the ladies' room, and I made a phone call. Just told a friend of mine what to take care of." When she continued to look at him speechlessly, he added, "I did it so you could stay here longer with me. Is that so bad?"

"How long are you gonna stay?" she asked.

"I don't know."

"Where will you go after you leave?"

"Surador. I've got work to do down there." He cupped her face with one hand and gazed at her tenderly. "See, Kat? We're both nomads. But even nomads can find ways to be together. I'll be back. I'll find you."

Suddenly the future was a lot less happy. Kat slid her arms around him and rested her head on his shoulder. "I'll miss you," she whispered.

"I'm not gone yet," he said gruffly, and stroked her hair.

*It feels like you are,* Kat told him silently.

•   •   •

KAT CARRIED AN armload of kindling back toward camp, barely limping now that she'd had several more days of Nathan's rather untraditional—but highly enjoyable—form of doctoring.

Sunset made long shadows hang from the trees, and bats darted across patches of sky overhead. She thought about all the Cherokee legends Nathan had told her of monsters and giants, elves and witches.

Kat chanted under her breath. "Lions and tigers and bears, oh my! Lions and tigers and bears, oh—"

"Hello," a bass voice said politely.

Kat dropped her kindling. Her heart jamming her throat, she swung around on the trail and faced an incredible sight. Oh Lord, Nathan was right. There *were* giants.

He didn't look Cherokee, but he could have been birthed by some Cherokee mountain. He stood there watching her, his neatly cropped black hair brushing a tree limb easily seven feet from the ground. He had shoulders a bodybuilder would die for, but otherwise he was streamlined. Big as a freight train, but streamlined, with a handsome, somewhat angular face.

Kat exhaled a little. No mythical giant would be dressed in a blue T-shirt, khaki trousers, and hiking boots. But she didn't like the fact that he had a knife the size of a small sword lashed into a leather scabbard on one side of his belt.

Kat backed away slowly, her hands balled into fists. The giant's eyebrows shot up. "Wait."

"I'm little, but I'm tough," she warned in a low, fierce voice. "And I'll take a prize or two before you squash me."

He stepped forward, holding up both huge hands in a placating gesture. "I'm—"

"Dead meat," she interjected, and whipped out the Beretta that had been hidden in the front waistband of her shorts, under her floppy T-shirt. Kat pointed the gun at the center of his chest.

"Facedown on the ground. Spread-eagle. Say a word and I'll turn you into cheddar cheese . . . Swiss cheese."

Kat grimaced. She was so intimidating. She couldn't even get her cheeses right.

The giant shrugged, sighed, and lowered himself with surprising grace to the forest floor.

"Eat the ground," she ordered, feeling desperate with fear. He sighed again and stuck his face into dark humus that was damp from an afternoon rain.

"Yo, Kat!" Nathan called from somewhere in the woods near camp. He sang coyly, "Here, kitty, here, kitty!"

"Naaaathaan!" she screamed. Within seconds she heard him crashing through the forest, taking a short-cut to the trail.

He burst onto it, his hand wrapped around the hilt of his bowie knife. "What?"

"I caught this guy on our land!" *Our* seemed appropriate. It had just popped out.

Nathan ran up to her, halted in midstride, and stared at the captive, who still had his face buried in the forest floor.

Kat watched in consternation as Nathan dropped the knife, clasped his stomach, and bent over laughing. "D-Drake L-Lancaster." He wheezed. "Caught by my Katie."

Oh no. Drake Lancaster, Nathan's co-worker? She stared at the huge man in horrified embarrassment. He remained flat, but his back quivered with laughter, and he raised his head slowly.

She's perfect for you, Nathan."

DRAKE RETURNED FROM his room in Gold Ridge early the next morning, met them at the site of the Blue Song home, and squinted at Kat in amusement when she solemnly apologized one more time.

Then he stripped down to hiking shorts and boots, grabbed a shovel, and attacked the house site like a human bulldozer. Nathan wore only jogging shorts and his hiking boots, and Kat felt positively over-dressed because she had to wear a bra and T-shirt with her shorts.

But after Drake returned to the inn for the day . . .

She followed the two men, picking up the things they unearthed, smiling when Nathan looked over and made clucking noises at her.

She really did feel like a little hen searching for goodies, and she found plenty to cluck about. By noon she'd stacked twenty window sash weights in a neat pyramid beside a smaller pile of nails, hinges, and miscellaneous metal.

But her big find was four buttons and a handful of musket balls.

"Nathan!" She went over to him excitedly and pre-sented the items in her cupped palms. "Look! They were all in the same spot!"

After carefully scratching dirt off one button with a twig, Nathan's expression became pensive. He held it so that a stripe of sunlight would illuminate the fea-tures.

"It's got a U.S. Army insignia."

She frowned. "But what would that be doing near the musket balls? Nathan, are you saying a soldier was killed here? But there's no skeleton!"

Drake came over and examined the items. He was a very quiet, private person. Kat had already noticed, and he seemed to feel awkward around her, though he certainly wasn't shy. She judged he was just self-conscious in the manner of large, brutal-looking men who were accustomed to being feared whether they warranted it or not.

As he volunteered technical information about the musket balls, Kat eyed him curiously. Nathan had said that he coordinated on-site security for Tri-State mines, and it was obvious he was a weapons expert.

"So what you're saying," Nathan observed when

he'd finished describing the balls, "is that these probably hit hard objects—stone or metal—not people."

"Yes. If the buttons fit the time period when the Cherokees were removed, then it's possible the army was up here, and these could be musket shots they fired inside the house."

Kat gave Nathan a troubled look. Her heart felt like a fist in her chest. "Damn," she said softly.

He laid a hand against her cheek. "There could be a lot of explanations."

"Yeah, I know. But that one jibes with history. There was a lot of violence when the Cherokees were rounded up."

"Well, could be that soldiers came into the house after the family left," Drake offered. "And shot the place up just for the hell of it. One of them could've left a jacket behind. The jacket rotted but the buttons didn't."

"But I thought white settlers took over the deserted houses and cabins," Kat said. "Why would they let this one sit here until it fell down?"

Nathan stroked her cheek. "Justis owned it, remember? Nobody'd try to move into the house if the place was claimed by an important man like him."

"Great," Kat said bitterly. "So the only thing that saved the place was the fact that he stole it from Great-Great-Grandmother's family. Real noble of him. I wonder why he didn't move his white wife up here. Heck, maybe he did."

"Aw, Katie, it wasn't like that."

Kat stared at him. Whenever he spoke in that strange, certain way, calling her Katie, a feeling of trust came over her.

His eyes locked on hers as if he were trying to remember something and looking at her helped. "Don't know," he said after a few seconds, wearily, and the intensity faded from his eyes. "It just seems to me that Justis was most likely a decent man. Maybe I want to like him for your sake."

She smiled a little then. "That's a good enough reason for me, sweetcakes."

"Let me take these buttons and musket balls into town," Drake told them. "There's a gun shop there run by an old codger who knows local history. He might confirm the button ID."

"Yeah, okay," Nathan answered. Looking at Kat, he said, "I'll walk to camp and bring back some lunch. Why don't you sit down and prop your ankle up on something?"

She nodded. "I'd kinda like to be alone here for a while." Kat looked around wistfully. "To think."

Drake got into a mud-spattered Jeep and drove away. Nathan hugged her tenderly, then swung off down the front side of the ridge, his proud, athletic stride holding her gaze until he was hidden by the trees.

Kat sat down on a log and stretched her injured leg out. Well, she had Nathan, she had her land, and even if there was a lot of sadness connected to her family's history she was going to love living here.

Especially if Nathan would live here with her.

Kat propped her chin on her hands and stared at the ground, trying to re-create the Blue Song house from its ghosts, wondering what had happened the day the soldiers came. How had Katlanicha escaped? When had she met Justis? Some things would always be a mystery.

A few minutes later she lifted her head at the sound of a vehicle driving up the trail. Hmmm, Drake must have forgotten something.

But the car that pulled to a stop a few yards away from her sitting place was a fancy, late-model station wagon. And the person who got out was not Drake.

Kat rose in surprise as a statuesque, curvaceous young woman came toward her, head up, eyes imperious, majestic even in soft leather boots, jeans, and a ruffled white blouse. The woman's dark eyes and ethnic features, her bronzed skin and long black hair convinced Kat she was about to meet a fellow Cherokee—and an extraordinary-looking one.

"Hi ya," Kat said, cheerfully impressed by the stranger. This babe could make a mint if she ever wanted to wrestle.

The woman stopped less than two feet from Kat, tried to freeze her with a dignified glare, and said softly, "Tell me where he is, and then get out of my sight."

S HOCK MADE A raw and brassy taste in Kat's mouth. She jammed her hands into the front pockets of her cutoffs and the soft denim bunched under her clenched fingers.

"If you were important, I'd have heard about you," she told the woman.

Dark eyes gleamed fiercely. "Where is he?"

Kat shook her head. *Please, this isn't happening. Nathan couldn't have another lover.* She lifted her chin proudly. "I don't know what you were to him, but it's over now."

"Oh? Just let me talk to him. Is he even here, or did he desert you the way he deserted me?"

A tone of despair rang through the visitor's voice. Kat looked at her wretchedly. "He walked over to our, over there"—she pointed limply—"to get something from camp. He'll be back."

"Are you the one he bought the bra for?" The woman measured Kat's chest size with a gaze that held anguish. "No, you're too big." Her shoulders slumped and she said in a small, stunned voice, "Oh lord. He's got another one besides us."

Weak-kneed, Kat hobbled to the log and sank down numbly. "I don't believe it."

"Believe it. I saw the bra. It had a pink bow tied on it." Moving wearily, ramming her hands through hair even longer than Kat's, the woman lowered herself to the ground and sighed in defeat. "How long have *you* known him?"

"A few weeks." Kat tried to ignore the dread knotting her stomach. "How about you?"

"A few weeks. He left without saying good-bye—three weeks ago. I thought he'd come back, until I heard about you."

They traded stricken looks. The visitor shook her head and struggled noticeably not to cry. "I've known other men who had a thing for Cherokee women, but I thought he was different. I thought he was sincere when he said he loved me."

Kat wanted to die. Nathan had never said that to *her*. "I just cannot buy this story," she said with renewed defensiveness.

"Me either," the woman said with a catch in her voice. "He seemed so special. I've never met anyone like him before. I mean, it was like I'd known him all my life."

Kat covered her face. "Oh no, it's true."

"I'm from the reservation up in North Carolina. Where are you from, around here?"

"Miami."

The woman made a soft sound of misery. "He *said* that he traveled a lot."

Kat got up and moved away, trembling. "I can't talk about this anymore. I don't want to be bawling my eyes out when he comes back."

"No." The visitor sniffed tearfully. "You're right."

"I guess we should introduce ourselves," Kat said, her throat on fire. "My name's Kat Gallatin."

"I know. Erica's cousin." She held her head and looked at Kat with despair. "I'm Echo Tall Wolf."

"Not from Grandpa Sam's family!"

"Yes. That's how I heard of you."

"Oh no!" Kat hugged herself to keep from crying out loud and turned her back. "N-no more talk."

"R-right."

Kat limped farther from her and leaned rigidly against a dogwood tree. She and Echo Tall Wolf waited in silent, shared misery that seemed to last an eternity.

Finally Kat heard the rugged sound of a powerful engine and knew that Drake Lancaster was returning. She turned around and saw Nathan top the ridge, his knapsack hanging jauntily over one shoulder.

Great timing, harmonica man, she thought. Now Drake can be our audience.

She walked over to Echo, who got up hurriedly, brushing leaves from her jeans and looking from the approaching Jeep to Nathan. "I guess we're going to have an audience," she said grimly.

"Yeah. A friend of his."

"Well, it couldn't be any worse than it is already."

They stood side by side, waiting.

After he studied Echo Tall Wolf for a second, Nathan looked at Kat quizzically. His stride casual, he never faltered. Kat couldn't take her eyes off his lean, tanned body covered only by shorts and hiking boots, the body he'd shared with Echo Tall Wolf only a few weeks ago. She was dimly aware of the Jeep door slamming as Drake Lancaster got out.

"He's always so damned calm," Echo murmured hoarsely.

"Yeah." Kat gritted her teeth. Nathan didn't look more than a tiny bit intrigued to see two of his lovers waiting where only one had been before.

Drake strode toward them, frowning, one enormous hand clenched lightly over the front of the T-shirt he'd donned for the trip to town. He and Nathan reached them about the same time and stopped.

"Who'd you give the bra to?" Kat asked coldly. "You know, the bra with the pink bow on it?"

"Bra?" Nathan asked.

"What kind of work do you really do?" Echo interjected.

Kat touched her arm and their eyes met. "He's a geologist."

Echo gasped. "He told me that he was a biologist studying pollution for the forestry service."

"What are you talking about?" Nathan demanded.

Drake gestured for attention. "The bra was for Tess Gallatin."

Kat and Echo wailed at approximately the same time.

"Thanks for telling me the truth," Kat muttered. "Somebody needs to." She sighed heavily. "My cousin Tess. My own cousin. Poor Tess probably didn't know there were other women, either."

"I'm sure your cousin Erica would have told me if she'd known," Echo said. "But even Erica thought I should have faith."

Kat trembled. How did Drake know about the bra? Oh no! Holding out her hands in supplication, she asked Nathan. "Do you guys discuss *everything* about your women?"

"No, wait, I'm—" Nathan began.

"How could you say that you weren't involved with anyone but me," Echo demanded, "when all the time you and Tess Gallatin were meeting in some cave in the woods? How could you do that to me? How could you do that to Kat?"

"Hold on," Drake said. "I—"

"Please be quiet," Kat told him. The man had no business butting in. "Echo?"

She looked at Echo, who explained raggedly, "In the morning he'd say that he had work to do, then he'd ride a horse off into the mountains and come back late in the afternoon. He and Tess were sharing a cave, a *cave.*"

Kat looked at Nathan tearfully. "Do you get your jollies livin' with Cherokee women in the woods?"

Nathan dropped his knapsack. Gazing at her open-mouthed, he held up both hands in defense. "I am totally confused."

"Please tell me this isn't true."

"Tell us *both*," Echo added fiercely.

"Dammit," Drake said loudly, "I don't know what's going on here, but there's no other woman!"

"How do *you* know?" Kat demanded.

"I'd remember if there was more than one who could cause this much trouble!"

"I would, too," Nathan said blankly. "Especially if I knew what the hell we were talking about."

Kat pressed a fist to her lips. Sorrow nearly strangled her. "I wish you'd tell the plain truth. I only want to hear, 'Yes, right before I met you I was involved with Echo Tall Wolf,' Or 'No, I wasn't.' "

Drake suddenly seemed a foot taller. "*What?*" he asked softly, with a lethal tightening of his body.

"Yes," Echo agreed with fierce control, "Just say it—did you leave me for Kat?"

Nathan's eyes turned the color of dark storm clouds. He gazed at Drake very, very intensely, as if waiting for answers. Drake returned the look in kind.

Kat was so upset that a stab of confusion was forgotten right after she noticed it. "Drake," she said as calmly as she could, "this is sort of private. Could you leave us alone with Nathan?"

"No, we're talking to Drake. You mean Drake," Echo interjected.

"No, I mean"—Kat turned to stare up at her—"I mean Nathan."

"Drake," Echo said softly, her dark eyes wide.

Kat shook her head slowly. Her heart was denting the inside of her chest. "Nathan."

Echo pointed a trembling finger. "You and Nathan?"

Kat nodded. "You and Drake?"

Echo nodded. "I came down here because Grandpa said Drake was in Gold Ridge with you."

"He works with Nathan. Nathan asked him to come here."

Echo clasped both hands to her heart and stared at Drake Lancaster, a desperate expression on her face. *"Colanneh*, I'm sorry I doubted you."

Kat made a strangled sound and didn't know whether she felt like laughing or hiding in embarrassment. Nathan's angry gaze told her laughter was *not* an option.

Echo continued to stare at Drake, who surveyed her with a troubled gaze. "What was I supposed to think after you disappeared without saying good-bye?" she asked softly.

"I left word that I'd be back. I said you had nothing to worry about. Why didn't you believe me?"

Echo shook her head. "Too many mysteries."

Drake stuck out a hand. "Come with me." To Nathan he said, "We'll be back after I explain a few things."

"Fine." Nathan's voice was flint-hard, and he spoke without taking his accusing gaze off Kat's repentant one.

"It wasn't Kat's fault," Echo called as Drake led her to the Jeep. "It was all so confusing."

Nathan didn't speak again until after Drake and Echo drove away. Then, his eyes full of reproach, he said, "I don't know how this mess started, but I do know that you don't trust me worth a damn."

"Aw, Nathan, I *do*. It was a misunderstanding—a strange woman comes here looking for the man who deserted her, and she never mentions a name, and how was I supposed to know that she'd known Drake up in North Carolina?"

"But the first thing you thought was 'Nathan lied to me.'"

Kat lifted her chin and eyed him proudly. "No, not that. I've never asked you for any promises and you've never said I was the only woman in your life. I know better than to expect too much."

"Then why'd you make a fool out of yourself—like I belonged to you?"

Kat realized that she'd talked herself into a corner,

and in doing so she'd provoked the truth from Nathan. He didn't want her to be possessive, or he wouldn't have asked his question so fiercely.

"For as long as you're part of this"—she gestured weakly at the land—"I feel like you belong to me."

He searched her face, his gaze shuttered. "Sounds like you only care about the land."

Words caught inside Kat's throat. "No, I care about you a lot, but I know the land will always be here, and you won't."

"You watch out for yourself first," he said between clenched teeth. "That's a smart way to live. That's the way I like to live, too."

Later, she would replay those words and die a thousand small deaths. But right now she had to salvage as much time with him as she could. "You're welcome to stay here as long as you want," Kat assured him. "I love . . . your company."

"Good. Real good," he said, breathing harshly, with something tormented and urgent rising in his eyes. "I'll be around here a lot—probably a hell of a lot more than you will be, for the next, oh, twenty years."

Kat shook her head, feeling dazed. "What are you talking about?"

He swept a hand at the magnificent woods, at the Blue Song homesite, at the valley and stream. "I own all the mining rights. I've waited a long time to dig the gold out of this land."

As she backed away, her hands pressed to her mouth, he added hoarsely, "And believe me, you won't want to live here then."

"You can't own the mining rights."

"Holt Gallatin signed them over to my great-grandfather in 1910." His voice was harsh, but sorrow clouded his eyes. "A ninety-nine year lease. All mineral rights. The Gallatin family doesn't even get a percentage of the profits."

"No!"

He held out his hands to her. "Kat, I didn't mean

to tell you like this. Dammit, I wanted to wait until you—''

''Were so crazy about you that I'd be on your side! Everything you've done—buying me things, acting like every word I said was important, doing all those things to please me in bed—it was only to get me on your side!''

''Dammit, no.''

''Just like ol' Justis must have done to my great-great-grandmother! What a joke that must have been to you!''

Full of tension, he stepped forward swiftly and grabbed her arms. ''I wanted you on my side, sure, because I didn't want to hurt you this way. I care about you too much to watch you lose everything you've dreamed about.''

''But that won't stop you from taking it!''

He shook her lightly. His voice was agonized. ''I promised my grandpa. I promised myself for my father's sake. It's something I've gotta do.''

Shock and disappointment whirled in her head until she could barely think. ''I trusted you. I trusted you in ways I've never trusted a man before.''

''You still can.''

She pulled away from him and pressed her hands to her temples. ''I don't understand how you got our mineral rights. And what's your grandpa got to do with it? How'd my family hurt him?''

Nathan reached for her hand. ''Let's sit down.''

''I can't sit down.'' She stepped back. ''Don't touch me.''

He stood there looking as miserable as she felt. ''You gonna listen? Listen good, so maybe you can understand that I'm not a greedy bastard looking for excuses to tear up this land.''

''I'll give it a try,'' she shot back. ''Talk.''

''Holt Gallatin—Blue Fox—took up a one-man war against my family,'' Nathan told her. ''After he killed my great-great-grandpa Nathaniel, the one who fought against Justis Gallatin in the Civil War, Holt went on the lam. Had to, since he was wanted for murder.

"The Indian Territory wasn't much more than a lot of empty land with plenty of places to hide, and there weren't enough U.S. marshals to track down a smart man who had help from the Keetowahs."

"The Cherokee society that hated white people?"

"Yeah. So Holt was able to ride over into Arkansas, strike at my family, and then go back to the Cherokee Nation and hide with hardly any chance of getting caught. He and a gang of Keetowahs robbed and murdered all over western Arkansas for almost twenty years. And the Chathams were their prime targets."

"You mean Holt killed other Chathams besides Nathaniel?"

"No, but he wounded a few and crippled one. And he tried to ruin any business a Chatham touched. He stole cattle, burned down stores, robbed a bank managed by a Chatham—in short, he was a curse that plagued my family for two decades."

"Then what?" she asked wearily, hugging herself.

"U.S. marshals chased him out of the Territory. Whites were moving in; there was talk about statehood—"

"The government was stealing land from the Cherokees again."

Nathan nodded slowly. "Yeah. I'm afraid that's right."

"So the thieves chased a thief off."

"A murderer," Nathan corrected, but without victory. "Holt was a bad man, one of the worst, Cherokee or white."

Kat slowly walked to an old tree and leaned against its gnarled trunk. Her eyes burning, she stared up into the thick foliage as if seeing something besides Nathan's grim face when he told her he intended to mine her land. "What happened after Holt left the Territory?"

"He disappeared for the next twenty years. I guess everyone in my family thought he was dead."

Nathan kicked at a broken limb on the ground. "But then Holt showed up again. He was getting old, he wanted to settle down on some land Justis and Katherine left him, and he had a young wife and two children—your grandpa Joshua, and Dove." Nathan looked disgusted. "Holt had wrangled some sort of amnesty from the U.S. government. I don't know how he did it, other than that his brother had some influence in Washington."

Kat nodded. "Silas Gallatin. He was Tess's great-grandfather. I think he became a pretty important man out in California."

"Holt didn't think his family would be safe in Oklahoma with a whole bunch of angry Chathams just across the Arkansas border. He wanted to bribe my family into forgiving and forgetting."

Kat groaned in frustration. "So he bargained with Eli Chatham, your Great-Grandpa—for peace."

"Right. Holt gave him the mining rights to Katlanicha's land in Georgia. This land."

"But you said that Holt killed Eli."

Nathan laughed grimly. "He did, about ten years later. Those two old men never stopped hating each other. Holt came to Arkansas and called Eli out. They had a gunfight—one of the last bona fide, Main-Street-at-dawn-duels in the state of Arkansas. 1921. It made the local newspapers."

Nathan paused, and she looked at his brooding expression carefully. "And what happened to my great-grandpa then?"

"Nothing. He was shot, too. He died a few days after the fight."

Kat sagged inwardly and sat down on an exposed root at the base of the tree. "So your grandpa wanted revenge for his daddy, Eli's death. Why didn't he mine our land himself?"

Nathan came close and squatted down on his heels. Gazing into her eyes with a sorrowful expression on his face, he said softly, "Because Dove Gallatin was his mistress and he never stopped loving her."

"Oh no, no." Kat stared at him as a sick feeling of defeat grew in her stomach. "Not Dove. Erica told me all about her. She was an old maid. She lived in North Carolina."

Growing agitated, Kat waved her hands anxiously and rushed on without pausing for breath. "Everyone loved her. They said she had powers. When she got too old and sick to be happy, she willed herself to die. She left us each a family medallion because she *cared* about the Gallatin family—"

"Whoa, whoa. That may be all true—except she was no old maid." Nathan sighed, gazed at the ground, and ran a hand through his hair as he thought for a moment.

"Don't try to be nice," Kat said fiercely. "You and me got no reason to be nice to each other anymore. Just say it like it is."

He looked up at her with anguished, angry eyes. "Right. All I know is what Grandpa Micah told me, and he was no saint, at least not by the time I came along. Dove and him carried on for years behind my grandmother's back. Dove got pregnant, and out of spite she went to my grandmother and told her about the whole affair."

"I can't believe this," Kat whispered.

"Believe it. My grandmother killed herself over it. She left a baby son behind."

"Your father," Kat supplied weakly.

"Yep. My father. Grandpa Micah felt so guilty over what he'd done to his wife that he went straight to hell in a liquor bottle."

"What happened to Dove?"

"She ran off to England with an RAF pilot she knew from God knows where. Married him."

"And her baby?"

"Died of whooping cough before it was four. The pilot was killed during World War Two. That's all I know about Dove. She ruined my grandpa and deserted him."

Kat dug her nails into her palms. "So this Gallatin-

Chatham feud came closer to you than I knew. It *is* personal."

He nodded, his cold gray eyes directly on hers. "My daddy had a drunk for a father. Grandpa lost just about everything he owned; he didn't give a damn how his son grew up, and because of that my daddy grew up worthless. He was a no-account drifter and he died in a bar fight when I was fifteen."

Even though this information about Nathan's background shocked her, she could only manage to retort, "Are you blaming my family for every rotten thing that ever happened to a Chatham?"

"I'm not blaming you or your cousins for anything. I'm simply saying that four generations of my family have been hurt by one Gallatin or another. It's only fair that this land should pay some of that debt back."

Kat stood up proudly. "We won't let you do this. You can't drag out a claim that our kin signed back when our grandparents were kids. It won't hold up in court."

He rose with slow, coiled emotion. "It's legal. I've had it checked out. There's not a damned thing you can do about it."

"I'm a fighter."

"You're a fake fighter. You put on war paint and play at being mean. This match against me is too much for you. Give it up."

He held out his hand to her suddenly, and Kat was surprised to see it tremble. "I'm not doing this for the money, Kat. I don't need the money. I do need you. I want us to be together despite this mining thing. I know that's a lot to ask."

"That's not just a lot to ask, that's impossible," she said softly, almost choking on the words. "My cousins would never forgive me and I'd never forgive myself. Oh, don't worry, I'm not through with you—not in court, anyway."

She left him standing there with his hand out as she walked away.

• • •

DEPRESSION CREATED A filter around Kat, diffusing the world until nothing made much of an impression when it reached her eyes, her ears, her emotions.

"Erica?" Kat murmured into the phone, her voice raspy and low. She leaned wearily on the big antique desk that belonged to their lawyer in Gold Ridge, her shoulders slumped, her head down. Now she knew how warriors must have felt after a lost battle.

Drained, lifeless, empty.

"Kat? What's wrong? Are you sick? When I got your message I was worried. You sound sick."

Kat knew she wouldn't cry. She had only a few tears left, and she was too tired to use them. "There's something we never knew about the gold on our land. The lawyer didn't even know. I guess Dove Gallatin knew—maybe she thought we could fix the problem."

"Whatever it is, relax," Erica said patiently. "Our Cherokee relatives are buried on that land. Katherine Blue Song's family—her parents and three sisters. Tess's medallion says so. Grandpa Sam just finished deciphering it. I don't see how we can lease the mining rights, knowing that, so it doesn't matter about the gold."

Kat found her last tears. "Erica, we don't have any say-so over the mining rights. We never have."

"What?"

"My great-grandfather"—Kat paused to exhale heavily. "Holt Gallatin, he was trying to bribe his way out of trouble, so he signed the rights over to a man named Eli Chatham. A ninety-nine-year lease. There are twenty years left on it."

"Oh, Kat, no. I can't believe Dove's father would do that! Listen, Dove wrote down a lot of family history. It's all in Cherokee, and Grandpa Sam is still working on it. But I do know this much—Dove could predict the future. Dove wrote a poem about me that came true."

"Erica, I don't believe in all that kind of stuff."

"Dove gave us our medallions for a reason, Kat. Mine says that our great-great-grandmother went on the Trail of Tears to Oklahoma, with the rest of the tribe, but Justis rescued her."

"Oh, Erica, Justis didn't care about Katherine—Katlanicha."

"Yes, he did. I'm convinced of that. There's so much love in those medallions, Kat. Mine also says, 'A wolf will find his mate, no matter how far she roams.' Kat, I'm going to marry James Tall Wolf. Do you understand? My medallion held a prophecy."

Kat pounded a fist on the desk, "Erica, you're not listening."

"I don't know what Tess will make of hers. I've sent it back to her with the translation of the message. We'll just have to wait and see how she reacts. When Grandpa gets your medallion figured out, I think we'll see some kind of pattern. We were meant to have the land, we were meant to take care of it."

"My great-grandfather sold the mining rights and there's nothing we can do about it!" Kat yelled. "That's all that matters! He sold the rights to Eli Chatham. Later he and Chatham killed each other in a gunfight. And now Chatham's grandson owns the rights!"

"Kat, honey, there has to be a way out of this," Erica said calmly, though there was a slight tremor in her voice. "Damn, I wish you weren't there alone. I can tell you're frantic."

"I'm sorry for yelling," Kat said hoarsely. "But listen, you don't understand. This isn't business, this is revenge." She explained the Gallatin-Chatham feud.

Erica groaned. "Kat, are you saying that this Chatham character blames us for all of that?"

"No, Nathan's real sorry for us, but he promised his grandpa, and he has a lot of honor."

"Whose side are you on?"

Kat felt a cold, shriveling pain wrap around her rib cage. "Ours. I'm a Gallatin. I gotta put the land first."

Erica asked gently, "Is there something I ought to know about you and Nathan Chatham?"

Swiping at her eyes, Kat exhaled sharply and said, "Nah. Listen. Micah Chatham put it in his will that nobody could mine our land until after Dove died. Now Dove's gone, and Nathan Chatham says he's going to, to—" Her voice cracked. "Do you know what 'heap leaching' is?"

"Oh Lord," Erica said raggedly, and Kat realized that her cousin was crying, too. "He'll turn our land into a gravel pit full of chemicals." She took a calming breath. "James and I'll drive down to Gold Ridge tomorrow morning. We can buy this Chatham bastard off or stop him in court. Kat, I know we can."

"Sure. I'm staying at the Kirkland Inn. See ya there."

She hung up the phone and sat thinking dully, *There's only one chance of changing Nathan's plan, and I'm the only Gallatin who can take it.*

HE WOULD NEVER forget this day, no matter how hard he might try—Kat's face when he'd told her the truth about his pledge to his grandfather, her wilted little questions, and finally the way she'd just turned and limped to her car, without looking back.

All of it was branded into him, and the brand would be painfully raw for a long, long time.

Nathan capped the bottle of bourbon and tossed it aside. He couldn't remember the last time he'd gotten drunk, but it'd probably been for a celebration of some kind. Well, that's what tonight was—a celebration of family revenge, family honor, and the evolution of Nathan Chatham, idealistic geologist, into Nathan Chatham, heartless bastard.

Nathan rubbed his face wearily, slung another piece of wood at his campfire, not caring that his boozy aim made it miss the fire entirely, and stretched out on his side, propped up on one elbow.

His head swam. He shut his eyes and saw Kat's

face. No, Katie's face. More often than not he thought of her that way. How could he win her after today? How he could make her understand that nobody would ever love her more than he did, despite the debt he had to settle for his family?

She was meant to love him back, but like before, it would take time for her to admit that, maybe even to herself.

*Love him like before?* Nathan cursed softly and rubbed his forehead again, as if he could force thoughts that made sense inside his brain.

*Katie, give me a chance, gal. Katie.*

"Nathan."

He opened his eyes groggily and saw her kneeling on the ground near his feet. Startled, he looked at her without speaking, slowly taking in the fact that she'd walked a half mile through the woods at night, alone, to come to him, that she wore the white dress he'd bought her, and that she'd crimped her hair somehow so that it cascaded around her in ebony waves.

She was so beautiful that he ached inside, so unreal in the firelight that he rubbed his eyes and checked to make certain she was still there, her hands calmly in her lap.

Maybe he was looking at a wishful thought.

But she rested a hand on his leg, and her touch seared him even through his buckskin breeches. "I love you," she said in a firm, somber voice, her eyes never leaving his.

Nathan blinked twice, shook his head, and almost said *I love you* back. But then he remembered the look of desperation on her face earlier that day.

He laughed hoarsely. "You love this land."

"I love you *and* the land. That's why I'm asking you for a deal."

"Love." Nathan said something so obscene that her hand trembled on him and she looked a little frightened. "Don't ever use that word to me," he warned. "It has nothing to do with what you want."

"Okay. If it bothers you so much, then you'll never hear it from me again."

"Good." He eyed her wearily, with dismay, finally asking, "So what's your deal?"

"Anything you want from me, for as long as you want it. I'll go wherever you tell me to go, do whatever you want me to do, work for you, sleep with you, wash your truck, clean your house—I guess you've got a house somewhere, don't you?" She smiled, but to Nathan it just made her look sadder. "How many men would turn down a nice slave?" she asked.

He stared at her in amazement. "This man would. I remember you saying, 'I don't want to go through the rest of my life being used.' "

"It's not the rest of my life. It's for as long as you want."

Nathan leaned on both elbows and let his head drape back. It made him dizzy. What he was thinking made the sensation even worse. *I wanted you then, I want you now, I want you forever.*

"And I'd give back the mining rights to your land," he said, tilting his head forward.

"I don't expect you to do that, Nathan. I guess I understand why you've gotta do what your family deserves." Her voice sounded old, defeated. "But maybe you could postpone the mining for a few years. You know—give me and my cousins some time to enjoy the land.

"Maybe Tess and Erica will have kids. If their kids could see this, you know, if the next generation of Gallatin kin could get even one look at where their people came from, where they're buried—"

"What d'you mean?"

"Katlanicha's parents and sisters are buried here," she explained, looking away from his intense gaze. "If you could give us a few years, maybe we can find their graves and move 'em. Tess's and Erica's children could see the old homeplace, and then you could do what you had to do."

"What about your children?" he asked grimly.

She shook her head and met his gaze again. "I don't think my prospects are too good. I don't get to know men too easy and I'm not marrying another 'safe' one so I can have children."

"You got to know me pretty easily," he reminded her. The hurt, angry look in her eyes made him wince. "I didn't mean it as an insult. Why am I different?"

"You just are." She frowned, looked down at her lap, fidgeted a little, and said finally, "We're great together. You said you want things to be right between us again. I know you're crazy about me in bed. And you like teaching me how to be a Cherokee."

"So we can go on like before if I give you a deal on the land?" he asked, feeling anger rise inside him like a snake. "You can fake it, even if you hate my guts?"

"I know how to make you laugh, and I won't get in your way much. If you want to travel to any of the crazy places you like to visit, you know I can go along and not be a wimp. How many women got so much to offer and ask so little in return?"

"You can fake it?" he asked again, his voice rising.

She shook her head. Her eyes were ancient and despairing. "I don't hate you. I couldn't do this if I didn't want things to be right between us, too. Maybe I hate myself for still wanting you."

His fury stalled, and he studied her shrewdly, wondering if she were telling the truth. If she was . . . Nathan felt his breath grow shallow with hope. He crossed his feet nonchalantly and tossed out, "I never kept a mistress before."

She shivered a little, but she looked him straight in the eye and said stoically, "Let's call it what it is. I wouldn't be your mistress. I'd be your whore."

The slow, sick press of air out of his lungs mingled with an admiration for her strength that made him want to cry. There was a great stillness in the atmosphere around them, as if the night had stopped to listen.

"I don't see it that way. I see it as a friendly compromise between two people who need to be together."

"Then you're sugarcoating it to be nice. Don't get me wrong, there're plenty of ways to be a whore in this world, and they don't have anything to do with sex. I've seen people trade themselves for a lot of bad reasons. At least I'm doing it for a good one."

"I don't want you on those terms. I want you as a friend and lover."

"Okay, if that's how you look at it."

He struggled not to pound a fist against the earth and tell her that he wanted her to love him despite this nonsense between their families. *She's giving you a chance to win her over. Don't be a fool. Take it.*

"All right. I'll take your deal. You're mine, body and soul, for as long as I want. Starting tonight. Tomorrow I'll have a lawyer draw up a contract."

"I trust your word."

"You're awful magnanimous."

"I don't know what that means, but I guess it's good." She was trembling noticeably now. "I only have one condition. I don't want my cousins to know I've got this deal with you. They'd try to stop me. I'll just tell 'em that I talked you out of mining our land right away."

Nathan chuckled harshly. "So you three Cherokee musketeers will have years to attack my mining rights with every legal maneuver you can find."

She looked at him for a moment, then said softly, "Yeah, that's the way I'm figuring it."

"All right. I like your honesty. You belong to me. Our secret. In return you get a five-year grace period for your land." He slipped the gold nugget from around his neck and handed it to her. "I want you to wear this all the time."

Her eyes gleamed with surprise. She took the sturdy gold chain and pecan-sized nugget, cupped them in her hand for a moment, then slipped the chain over her head.

Nathan caught his breath. The gold seemed to gleam

brighter just from being close to her. He squinted, shook his head to clear it, but couldn't rid himself of the illusion.

It was only right that she have the nugget, right that the warmth of her spirit should make it take on new life. After all, it was the one thing he could give back. It had belonged to Justis Gallatin.

T HE FRIGID MOUNTAIN water cut through her brooding thoughts and made her think only of getting warm again. That, unfortunately, make her think of Nathan's leg draped across her thighs and his arm lying relaxed and possessive under her breasts.

Kat put her soap and shampoo on a rock, sat down close by, and curled her legs to one side. Water closed around her waist, the stream capturing her, making her a part of the land it served.

She scooped water onto her face and held it there, the silver drops draining down her arms like tears. This bargain would ruin her, because unless Nathan fell in love with her somewhere along the way, she'd lose both him and any chance of saving the land.

The thought of losing either made her whimper softly; more so because it was Nathan she needed most.

"Kat."

She jerked her head up and looked over her shoulder. He waded across the stream to her, naked, carrying a towel in one hand with little regard for whether it hid anything or not.

He dropped the towel next to her shampoo and sat down behind her in the stream. His hands cupped her shoulders. "Morning."

"Morning."

"Why are you crying?" he pulled her hair back and cupped her chin in one hand, holding her face in profile as he studied it.

"I just splashed water on my face."

"I don't want you to go around miserable."

"Okay."

He rested a hand along her cheek, his fingertips trailing over her skin as she faced forward again. "I don't want you to ask me for permission to get out of bed, either."

"Okay, I won't do it again."

"I want things to be like they were between us before. Like there was no bargain. 'Cause there isn't a bargain. There's only a compromise between . . ."

"Two people who need to be together. I know. Okay."

His fingers curved over her shoulders and shook lightly. "Stop that. Stop agreeing to everything like you don't have a choice."

"What kind of choice do I have? I already said I'd do whatever you tell me, and you already said I wouldn't like some of it."

"I didn't do anything you hated last night, did I?" He pushed her hair aside and slid his hands down her back, stroking her spine with his thumbs.

"You were full of bourbon. You fell asleep five seconds after you grabbed me."

"Grabbed you?"

"Yeah. I felt like a teddy bear."

"Whatd'you think I was going to do?"

"Something besides fall asleep."

"Disappointed?" He soaped his hands and began washing her back, sliding his fingertips in slow circles.

"I don't know. Everything's so different between us now."

He stopped washing and rested his forehead against the back of her head. His hands closed around her arms. "Tell you what, Kat Woman. I'll treat you like a teddy bear until you're ready to stop thinking that way. You say when."

Breathing quickly, a familiar tickle of desire growing in her stomach, Kat couldn't ignore him. His concern for her happiness pretty much destroyed any doubts she'd had about his motives. Yes, Nathan cared about her, and he was willing to do anything to make her forget about the land problem.

She'd never forget, though. It would always be between them. But she hadn't been lying to him last night when she'd said that she wanted things to be right again, too. She didn't think they ever would be, but she had to try.

Her throat closed with anger. He could afford to be that word, *magnanimous*. He held everything in the palm of his hand—the future of the land, her future, her love.

"What if I'm never ready to make love to you again?" she asked.

He laughed softly and reached for the shampoo. "You will be 'fore too long," he promised, as his hands sank into her hair.

KAT AND ERICA sat in the Kirkland's intimate country tearoom at the same window table where they'd first discussed Dove's legacy, two months earlier, except that Tess wasn't with them. Beyond the window with its curtains of white eyelet the dogwood tree that had reached out to them with delicate blossoms now stroked its lush summer foliage against the panes, as if seeking to come indoors from the August heat.

Erica, tall and lanky, had changed over two months in subtle ways that Kat took a moment to analyze; it wasn't simply that she'd switched her unflattering gray suit for a tailored white dress or that she now used combs to pull her chestnut hair back from her face; it was her aura of happiness.

The source was no mystery. Ten minutes ago James Tall Wolf had left the tearoom to call his attorney about the mining agreement Holt Gallatin had signed with Eli Chatham. James was certainly tall and certainly one heck of a handsome, well-dressed wolf.

Kat had watched Erica's loving gaze track him all the way from the room. He'd stopped in the doorway to offer her one last bit of reassurance in the form of a wink and a smile.

Now *this* was how two people acted when they loved each other.

Kat reminded herself that Nathan's gold nugget was hidden under her T-shirt. It meant a lot, his giving her that piece of gold to wear. Of course, it was sort of like a collar on a slave, but she wouldn't think about that too much.

"I wish Tess were here, too," Erica noted, looking out the window at nothing. "But I don't think she's back in the country yet."

Kat shook her head in awe. "Should we call her Princess Tess now, ya think?"

Erica sighed. "I don't know. Until this problem came up with Nathan Chatham, I couldn't wait to see her and find out how she learned that her mother was queen of Kara. Now I can only think about our land."

Erica cleared her throat, reached into a large white purse, and retrieved a page torn from a magazine. "I have some information on Nathan Chatham for you."

Her voice was somber, almost regretful as she handed Kat the page. "I found it in an old issue of *Forbes.*"

Hands trembling, Kat laid the glossy, important-looking page on the table and stared incredulously at a color photograph of Nathan lounging in a cushy executive office, his moccasined feet propped up on a gleaming desk. Behind him a wall-sized window framed the unmistakable skyline of downtown Atlanta—the tall cylinder of the Peachtree Plaza Hotel, the Hyatt Regency with its famous restaurant room on top looking like a flying saucer that had landed on the hotel's roof.

Nathan wore tan trousers and a blue cashmere pullover similar to the one he'd had on the night she'd landed in his lap at the wrestling arena. His slight smile was confident; his spaniel eyes were half-shut in a knowing look; he was the essence of relaxed power. The cutline underneath confirmed it.

*Chatham's New Age sensibilities and old-fashioned business sense win him raves from environmentalists and a fortune from gold mines.*

"A fortune?" Kat repeated, frowning. "He might own our mining rights, but he's still just a geologist for Tri-State."

"No," Erica said softly. "He owns Tri-State. In fact, he owns the company that owns Tri-State."

After staring at Erica for several seconds while her mind tried to comprehend, Kat numbly looked down at the page and read, "This boy wonder has changed the nature of gold mining and reaped $300 million for Auraria, Inc., a company he started twelve years ago when Suradoran Indians led him to a vein of gold in the Amazon river basin.

"In a cooperative effort that has become his trademark, Chatham made money for both himself and the tribe, which has used its newfound wealth to bring the best of modern living to its people, while preserving ancient traditions. Twenty years from now, when the Suradoran site is mined out, Auraria, Inc. will restore the site fully. Unlike smelter refining, Auraria's heap-leaching method leaves virtually no permanent toxic effects."

"He sounds like an admirable man," Erica allowed. "Except in our situation."

Kat read the words again, then once more, then out loud. Then she stared blankly out the window and thought, *No wonder he has a nice truck.* That was the only way she could define $300 million.

"Ladies!" a voice called in a lilting English accent. "I understand from our charming lawyer that you can't wait to tell me something! I have quite a story, too!"

Kat and Erica twisted in their chairs to gaze at the elegant, darkly exotic young woman who smiled at them affectionately as she floated into the room close beside a ruggedly beautiful blond man.

Her eyes shining with joy, Tess Gallatin introduced her cousins to Jeopard Surprise, whom she described as "the man I adore entirely too much for his ego's good," a comment that made his rather guarded expression soften with pleasure. Kat noticed that he watched Tess with loving pride as she returned hugs and excited greetings.

Tess chuckled. "I've told him all about our land and our marvelous heritage. And I can't wait to tell you two about the winery Justis and Katherine started in California during the 1840's. It's all so romantic and exciting."

Kat and Erica traded sympathetic looks. Kat patted Tess's arm wistfully. "We better order a whole pot of tea, English. You're gonna need it."

SHIRTLESS, DRESSED IN his buckskin breeches and hiking boots, the tiny gold nugget gleaming in the top of his ear, sweat and grime streaking his hairy chest, Nathan was not what people expected a multimillionaire gold-mining executive to look like. Kat's heart rate accelerated at the memory of his slow, thorough attention to her hair that morning. Only Nathan could make her feel that she'd been satisfied as well as shampooed.

Kat was surprised to find him and Drake at work again on the Blue Song homeplace, with Echo clucking around behind them, picking up the things they unearthed, a large brown hen instead of a small one, Kat noted wryly.

"That's Chatham?" Tess said in amazement, as Kat guided the Mustang to the end of the old trail. Tess sat in the front passenger seat, or more precisely, in Jeopard's lap. Erica had her legs across James's lap in the Mustang's small backseat.

It was a good thing everybody was in love, Kat thought.

"Yep. He's, uhmm, he's sorta different. He's not such a bad guy. Like I told you, he helped me find the old Blue Song place."

"Drake!" Tess exclaimed, as the black-haired giant stepped forward and scrutinized their arrival. She turned her head and looked at Jeopard closely.

"This is news to me," he responded.

"Drake does some security work for Nathan Chatham's company," Erica commented from the backseat. Her voice was puzzled. "You know him, Jeopard?"

Kat glanced at Jeopard Surprise. "You know Drake?"

He smiled, revealing practically nothing, while Tess fiddled with the collar of his white polo shirt and was much less successful at looking inscrutable.

"Drake works for Jeopard sometimes, too," Tess said pleasantly. "They're old friends in the security business."

James, who'd been ominously silent since noticing Drake Lancaster, asked in a soft, grim tone, "Can my sister trust him?"

Jeopard didn't hesitate. "Drake would die for her. Yes, she can trust him."

"He has very good taste in women's lingerie," Tess quipped.

As everyone got out of the car Nathan tossed his shovel down, slipped a T-shirt over his torso, and strode over to greet them. He met Kat's eyes, and his somber gaze seemed to say, "So the war party's finally here."

Kat introduced him and watched her cousins' expressions carefully. They didn't think of Nathan as a monster, since she'd told them about his Cherokee knowledge and sympathies, but they didn't want him to destroy their land any more than she did.

Drake and Echo walked up. Looking contented, Echo strolled to her brother, and gave him a hug.

"Happy?" he asked.

She said something in Cherokee, smiled, and went back to Drake's side.

"Kat says you're giving us a five-year grace period," Tess told Nathan. "Why?"

Kat clamped her hands together and wondered how Nathan would explain. She didn't want her cousins to think she was in cahoots with him, maybe trying to get a share of the Blue Song gold. They must never find out about her bargain.

"I have a lot of interest in your heritage," he explained calmly, nodding to Kat as if she could confirm that.

"So the Gallatins and the Chathams have always feuded?" Erica asked.

"Yep. From Justis and Nathaniel during the Civil War to Holt and Eli to Dove and Micah." Nathan shrugged and looked at Kat too innocently. "Who knows? We might be the ones to end the feud."

"Why are you doing all this excavation work?" James asked in a quiet, authoritative voice. "What do you expect in return?"

"Nothing. I like Kat. We're friends. I don't have anything against any of you folks. But mining this land is something I have to do for my family, just as you've got to take care of your family's interests. I've got a mining lease that's legal. The transaction was even recorded in the courthouse records up in Arkansas. You can't fight it."

"Oh, we can," Jeopard interjected pleasantly. He held out a hand to Nathan. "But thanks for helping my brother in Surador."

Kat pressed her fingers to her temples and watched

as Nathan shook Jeopard's hand. What was this—a soap opera? Their lives had crossed one another's in such unusual ways before they'd all reached this common ground. Had Katlanicha foreseen this? Is that what the medallions were about?

"What does your medallion say?" she asked suddenly, turning toward Tess. "And did it mean anything to you?"

Tess smiled, and Kat noticed how Jeopard's hand strayed subtly into hers. "It said, 'A bluebird should follow the sun.' It brought me home to Jeopard."

Kat swallowed the lump in her throat. Tess's medallion had brought her to Jeopard; Erica's had brought her to James. "I bet when Grandpa Sam figures mine out it'll say something dumb like 'Buy two, get one free.'"

The smiles around her, including Nathan's, only made her feel worse.

WITH A FEW more Cherokees, they could start a village.

Everyone changed into casual clothes and came back to work on the excavation. It made Kat's chest swell with pride, watching her cousins and their men enjoy the discoveries as much as she had.

But it made her uncomfortable, too, having them so close to her and Nathan, having Nathan's necklace hidden under her shirt, trying not to look at him or touch him in any way that would reveal their true relationship.

Echo and Drake wouldn't talk about it to the others, and even they didn't know about Kat's bargain. What happened between a man and a woman was nobody's concern but their own, Echo had said solemnly. She and Drake, whom Echo now called *Colanneh*, the Raven, had agreed.

Nonetheless, Kat found that being around Nathan that day was difficult. The air always seemed a degree or two warmer between him and her, the emotions shimmering like an invisible web.

Heat. Lord, August was so sticky. Fanning herself, Kat left the homesite and walked past Nathan's truck to an ice chest Jeopard had bought in Gold Ridge. She got a soft drink, started to open it, then noticed a curious rock sticking up from the leaves a dozen yards away.

It had a rough square shape that made her wonder if it had been chiseled. Her drink in one hand, Kat traipsed over, still limping but not badly.

She reached the odd rock and saw that there was a large circle of similar rocks under the leaves. "Hey, guys!" she called, and putting her fingers to her lips, pierced the air with a whistle. "Look what I found!"

Then she stepped into the center of the circle, and the whole world gave way.

Cool. Damp. Close. Like a wet grave. Those reactions ran through Kat's mind as soon as she stopped falling. She looked up and found the top of the hole only a dozen feet overhead, but it might have been a mile.

Shaking, Kat laughed when she saw that she still held the soft drink can. She dropped it and hugged herself. This was no ordinary hole; it had carefully constructed rock walls. Under her feet—oh no, her injured ankle hurt like hell—the walls had caved in long ago, making a jumble of rock and mud.

Boots crashed through the leaves aboveground, followed by a louder crash as Nathan threw himself on his stomach at the edge of the hole. "Katie!"

"I'm okay."

"Get against the wall. I'm jumping down."

She pressed herself to flat stones and felt water trickle along her neck. Nathan rolled over the lip of the hole and dropped lithely beside her. They were chest to chest in the small area.

"Kitty Kat, I thought you'd lost one of your nine lives," he said gruffly, his hands stroking her head, cupping her face, then running down her arms as he tried to examine her in their narrow confines.

"I just hurt my ankle some." She wound her arms around his neck and he drew her close. Kat rested her head on his shoulder and wanted to cry, her emotions jarred free by the fall. "I need you," she whispered raggedly.

He brushed his lips over her hair and curved one hand over her head protectively. "I need you, too, gal."

"*Nathan*," a voice called in soft warning.

They looked up to find Drake peering at them anxiously. The others were coming. Quickly Kat stepped back as best she could. Nathan's fingers slid down her arm and he squeezed her hand in a silent good-bye.

Soon everyone was clustered around the hole. Nathan called up, "I'll put her on my shoulders and y'all lift her out."

"I'll do it," Drake said, and dangled a long arm the size of a tree toward them.

Kat laid her hands on Nathan's shoulders tentatively, as if she hadn't grown accustomed to caressing the ruddy skin under his T-shirt, as if her fingernails hadn't left marks in that skin at times.

"Can you climb onto my shoulders with your bad foot?" he asked.

"Us Flying Campanellis never forget how."

She scrambled up his body as if he were a ladder, almost smiling when her foot wedged a little too close to his groin. He muttered under his breath, "Wanta be a teddy bear the rest of your life?"

*No*, she thought with a fervor that shook her. She wanted to be in his arms, away from everyone else, being doctored in his Cherokee ways and soothed in his other ways, ways that men in every culture knew—or ought to know.

Drake pulled her upward as if she were a feather. James grabbed her around the waist with hands that had once crushed quarterbacks in professional football, but held her delicately. Jeopard caught her legs and deftly swung them out, his easy grace making her feel as if she were Ginger and he were Fred in a strange sort of dance.

The men put her fanny-first on the ground and she sat there looking up expectantly as Erica and Tess hovered over her. "I haven't had so much fun since I tagteamed with the Russian Roulette Brothers."

They laughed with relief.

"There's something down here!" Nathan called.

Kat was nearly the first one back at the opening. "You okay, sweetcakes?" she called, facedown at the edge of the darkness.

"Yeah."

"Sweetcakes?" Tess repeated.

"Sweetcakes," Erica mused.

"Aw, I call everybody that."

Nathan was on his knees, scooping mud from around the jumbled rocks. "It's a half-dry spring. Must of been a couple of feet deeper before it caved in. I think there's something wedged here, if I can just get it, there. Huh! A couple of spoons."

The sweetcakes business was temporarily forgotten as everyone crowded closer to the edge. "What are spoons doing in the bottom of a well?" Erica asked.

"Unless the Blue Songs dumped them there for a reason," James suggested. "Cherokee families hid what they could before the army came. If they were in a hurry they would have dumped things down the well."

"Get me a shovel!" Nathan called. "And a bucket!"

Tess and Erica nearly collided as they ran to get one. Kat started to rise, favoring her ankle. Nathan glanced up at her, said something jovial in Cherokee, and Echo put a restraining hand on her shoulder.

"He says, 'Make the hummingbird keep her bent wing still.' "

Kat eyed him, then chuckled with helpless devotion. "Okay, you bossy gopher."

From the corner of her eye she saw Jeopard studying her expression. Kat looked up at him, and he smiled quickly, as if to put her at ease.

A thread of alarm trickled down Kat's spine. What would her cousins think if they realized that she loved the man who was going to tear up their land and steal their gold? She didn't want them to hate her or think she wanted the gold.

"Hey, Chatham," she called to Nathan in an ugly voice. "Don't slip any of our spoons into your pockets."

He stopped examining the blackened, corroded silverware and stared up at her as if she'd just threatened to bury him in the well.

"Are you serious?"

"You better believe it. The silverware's not yours just because it came out of the ground."

The slow tightening of his face and body assured Kat that she'd accomplished what she'd intended—she'd made him forget about being nice to her.

"I don't want anything but what's due my family," he said in a soft, lethal voice.

"I can't tell. You got mighty funny definitions of what's due your family."

He tossed the spoons up to her. "Take 'em. And leave me alone."

"Can do." Her throat tight with sorrow for them both, she left him in the old well glaring up at her.


THE MEN TOOK turns digging, and by late afternoon the women had scrubbed over forty pieces of silverware, some bearing on their handles the still-legible Cherokee symbols for Blue Song. The heavy sterling was ruined beyond anything except sentimental value, but the cousins cried over the lost dreams it represented.

Then Jeopard's shovel found other pieces of sterling—a tea set, a soup tureen, a tray so corroded that it broke in two when he handed it out of the well.

"I hope there's no more," Kat said, her throat raw as she watched Tess and Erica hug separate halves of the tray. "This is like a funeral."

"Well, better find it all while you have the chance," Nathan warned. He stood on the sidelines, watching, his eyes cold.

"We've got five years," she shot back.

"Yeah. Consider yourself lucky."

He gave her a commanding look that reminded her why they had five years, and she crumpled inside. Oh, he wanted her to think that he and she had a friendly agreement, that he cared about her so much that he'd postponed the mining.

But she wasn't supposed to forget that he could change his mind if she didn't do exactly as she'd promised.

I'm a slave, she thought again, and the gold nugget lying between her breasts made her chest move heavily, as if it could smother her.

SHE AWOKE THE instant she heard the soft rattle of the key in the inn's old-fashioned door lock. Kat scooted up in bed, reached frantically for the night-stand, then remembered that she'd left the Beretta back in her tent.

But when the door opened, the faint light of a hall lamp fell across Nathan's face—angular and harsh in the shadows. Kat groaned softly with relief, her heart still in overdrive.

"What are you doing here? My cousins have rooms on either side of this one."

He shut the door, throwing the room into the deep ink of a moonless night. Kat quivered when she heard him lock the door. Then there was nothing but silence, a silence she listened to while breath pooled in her lungs.

Slowly he settled on the bed beside her, and she smelled the mingled traces of woodsmoke and a brisk, fresh scent that told her he'd scrubbed himself in the stream after everyone left.

"We can't sleep together tonight," she murmured, almost begging. "If my cousins figure us out they won't understand."

"Who said anything about sleep?" His voice was soft and gruff, whether from leftover anger she couldn't tell. "Lie back down."

Kat shut her eyes, analyzed the emotions that were making her vibrate with awareness, and admitted that she wanted him in bed with her, no matter what.

She slid down and put her hands beside her head on the pillow. His fingertips grazed her shoulder, skimmed over the soft cotton of her T-shirt, then trailed down her arm.

Kat tilted her head back on the pillow and heard herself breathing faster in the stillness of the room. It was an incredible sensation, to lie there in total darkness, knowing that Nathan was beside her but feeling only the provocative caress of his callused fingertips, not knowing what part of her he might touch next, or in what way.

He covered her hand with his, simply letting his hand rest there quietly atop hers, and the sensation was so exquisite that Kat made a soft keening sound.

"I don't mean to scare you," he said grimly.

"That wasn't fear you heard," she whispered. "I'm sorry I hurt your feelings today. I did it to make things easier in front of everyone."

"That's what I came here tonight to find out."

His hand tightened, then slowly slid away. A second later she felt its pressure on her stomach, his blunt, scarred fingers incredibly adept as they eased her panties down to her thighs, hardly brushing her skin, setting off storms of sensation when they did.

Kat bit her lip to keep from shifting in blissful agony as his hand touched her stomach again. This time there was the seductive whisper of cotton on her skin as he lifted her T-shirt, then the breath of night air scattering goose bumps on her bare stomach and breasts.

For a moment he stopped touching her at all, and it took considerable willpower for her not to reach for him. Then his fingertips surrounded her nipples with wetness from his mouth.

The combination was fire and ice as he rubbed them—just the tips, very slowly and very lightly—into peaks so hard they barely flexed under his caress.

"This woman is of the Blue clan," he whispered. "Her name is Katlanicha. I am adopted of the Deer clan, my name is Tahchee. Draw near to listen. Our souls have come together. I am *da-nitaka*, standing in her soul. She can never look away."

His fingers left her and she inhaled weakly, the sound a plea. A moment later, wet again, they slid between her thighs. He stroked the sleek skin and whispered over her soft cries, "Your body, I take it. Your flesh, I take it. Your heart, I take it."

He said those words again and again, a soft, guttural chant in rhythm with the movement of his fingers until sensation and sound mingled with the roaring in her ears and she heard nothing, knew nothing except waves of pleasure that made her body strain to follow the crests.

In the slow collapsing afterward, she heard him say, his voice tormented with restraint, "I am *da-nitaka*, standing in her soul. I have always been there. I will always be there. It was decided long ago."

Kat was still fighting for breath, her head lolled to one side on the pillow, feeling the dampness of her perspiration, when he rose off the bed. She turned her face to search for him hopelessly in the darkness, then sensed him and lay still, poised for whatever he did next, whatever he asked, anything.

His mouth brushed hers, his mustache tickling her upper lip as he drew away. Kat waited, too limp to move, every ounce of her energy tuned to him. When he unlocked the door, slipped out, and locked it behind him, she exhaled so long and slow that her body seemed to melt into the bed.

Spellbound, she fell asleep just as he had left her.

When morning came she found a note from him on the bedside table. It told her what she had to do that day, and she wondered sadly if this was only the beginning of the requests she would not like.

N ATHAN CERTAINLY LIKED to stay on top of his job. In fact he lived on top of it in a penthouse complex with a Jacuzzi, a sun deck, rooms full of native artwork from all over the world, a master bedroom that rivaled something from a Moroccan fantasy, and a huge garden room that looked toward the cityscape of Atlanta.

No, it wasn't a garden room, Kat corrected herself as she stood in the midst of vine-draped tropical trees, it was a *jungle* room.

"Do you have everything you need?" Nathan's administrative assistant inquired politely, in a lyrical accent the Jamaican tourist bureau ought to hire.

Kat turned toward the young man, studied his jeans, sports shirt, and dreadlocks, then concluded that *maybe* she wouldn't feel out of place in Nathan's mixed-up business/fantasy world.

"Yeah, I'm fine. Thanks for carrying my duffel bag up."

"No problem." He handed her an envelope. "Key

to the private elevator, key to the apartment door, a note with my phone extension downstairs. You're welcome to a tour of the company anytime. Just come on down."

"Thanks." No way, Kat added silently. The last thing she wanted was to be the prime source of gossip on five floors of Auraria, Inc.

After the assistant left she wandered around the huge apartment, listening to the lonely squeak of her Reeboks on polished slate, parquet, and handmade Spanish tiles, her hands sunk in her jeans pockets because she was afraid to touch anything.

Not that Nathan's place looked formal—no, it was warm, exotic, inviting—but it was so damned *expensive*. His note hadn't warned her. It merely had told her to go to Atlanta, move into the apartment, and make herself at home.

Well, sure, but she'd never lived in a Native Peoples exhibit before.

Kat went into his bedroom and stared at rich wall hangings, rugs so deep she could get lost in them, and a big bed filled with fringed pillows and canopied in dark silks. If she tried to describe this room to anyone it'd either sound silly or self-indulgent, but it wasn't. It was incredibly masculine in a way that made her think of incense mingling with the erotic scent of seduction, of low-burning lamplight glistened on naked skin.

She sat down on the bed and burst into tears. It was a perfect place for a slave girl to please her master.

Where the hell was Nathan? she thought with unslavelike rudeness, wiping her eyes. He hadn't even said when he planned to follow her here, or even if he would follow. She still ached inside from telling her cousins a lie. They thought she was back on the wrestling tour, doing ringside commentary until her ankle healed completely.

Fifteen minutes later the phone rang. Kat sidled up to a heavily carved bedside table and gazed warily at the black phone sitting there. It looked ordinary. Well, at least she could touch this safely.

"Hi."

"Ms. Gallatin, I'm Cassandra, from Neiman-Marcus."

"Okay."

"Are you ready to go? I have a limousine waiting."

"Go where?"

"Shopping."

"I don't shop."

"Uhmm, Mr. Chatham says"—Kat heard the Cassandra person rattling a piece of paper—"he says you're to spend at least three thousand dollars before the store closes this evening."

Kat sat down weakly and hugged a fringed pillow. "Oh. How many hours have we got?"

"Five."

*That was six hundred bucks an hour. She'd have to stand in the middle of the store and give away cash.*

"I can't," she whispered.

"Mr. Chatham said you wouldn't have any problem with the plan."

"Oh." This was an order from Nathan, then. A really odd kind of order. Was this another example of the stuff she was supposed to do whether she liked it or not?

Kat sighed. "I'll be right down."

*As soon as I get over being shocked.*

This was Nathan's guilt at work. He had a lot of regrets where she was concerned, because of the Blue Song land, and maybe his kindness was motivated more by those than by affection for her.

Well, they'd play this game then, this sad game, until one of them lost.


NATHAN PAUSED AT the apartment's double doors, his hand on the gold-plated doorknob, trembling. All right, so he was bullying her. Yesterday's Neiman-Marcus thing must have set her teeth on edge;

he could only imagine what she'd thought when she got up this morning and found a man waiting downstairs to take her shopping for a new car.

But she'd get used to all that, she'd see what kind of life he could give her, and she wouldn't be able to resist. He'd dazzle her until she couldn't think straight, and then he'd marry her.

He'd donate all the money from the Blue Song mining operation to charity, so she and her cousins might eventually forgive him for turning their land into a huge gravel pit. Then her family would be happy, his family would be revenged, and Kat would love him as much as he loved her.

It was simple, Nathan thought. So why was he worried?

"Kat?" he called nonchalantly, as he strolled into the apartment. The lights were low, and through an arched doorway he could see that she'd shut the garden room blinds against the afternoon sun. He walked into a den done in Cherokee art, plush earth tones, and with a floor-to-ceiling stereo system.

The harmonies of a soft instrumental tape resonated through the room.

"Kat?" he called, and wondered grimly if concern made his voice sound little like Buckwheat's on *Our Gang.*

"Hi." She floated into the den from the hall that led to his bedroom. Her lithe little body was draped in nothing but a robe of pale green silk which matched her eyes; her hair had been curled and fluffed and moussed into one of those sexy "I've just come from bed" styles.

The gold nugget gleamed at the V of her robe, and small gold-and-jade studs decorated her earlobes. When she swept up to him and latched her arms around his neck, he inhaled a sensuous designer perfume, something with a decadent name, he figured.

"I'm glad you're finally here," she whispered, smiling.

Nathan didn't know if he liked what money had

done to her basic feminine appeal, but he liked having her smile at him, and the knowledge that she was happy made him even more determined to keep her that way.

"Do you like—" he began, but she raised herself up and kissed him.

"I'm taking you to bed for the rest of the day," she whispered, and slipping her hand into his, she did just that.

Night was in the room when he woke, his body still heavy and satiated from everything she'd done so slowly and so well. Nathan sat up in bed, feeling silk sheets slide down his stomach the way Kat's hands had done earlier.

But Kat was gone.

He threw a dark russet kimono—a gift from a Japanese business associate—around his shoulders and left the room quickly, his heart pounding with a strange dread.

*She's left me before.*

Nathan exhaled raggedly when he found her curled, asleep, on an overstuffed couch in the den. She's left me before? Kat had never left him—and he'd make sure she never would. Shaking his head at the idea, he went to her and knelt down.

She wore one of her silly *WOW-Wild Women of Wrestling* T-shirts, with her green silk robe jumbled over her legs like a blanket. Her face was streaked with dried tears and her arms were wrapped around one of the rusty, pitted window sash weights from the Blue Song home.

Sorrow and confusion tore at Nathan. Then he realized what she'd done—she'd put on a grand show for him today because she thought she had to repay him for all the damned gifts.

He almost choked on the knowledge that she'd made love to him for that reason. Oh, she hadn't faked her body's reaction, he was sure of that, but she'd faked her happiness.

His chest tightened with disappointment. Wearily

he slid his arms under her. She stirred, then blinked up at him with swollen, worried eyes.

"Sssh," he said, because it was all he could manage easily.

Nathan carried her and her whimsical keepsake to bed. She held it, and he held her.

SHE DRAGGED HERSELF around her beautiful prison, wishing she'd get over the awkward feeling. She'd lived here for ten days. In nomad terms, that was a long time.

Kat roamed from room to room, absorbed with thoughts of how cheerful Nathan had been before he left that morning. He had to fly to New York on business, and he wouldn't be back until tomorrow. He hadn't asked her to go with him.

Kat wondered if she weren't good enough to take to New York. She reminded herself that Nathan was proud of her, and now that she knew the kind of family background he'd come from—grandpa an alcoholic, father a worthless drifter—she had even less reason to worry that he looked down on her.

But a question kept nagging at her—Was he proud of her, or had he brought her here to spruce her up so that he *could* be proud of her? Heck, he'd sent the Mustang to a body shop so she'd have to drive the new Toyota she'd picked out. Maybe he wanted her retooled, too.

Kat went to her purse, got out a personal calendar book, and checked to see where the Wild Women of Wrestling tour was at the moment. Tonight in Jacksonville, Florida. She noted the name of the motel the tour always used in Jacksonville and placed a call to Muffie.

"Kat, when ya comin' back?" Muffie bellowed.

"Don't know." Kat tested her ankle and felt a little guilty because it was completely healed. "What's cooking?"

"We need ya, we need ya. Mary sprained her knee last night in Orlando. She's out for a couple of days."

Kat wiped a sweaty palm on the leg of her new designer jeans. Then she looked at the palm a moment and realized that she'd been hoping for an excuse to go back where she belonged, if only for a night.

"I'll be there as soon as I can get a plane."

"You got money for flying?"

"Sure." Kat shut her eyes. *Nathan wants me to be happy. Well, this makes me happy.* She'd leave word with his administrative assistant so that he'd know where she'd gone.

If Nathan was really proud of her the way she was, he wouldn't mind.


NATHAN REACHED THE auditorium—one of those concrete relics from the thirties, with gargoyles on the outside and lots of cracking plaster on the inside—in time to see Kat's entrance.

He almost groaned aloud. Was she so damned desperate to get away from him that she'd go back to this humiliating life? He made his way down to the front. Since this was a weeknight the place was only half-full, so he managed to find an empty seat in the third row.

Nathan stared hard at her and hoped that she'd spot him in the audience, but she didn't. He sat on the edge of his folding chair, his fingers digging into the dark trousers he wore with a white pullover.

He hadn't been in New York at all. He'd been up in North Carolina, talking Grandpa Sam into giving him Kat's medallion. Nathan wanted to present it to her himself, when the time was right. Grandpa Sam, being a romantic, had agreed. He'd just finished translating it, and he understood that Nathan was the man who was meant to love Kat.

But now this. Nathan cursed under his breath. He wouldn't lose her to this carnival, no matter how much she despised what he planned to do with her family's land.

"Hi ya, folks!" she yelled to the crowd.

Well, at least she'd given up the dime store pow-wow talk. But he winced inwardly at the silly face paint and gaudy warbonnet, at the tight leather top and fringed miniskirt which revealed too much of her to the men around him.

"Swing that wampum, Princess!' someone called.

Lady Savage grabbed her and she punched in retaliation. Lady Savage dragged her into the ring and they went down in a heap of flesh—most of it belonging to Lady Savage.

There was a giant redneck next to Nathan, his tractor cap emblazoned with the bottom half of a woman's bikini-clad body and an obscene slogan. He stood up, cupped his hands around a mouth full of gold-capped teeth, and yelled, "Shake that booty, Princess!"

Nathan stood also, swung the man toward him, and laid a fist into the mother lode.

There was general chaos after that, and Nathan was dimly aware of the redneck's fist crunching into his face and of the man's slow, pained collapse as he got a knee in the groin. A small, gleeful war broke out among the men around them.

The security guards showed up, some of them carrying billy clubs. Nathan went down seeing stars after a club slammed into the back of his head. With people stepping on him, he was only vaguely aware when someone grabbed his arms.

"Help me pull, Muffie!"

A second later he was out of the chaos, feeling the cool concrete floor of the auditorium under him, his head in a soft, sweaty lap. He'd recognize that lap anywhere.

"Katie, gal," he said groggily, trying to blink away the blackness over his eyes. "You didn't think they'd hang an old buzzard like me, did ya?"

That didn't make sense. He couldn't figure out why,

because his head was still celebrating the Fourth of July, but he heard Kat say desperately, "He's addled. We've gotta get him to a hospital."

That jarred him back to reality. "Hate hospitals," he muttered. "Everything's too clean." The blackness receded and he gazed up into Kat's face.

"Are you in there, Nathan?" she asked in a small, ragged voice. She bent over him, tears smearing her war paint, her hand stroking his forehead with quick, worried movements. For a movement she searched his eyes, then exhaled with relief.

"I came to get you out of all this," he said weakly, and shut his eyes against a wave of dizziness. He felt her small, gentle hand dabbing a cloth under his nose. "Bleeding?" he asked.

"Yeah," she whispered. "Like a stuck pig. A handsome stuck pig, though."

"I started the fight."

"Why?"

"Jerk said something . . . ugly about you."

Her hand stopped moving. "And you were ashamed."

"Not ashamed." He tried to shake his head. "Always take care of you. Always have. Always will."

She called his name softly and kissed him on the forehead. "Let's go home, sweetcakes, and I'll take care of you."


IT WAS LONG past midnight before they got back to Atlanta. She kept one arm around his waist and watched him anxiously as she guided him through his penthouse to the bedroom.

"You walk okay for an addled man," Kat noted.

He nodded, peered at her over the bandage covering his scraped nose, and smiled gingerly. "Thanks."

After he lay down, Kat pulled his clothes off and brought him a handful of ice wrapped in a washcloth. She sat beside him and held the ice to his face. "What am I gonna do with you? You can't go around beating people up on my account.''

His voice was muffled, but firm. ''I won't be fighting again because you won't be wrestling.''

Kat counted to ten. After all, he was hurt and addled. ''That an order, master?''

He pulled the ice pack off his face and looked at her. ''I never got the feeling that you like to wrestle.''

''I like to work. I like to be around people. I can't sit here alone all day.''

''Go to college.''

Kat shook her head. ''College is one more thing you'd have to pay for. I want to wrestle—just part-time, okay? You keep saying that you want me to do what makes me happy.''

''Not wrestling.''

''So it *is* an order,'' she said grimly, tingling with anger.

''Yep. If there's no other way to stop you from being a proud fool, then it's an order. Here's another one. Go down to Georgia State University tomorrow and get a catalogue and admission forms. I want you enrolled in college.''

She got up from the bed and gazed at him with barely concealed fury. ''I won't do it.''

''You will do it. Or you won't ever get your medallion.''

Kat listened in amazement as he explained that her legacy from great-aunt Dove was now in his possession. ''How'd you con that sweet old man out of it?'' she demanded.

''That's a secret between Grandpa Sam and me. It was no con.''

Her teeth clenched, she said, ''Don't ever tell me I'm free to do what I want again. And don't ever try to make me think I'm not your slave.'' She backed away a few steps, clasped her hands, and bowed low.

He threw the ice pack onto the floor. ''Dammit, stop that!''

''You won't need me in bed tonight, master. You're

in no shape to enjoy me. Your nose is bleeding again, for one thing. Can I have the night off and sleep in the guest room?''

''No! I want you in this bed now!'' His face was contorted with pain from yelling. He looked miserable, and a stab of concern nearly dissolved Kat's anger.

So this was what it meant to love someone. Even when she wanted to strangle him, she didn't want him to hurt.

''Naked?'' she asked.

''Buck-naked! If it's good enough for me—''

His eyes flickered shut and he winced from pain. Kat dropped her jeans, T-shirt, and underwear, retrieved the ice pack, and crawled into bed beside him.

''Just keep your mouth closed, Chatham, and maybe I won't punch you myself.'' She pressed the pack to his face, bending close to him with her bare breasts flattened on his shoulder.

He raised the hand next to her, fumbled for a moment, then finally grabbed one of her knees and held it tightly. ''I'm trying to do what's best for you.''

''I said keep quiet,'' she ordered. Kat reached across him, turned out the bedside lamp, then gently pulled his head to her breasts and held him. ''Go to sleep. I'll keep the ice pack on your face for a while.''

''I'm trying to do what's . . . best,'' he repeated, but his voice was drugged with pain and exhaustion.

*Then love me*, she told him silently.


THE PHONE RANG. Good, something to do. There were about a dozen extensions in Nathan's apartment; half the fun was just deciding which one to use. She turned Geraldo Rivera off in the den and went to the jungle room to pick up the phone there.

''Chatham residence.''

''It's Echo.''

Kat froze. ''Yeah?''

''Kat, are you with Nathan Chatham?''

There was no point in bluffing. "I'm with him," Kat said wearily.

"Tess and Erica tried to find you on the wrestling tour. My grandpa finished translating Dove's papers, and there are a lot of things you need to know."

Kat breathed in shallow gulps. "They tried to find me?"

"And they couldn't. Because you never went back to the tour, did you?"

"No," Kat said, defeated.

"So—"

"They suspected me and Nathan all along, didn't they."

"Yes."

"How'd you trace me here?"

Echo sighed. "Give Jeopard Surprise twenty-four hours and he could probably find Jimmy Hoffa and Amelia Earhart."

Her knees weak, Kat sank onto a chair. "So they think I double-crossed 'em?"

Echo's voice was regretful. "Yes, they do."

Kat shut her eyes and thought, *Now I'm going to lose my family, too.*


WHEN HE GOT home that night Nathan found her sitting in the dusky light of the garden room, dressed in a beautiful gray jumpsuit and matching pumps, her hair pulled up in a sleek braided coil, her face utterly composed and unfathomable.

"Good day?" she asked, and got up to kiss him.

"Yeah."

She hugged him—no, she let him hug her, and as soon as he loosened his grip she moved away, not with distaste, just not particularly interested in being near him.

"Hope you're hungry," she said pleasantly. "I called one of the restaurants over at Lenox Square and ordered everything short of a side of beef. Real gourmet.'' She chuckled. ''Everything has parsley on it. Head for the dining room and I'll cart it to ya.''

''You okay?'' he asked, sliding his hand around her arm to halt her easy stroll out of the room.

''Sure.'' But though she looked up at him with a smile, her eyes squinted as if in pain.

Nathan took her face between his hands and rubbed his thumbs across her lower lids. They felt hot and a little puffy. ''Have you been crying?'' he murmured.

''Nah. I sat in the Jacuzzi too long, that's all. Makes me bloat.'' She grinned at him.

He wasn't sure he believed her, but he didn't press for details. Nathan chucked her under the chin. ''We've got to find something to keep you out of the Jacuzzi so much. Did you go down to Georgia State today?''

She shrugged. ''Sure, I got a catalogue. No hurry. You tired of me already?''

''Nope, but whatd'ya think I brought you here for? Just to order food and look pretty and ravish me every time I come home?''

The smile that stayed on her mouth didn't do a thing to hide the discomfort creeping deeper into her eyes. ''Whatever you want.''

Frustration jabbed at him. ''I want you to act like this is your home and I'm your friend.''

''Okay. I can act that way.''

He made a growling sound of disgust. ''I don't mean *act*, dammit.''

''Then tell me how I'm supposed to *feel*. I've never lived with anybody before, except when I was married.''

Nathan said loudly, ''Well, pretend that we're married.''

She trembled and stepped back from him. ''Nope,'' she said in a soft, fierce voice. '' 'Cause we're not married and we're never gonna be married. I'm going to stay here as long as you want me, and when you say leave, I'm leavin'.''

Stunned by her vehement words, he gazed at her

silently and watched her struggle to regain her calm façade. The fact that she was able to do it nearly tore him apart, and dull fury poured into the wound.

"If I want an actress I'll hire one," he told her.

"If you want dinner you better come get it," she answered, and left the room.

A minute later, after he got his anguish under control enough to speak normally, he walked into the kitchen to talk. This was not the Kat Gallatin he knew, the woman who had a deep and true need for him.

She stood at a counter putting baked fish on a platter. When she heard his footsteps on the tile she turned, smiled carefully, and said, "I'll learn how to cook, if you say so."

Nathan halted, his control evaporating in light of her continued nonchalance. She just wanted to do her part and be left alone. In front of an audience she could play Princess Talana and fake fear, anger, or pain. In front of him she could play his happy lover and fake contentment.

"Take the night off," he said with sick disappointment that made his tone cruel. "I'll go out to get dinner—and anything else I need."

He left the apartment with the memory of her haunted eyes as his only victory.


NATHAN HAD WALKED less than a block from the building when the fat yellow cab made a U-turn across three lanes of city traffic and bounced off the sidewalk in its careening journey toward him.

It screeched to a stop too close to his legs, and the dull agony simmering inside him exploded into violence. Nathan vaulted around the front of the cab and jerked the driver's door open.

"Get outta there, you SOB!"

"Get in this car, you SOB," a female voice demanded.

"Immediately," another said.

Nathan bent down and looked past a terrified driver

into the back. Tess and Erica leaned toward him, poised like two dangerous tigers just waiting for an excuse to pounce.

"We came to see our cousin," Erica said.

"But you'll do nicely," Tess finished. "Get in."

Nathan gave them a grim smile, nodded, and went to the front passenger side. He was ready for another good fight.

TWO BEERS, TOO little sleep, then when she did sleep, rotten dreams. Kat woke the next morning with a pounding headache and a thick cloak of misery around her.

She dragged herself off the couch, looked down at the wrinkled mess of her jumpsuit, and turned around in a circle, feeling groggy and trying to put the world right.

Her hair was in her eyes—that was part of the problem. She pawed it aside, then realized that it had been braided atop her head when she'd gone to sleep. Now it was undone, and someone had brushed it very gently so she wouldn't wake up.

She wobbled in place, her heart twisting, then called out plaintively, "Nathan?" She had a desperate need to feel his arms around her.

Kat hurried through the rooms, bumping into things because her head hurt and she was upset. He wasn't anywhere, and the closet door stood open. Kat stared at it and couldn't bring herself to see if his clothes were gone.

Aw, why would he leave his own place? He'd tell her to leave. But fear churned inside her as she went back to the den. Now she was awake enough to notice that her hairbrush lay on the teakwood coffee table by the couch. Under the brush was a sheet of Auraria, Inc., letterhead with a handwritten note from Nathan.

"*Kat.* The mining rights are yours, now—yours and your cousins'. I found out some things that put the family feud in a different light. Tess and Erica are staying at the Peachtree Plaza, waiting to see you this morning. Don't worry. They know the truth now, and they're proud of you. Our deal's done. I'm going to Surador. You're free, Katie.''

Kat lay back on the couch, tears scalding her eyes. ''Not free,'' she whispered. ''Just alone.''

TESS AND ERICA grabbed her duffel bag, then drew her into their hotel room and hugged her. She immediately began to cry. "You don't hate me?" Kat asked.

"For trying to rescue the land?" Erica asked, sniffling.

"And falling in love with a sweet man like Nathan?" Tess added.

"How do you know I'm in love with him?"

They led her to a couch and sat down on either side of her. "We suspected it that day at the homeplace."

"We *know* how people look at each other when they're in love."

"We're really quite expert on it, both of us."

Kat smiled at them wanly. Nathan didn't love her, but she couldn't bring herself to say so at the moment. "Why did he give us the mining rights back?"

"Because he loves you."

"And because it's the only honorable thing to do,

now that he's seen the other side of the Chatham-Gallatin feud.''

Kat wiped her eyes and looked from Tess to Erica in surprise. ''Another side?''

''The family history Dove wrote down. Grandpa Sam finished translating it,'' Erica explained. ''We told Nathan. He said it was too detailed and made too much sense not to be true.''

She took Kat's right hand. Tess took her left one. Kat looked back and forth between them, scrutinizing the solemn excitement in their eyes. ''What did Dove say?''

Tess smiled. ''Your great-grandfather Holt didn't shoot Nathaniel Chatham, but he was a prime suspect because everyone knew the Gallatins despised Nathaniel.''

''Nathaniel was the Union officer who captured Justis in the Indian Territory during the war,'' Erica reminded Kat. ''His men took everything the Gallatins owned. The only way Katherine could save Justis from being executed was to bribe one of Chatham's men with the three medallions. After Justis escaped, Chatham found out about the bribe and confiscated the medallions.''

''That's what the big scandal was about,'' Tess noted. ''Chatham was accused of taking part in the bribe, because he also had a gold nugget that belonged to Justis.''

Kat frowned, trying to sort everything out. ''So Chatham kept our medallions?''

Tess nodded. ''At least that's what everyone thought. It couldn't be proved. But it's why Holt was accused of ambushing him, a few years after the war. The Chatham family started a campaign to have Holt arrested and tried—''

''And for a Cherokee, that meant automatic death,'' Erica explained. ''So Holt became an outlaw. He had to.''

Kat looked at her askance. ''So he *did* go around blasting people?''

"No, he went around robbing every business the Chathams owned. Dove said he never shot anyone except in self-defense, not in all the years he tormented the Chathams."

"Until finally they sent a small army of U.S. marshals after him," Tess interjected. "Holt had a log fortress hidden in the hills. The marshals found it, and when Holt refused to surrender, they burned the place to the ground."

Kat felt Erica's and Tess's hands squeezing hers tighter. Erica looked at her sympathetically. "But the horrible thing was, Holt wasn't there. His wife was there, and his five children, and they'd lied to the marshals to throw them off Holt's track."

Kat winced. "So that's why Dove and my grandfather Joshua were born so late in Holt's life. They were his second family. Poor Great-Grandfather."

Tess nodded. "Right. And after that, Holt waged war on the marshals *and* the Chathams."

"Finally, thirty years after Nathaniel was shot, a witness came forward and said that Holt wasn't responsible."

"So Great-Grandpa was cleared of the murder charge, and he turned peaceful?" Kat asked.

Both cousins nodded. "But he never forgot that the Chathams had his mother's medallions," Erica said. "When he was an old man he and Eli, Nathaniel's son, tried to call a truce. Eli said he'd give the medallions back if Holt would sign over the mining rights to the Blue Song land in Georgia."

"So that's why Great-Grandpa did it," Kat said softly. "But why'd he and Eli have a gunfight years later?"

"They just plain couldn't stand each other," Tess said, imitating Kat's sideways twang.

"So they killed each other. Dove inherited the Blue Song land and the medallions."

Kat sighed. "She got Eli's married son, Micah, too."

Erica straightened proudly. "Well, I believe in Dove. I live in her house now, you know, and I think that she told the truth about everything, including Micah."

"So what'd she say?"

"Oh, they were having an affair, all right," Tess admitted. "But they'd been in love for years before Micah married someone else. Eli wouldn't let his son marry a Gallatin—he threatened to disinherit him, and apparently Micah was *not* gallant enough to forgo money to marry Dove."

"Dove made the mistake of still loving him," Erica noted. "But I think we can forgive her for loving too deeply, can't we?"

Kat nodded. "Then she got pregnant—"

"And she went to England to save everyone some grief."

"But Micah's wife learned the truth, anyway. End of story."

Kat looked at her cousins with tears that matched their own. "But what happened after Dove's baby and her English husband died?"

"Dove came back to the States and settled on the reservation in North Carolina."

"Did Dove say anything about Justis and Katherine? I guess they'd passed on before she was born."

"Yes, but she wrote down what Holt told her," Tess said softly. "The only reason Justis had to have a white wife was to keep Katherine's land for her. In the state of Georgia any man who married a Cherokee was considered a Cherokee, too. He would have lost everything, including the Blue Song land."

"And Amarintha Parnell needed a respectable husband," Erica said. "who was willing to give a respectable name to a baby that wasn't his."

Kat sank her head in her hands. "So Justis kept up a show for Katlanicha's sake."

There was a knock at the door. "Must be the pot of tea I ordered," Tess murmured, as she crossed the room. "We can certainly use it."

The waiter tromped inside, loaded with a full tray,

and immediately tripped over Kat's duffel bag. As everyone tried to help him up, he grimaced.

"Are you hurt?" Tess inquired.

"My foot hit something *hard* in that bag. I think I broke it."

"Your foot?" Erica asked.

"No. Whatever's in the end of the bag."

"My sash weight!" Kat cried. She pulled the bag open and dug clothes out of it desperately. "It was so rusty and frail. And it's hollow, Nathan said. If it's broken—not today, please, not today, I can't take it—"

Kat stuck one hand into the bag and hit a pile of metal fragments. Swallowing tightly, she finally managed to say, "It's broken into about a hundred little pieces."

"There are two dozen more of those weights back at the homeplace," Tess said gently.

Erica hugged Kat's shoulders. "That's right."

*But this is the first one Nathan and I found together.* Crying silently, Kat pulled a handful of broken metal out of the bag.

The coins caught the light and held it—golden, ageless, and shimmering with dreams that had finally come true.


KAT HAD A quarter of a million dollars, her share of the modern market value for 850 gold coins minted before 1810. Hidden inside twenty-five hollow iron sash weights, the rare coins were expected to send collectors all over the world into a frenzy. There were an additional thirty coins, but each of the Gallatin cousins kept ten for sentimental reasons.

Nathan put the newspaper down and wished he hadn't gotten this news on his first day back from Surador. He'd lived for this day, hoping that time and restored mining rights had helped Kat forget that he'd tried to manipulate her into staying with him.

*And that he had every intention of manipulating her again.*

Nathan smiled grimly. The medallion would help him win her. He was the only person who knew what it said, who knew what great-great-grandmother Katlanicha had been waiting all these years to tell them.

*"LISTEN!* HIS NAME is Tahchee. He is adopted of the Deer clan. His body, I take it. His flesh, I take it. His heart, I take it. Bind his soul to mine, never to turn away. I am *da-nitaka*, standing in his soul. It was decided long ago."

She'd said those words several times a day for the past three weeks. If anything could make Nathan come here on her terms, they would. The conniving rogue was home from Surador, and if he wanted his gold nugget back, he'd have to beg for it—and bring her medallion to trade.

If he didn't, she'd have to think of another way to get him to come to her.

The brisk September air made her glad she'd donned a long-sleeved work shirt, plus knee-high socks under her jeans and Reeboks. A breeze carried whispers of fall through the trees, and a hawk swung overhead, black against a deep blue sky. Kat watched it quietly.

The hawk floated for a moment as if suspended in time, and then glided out of sight.

Carrying rough sketches of her house, Kat shut the door of the camper she'd rented and walked along the ridge to the old homesite. It was cleared now, the crumbling fieldstone foundation showing where the Blue Song house had stood and also showing, with the blackened rocks, that it had burned the day the soldiers came.

She, Tess, and Erica figured that even Katlanicha and Justis hadn't known about the sash weights full of gold coins. Justis would have had plenty of opportunity to gather them during his trips back to Georgia to visit Amarintha Parnell, and he surely wouldn't have left the sash weights lying around on open ground, thinking that no one would steal them.

Obviously Katlanicha's parents had hidden the gold coins when they built their house, before their children were born.

So the land was a legacy from Katlanicha Blue Song, who became Katherine Gallatin but never forgot her Cherokee homeplace; and the coins were a legacy from the Blue Song family.

Kat stood in the center of the old homesite, thinking how the house was going to rise from the ashes like a phoenix, restored as close to the way it'd looked before as she could determine, though maybe it'd be a little bigger—there had to be plenty of room for Tess and Erica to visit with their families. They expected to build places here someday, but for now she'd be the only Gallatin on the property.

Well, not the only one, but the only flesh-and-blood one. Okay, so she really didn't believe in ghosts—she simply liked to think she wasn't alone here. Nothing odd about that.

Kat shut her eyes and pictured the house finished before Christmas. Her first Christmas in her old home. Her old home?

*"Osiyo,* Katlanicha."

She dropped her sketches and whirled, searching the woods. Nathan, dressed in his buckskin breeches, moccasins, and a light gray sweater the color of his eyes, was leaning against an oak, his arms crossed nonchalantly over his chest as he watched her.

Her medallion gleamed on the end of the long gold chain he wore.

Her heart racing, Kat pulled the chain with the gold nugget out of her shirt. *"Osiyo,* you sly-footed hellion."

He smiled slowly and walked toward her, every step a measured enticement telling her that he read the welcome in her eyes. But this feud wasn't over.

Nathan stopped too close for her comfort and said in a droll voice, "You're a rich little hummingbird now. You've got money, you've got your land, you've got your home—and nobody can ever hurt it again. That's what Katherine and Justis intended. You don't need to know what your medallion says. Everything's settled.''

Kat shook her head sadly. ''You and me aren't settled. You left me. You didn't want me anymore. And now I don't know what I expected when I saw you again, but it looks like you came here only to make me feel bad.''

''Nope. I gave you freedom so you'd forget what I'd done to you. Then I came here today to tell you that you can't forget me.''

Feeling a little dazed by the way he was looking at her, she took a step back. ''You wanted me to forget.''

He stepped forward. ''Nope. You can't forget. You'll never forget.'' Suddenly he was touching her, slipping one arm around her, pulling her to him while he nestled a hand into her hair. ''You'll always need me, Katie.''

*Katie.* His hand. Her hair. Oh no. Kat shut her eyes and put her arms around his neck, then raised her mouth and caught his in a long, spellbound kiss.

She rested her forehead against his shoulder and felt the swift movement of his chest, the harsh grip of his hands on her, her own body trembling. ''Needing and having are two different things,'' she whispered.

''No.''

Tilting her head back, she looked at him wretchedly. ''I'm going to college. I've already talked to the people at the one in Gold Ridge. They say all I have to do is take some catch-up courses first.''

''Yeah? So?''

Kat frowned. Was he dense? ''So maybe I'll be educated enough for you.''

''Good God, who said you weren't?''

She studied him closely. ''Are you ashamed of me for being so low-rent? Tell the truth.''

With a soft groan of dismay he took her face between his hands. ''You're not low-rent, sweetheart.

And if I were any prouder of you, I'd be hard to live with.''

Giddy and confused, she said solemnly, "You *were* hard to live with in Atlanta. I didn't know you anymore.''

"Is that why you stopped wanting me?''

She cried out sadly. ''I didn't know how to treat you. All those gifts, all that fancy stuff . . . I just wanted my old Nathan back, the one who roamed the woods and took buck-naked baths outdoors.''

"I can manage that for you.''

She pulled away, shaking her head and sweeping a hand around her. "You'd have to live here with me.''

"Best invitation I've heard in years. I accept.''

His eyes gleamed like old silver as he grabbed her hand. Without a word he pulled her along beside him as he headed for the front of the ridge.

Openmouthed, Kat stared at him, wondering what gave his eyes such a compelling purpose and set his mouth in a knowing little smile.

He stopped at the edge of the ridge, gazed out over the valley as if mesmerized by its beauty, then rested his fingertips on her medallion and looked at her the same way he'd looked at the valley.

"Do you want to know what your medallion says?'' he asked softly.

Kat caught her breath. "Oh *yes.*''

He shut his eyes for a moment, then locked his gaze to hers. His fingertips caressed the Cherokee symbols. ''Taken from the land, given back to the land, this gold will bring us home.''

His eyes never leaving Kat's, Nathan turned the medallion and touched the symbols on the other side. ''I will know him by the gold over his heart.''

Kat shook her head, puzzled. Nathan lifted the gold nugget from her chest. "This belonged to Justis.''

She gasped lightly and clung to him with both hands. Kat looked down at the nugget he cupped reverently in his palm. "This belonged to Justis? This is the nugget your great-great-grandpa took from him?''

"Not 'took from him,' " Nathan corrected gently. "Justis gave it to him to send to Katie after he was executed. Justis didn't expect to escape." Nathan paused. "This nugget's stayed in my family over a hundred years. I've worn it all my life."

Kat looked up at him and asked in a small, awed voice, "I will know him by the gold over his heart. Are you asking me to believe—"

"I'm asking you to marry me, Katie."

She quivered with emotion, took his face between her hands, and searched his face until she knew she wasn't imagining what she saw there. "That night when I asked you to make a deal on the mining rights, I said that I loved you," Kat whispered. "You didn't believe me. Will you believe me now?"

His voice was gruff. "I'll believe you. Say it again for me, Katie."

"I love you, Nathan." She swayed against him, and he held her tightly. "And I'll marry you."

"Good. I love you, too." He kissed her, then murmured against her lips, "That sounds so right I know I've said it before." He chuckled hoarsely. "Maybe I've just thought it a lot."

"Maybe," she agreed. "But I've been waiting forever to hear it."

H E HAD LOVED Katherine Blue Song Gallatin for twenty-five years, and when he died tomorrow he would love her for eternity.

Justis Gallatin squinted both from the hot Arkansas sun and the blinding pain in his left arm, shattered by a Yankee bullet. His head aching with fatigue, briny sweat slipping through his mustache and into his mouth, he settled closer to the trunk of the aged pecan tree. The tree was his salvation and his tormentor; he was bound to it by six feet of thick iron chain which led to tight shackles around his booted ankles.

A shadow fell across Justis's face. He lifted his head wearily and met a sympathetic gaze. Justis smiled thinly. "A hot day in hell. Good work, Colonel."

"You ought to know."

The blue-coated colonel squatted by him, handed him a canteen, and accepted a nod as thanks. Justis filled his stomach with the cool liquid.

"Major Gallatin, if there's any message you want sent to your family, you best tell me today."

Justis slid his good hand inside the neck of his shirt and, ignoring the agony every movement sent through his body, lifted a chain with a gold nugget on it over his graying hair. He handed it to the officer.

"That came from my wife's land in Georgia." Justis shut his eyes for a moment, picturing the old Blue Song place, thinking of all it meant to Katie and all he'd done over the years to keep it for her.

He gazed intently into the colonel's eyes and said simply, "Tell her I'll be waiting there."

SHE HAD LOVED Justis Gallatin for twenty-five years, and she would love him for an eternity more. She would not let him step into that eternity alone and before his time.

Her pulse hammering with fear, Katherine entered the army tent and stood before the makeshift desk of a bearded, grim-faced Union officer. Colonel Nathaniel Chatham of the 1st Arkansas Cavalry stood and bowed slightly; he was obviously surprised as he took in her regal demeanor.

"I'd heard that you were beautiful and refined for a Cherokee woman," he said. "But the rumors don't do you enough credit, madam."

Katherine ignored the compliment. "You have no right to hold my husband prisoner here in Arkansas. He's a citizen of the Cherokee Nation."

"He's a white man. Living in the Oklahoma Injun lands doesn't change that."

"He's a citizen by marriage. He has sons who are half Cherokee. He served in the tribal government before the war." She paused, struggling to keep her dignity despite the growing terror for Justis's safety. "We're not part of your war, sir. Let him go."

Chatham stroked his graying-brown beard and gave her a hard look. "Madam, there's no use in trying to protect him or yourself. I know you were both born in Georgia. I know you've got Southern sentiments."

The colonel arched a brow. "And I know that your

husband is secretly an officer in the Confederate army. He and his Injuns spent the past two years bush-whacking Union troops all over Indian Territory."

"Because those troops didn't belong there."

"*No*. Because you Gallatins wanted to save your way of life. You owned fifty slaves. That showplace of yours over at Tahlequah was one of the biggest farms in the territory."

Katherine glared at him. "We've never owned slaves, Colonel. Those were freemen who worked for hire."

Looking stunned, Chatham studied her. Then he grimaced. "Doesn't matter. Major Gallatin is going to hang."

A rush of queasiness made lights dance in front of Katherine's eyes. She took a steadying breath. "Your troops have confiscated everything we owned. You ordered them to burn our house. My youngest son is in hiding because he shot a soldier who was trying to harm me. He's only thirteen years old, just a child. Haven't we suffered enough?"

"Madam, last month Injun soldiers killed my two eldest sons at the battle of Honey Springs." He paused. "And they scalped them."

Despair settled coldly in Katherine's chest. "My eldest sons fought for the Union," she told him. "One is dead and the other is in a Confederate prison."

"Your husband is a Reb and your sons enlisted for the Union side?" he asked, amazed.

"Yes. They went East and joined a regiment there so there'd be no chance of them fighting their own father one day." She paused, her throat aching. "It was an act of conscience and honor."

She and Chatham traded awkward, almost sympathetic looks. Katherine wondered if he had a kind-hearted soul beneath the bitterness war had brought him.

"Please, Colonel," she whispered. "I beg you to let my husband go."

He looked away wearily. "I'm a man of duty, madam. I can't turn a prisoner loose."

"Duty," she repeated with disdain. "You destroy my family and my home for duty." She raised one hand and pointed at the colonel, then murmured an incantation in Cherokee.

He glowered at her. "Madam, I've heard stories about your witchcraft. I'm not swayed by it."

"I'm a seer, not a *tsgili*. I cast no spells. I see what God intends. There will be a bond of darkness between my family and yours. Only God can change that."

She turned and glided from his tent, leaving him spellbound.

IN HIS MIND Justis relived his memories—the first time Katlanicha Blue Song, wary and full of fight, had shared his bed; the day she had admitted that she loved him as much as he loved her; the marriage that had produced four fine children.

They had shared all the happiness that came from living *da-nitaka*, so close in spirit that they stood in each other's souls, and he loved her more now than he had the day they'd met.

"*Osiyo*, Father," a voice whispered behind him.

Justis turned slowly, all his senses alert. In the moonlight beyond the tree crouched a lanky, handsome boy dressed in buckskins, his black hair streaming down his back.

Pride and love mingled with fear in Justis. "Holt. Get out of here, Son. There's nothing you can do."

But Holt slipped soundlessly forward and fiddled with the manacles. With a sharp click they fell open. "Mother bribed a soldier to get the key."

Justis clasped his son's arm. "Your mother—"

"Is waiting for us." Holt's teeth flashed white in the darkness. "Put your good arm around my shoulder, Father, and let's leave this place behind."

SHE HELD JUSTIS'S head in her lap as Holt drove the wagon through the darkness. Crying silently, Katherine stroked a wet cloth across her husband's face.

He reached up and grasped her hand. "You weren't worried that those Yanks would hang an old buzzard like me, were you, Katie gal?" he whispered hoarsely.

"Sir, you gave me a fright." She bent over him, kissed him tenderly, and whispered, "How would I live without you?"

They were silent for a long moment, their lips not quite touching, his hand squeezing hers more tightly as he struggled for composure. Finally he asked, "Where'd you get enough money to bribe somebody for the key?"

"I traded the medallions to one of Chatham's men."

"Katie."

She shook her head. "Saving you was more important than saving some gold pieces from the old homeland. They were just a silly notion of mine, anyway." She slipped her hand inside his shirt, then gasped.

"I gave the nugget to Chatham," Justis told her. "He was supposed to send it to you after I was dead."

She stroked his chest. "Oh, husband. Then we have nothing left of the land but memories."

He drew her closer with his good hand. "The land will always be there waiting for us," he promised gently. "We'll go back."

Katherine rested her forehead on his and laid her hand over his heart, her fingers as light as a spirit.

*Someday.*

*Deborah Smith told the compelling love story of Katherine Blue Song and Justis Gallatin in* BELOVED WOMAN, *a Bantam Fanfare novel published in April 1991. If you missed it, be sure to ask your bookseller for this unforgettable historical novel.*

# FANFARE

Enter the marvelous new world of **Fanfare**!
From sweeping historicals set around the globe to
contemporary novels set in glamorous spots,
**Fanfare** means great reading.
Be sure to look for new **Fanfare** titles each month!

## On Sale in August:
## GENUINE LIES
### By **Nora Roberts**
author of PUBLIC SECRETS

*In Hollywood, a lady learns fast: the bad can be beautiful,
and the truth can kill.*

## FORBIDDEN
### By **Susan Johnson**
author of SWEET LOVE, SURVIVE

*Daisy and the Duc flirt, fight, and ultimately flare up in
one of the hottest and most enthralling novels
Susan Johnson has ever written.*

## BAD BILLY CULVER
### By **Judy Gill**
author of SHARING SUNRISE

*A fabulous tale of sexual awakening, scandal, lies and a
love that can't be denied.*

### THE SYMBOL OF GREAT WOMEN'S
### FICTION FROM BANTAM

Ask for these books at your local bookstore.

AN 323 8/91